The Classic Grill

A TALE OF
GREEK GODS AND
IMMIGRANT HEROES

a novel

Nancy Econome

Joela! To my favorite
Beta-reader + friend.
Thank you for all
your support!
I hope you enjoy!
Nancy

Published by Kafeneon Productions

Excerpt from "Hidden Things" from THE COMPLETE POEMS OF CAVAFY, translated by Rae Dalven. English translation copyright © 1961, and renewed 1989 by Rae Dalven. Reprinted by permission of Houghton Mifflin Harcourt Publishing Company.
All rights reserved.

Cover photo credit: Ancient Greek Plate
https://commons.wikimedia.org/wiki/File:Eos_Memnon_Louvre_G115.jpg
Public Domain photo
File: Eos Memnon Louvre G115.jpg; Former collection of
Charles Hippolyte de Paravey; purchased in publication auction, 1873;
Source/Photographer; User:Bibi Saint-Pol, own work, 2007-05-09

Knife and Fork photos from iStock by Getty Images file ID 183038818
Coffee Cup icon from iStock by Getty Images file ID 902883172

Book design: Happenstance Type-O-Rama
Cover design: Nancy Econome

978-1-7344288-0-3 (paperback)
978-1-7344288-1-0 (eBook)

www.nancyeconome.com

Printed in the United States of America

For my mom Georgia
who never gave up on this story,
me or anyone else

ONE

"Resist!"

A young woman's face slammed against my windshield.

"No human is illegal!" Her voice was a harsh, dry croak, muffled by the barrier of safety glass between us. The police, cocooned in thick plastic riot gear, peeled her skinny frame from my old Toyota and casually tossed her to the ground.

Why was this woman shouting at me?

Sitting behind my steering wheel on the Golden Gate Bridge, I was trapped between a tourist bus and a stretch limo, the private tourist transit for those who can afford it. My rumbling stomach counted the minutes as I crept forward inch by inch. I was returning from an appointment at UC San Francisco Medical Center, where a doctor lectured that my prostate cancer would not be the thing that killed me. But what do doctors know?

I cursed myself for not taking the Bay Bridge to my home in Vallejo, but I wanted to catch a glimpse of the churning gray waters and roll down the window to sniff the salty, cold wind blasting from San Francisco Bay. Instead, I stretched my neck to search for the young protestor. Squinting, I watched the police usher her to the east walkway — the side of the bridge people sometimes jumped from. She grabbed a sign reading, "Never Again Is Now!" stapled to a wooden post. She and her group continued their resistance, their chanting, making their point. Looking across two lanes of traffic, I felt she was staring at me. As if I, an old retired man, held hostage in a hunk of metal on wheels, could actually do something about their cause.

"We Are All Immigrants!"

"Immigrants Make America Great!"

"Resist!"

I couldn't help but think she chose my car, expecting I would jump out and join her. She couldn't see I was older than her grandfather could possibly be and lucky the doctors still let me drive a car. Why did she pick me as her connection in this bumper-to-bumper chain of gridlock? Did she know I understood a thing or two about immigrants?

As the traffic crept away from her, I realized my personal protestor had refocused my attention from my stomach to my heart, a space I had not inhabited for a while. But then, it is my personal belief that the stomach and the heart are linked somewhere deep in human chemistry.

Looking north, my thoughts were caught in the ocean breeze and, like a kite, floated across the bay to my family. What would they have thought of this protest? They were all gone now. So I shook off the spirits of the past as well as my fantasy of a savory lunch, served on a real plate — not in a paper wrapper. I decided to grab a quick bite near old downtown Vallejo, close to where my house stood, the home my family had occupied since the Great Depression. A simple sandwich would be cheaper, but I was certain it would not live up to my father's version of a good, hot lunch. Gravy preferred.

I rolled away from the Golden Gate Bridge and about twenty-five miles up the highway, turned east at Novato. I relaxed and glided on the skinny two-lane highway cutting through the soft blue and green marsh-lands — the spongy, shallow end of San Francisco Bay. That part of the trip never failed to fill me with beauty and peace until I was locked in another traffic snarl near the Mare Island Bridge. But that was automobile travel in northern California. I should have packed my lunch.

Traffic finally released me from its claws and I rolled down Sonoma Boulevard, which used to be the main drag in Vallejo. My cantankerous stomach and my Type 2 diabetes reminded me I had to eat — now. I pulled my car into the parking lot of a run-down fast-food place. Shuffling across the uneven gravel walkway with my cane, I swung open the doors.

I could hear a young woman behind the counter speaking in low tones to the cook in the assembly line of a kitchen. I couldn't quite tell if her accent was Spanish or Middle Eastern, but then my hearing aids never did work properly. Damn things. I walked to the counter, my bones creaking like the joints in the wooden floor of my old family home. I set down my orange plastic tray and waited for her attention.

I instantly felt sorry for this girl — more girl than woman. She looked worn out and was probably only seventeen. Her red polyester uniform hung on her petite frame as if she was a clothesline. The only clue to her personality was an elaborate sweep of black eyeliner slashed along her eyelashes. Maybe it's the style now — but how would I know? The aroma of potatoes boiling in the deep fryer was intoxicating until I remembered they were pre-cut, frozen for months and delivered in twenty-pound bags. Not like we used to make them at our restaurant. We hand-peeled every damn potato.

"Hotcakes," I said, ignoring my carbo-count for the day. "And a cuppa coffee. Please."

The young woman did not react. Did they even call them hotcakes anymore? I didn't need to make her shift more miserable.

"A hamburger then." It was lunchtime anyway. I paid with my customary exact change and used my lead-pipe of a cane to guide me to a seat. The young woman, who I called Dark Eyes to myself, followed me with quick, quiet steps.

"You forgot your coffee — and your number!"

She dropped a small plastic stand emblazoned with the number thirty-eight on my table and carefully set down my small cup. As she turned away, I'm quite sure I heard Dark Eyes mutter *Dādā*, the Punjabi word for grandpa. In this neighborhood I have to be up on my Spanish, Punjabi, Tagalog and a little Vietnamese, the way I used to be quick with a few Italian phrases and some Yiddish. But that was long ago.

Dark Eyes padded back to the counter in her worn-out athletic shoes.

I had seated myself near the only customers in the fast-food restaurant, a frazzled father wrangling a boy and a girl in soccer uniforms, likely his part-time custody. I glanced over to see the young boy pushing away the open-faced hamburger. "She got it wrong. Take it back!"

"Forget it, Aiden!" The dad was pleading now.

"They don't even speak English here!" the boy grumbled. The dad slapped the burger together, exhausted. I leaned over to speak to the family in a soft voice.

"In some of the best restaurants, they never did speak English." I kept my eyes lowered, so I did not look intimidating.

The dad smiled, moving away from me — or maybe that was just my imagination. He probably wondered when I was going to ask for money and I'm quite certain he hoped I would go away.

Looking at the little family, I realized I missed my people, my family. I hadn't thought about them in a while, but this was the second time today that their spirits came rushing at me. Like the scent of roasted lamb and rosemary potatoes could hit your gut after a long Greek Orthodox liturgy and a walk back home, I was hungry for my Greek self. And I always found it when I opened the door to my family's restaurant and my father's cooking.

I slowly sipped my coffee and the whining from this twenty-first century seemed to fade. Just for a second, I was back at my father's restaurant. I was home.

"My family's restaurant was The Classic Grill. Used to be two blocks down the street there and around the corner." I pointed outside, through the orange-tinted window clouded with cling-on signs for the Western Cheeseburger Special. I could almost envision the crisp awning outside our restaurant and the red neon sign with tiny sparkling lights around it.

"That's where we made a delicious hamburger steak. And a hot turkey sandwich with gravy." I looked at the kid's untouched hamburger. "And our cooks could hardly speak English. It was my family's restaurant and we practically lived there."

My audience of three was quiet, not knowing if they should fear me or dare to listen.

"But I can't tell you about the restaurant without talking about my brother Demo. Demosthenes. He was my hero. Of course, you'll also want to know about my father, Achilles. He ruled our restaurant and everyone in it. And I am George. And this is the way it was — as I remember it."

TWO

In early 1942, the war had begun. Everyone was worried. About Hitler, Hirohito, Mussolini and everyone's sons coming home horizontal, under a flag. Although my father did not appear worried, he always churned on the inside. As the Greeks say, *"San ti vuta!"* Like the butter churn. But it didn't matter. I worried enough for the both of us. In fact, I worried for our whole Pappayannis family.

My father always struggled with the heavy brass lock on the restaurant front door. His daily key jiggling was as familiar to him as flipping eggs in one of the buttery frying pans in our restaurant kitchen. My father had a knack for making things work — or maybe work was all he knew.

The door to the restaurant squeaked open, as it did every morning, and my father hauled in a fragrant box of French bread he had purchased from the bakery. The whisks, bowls, saucepans and spoons awaited his touch. I knew my father felt his restaurant, The Classic Grill, was more his home than the small house he occupied with our mother Chrisoula, my brother Demo and me. At times, the restaurant was a madhouse. And at moments like this, it was my father's sanctuary.

My father was a native Greek but we did not serve Greek food at The Classic Grill. My father's instincts told him that in 1942 Vallejo, everyone needed a good American meal. And he was there to supply it. Each day he would affix the menu on the board with the same tarnished thumbtack he had used for decades:

TODAY'S MENU — FRIDAY JANUARY 16, 1942

T-bone steak	$1.25
Juicy Salisbury steak with brown gravy	$1.05
Pan-fried potatoes	$.30
Hot turkey sandwich	$.50
Bread pudding	$.15
Custard pie - per cut	$.15
Hot French bread	$.05

My father's restaurant was located a few steep blocks from Mare Island Naval Shipyard and he loaded his menu with food that would fill a worker's empty stomach. Hungry men and women who labored at The Yard would treat themselves to what seemed like home cooking. His customers had immigrated to the U.S., had enlisted or were drafted into the Navy from small towns and major cities across America. Officers and swabbies. Navy nurses and doctors. Locals too. Anyone looking for a good meal at a good price.

My father would often take stock of The Classic Grill. He'd built up the restaurant over the twenty-two years he'd owned it. The glow from the long bar created of pounded nickel pleased my father. It looked rich and he got it cheap. The black and white mosaic Greek key design on the entryway floor was the only ethnic touch in the place. My father assumed the customers would view it as classic and not necessarily Greek, which in those days screamed "poor immigrant."

My father slowly walked to the kitchen, his place in the world. If there was one thing a Greek man knew how to do, it was cook. And make money doing it. My father had a vision for the day and a plan for the future. But the future depended on his son, my brother Demo. His *protoyos*, his first son. Demo was the secret ingredient my father needed to put his plan into action. Never me. Demo always got my father's heat and would have gladly abdicated the responsibility to me. I was nearly two years younger. After all, Demo was the first to be educated here in the United States, in an authentic school with books, desks and English-speaking teachers. Demo's high school and someday college education anointed him to be my father's businessman. The luxury of formal schooling, however, was nearly inconceivable to my father. Higher learning was only a dream for which he had no time or opportunity. When the subject came up, my father would quickly dismiss his jealousy that we, his sons, could read and write while he could not. He didn't hide his illiteracy, but it was clearly a dent in his pride.

No matter. My father knew his plans were big. As he tied on a fresh apron, his thoughts were weighed down by Demo. No matter how my father explained his plans to my brother, he could not sense enthusiasm reflected back. My father must have suspected Demo's hunger, his *peina*, was as great as his own — but for something else. He did not want to believe it.

My father began to brew the coffee for the morning crew, exclusively using only Milo Coffee to support the company owner, a fellow Greek immigrant he had never met. The familiar smell of the coffee comforted him, yet uncertainty tightened his stomach. He desperately needed Demo, the only force in his universe he could not rein in.

Instead of pouring himself a cup of American brew, my father quickly poured a demitasse cup of water into a small brass *briki* with a long handle. Greek coffee was more work to make but he needed a strong jolt. He added the ground coffee and sugar, and as the brew came to a boil, he noisily shook the *briki* over the burner. As my father poured the thick, dark liquid and took a sip, he was resolute. Demo needed to soon realize my father's was the only plan for our family's future.

As my father cracked the first of a dozen smooth brown eggs for the morning rush, he knew he had sacrificed too much for Demo to lack enthusiasm for his brilliant plan. *Demo. Always Demo*, my father grumbled to himself. He cracked the last egg with a thwack instead of an expert gentle tap and the eggshell shattered into pieces. My father silently cursed his mistake, vowing he would make Demo into what he — and his business — needed.

After the breakfast rush quieted, the midday sun had broken up the dull, grey fog. A thin man in his late fifties unfolded his spindly legs from a Chevy coupe that had pulled up to the curb in front of The Classic Grill. Theo Vasili, my uncle, planted his dusty workboots on the sidewalk and nodded in appreciation to the driver, who had given him and his worn suitcase a free ride. He passed a nearby newsstand displaying the *Vallejo Times-Herald*, the headline shouting, "NINE DIE IN ARMY BOMBER CRASH — AUSTRALIANS JOIN SINGAPORE BATTLE."

My uncle, a certified drifter, worked an occasional day or two in Reno but mostly took the jobs my father provided. Now he was back in town. His spirit was in good shape, but his years laboring in the silver mines of Nevada had rewarded him with a limp and more than a little emphysema. Lighting a cigar that did nothing to soothe his lungs, my uncle opened the door to The Classic Grill. As he pulled back the brass door handles of the restaurant, he leaned over and turned the sign from "Breakfast Service" to "Lunch Service."

Theo Vasili ambled through the long, narrow restaurant to a set of swinging doors that opened to the kitchen. Passing through them, the familiar orchestrated chaos enveloped him. Facing the outside world, The

Classic Grill dining area was an orderly, busy American-style restaurant. But behind the doors, a hectic engine room was busily at work and only Greek was spoken.

"Ella! Ella!" was the hurry-up cry from my father in the kitchen.

My brother Demo and I worked in the back kitchen. Demo sat at my father's desk located in a tiny office with no door. As usual, I positioned myself behind the busy vegetable station. As my uncle strolled past the energetic hive of the central kitchen, my brother and I rushed to greet him. Demo and I hugged our bachelor-uncle, who easily dispensed love and attention to us along with stories of card sharks, prize fights, wicked women and his meanderings through the wilderness of northern California.

My uncle slowly released himself from our proud Greek-men's embrace. He breezed past a high shelf in the back of the kitchen that displayed a byzantine icon of St. Nicholas and a tall burning candle nestled in red glass. A sepia photo of two young men standing in front of an old-fashioned hotel took center position on the shelf. My uncle nodded his head in salute to the poster of Roosevelt's Four Freedoms that was thumbtacked to the wall, covering the peeling paint job.

Seeing that everything was in its place, my uncle wandered through the swinging doors to the front counter and rested himself on a red leather swivel stool. At that moment, the restaurant door squeaked open and another man strolled in. Taki, with pencil-thin mustache and worn fedora, slid into his customary seat next to my uncle. Where Theo Vasili was wiry and lean, Taki was compact and fit for his age, which I judged to be about sixty. A body perfectly suited for picking olives and herding sheep.

Taki leaned into my uncle. "Broke again?" he asked.

Theo Vasili puffed his cigar and shrugged.

"Ella, kafé!" Theo Vasili cried out for coffee to no one in particular in the back kitchen. My father immediately pushed through the swinging doors to wait on his cousin and his friend, otherwise known as The Counselors. My father assigned them that nickname as they offered opinions on everything that passed their purview at The Classic Grill.

"Vasili, English out here!" my father admonished.

Taki took off his hat and motioned for coffee. While Taki unfolded his newspaper, my father poured two cups while closely surveying my uncle's face, looking for clues of the damage.

"How much you lose in Reno?"

"Hundred. Maybe two…" Theo Vasili seemed indifferent to the amount.

"*Xáderfo*, cousin, forget the cards. And the girls." He pointed to an apron hanging on a nearby nail. "The dishes, they wait for you."

The lunch crowd trickling in siphoned off my father's attention from my uncle and his financial losses. Mare Island workers as well as plumbers, shopkeepers and construction crews streamed in for a hot lunch served up quickly.

"Chrisoula! Menus!"

I carefully watched my mother, Chrisoula, a dark-haired, shapely woman in her late forties who, in her younger years, was the beauty in her village, Silimna in Greece. She maneuvered through the kitchen where six or seven cooks fried fish, tossed salads and roasted lamb. She snapped up a small stack of paper menus to warmly welcome a new group of customers clustered near the front door. Her ready smile and genuine friendliness left behind her Greek village past and took on the full force and grace of an American woman in business.

At the kitchen door, my father closely inspected a waiter's tray before it was whisked away to the customer.

"Never no gravy on the edge! Must be perfect! Go!" My father scolded the waiter while marching into the kitchen. Hands on his hips, my father was a captain surveying his ship. No one escaped his critical gaze or his complete control. My father grabbed the carving knife from a cook's hands.

"Away from the bone! Like this!" The slices melted off his knife onto a large wooden cutting board.

"Chrisoula!" he shouted over his shoulder. "You take bank deposit?"

Switching gears, my mother observed the exasperated cooks who made a living while enduring my father's interference. "*Neh*, yes, I go before they close."

My mother was my father's counterbalance, the calm, well-reasoned weight that kept my father in check — most of the time.

"*Kalí týchi, mágeires!* Good luck, cooks!" she shouted.

In the back of the kitchen, Demo and I watched our mother step out of the back door in a swirl of femininity and strength. Our hearts went with her. She was the lifeline between our hard-line father and the rest of the sane world. Generosity came naturally to my mother and I sometimes wondered how she and my father remained close as a couple. My mother believed that love, her love in particular, could overcome the mistakes in the lives of people around her. She fiercely willed it so.

Demo, seventeen-and-a-half years old at the time, held a rusty clipboard and wore an apron that was wrapped twice around his tall, thin frame. Demo moved like a dancer, even when he was sifting flour or sorting out my father's paperwork. He was graceful compared to me. I was just a human potato-peeling machine behind the eternal mountain of hard brown spuds. I'm pretty sure that's what my father thought of me. My brother looked like one of those young curly-haired gods playing the lute on a Greek ceramic vase with women and men circling around him. I was just a kid, but I knew it in my soul — my brother was beautiful. Man or woman, you couldn't keep your eyes off him.

THREE

I looked up to my audience of three. The boy had quit whining and was staring at a handheld video game that rang out annoying, high-pitched sound effects. The dad was listening to me, eating his cheeseburger and the daughter rested her head on her arms. I couldn't tell if she was waiting for me to continue my story or to hurry and finish.

"At the time, I didn't know that place was special," I said to my small family audience. "I didn't know my people were caught between the ancient world and the new one. And I certainly didn't know how things would change. I wouldn't have wanted to know anyway."

Dark Eyes placed my hamburger in front of me and whisked away my plastic number. She left for an instant and returned chewing on an extra-long straw stuck in a soft drink cup. She said nothing, then sank into a nearby seat, balancing on the edge so that she wasn't officially "sitting down on the job."

"We Greeks invented heroes, you know. My brother Demo was my hero. And I loved it when Demo found his ancient self."

I savored the thought. I'm not sure my audience understood, but they listened anyway. The coffee had warmed my voice so I continued with my story.

"I knew I needed to help my brother — and my father at the same time. If they would let me."

FOUR

"How much more you got?" Demo whispered. He leaned over to me, a pencil stashed behind his ear.

I cocked my head toward a pile of potatoes mounded two feet high in a giant aluminum tub. Nearby, a massive pile of fresh green pea pods awaited my experienced sixteen-year-old hands. I raised my eyebrows and shrugged. Just for a minute, I wanted to run away from the restaurant and become swept away into Demo's imaginary world. Demo loved the lives of ancient Greek heroes, worrying about Ajax's emotional state when he mistakenly killed a herd of livestock, hoping he was destroying Odysseus and Agamemnon. Wondering how Dionysus felt when he returned to Thebes in the Bacchae. I never said so but I always thought Demo was Dionysus come to life.

Suddenly, infused with an ancient spirit, Demo flung the clipboard to the floor and leapt onto a lettuce crate. He chanted:

> There are many strange and wonderful things,
> but nothing more strangely wonderful than man.
> He moves across the white-capped ocean seas
> blasted by winter storms, carving his way
> under the surging waves engulfing him.

Eyes electric, Demo jumped from the crate and moved to a stack of clean white tablecloths, throwing one over his shoulder like a toga.

"Bravo, Demo!" The balding cook Petros applauded Demo's performance, tapping his wooden spoon on the boiling pot of spaghetti sauce. I'm not sure he understood Demo's speech from the Greek play *Antigone*, but he loved the entertainment.

I happily applauded while the kitchen crew looked up with smiles when their hands weren't busy clapping. My father stormed through the swinging doors and immediately everyone returned to work.

"*Pántote to drama* — always the drama!" My father sighed. "*Stamatísei!* Stop this, Demo!"

Steaming mad, he marched back out to the dining room. But Demo was just warming up.

> I did not mean to let a fear of any human will
> lead to my punishment among the gods.

Antigone again. I was learning which play was which. Many nights, Demo stood on his twin bed, tapping into the spirits of ancient Greece for me, George, his brother, his audience of one.

My father angrily crashed back in. The kitchen crew's attention kept shifting as if they were watching a tennis match.

"Enough! *Doulepséh!* Work!" He stormed back out to the dining room.

Demo finished his ancient soliloquy. He dramatically posed his final lines to Petros, who by this time, kept an eye out for my father.

> When someone has to live the way I do,
> how can I fail to find a benefit in death?
> For me meeting this fate won't bring any pain.

The crew burst out into hearty, noisy applause. Petros turned to Yannis, another cook. "What he say?"

"He say...he is our Demo!" Yannis shrugged, smiling.

Demo took a slow, graceful bow. Now that he had returned to earth, at least for a moment, I cast a friendly glance at my brother.

"C'mon Demo," I said enthusiastically. "Let me finish and we'll get out of here. You and me."

Demo unwound himself from his over-sized apron, slipped on a windbreaker and headed toward the back door. I'm sure my face dropped from the Comedy mask to the Tragedy mask of ancient Greece.

"Comin' back?"

"Pop can handle it. Always does." Demo surveyed the kitchen chaos and winked at me. "I'll come get you later."

My older brother, my everything, walked away, and I turned back to my potato peeling. Although I loved our restaurant and usually liked the work, I wanted to run away with him. But my motionless feet anchored my heart in front of the tureen of potatoes. I couldn't disobey my father, but Demo had no problem in that department. I actually think my father had come to expect Demo's disobedience, his lack of interest in our daily special.

Tetsuya, a Japanese man in his early fifties, was the only non-Greek in the kitchen. Each morning soon after we opened, the produce vendor would arrive at the back door of the restaurant and announce the day's specials. Tetsuya always closely inspected the freshness of the vegetables and fruit, then judiciously spent his allotment of my father's budget to buy them. He was in charge of steaming, sautéing and boiling all vegetables. In addition, he was the only person — other than my mother, Demo and me — who had a set of keys to the restaurant. My father trusted Tetsuya completely. He was family.

I could hardly contain myself. "He's always gone now," I blurted to Tetsuya.

"Restaurant work not for everyone." Tetsuya gently patted my back. "My father, he thought to cook was womanbusiness."

I looked around the kitchen of nearly all Greek men.

"That's all we know." I was nearly in tears.

The lunch rush was coming to a fever pitch. I heard my father shout orders as the cooks and waiters hurried from one station to the other.

"Over here!"

"You forgot their order!"

"Not hot enough!"

"Give them their check!"

"Soup, it need lemon! Always more lemon!"

Back in the kitchen where I was stationed, the atmosphere was more claustrophobic than ever. Mr. Chris, a Greek with an electric-red crew cut, tossed down his scrub brush and picked up a violin and bow. Softly yet clearly, he began to play a lively Mozart concerto. I had grown up in the back of the restaurant so I knew all his songs. Through the swinging doors I could see my Theo Vasili and Taki listening to the violin music from their official seats at the counter.

Taki checked his watch. "Apollo and his lyre."

"Twelve-thirty," Theo Vasili nodded. "He on time."

"He gonna play *Miserlou*?" Taki asked no one in particular. "It my son Nikko's favorite!" He crossed himself with three pinched fingers, touching his head and shoulders. "God keep him safe in the Army."

Surrounded by waiters in the kitchen my father exploded, "Where is Demo? He need to be here! Lunchtime now!"

Calmly peeling carrots, Tetsuya ignored my father's anxiety and turned to Mr. Chris. "I would like to hear Tchaikovsky!"

"Stop!" My father covered his ears with his palms. "*Mana na xatheí!* My mother should perish! Customers think we crazy back here!"

Mr. Chris stopped playing, and I laid a protective hand on his shoulder. "The lunch rush makes him nervous!"

Mr. Chris told me he had studied with a music teacher in Greece. But his family fell on hard times and he was forced to come to America. Dishwashing was the only work he had found in twenty-seven years. His first love would always be music, his day job was incidental.

Turning back to his vegetables, Tetsuya mumbled, loud enough for Mr. Chris to hear.

"He never play Tchaikovsky for me."

FIVE

Hours later, after we closed The Classic Grill for another night, there was near silence. I heard my mother tossing a leafy green salad in a large stainless steel kitchen bowl while thick lamb chops sizzled, piled high on a platter. This was my favorite time of the day, when my family and the kitchen crew gathered around the table. Attacking our home cooking with gusto, we gossiped about the customers and discussed the special for the next day.

"The mayor." My mother delicately bit into a crispy lamb chop. "He here today."

Mr. Chris looked up. "Again?"

"He want something this time." My father had picked up the mayor's scent, his questionable intentions.

I read a cookbook while I ate.

"Pop, we should try Lamb Fricassee. You used to make it. I saw it on an old menu."

My father ignored me and looked around the table.

"George, where your brother?"

I shrugged. How was I supposed to know if Demo was in a theatre, at the movies, writing a play or lying on his back, dreaming of the day he would appear on stage in *Prometheus Bound*? My father slammed his fist onto the table causing the plates and glasses to jump. My mother, accustomed to his rage when talking about Demo these days, steadied the platters of food and the glassware.

"*Demosthenes Nicholau Yannis Pappayannis! Pou eísai*? Where are you?" My father walked around the table and dramatically gestured. Demo wasn't the only actor in the family.

I knew what was coming.

"Demo he take over this business and make it famous all over the country. In every city we make the same restaurant! A son, a nephew, a cousin, a friend of the Pappayannis family will own and operate every one!"

My father stopped his pacing and planted his hands on his hips. "My idea — it make this family want for nothing!"

Mr. Chris chomped away on his lamb chop, then looked up. "Who want to eat the same food in every city?"

"With same menu?" Tetsuya shrugged.

"People want different!" As an experienced drifter, Theo Vasili would know what American people wanted.

"My plan is good! The finest dining this country has seen!" Once again, my father pounded his fist on the table to end all discussion.

My uncle had listened to these words hundreds of times.

"With gold leaf on the ceiling — like a church! The freshest food from the garden to the plate." Theo Vasili gave an excellent rendition of my father's grand hand gestures.

Looking away from my father, Mr. Chris whispered to Theo Vasili, "He no got lotta big money."

My father stood up and walked to the windows, staring out to the street.

"Chicago! New York! San Francisco! Boston! Denver!" He reeled out the restaurant locations just as he had last week. And the week before. "This is future for the Pappayannis family. And Demo, he the one to do it! My first son!"

Satisfied, he sat down and poured a glass of wine, reflecting on his plans with pleasure. I sank down in my seat, feeling just like the food bits we scraped each night from the dirty plates into the trash barrel.

"College for my son! Demo will be brilliant businessman. He learn everything!"

Theo Vasili ventured to toss out a truth, however unpopular.

"Demo, he like the drama. He is…Demo!" Theo Vasili threw up his hands. "He not so much like the restaurant business."

"I love it," I said quietly. Softer still, I added, "Send *me* to college."

My father did not hear or pretended not to. He stood up, towering over us.

"Nothing keep me — this family — from the dream!"

My father's angry glare dared anyone to pipe up with another "truth" that might alter his reality. I knew he envisioned Demo carrying a briefcase, working with real estate men and reveling in receipts and financial forecasts. I could envision myself with that briefcase or wearing a chef's toque — or both, but I didn't dare to speak up. I would only be asking for trouble. Why tempt a hungry tiger with substandard meat?

My father snapped back into reality.

"Who want more lamb chops?"

No one looked up.

"Fage!" my father ordered. With exasperation, he dished out lamb chops randomly to the plates of his family and crew. "Eat!"

Gnawing on a juicy lamb chop, I stopped listening, my mind following Demo's path out the door. Even before we'd begun our late evening meal, I knew he was long gone. His Greyhound bus ticket had whisked him to the East Bay, Berkeley in particular. Not to wait in line at the University of California, anxious to secure a position as a college freshman. I knew that my brother was communing with the ancients, listening to the Greek chorus chant its story to the audience without the real-life intrusion of my father's business obsession.

Last time he went to Berkeley I tagged along with him as we visited the closest thing to ancient Greece, in northern California. That afternoon, I soaked up the last long rays of sunlight that were casting a soft glow of apricot and pink on the stone formations of the Greek Theatre burrowed in the east side of the Berkeley campus. Doric columns soared behind the wide stage and concrete slabs fashioned into smooth seats were stacked in layers within the amphitheatre. It was a modern replica of The Epidaurus Theatre in Greece. High in the top row, Demo was strolling about the theatre while I sat below, watching my brother.

> The mountains look on Marathon
> And Marathon looks on the sea
> And musing there an hour alone…

I could see that Demo could not determine exactly to whom the voice belonged, but it seemed to resonate with the character and cadence of a well-rehearsed actor. I watched as Demo viewed a small man wearing a long, sweeping topcoat, a few sizes too big. He walked about the stage, recounting the Lord Byron poem. He was closer to me than Demo and his angular frame reminded me of a shorter, more energetic version of Theo Vasili.

> I dreamed that Greece might still be free
> For standing on the Persian's grave,
> I could not deem myself a slave.

Like a Greek mountain goat, Demo picked his way down the theatre structure to reach the old man who watched him descend.

"Been to the Epidaurus?" He looked at my brother.

Demo shook his head.

"Best place in the Western world. One for your list."

I watched as Demo examined the small, aged body connected to the thunderous voice that had ricocheted off the stonework. The man's intense dark eyes drifted to the upper rows of the theatre. Perhaps the elderly man was imagining he was performing in Greece. His clothes were rumpled but the cigar hanging oddly from his lips was the expensive kind that Theo Vasili smoked when he won big in Reno. Demo could not determine if this man was an actor or a well-rehearsed wanderer.

"But I'm Greek — born here — California. Never been to Greece. The old-timers, they don't want to go back." Demo kicked a few stones under his feet. I wondered if the same dusty terrain surrounded the Epidaurus Theatre, only a few hours from our mother's home in Greece.

The old man sat down, poured dark liquid from a small flask and tossed it back.

"Greek by birth. Lord Byron could only dream it!"

Demo looked around the theatre. "I love the ancients — Sophocles, Euripides, Aeschylus. He spoke the words with quiet reverence. "I want to be…an actor."

Bracing himself for a lecture about selecting a more practical career, I watched Demo examine the old man's reaction to his words.

"I could think of nothing better for a young Greek man to do." The old man looked Demo over. "And your parents? They want you to live the life of an actor?"

"They don't — my father — we all work at my family's restaurant."

Demo gave me a knowing look as the sun slipped into San Francisco Bay and blazed an orange glow onto the tiers of concrete seating. I knew Demo had promised himself he would someday perform at the original Epidaurus Theatre. He was hungry to plant his feet in the land of our ancestors — those spirits he sensed when as he acted out the dramas.

The old man sat back and smiled. He pulled his long coat tighter around his thin body. "Ah…the ancient and the modern collide. Comedy, drama — it's all yours! Your people wrote it first."

"I want to learn all of it." Demo was infused with new energy and intensity.

The old man quickly stood up, gained his balance, shuffled close to Demo and laid a hand on his shoulder. "Screw up your courage! Be the hero Lord Byron would be proud of."

The old man cautiously found his footing out of the Greek Theatre. I watched as Demo remained standing in the empty bowl of concrete seats. I imagined he was waiting for a Greek chorus to begin a doleful, rhythmic chant to introduce the next ancient play.

SIX

I faced my fast-food restaurant group, which had increased by one. This time the cook slipped in from the kitchen and added himself to the mix of those listening hard to my story. A Latino man in his early twenties was dressed in the international outfit of cooks: pants with a small grey check pattern and a uniformed white coat. He lowered his tall frame into the plastic seat and waited, attentive.

"Demo later told me those words of encouragement at the theatre lit the small sparks inside him that my father tried to extinguish every day. Those few moments kindled his ancient Greek self. That's all he needed."

I looked up at my audience and could tell they were not happy with my father's ways.

"Before you dislike my father, let me tell you a little more. He was a difficult man, true. But the softer side of me learned to appreciate, some-times envy, his hard-as-nails spirit. I wondered if I had the stuff to make it in his rough world, improvising, filling in, always a half-step away from empty pockets. Only time would tell if I was tough enough to make it in the modern world."

SEVEN

I opened the back door of our restaurant kitchen and my eyes fell upon a familiar face. It was Saturday and Josef patiently waited for my father. He was a small man with dirty, swarthy skin who was never without his worn-out canvas bag—always empty—in hopes that my father would fill it. Josef, who spoke with a heavy Czech accent, said he had dogs at home, probably in a lonely alley somewhere, and declared he only wanted scraps for his hungry pets. My father allowed Josef to search our garbage barrels for chunks of steak and left-over fried chicken for "his dogs." But before Josef turned to leave, my father handed him an armful of sandwiches which Tetsuya had hurriedly constructed—a batch that should have kept Josef satisfied for days. I watched this small kindness each week and finally asked my father why he didn't tell Josef to get a job or at least insist he work around our restaurant. My father didn't answer me directly, but bits and pieces of his early years occasionally fell out of his mouth and I fit them together the best I could. I finally understood why my father could not let another immigrant go hungry.

My father arrived in the United States in 1904, at the age of fourteen. His first job as a shoeshine boy was arranged by his *padrone* who received my father's wages in exchange for paying room and board. After two years, my father was released from this arrangement of servitude. He was free.

His next job was selling fruit from a cart in Chicago. He graduated to swinging a giant sledgehammer as he helped build a railroad in the bitterly cold Colorado altitude. His heart burned for the warmth of his Mediterranean home of parched rocky hillsides dotted with hearty olive and lemon trees. But he frequently flashed on the sawtooth memory of the family's paltry wheat storage that never stretched throughout the winter season. As the grain supply dwindled to nothing, his mother and sisters began to forage for wild grasses and root vegetables to satisfy the family's hunger until spring. Even as a young child, my father saw no path to an easier life, no hint of security to look forward to. He envisioned a lifetime of back-breaking labor only to exhale his last breath in a heap of village dust, his children no better off than he was.

His family hatched a salvation plan and *amésos*, instantly, it was set into motion. My father, Achilles, the first-born son, would be sent to America to make good for the family. It was decided the younger brother, Christos, would stay behind to care for the homestead and parents in years to come. Other young men might have harbored sticky sentiments about leaving their childhood friends or missing their mother's love while preparing to leave. But there was no argument from my father who, in truth, was only a child. Any emotions tethering him to the family were obliterated the day before his parents secured his trans-Atlantic ticket.

Unknown to his parents, my father came upon his older sister Voula late that night, hastily loading personal belongings into a woven sack. My father's stomach clenched with apprehension as he realized she was packing her few possessions to leave home. The fifteen-year-old Voula collapsed in tears, admitting that she had made arrangements with a foreign man who helped girls get jobs in Piraeus. Voula learned of another older village girl who had also signed up for the distant work arrangement, but regularly sent money to her parents.

My father instantly understood that Voula's wrenching hopelessness caused her to sacrifice herself to prostitution to help the family survive. The thought repulsed him beyond his imagination. He placed his hands firmly on her shoulders and vowed on her life that if Voula was patient he would become a funnel for cash to lift the entire family out of the dust. Without his financial help, the sheer cliff of three dowries was insurmountable for his family. The next day, two worn Persian carpets and his parents' thin gold wedding bands were exchanged for a one-way passage to America. The extended family had gathered enough money to purchase another ticket for my father's first cousin, my uncle, Theo Vasili, another body who could earn money and keep the rest of the family afloat. With his ticket in hand, my father's parents, in their own desperation, practically shoved their son out the weather-beaten door of the earthen-floor home.

My father was the young, green tendril on his family tree, a shoot launched into the great unknown, protected only by his mother's prayers to the Virgin Mary and perhaps benevolent St. Nicholas. He would stretch his physical stamina and emotional constitution to travel and work in the uncharted territory of the United States. Desperately reaching toward the sunlight, he sought a way to make honest money — and lots of it.

That promise to Voula haunted my father. He talked about it regularly — even after he had fulfilled the dowry debt and paid the mortgage in full on the family home in Greece. The phrase "on Voula's life" was familiar to Demo and me around the dinner table. My father felt he could never send enough money to wrap his family in the security they deserved.

My father found some peace with his exhausting labor on the railroad by repeating to himself that it was only temporary — better than farming an anemic plot of soil for decades or herding sheep for a lifetime in the lonely hills of Greece. As a young immigrant, my father's outer shell was toughened by questionable Americans and Greeks who materialized at every turn. A seemingly respectable Greek man offered to protect my father's hat and small bundle of clothes for a nickel, but when my father turned his head, his belongings quickly disappeared. He learned to inspect rooms for roaches and mice before he paid the ten-cent rent for the night. He avoided devious women attempting to reel in a lonely-looking young foreign man, far from home, by advertising a warm heart and then some. My father learned to walk the buckboard streets of western towns, head down, hands shoved in his pockets to protect his money before a stranger helped himself. His mind sharpened and his skin hardened. Some might say his heart grew a callous layer. But my father knew he could not expose a spineless constitution or a soft brain to a world that could pull him apart like a turkey vulture would — and devour the pieces.

As a sturdy, lean teenager, he survived the sweaty, intense railroad work, but his mind wandered to a more civilized life. My father was still formulating his future in the new world, not quite clear on his outcome. But he knew his plans were big — they had to be. And swinging a sledgehammer wasn't one of them. He often told this part of the story without missing a detail: one early evening, after ten hours of clanging the hammer against the rails, he teetered on the edge of exhaustion. Far down the track he saw a railroad camp cook flipping a steak in a hefty black skillet. At that moment my father's life came into focus.

That, I can do. He whispered to himself, his mind drifting down the track, away from the brute labor. *And better.*

From that instant, my father knew that food, plates, cooks and customers would be his life. Cooking and eating was an international language. "Always a customer for eating food," he would repeat. And he felt at home in a kitchen, always a safe and respectable place for a Greek man. Cooking would be his passport to making a solid living and maybe someday much more. In that one moment on the railroad line, my father devised his life plan. He set his mind to work to his breaking point. And then work harder.

EIGHT

Like the people in the crowded, smoky *kafeneons*, cafés, that my father left behind in the villages of Greece, everyone at The Classic Grill, a breakfast-lunch-and-dinner restaurant, had an opinion. Of course, no one held back when it came to sharing it.

The Counselors, Theo Vasili and Taki, sat at the counter slowly drinking their coffee. It was the long sluggish after-lunch period at the restaurant. The air was heavy, and when the door opened the rush of fresh air was a welcome relief. Even Mr. Chris moved slower than usual, his elbows buried in his dishwashing suds. I meticulously swept the floor from the back of the kitchen to the front counter, knowing my father would inspect every inch. I hoped my work would stand up to his hawk-like scrutiny. I had to be good enough.

The front door to The Classic Grill squeaked open and a woman in her mid-twenties entered our restaurant. She did not amble or stroll. She floated. She was the Helen of Troy in our Navy town: elegant, strawberry-blond, beautiful. Her even features seemed alien to the faces of the old Greek men at the counter — as if she had walked into the wrong restaurant. Theo Vasili and Taki took a long look, pretending not to notice. But they looked again. And then they stared.

"Like the one I leave in Reno," Theo Vasili sighed. The pain of her beauty was almost too great for him to bear.

"Like the one I leave in Kalamata," Taki lied. He hadn't been near a woman since his wife Maria died seven years ago. Nowadays, the closest Taki got to a woman was standing near Mrs. Pappas in the serving line at the funeral luncheons. And she smelled of oregano and rosemary, not the soft, spicy perfume of this woman.

From the back of the kitchen I watched my father notice the young woman through the circular window of the kitchen door. He hurried to the counter looking over his shoulder to confirm that my mother was not in the restaurant. As I swept my way to the counter, I could hear everything. Seating herself at the counter several stools away from The Counselors, the woman settled in. She set her small, girlish handbag on the counter. My father dried his hands on his apron.

"Good afternoon. Menu?"

She smiled. "Coffee. Black."

I watched my father pour with one eye on her. I thought I recognized her from several earlier visits she had made to the restaurant during the busy lunchtime when my father and I were too occupied to personally serve her.

"Welcome to The Classic Grill. My restaurant."

As my father's eyes drank her in, he nearly filled the coffee cup over the rim. For years, I had overheard Greek men talk about these American girls who were such magnets to them in this new world. Just to gaze upon light eyes and a delicate face and hands was like a holiday for their soul.

The few words she uttered so far were like bites of baklava — rich sexuality dripping with honey, lightly layered with the freshness of youth. How old was this woman? And what was she doing in Vallejo in this restaurant? She was a bolt of fine French silk lost in a pile of rough, raw Greek wool.

She sipped her black coffee slowly.

"Don't know many people in town. I'm Daphne."

Her slim fingers plucked a cigarette from her Lucky Strike pack and she lit up. Even the crinkle of the cigarette package attracted my father's attention. She held her cigarette in one hand and extended the other for a gentle handshake.

My father cleared his throat and cast a glance at Theo Vasili. As my father shook her hand, I wondered if she noticed the calluses on his palms or his rough skin from so many years washing dishes.

"Except for my cousin Vasili here, I no like smoking in my restaurant. Not good to taste my food. But you new."

Daphne smiled and exhaled smoke like a strawberry blond dragon.

"And the coffee. It free today!" My father seemed to extend the conversation, for once not allowing his next task to move him to the kitchen.

"Thanks. And you are…" Daphne asked. The Counselors followed the conversation while pretending not to listen. Unexpected entertainment on a sleepy afternoon.

I could tell my father was embarrassed that he had missed the opportunity to present himself to her in a dignified manner. He coughed up his name.

"Achilles. I am Achilles."

"Achilles...hmmm..." Daphne smiled gently. "Wasn't he a brave Greek warrior?"

My father puffed out his chest a little, but Daphne didn't seem to notice as she looked around the restaurant.

"Been in business for a while?"

"Twenty-two years. But soon we make another restaurant. Then another. In every city. With the best food you can believe!"

Taki chuckled from his place down the counter.

"Now, who is the dreamer?" Theo Vasili grumbled in a low voice, into his coffee cup.

With introductions over, Daphne, Theo Vasili and Taki all bobbed their heads to sip their hot coffee. Suddenly, like a ceramic plate shattering on a tile floor, Mr. Chris' voice called from the kitchen, destroying my father's magical moment.

"Achilles! *Ella! ELLA!*"

Mr. Chris' cry was panicked and he uncharacteristically spoke in Greek, which he knew was against my father's rule. In fact, he was shouting in Greek.

"*ELLA!*"

My father smashed into the swinging door separating the kitchen and dining room, nearly trapping me behind the door. In the rear of the kitchen, two men in cheap gray suits hovered over yellow notepads. The tall man, who seemed to be the boss, was pencil-thin and nervous. The other was short and perspired heavily over his notepad which was held tight in a clipboard.

"Yawh -nis, - uh - John Pappa-yawnis?" he dreadfully mispronounced our last name.

"Yes. But I am called Achilles. What is this?"

"We're from the Federal Office of Immigration. San Francisco. We hear you hire illegal workers here."

My father summoned all the indignation he could muster. "Of course not! They are all...uh, what exactly you mean, this — illegal?"

The short over-stuffed official chimed in. His eyes searched his notes on the withered yellow paper. "We've been told you are hiring workers without their proper immigration papers."

My father looked around to find that most of his cooks and dish-washers had vanished. The kitchen screen door was pushed open to the alley, swinging in the breeze. Only Tetsuya remained, peeling cucumbers, humming under his breath. His own immigration papers were in order.

I saw my father instantly transition into an attack, his best card to play at this moment. He stood erect and sucked in a breath of indignation.

"I make my business by the rules!" he thundered and threw up his hands. "I citizen here! Why you treat United States citizens like this? Hrumph!"

He held up his index finger the way he had seen judges and professors gesticulate in the movies. Spencer Tracy meant business with gestures like this.

"I love this country and do everything right. United States a democracy—a Greek word!"

His brave front seemed to be enough for the moment. My eyes followed my father as he walked quickly to his tiny, tacky office, which housed his small desk. He spun around to find the officials had followed him and had crammed themselves into the room.

Sweating a little, my father's tone softened. "Why you do this? Just a couple of dishwashers."

The thin bossman checked his paperwork and read aloud.

"The mayor said to check the status of the workers at The Classic Grill. He reported it to the Frisco office. So how 'bout it?"

My father's back was pressed to the wall in the small office area. He began the pointless search for papers in the nearest file drawer.

"This gonna take time." My father looked up. "You hungry?"

Back in the kitchen, Tetsuya and I jumped to lay out platters of freshly roasted lamb and pasta drizzled with hot brown butter over *mizithra* cheese. An hour later, the two officials sat at the counter, jackets off, ties loosened, each wiping clean a platter of food with pieces of French bread, signaling for more coffee. The thin official checked the placement of his bib-like napkin behind his collar and tie.

"Any more of these noodles with that tangy cheese? This is great!"

The overstuffed assistant loosened his belt buckle. "I didn't know lamb could taste this good!"

My father slowly made his entrance through the swinging doors from the kitchen. He walked toward the officials and refilled their cups.

"Greeks roast the lamb," he lectured with pride and purpose. "English boil the mutton. Not the same."

My father slowly walked to the cash register area and reached for a battered cardboard box on a high shelf. He slid it down the counter toward the officials.

My father smiled. "You look at my paperwork when you finished. It all here."

Sluggish after their marathon consumption, the officials tipped back the box lid and glanced at the mounds of greasy files, unkempt paperwork and used-up adding machine rolls. Mixed in were grungy payroll ledgers that were hardly recognizable. A look of horror spread across their faces.

Finally, the master of the situation, my father stood in front of them, his arms outstretched behind the counter. Now my chest puffed out a little too. I was proud of my father's quick thinking — seems like he had practice at wiggling out of tight situations.

"So you like my place?" He opened his arms wide as if he was presenting a newborn baby to the Greek Orthodox church for the first time. The officials nodded, their mouths full.

Without taking his eyes off the two officials, my father slid a napkin with The Classic Grill embroidered on it towards them.

"I want to keep it," he rumbled in a low voice that no one but the officials and I could hear. "Tell your Mayor."

Almost imperceptibly, the thin official slipped the fifty-dollar bill which was tucked inside the napkin into his pocket. He shoved the unsightly box of paperwork down the counter, far from his sight. Both men searched their pockets for a few coins which they slapped on the counter for a tip and then hurried out the back door.

Theo Vasili and Taki hadn't moved from their customary places during this chapter in the daily Greek drama. My father filled their cups for the hundredth time today.

"What do they care for my dishwashers?" My father indignantly crossed his arms over his apron.

Taki rested back in his stool at the counter.

"You know the mayor's restaurant across the street?" He pointed to The Restaurant St. Charles with his thumb. Theo Vasili nodded his head vigorously. I polished the counter where the officials had sloppily inhaled their lunch, soaking up the local business chatter from these older, more experienced men.

"Their food — *san laspi* — like mud!" Theo Vasili nodded in agreement. "So the mayor...his brother, he own the restaurant. And business not so good. The mayor, he no like you. No like your restaurant. Now you have government men at your door. *Etzi!* That's the way it is!"

My father appeared to muse on this a moment but quickly noticed that Daphne was still lingering over her coffee at the counter. He rushed to refill her cup.

"You gotta eat, Miss... uh... Daphne," my father chattered nervously. "I fix you something nice."

"You're so kind." She purred like a kitten, happy to have a saucer of cream gently set out just for her.

"Yes, my name Achilles. I am Greek. We all Greeks here!" My father said motioning to the crew. The Japanese Tetsuya waved and smiled from the kitchen interior. My father leaned in toward Daphne — but not so close that she could detect the scent of roasted lamb and oregano. Just possibly, he could extend her a lifeline so that she might return.

"This is our home." His words were quiet, almost tender. "Now it is yours."

Daphne flashed her knockout smile and daintily sipped her coffee, her eyes never leaving my father's.

I recorded all of this in my memory, thinking I might need this information, someday in the future.

Moments later, the kitchen back door swung open and my mother entered, hauling four pink pastry boxes wrapped with string. "*Nah!* Here!" Proudly she presented the boxes so that we could only imagine the sweet perfection within. "One chocolate cake, one apple pie, two custard pies. *Ftani!* Enough! That should do until Friday." She began to open the boxes. Each pie or cake would find a place on its own glass pedestal stand which would then be covered by a glass dome.

Tetsuya nodded in her direction. My mother walked around the kitchen and inspected the bubbling liquid in the soup pot.

"Clam chowder today?" She tasted it. "*Nóstimo* — delicious!"

I loved my mother's presence at the restaurant. Since I was invisible to my father, having my mother nearby made me feel like I was an important part of our family effort at The Classic Grill. Quickly moving to the kitchen, I hugged her and peered over her shoulder at the perfect chocolate cake she had baked.

"Did you use the imported cocoa?"

"Since when you the expert?" She laughed at my curiosity. "Yes, always the imported cocoa. I make these cakes before you born."

My mother looked around.

"Before all of this."

Mr. Chris picked up his bow, looked around to see that my father was occupied in the dining room and began to play the violin.

Tetsuya looked up from his work. "Maybe Tchaikovsky, just once."

But this time it was a Greek song. Fussing with her pastry, my mother hummed for a moment and then broke into an old village song, accompanied by the violin.

As much as I loved my mother at the restaurant, I loved her more when she sang. Her voice was smoky and low. Whenever the old Greeks in the neighborhood gathered over a bottle of *retsina* and a game of backgammon, they would ask my mother to sing the old folk songs. Her voice, quivering like a cello string, always brought them to tears as they remembered their stony huts or beloved parents back home in Greece.

I believe my mother's optimism had attracted my father to her. Only my mother could get away with singing and traveling with mandolin minstrels in central Greece and not be called the vulgar names shouted at immoral women. Her spirit was simply honest and kind and the ugly village gossip could not stick to her. I often thought that if Demo was my modern-day Dionysus, then my mother was Xenia, the embodiment of the unending generosity and hospitality so treasured by us Greeks.

"Chrisoula, you think this is the Golden Gate Theatre?" My father rushed in, glaring in disbelief. He hurried out to the counter to fetch more coffee for Daphne. My mother watched closely from the kitchen.

"Poor. Lonely. Looking for a home." My mother sighed as she observed her husband giving an extra helping of thoughtfulness to the beautiful young woman at the counter.

"Another one."

NINE

"At that time I knew how Demo felt when he was away from the heavy iron skillet my father kept us under at The Classic Grill. In San Francisco he was free."

I looked around, quite amazed my little group was still with me — and getting bigger. A teenager with oceans of pink blemishes splashed onto a pale complexion had swabbed the entire beige tile floor while listening to my story. He took a break to rest his elbow on his mop and listen intently, especially to the part about Demo.

"As for me, I admired my brother for the way he pressed on to find his voice. I still didn't have one yet and was too afraid of my father to try. Instead, I learned to watch. Watch everything."

I looked at these kids and saw they did the same. They seemed interested in my story but they didn't offer any threads of their own. Just like me at their age. I figured I'd better hurry and tell them more about Demo in case their interest lagged. Besides, I wanted to talk about him one more time.

TEN

Demo stood on the deck of a ferryboat, plunging his hands into the pockets of his wool Navy pea coat. He'd been riding this ferry alone since he was ten years old. But one thing never changed — the fog of San Francisco Bay. January, April, July, November — it didn't matter. That wicked chill could penetrate the thickest wool coat or sturdiest work boots. Demo loved to tread along the top deck without a hat, no matter how bitter the temperature. The low San Francisco skyline welcomed him through the thick fog and mist. The glimmering lights of early evening signaled activity, nightlife, a cosmopolitan outlook and the Geary and the Curran theatres.

Hungry for everything but flipping omelets and balancing the books at The Classic Grill, Demo walked down the gangplank to the pier and worked his way up Market Street. As he walked between the ominously dark cement buildings on Montgomery Street, a fierce wind began to blow down the street like a manmade wind tunnel. Demo sank into his jacket and slowly began to relax. No one knew him here. He was no one's son, no longer a schoolboy. He could possibly pass as an adult. Demo was on his chosen turf and he slowly let out a sigh of relief.

In the dark, luxurious Geary Theater an hour before curtain time, Demo found his seat and, for the first time in weeks, cracked a slow smile. Golden wood carvings framing the stage and the green velvet fabric hanging from above was just the tonic Demo needed to refresh himself from his life in Vallejo and the restaurant. This was his home and this was his landscape. His soul was reset. And today, *Medea* by Euripides starring Judith Anderson was on the bill. Demo could imagine himself in the lead role madly weighing whether to kill his children to avenge the husband who had brazenly brought home a new young bride. Demo could taste it. A dramatic role, lead or otherwise, was his inner vision and he felt he had no option but to live it out.

Demo could taste it. A dramatic role, lead or otherwise, was his inner vision and he felt he had no option but to live it out. Demo always knew his spirit had been created to become a vessel for characters needing to tell their story. He desperately wanted to give them oxygen and a voice, and by doing so, find his own. The desire was all-consuming, almost suffocating. Demo needed what he found in San Francisco playhouses. And he wondered what was beyond his local metropolis. Perhaps someday he would perform on stages in New York, London, Paris.

Demo settled in, a blotting paper for every nuance and technique he could possibly absorb from his cheap seat in the balcony. His stage was set. His life was theatre and the rest was something to wrestle away from — the sooner the better.

A few hours later, Geary Street was flooded with people chatting excitedly about the play or strolling to the bars for a post-performance cocktail. Demo exited in a trance-like state, the lines from *Medea* resonating in his head.

> ...thou hast a city here...some joy
> in life and friends to share thy
> thoughts, but I am destitute, without
> a city, and therefore scorned...

ELEVEN

The front doors of The Classic Grill crashed open — both of them at once. A tempest roared in as my mother, who usually entered through the back door, burst into the restaurant. Her hair, a wavy chestnut brown, flew behind her as she sought my father's attention. Her serious walk said it all: there was trouble and she had the news.

My mother, chest heaving to find words and breath, spilled it.

"I saw it! You must come!"

My father strolled over to my mother and handed her a small stack of paper menus I had just printed on our Hectograph machine. Daphne occupied a stool near the kitchen, sipping a steamy cup of coffee. Without a word, my father presented her a plate of eggs and toast, without a check.

"Lunchtime now! *Ella!*" he commanded her, silently concerned at his wife's upheaval. Was she remotely sensing the extra helping of attention he gave to Daphne? Were they so inherently connected after twenty-five years of marriage that she could feel his attention wandering from afar? *Only slightly wandering, just looking,* he reminded himself.

"Achilléas!" My mother howled to my father as if barbarians had come to steal her baby while her inattentive husband was smoking on the porch, drinking *mavrodaphne* liquor.

"Achilléas! They read it to me! You must come! Now!"

My father pulled off his apron and quickly followed my mother out to the street. Seeing drama like this, the two Counselors were not far behind. I sprinted from the back kitchen and busted through the front doors into the street joined by Tetsuya, Mr. Chris and a few of the cooks.

Like a mighty crossing guard my mother led our small, anxious Greek contingent past the downtown Vallejo storefronts to a busy intersection and crossed the street. We halted abruptly in front of a large plate glass window with the name Restaurant St. Charles painted in elaborate gold-leaf calligraphy.

I could swear to the Virgin Mary, Athena and any goddess who was listening that the emblazoned gold letters on the window were not there yesterday. That lettering was shiny and new. And it was suspiciously expensive to be displayed during wartime. Inside the window, two large American flags were displayed and red, white and blue bunting surrounded a large hand-painted sign with thick red letters.

I looked around me. Our group looked like a collection of long-faced Byzantine icons who had just witnessed the martyred death of a fellow saint. Each face, with a substantial ethnic nose, a generous mouth and a smooth olive complexion attempted to grasp the meaning of the window display. As usual, my father was the first to react.

"George, read me this! What it say?"

Knowing the pain my words would evoke, I took a breath.

"EAT AT A REAL AMERICAN RESTAURANT!" I lowered my voice, ashamed. Softer still, I continued.

"DON'T EAT AT THE GREEKS — THEY ARE NOT AMERICAN."

Seconds or hours ticked by. Finally, Taki broke the silence.

"The mayor, his brother — they mean business."

My parents continued to stare straight ahead, motionless, in front of the window like the painting American Gothic I had seen in my history class. In this case, not so American. I could feel my father's anger turn up from simmer to boil.

"How I not American?" he demanded. "I American in *ee psychí*, my soul!"

I had heard my father angry before, like the time the meat salesman cheated him on the price of New York steaks or when the electricity bill unexpectedly went through the roof. But this time, his entire being was subject to ridicule. He looked sickened to the core. In two sentences this sign made a mockery of my father and his decades of labor creating his business. An American business, or so we thought.

We continued to stare at the window, like children who've been shamed in the schoolyard but are not sure why. The sense of hatred, toward my family, my parents' Greek friends and me, ripped at my heart and my stomach. We were not wanted by the so-called "leaders" of this town. After twenty-two years in this restaurant and two generations, we were still seen as dirty, opportunistic outsiders from a strange land.

Finally, my father erupted.

"*Ftani!* Enough! We go!"

This time our group followed him walking single file across the street, following the same path we had come. We made a slow, gloomy return. The front door of The Classic Grill swung shut with less exuberance than it had been opened with only a few minutes before. The air in the restaurant seemed muggy. It was hard to breathe.

Dejected and confused, my mother and the kitchen crew shuffled about, not immediately returning to work after the St. Charles gut punch. For a change, my father offered no direction. He paced in circles. How could he have missed the signs that he was hated in this town?

Finally, his fuse detonated.

"They say we not Americans!"

Tetsuya laughed with an unusually harsh edge. "That one, I know."

"The sign—it say no to eat here!" My father could bellow loudly as there was no one in the restaurant besides Daphne. Her aura seemed temporarily overshadowed by my family's identity crisis.

"We call police!" Mr. Chris offered.

"The mayor—his cousin is the top of police." Taki shook his head. "He the boss. So, what you gonna do?"

My father's personal earthquake could have toppled the Colossus of Rhodes.

"I work in this country since I come in 1904. I shine the shoes—work the railroad. I wash dishes all the day! I sell vegetables from the cart and sleep in the kitchen in the night. I save to live off nothing! Then I make this restaurant. And I make it good. What they mean *American* restaurant? I more American than this mayor. And his brother. Who are they? Irish? English? They no know how to cook!"

He railed on for some time and I took those moments to sprint three blocks to our family home. When I returned my father had set up several shot glasses and poured whisky into each. He snapped up the first glass and tossed the whiskey down his throat with a jerk. I walked to the back of the restaurant with a small vegetable crate that I had hauled from our house.

"I pay the taxes this mayor live off!" My father knocked back another shot, slamming the glass down in frustration on his cherished bar.

Back at his rightful place at the counter, Taki took a sip of his cold coffee. He dared not ask my father to warm it with a refill.

"Your business—it good. For his brother—it stink. Now you not American." Taki slurped the last drops in his cup. "Welcome to America. Call you names. Ruin your business. Now—go home!"

It was bad enough to be called an outsider when I knew my father felt he was part of the loose-knit local business community. But this public ridicule aimed to harm our family business—all my father had worked for—was unthinkable. I knew my father truly loved this country that had wrapped its arms around him and allowed him to make a buck.

Like Jimmy Stewart arguing his case in *Mr. Smith Goes to Washington*, a movie he had seen with my mother at The Empress Theatre several years ago, my father couldn't keep his sense of injustice bottled up.

"This is my home!" my father shouted and then pointed to Tetsuya, then Mr. Chris. "This is his home! And his home! These *xénie*, these strangers. They say we don't belong! I have business in Vallejo before them. They no own this town!"

Theo Vasili lit up his Cuban cigar. "They own Vallejo like sack of lemons." Reaching for a shot glass, he took a small, loud slurp.

My father was now standing in the center of the dining room like an actor making the most of his monologue. I quietly worked in the back of the restaurant and my father, as usual, did not notice.

"I no go back to Greece to plow stones and work for nothing. Never I go back!" Everyone's eyes were locked on his every move. In the silence, Taki reached for a shot glass and tossed back the whisky. The tension was thick like the morning oatmeal we accidentally left on the back burner.

A voice cracked the quiet. A sweet voice that did not belong to the old Greek men's club.

"So, you gonna fight?" Daphne arched her eyebrows, waiting for an answer. "You know, Achilles, the brave Greek warrior?"

My mother was stunned. My father froze. The kitchen crew watched what would happen next. I stood at the far end of the restaurant where I was working, unable to breathe.

"Fight?" my father asked hoarsely, shaking off his astonishment.

"Fight what the sign says." Daphne spoke matter-of-factly, her eyes unblinking.

My mother's eyes locked onto my father, registering his reaction. An American young woman just offered my father, a veteran of the business world, a piece of advice. No matter that it might even be good advice.

"Yes..." My father replied, adding nothing more.

He was wise enough to keep his eyes off my mother. Drawing in a breath, he tilted his chin up in Greek resolution, but I sensed an almost imperceptible hesitation.

"Yes! We fight! Of course we fight!" he announced without his usual conviction. Suddenly his eyes met Daphne's.

"Achilles never lose!" Jimmy Stewart was still on stage and my father mustered all the certainty he could. "I need good plan. Where my Demo?"

Taki rolled his eyes. "Reading a poem, under a tree." He reached for the last whisky shot. After all, today the drinks were free.

"Where in the hell is my Demosthenes?" my father shouted, his voice tight.

Nearly always calm, Theo Vasili strolled over to me at a back table, puffing on his cigar.

"*Keeta!*" cried my uncle, motioning to my father. "Look!"

On a table in the back of the restaurant I had laid out a tarnished doughboy helmet, a few U.S. Army medals that hung from red and blue grosgrain ribbons and a large framed photo of a World War I soldier saluting in his crisp uniform. An American flag folded into a triangle was tucked in the mix. I had also sprinkled in a few basketball trophies and track medals Demo and I had won at sporting meets at our local junior high school. They somehow seemed to fit. My father picked up the dough-boy helmet and examined it.

"From cousin Costa when he fight the first war." His voice was quiet. "George, where you get this?"

I overflowed with pride and stood at attention near my treasure trove.

"The big trunk in the attic. Demo and I used to play with this stuff. Pop, it's absolutely, positively, one hundred percent..."

For once I looked directly at my father, unafraid.

"...American!"

TWELVE

Dark Eyes wiped what might have been a tiny tear from the corner of the thick black wing around her eye, being careful not to smear the paint job. She glanced at the counter to see that she had two customers.

"Why'd they do this to your family?" She pouted a little. "You were a nice family."

"Seen that before," the cook said quietly as he and Dark Eyes made their way to take the order for the couple at the counter.

"Wait for me!" She rushed behind the counter and called softly to me over her shoulder. "I want to hear you tell it."

The young soccer-player girl had rested her head on her folded arms but stared wide-eyed at me, no longer afraid of my wrinkled skin and croaky voice or the fact that I was a stranger talking to strangers. Her older brother walked around the restaurant carefully placing one soccer shoe into each tile on the floor without hitting the cracks. He looked up.

"So, like, what happened?" he asked, not wanting to show too much interest. "To your restaurant?"

THIRTEEN

I remember the faces of my father, mother, Theo Vasili, Taki, Tetsuya, Mr. Chris and the cooks as they stared into our own restaurant's large glass window from the street. This time their faces staring into the window seem pleased and proud. This time hurt had been replaced by something else — something of our own making. Retooled and reshaped until it was their own homemade memo to America. To us, America was a roasted chicken — tasty enough when simply roasted. But basted with lemon, olive oil and Greek oregano — simply divine.

Inside our restaurant window, our own large American flag served as a striking red, white and blue background. In front of it, our family's Army medals and the large photo of my uncle Costa saluting the flag sat on a low table. Surrounding the table were Demo's and my gold-painted sports trophies to add extra American pizzazz. Not military, but close.

This time, the handwritten sign in the window read, "ALWAYS An American Restaurant."

"Perfect!" Theo Vasili puffed on his cigar, admiring the window.

Looking at the photo of the soldier, Taki leaned into my uncle. "Costa hurt in the war?"

Theo Vasili smirked. "He break the arm working in the kitchen. He slip and fall!"

Both old men snickered, then stood back with the rest of the group to appreciate the display.

Still wearing his long white apron, his arms crossed in front of his body, my father stood motionless like a marble Ionian column. I understood that look. His body might be stationary, but his mind was racing to form his next plan. He quickly snapped out of his trance.

"Now, who is American? Best idea I have."

My father handed his Kodak Brownie box camera to one of the cooks who aimed the lens toward The Classic Grill crew. We arranged ourselves around the window, our Greek faces proudly endorsing our American display. We had reclaimed our connection with our adopted country on our own terms — no caption needed.

Pride must have radiated from my body like the gold halo surrounding St. Nicholas' white head on the icon on the kitchen shelf. I had calculated one step ahead of my father. Finally, I was the businessman he had always wanted.

Tetsuya gave me a quick, gentle hug. "You do good Georgie." He walked inside the restaurant doors and back to his vegetable station in the kitchen.

"Bravo, *Giorgi!* Bravo!" My mother kissed my forehead and squeezed my arm. I hugged her, then followed my father like a puppy and waited outside the restaurant for my reward. Or at least a pat on the head. Instead, my father walked to Theo Vasili and lit his cigar from his cousin's smoke. Puffing it, he absorbed the good will of his American message to the world, especially to the Restaurant St. Charles.

I shoved the disappointment into my pocket. Head down, I industriously began polishing the brass door handles of the restaurant, so my hands were busy and my lips didn't tremble. I knew my father was ready to work now, so I opened the front door, awaiting his entrance. Having freshly renewed his vows to America, he took a majestic stride inside, then spun back around.

My father stared each of us in the eye, one by one. "We do better!" The long cigar that he smoked "only to help him think" punctuated his words.

Then he turned to Theo Vasili, the cousin with whom he had sailed to America. The rambling cousin he had many times bailed out of jail. The cousin he kept employed. Who was his willing partner, no matter the scheme. Who knew my father to the core — better than anyone.

"We start today!"

We were left standing in the street as the door to The Classic Grill swung closed behind him. As we admired our new window display, we wondered just what was about to begin.

FOURTEEN

My father paced behind my mother as she peeked over the sturdy O'Keefe & Merritt oven door, inspecting her *koulourakia*. Her twisty cookies crowned with golden sesame seeds had puffed up in the baking pan. The house smelled of the rich vanilla and butter and sugar she kept to a minimum, because of rationing. To keep her baking on schedule, my mother's quick steps were like the dance of a honeybee, small circles from oven to pantry to utensils to mixing bowl. My father's straight line pacing was the wrong geometry for this small kitchen and for my mother's sensibilities.

Although my father was the king and master at The Classic Grill, my mother ruled her own kitchen. She had been the family cook since she was tall enough to reach the large aluminum *cazani* pan and knead the dough for the weekly bread baking. In fact, that aluminum *cazani* pan was the beginning of the end of childhood for my mother. She didn't often speak of her early years but this particular tale cut into my heart and I remembered every word.

My mother told the story of her younger self, thriving in what I imagined to be the verdant garden of Babylon. But her village was only Silimna, nestled in the rocky hills of the Peloponnese in Arcadia, central Greece. As the treasured daughter in the family, my mother lived a carefree childhood, swinging on the time-worn wooden arbor and tasting the sweet apricots and figs of late summer from the family *kípos*, the ample garden from which most family meals materialized. My mother told me that her mother, my Yiayiá, was a gentle, quiet woman who my mother claimed possessed powerful communication with her luscious fruit and earthy vegetables through what my mother believed to be personal vibrations. My Yiayiá would sink her feet into the dark soil near her blossoming plants and urge them to grow. A touch, a word, a glance from my Yiayiá and, my mother swore, the plants shot up and bore fruit in response.

Yiayiá's plants were not the only beings to flower and flourish. That special touch was magic to my mother whose real name was the common "Stamata," being traditionally named after her paternal grandmother. My Yiayiá saw her daughter as the most precious being in her world and doted on her by sewing beautiful dresses with the finest fabric she could afford so as to envelop my mother in devotion. My Yiayiá ignored tradition and began calling my mother Chrisoula, "golden one," and the name Stamata was left behind. In turn, my mother was the lifeline to happiness for my Yiayiá who had mostly known hostile silence and an occasional violent demand for satisfaction from her husband.

My Yiayiá began her married life at twenty-four years old — an undesirable age for late Nineteenth Century nuptials. As destitute Greek immigrants who fled from Constantinople, her parents could only amass a scanty dowry for my Yiayiá's arranged marriage. They provided no cash, only a few blankets and a set of cooking pots. My Papou, her groom, was fifteen years older and had tended sheep most of his life. He lived solo with his flock, never quite reading the needs of people — most of all, his younger wife. From what my mother told, her father knew only a harsh life of struggling for a living and heavy drinking for relief. He had no experience with tenderness and therefore never offered any to my Yiayiá.

My Yiayiá never trusted her husband after the beating he dispensed several months into their marriage. She cut an unspoken deal with the man for whom she bore the weight of marriage as well as children: no complaints, no beatings. She would not risk her wellbeing — and certainly not her daughter's — for additional undeserved punishment. So she excelled at all things domestic. My Yiayiá even remained silent when my Papou did not return home after a night at the taverna. She turned to my mother, Chrisoula, for the happiness she would never find with my Papou.

One drunken night, my Papou crashed home, apparently not finding satisfaction in a group of small huts outside the village where desperate women squeezed out rent money from sexual encounters. My seven-year-old mother had been sleeping near my Yiayiá that evening when her father, reeking of harsh *spiti krasí*, the taverna house wine, tried to wake the sleeping child. His hands began to slowly move in the wrong direction on my mother's small limp body. A sharp swish sound suddenly cut the darkness. My Yiayiá stood over her husband, more than ready to cleave his hands from his arms with his own large hunting knife, just like she butchered lambs for Easter dinner. His wandering hands froze, as did any remaining attachment to his wife and daughter. After that moment, my Papou ate meals with his eyes cast downward and only occasionally slept at home. And the meals his wife transformed from the plants in her garden were always served up on schedule.

From what my mother could remember, my Yiayiá was also a medicine woman. She tended her flock of sick villagers, as her husband tended his few sheep in the herbed hills surrounding their whitewashed stone house. My mother watched with curious eyes as my Yiayiá used her vibrations and hundreds of years of herbal remedies and potions passed down to soothe fevers, slay infections and set broken bones. Many were cured. Few perished. The wounded limped in and sipped her teas and brews, or received a treatment of *vendouzes*, the small cups heated and applied to the aching back, hip or shoulder. The cured gingerly walked out of my Yiayiá's tiny home, having paid nothing.

Another sister, Magdalini, was born but the new pink, velvet-skinned baby was the last happiness my mother knew in the stone house that soon turned cool, then cold. My mother had been sent to the village schoolhouse at about age six. Two years later, in her second year of schooling, my Yiayiá, who had healed everyone else, could not keep illness from her own scrawny body. A few cruel village widows who wore the eternal black uniform of mourning, claimed the Evil Eye had cursed my Yiayiá's soul because she dared to cure the locals. They said the Evil Eye had drilled a hole in her vibrational field and dragged her into the black silence. My mother held her own mother's body and begged her to come back, even sleeping with her mother's corpse for a night, only holding onto hope as her mother's body grew cold. After my Yiayiá succumbed, my mother's world of heart and home was shattered forever. In a few weeks, her baby sister, Magdalini, wearing the dress my mother had crocheted with her own small hands, breathed a last soft breath. She was gone.

At eight-and-a-half years old, my mother instantly became the domestic head of the house, more like the head of hotel housekeeping. My mother said she did not cry over my Yiayiá's death because her father would not allow it. He simply looked her over and said, "It's your house now."

She did her best to mimic her mother's "serve and be saved" philosophy. Chores done, food on the table and you were left alone. No mourning period for a little girl who had lost her mother and sister, most likely to pneumonia. With the dirt still fresh on the dual graves behind the ancient St. Sophia Church in the center of the village, my mother was expected to fetch water, tend the garden, cook meals and bake loaves of bread from scratch. She was automatically pulled out of school and her days and nights were now jammed with domestic duties. Just a few weeks before her mother's death, it had become delightfully clear to my mother that letters on a page could become words which could become thoughts which could catapult a reader into a new universe. But that revelation quickly faded as did the memory of her mother's tranquil voice.

Having no schoolwork to occupy her day, my mother slowly developed the touch of the goddess Demeter in the garden. She recreated her mother's magic by growing sumptuous vegetables and fruit. Her cooking was simple and manageable. But the weekly bread baking ceremony was the roadblock in my mother's housekeeping. Despite her best efforts, she could not reach to the bottom of the *cazani* pan to mix the flour into smooth and shiny dough. Her father ignored her requests to build a wooden *skamni*, stool, to stand on. Finally, after days of my mother's praying to the large icon of St. Sophia herself, Andromache, an outcast from the gossipy village women's group, happened to stop by my mother's fertile garden and admire her handiwork.

My mother always believed that both she and Andromache must have appeared odd in comparison to the parochial village norms. My mother was a young girl working as an adult woman with no time for girlhood games or teenage romances. Andromache, over six feet tall, seemed not quite a female, but did not possess the harsh ego of a village male. Maybe Andromache felt drawn to heal my mother's wounds or maybe my mother's house was just a safe place in the world for a few hours each day. Little girl and tall woman-man opened their hearts to each other. They baked bread together, Andromache always kneading the dough my mother could not reach in the bottom of the *cazani* pan. While the bread baked in the round communal ovens in the center of the village, Andromache taught my mother enough math to calculate prices at the market. For the rest of her life my mother would always light a candle or say a prayer in church for Andromache, a fellow outcast, who helped my mother when she needed it most.

By eighteen, my mother had swept enough earthen floors and crushed enough wheat for a lifetime. Her father did little besides tend his few sheep and drink away the drachmas from the annual shearing and slaughter. He had certainly saved no dowry money for his daughter's possible marriage. She felt her future closing down like the altar doors in church when the priest cried out, "The doors! The doors! In wisdom, let us attend!" In the liturgy, the doors in front of the altar would creak closed and only the priest and other male helpers were allowed behind them. No women could pierce that spiritual barricade.

One crisp spring afternoon, my mother was again on her knees, alone in the village church, desperately praying to St. Sophia for a new life with specifics she could not articulate. She had prayed intensely but gave up when hunger took over as she was exhausted from hours of scrubbing laundry in a large wooden tub. Still on her knees, my mother scrutinized the landscape of the aged church doors adorned with gold leaf and melancholy icons of Archangel Gabriel and the Virgin Mary. At that moment, the idea came upon my mother that there were *two* sides to a door. A door could shut out and strand a person pleading for entry to the familiar. Or if shut from the outside, a door provided unlimited, uncharted freedom. My mother said she felt St. Sophia had lent her wisdom and a pair of wings.

Tempting the rumors and the Evil Eye, my mother packed her meager wardrobe into a knitting bag and slyly left the house before her father returned for dinner after too many glasses of wine and hashish. Once out of her housekeeping chains she latched onto a band of musicians who traveled to Sparta to play at a taverna. Her glorious alto singing voice and cache of old folk songs were her ticket out. She fended off all male advances, as a bad reputation was a deal breaker for girls her age if they wanted to eventually marry a good man, or any man at all.

Most summer evenings that year, my mother sang the old folk songs to violin and mandolin accompaniment in the steamy garden taverna with its gravel floor and cheap retsina wine served in handmade wooden cups. She closed her show with *Toh Yilekaki, The Little Vest,* that left most of the audience wistfully remembering their village homes and ordering another drink. A small crowd of suitors met my mother behind the little stage every night, but there was only one man she could not ignore.

Always a straight shooter, my father's opening line was both a proposal of marriage and a plan to immediately return to America. Like many other Greek men, he had financially established himself in America but journeyed to Greece to seek a wife before returning. He knew what he wanted in a Greek wife who would navigate America by his side. No silly village girl who clung to her parents and who could not envision an adventurous, independent life. For three nights my father had observed this fine woman sing. He longed to warm himself on what he judged to be her inner hearth of optimism and strength. His vision was to earn more money to add to the stash he had saved from a decade of cooking and dishwashing work in California. And now he would create a restaurant with his new wife, if my mother would have him. My father told her he always looked forward, never back. He needed my mother for his wife. Right then. He was leaving for America in a week and he begged her to join him.

Familiar with making lifetime deals with a man, my mother dragged him to a small table at the taverna and bored her eyes into him desperately trying to read his character and motivation. At a time like this, she longed for her own mother's intricate knowledge of vibrations and positive forces in the universe. Had my father's soul been warped by the peasant philosophy of man-as-king? Would her new role be wife, not slave? My mother appreciated my father's honest talk and quickly negotiated three things: her husband would be faithful. Period. Her husband would respect her and the work she did. Most of all, she demanded, their family would be strong. Unbreakable no matter the circumstances. She could only imagine a family drenched in love — enough to backfill a lifetime of affection that she and her mother were denied. My mother asked for nothing more. But nothing less.

With an exchange of drachmas, a nearly authentic birth certificate and passports were minted. My parents quickly married at a church in Piraeus and the page turned for my mother, who by this time could read every word on her roadmap to America, her new world. She had slammed the doors on a life spent on her hands and knees. She would work — and work hard — but she would stand proudly next to her husband in America.

After that, my mother, always known in America as Chrisoula, did not knead her own dough and bake her own bread — not even on holidays. In fact, my mother purchased her bread at the expensive Italian bakery downtown. This was one extravagance of which my father wholeheartedly approved.

FIFTEEN

"And that is the story my mother told. My parents made a deal in Greece and came to America to make good on it." I sat back and watched the faces of my little group.

Dark Eyes was back and had pulled another young woman over to our table. Maybe originally from Eritrea, maybe from Egypt. She whispered to Dark Eyes to catch her up on the story.

With a new member in our group, I suddenly felt embarrassed that I had not asked their names. If these kids were kind enough to listen to a craggy old man talk about his family, I should at least know their names. Thankfully, Mariam, our newest member wore a name tag, so that was a start. I announced my name, George, and shook hands with Dark Eyes who was Aman, Jesús the cook and Jason the kid with the mop and bad, pale complexion. The dad with the kids was Zach and we already knew Aiden was attached to his video game. Zach introduced his daughter Addison who seemed to follow my story.

Right away, Mariam spied that my coffee cup was empty and jumped up to refill it. Once we were settled again, I couldn't help but continue. It had been so long since anyone wanted to hear me talk about our family — or anything else for that matter.

SIXTEEN

Perched on a tall wooden kitchen stool, our neighbor Irini giddily soaked up the exchange between my mother and father, hardly helping with baking *koulourakia*, the task that day in my mother's kitchen. She was an aged Greek woman wearing the all-black mourning vestments. Irini reminded my father of everything he detested about Greek village life — the gossip and the scraping for every morsel not owned or nailed down. She read fortunes whenever she had a gullible victim. My father could not understand Irini, or anyone else, whose purpose in life was to worship death and the past. My father had little time for self-reflection as he was in complete synch with America. Here he could quickly reinvent himself and nimbly move forward to making a profit.

He continued pacing while my mother calmly rolled and twisted more *koulourakia* and sprinkled them with sesame seeds atop a slathering of slick egg yolk. Her cookies, aligned in perfect rows on the baking pan, were a product of centuries of culinary know-how.

In an attempt to interrupt the rhythm of his relentless pacing, my mother pulled out the *briki* to noisily make Greek coffee. She purposefully shook the brass long-handled pot hoping to build a wall of noise between her and my father's uneasiness.

My father tried to speak to my mother in low tones, without Irini hearing.

"Like I told you, Chrisoula *mou*, it is time to make the new restaurant." He spoke louder to reach her over the *briki* noise and glared at Irini whose eyes followed my father like a vulture waiting for a morsel of meat. "I go to the bank."

Passing a mirror he straightened his slightly out-of-date tie that he customarily wore to funerals. He checked his salt and pepper hair and mustache to make certain he looked as dignified as possible. An established look was a winning hand. My mother warily studied him primping and attacked a new batch of dough in the mixing bowl. She pinched the dough and nimbly rolled it between her hands to form a thin rope and then a twist.

"The bank give us money for this new restaurant? They think this is good idea?" Her movements punctuated her words. Had he already been to the bank without consulting her? *Collateral* was an English word my mother had learned early on. She'd quickly computed that the only possible fodder for that ravenous beast that Americans called collateral would be The Classic Grill restaurant and the family home. Now she hurried to the oven and pulled out a sheet of toasty cookies, moving past my father.

He swiped one *koulouraki* and tasted it. "They are done!"

"Another minute," my mother countered, in no mood to agree. She shoved the baking pan back in the oven. Frustrated on both the cooking and financial fronts, my father threw up his hands and let out an exasperated sigh.

Irini cackled as she nibbled a cookie from an earlier batch and watched the show. "What does he know of *koulourakia?* A man..."

My father gave her a dark glance, wishing she would vanish.

"What if the big restaurant no do so good?" My mother folded her arms. "It wartime now."

My father sensed the ebb of my mother's enthusiasm for the new restaurant and quickly tried to buoy it up. "It will be a palace for Athena herself! You will see!"

Irini set down the half-eaten *koulouraki.* Her bony hands illustrated her thoughts.

"We are little Navy town. No rich peoples here...*prosechseh*, be careful with the money!" Irini hissed.

Irini's words once again were validation to my father as to why he was thankful to leave the old village ways behind. Always someone to tell you it couldn't be done. Always a jealous someone to strangle an infant idea before it could inhale its first breath. In America you could succeed or fail by your own ingenuity or lack of it. You navigated your ship by your own stars. Agitated with Irini butting in, my father looked at my mother but could not read her reaction.

"I want this now! I will have it!" My father had never truly demanded anything of his wife, my mother. With a quick glance, he could see that his words had pushed my mother away, her small boat drifting in another direction.

"Chrisoula?" He spoke more softly now, attempting to reach her in any way he could. My father craved a sliver of light to crack open the locked gates blocking his pathway to the bank. My mother moved to the stove and again noisily shook the *briki*, jangling my father's nerves. Her eyes lifted to meet my father's. She did not challenge him, which she knew would be disastrous. She locked him in her characteristic truthful gaze.

"We not young, *Achilléas*. You want we risk everything?"

"I no wait! This my chance to take!"

My father walked to the wooden hat tree and pulled on his overcoat and gray fedora. "I get the money! Now!" He smashed his hat onto his head.

In the corner, Irini rocked her body on her kitchen stool. "Tsk, tsk, tsk. Big restaurant! Big chance! *Toh mavro mati ketai polla leptah!* The Evil Eye watch big money!" She channeled all the negative energy from her webby world of voodoo, charms and Greek black magic.

My father grabbed the fluted crystal knob of the front door, purposely ignoring the vexing Irini. He stood in the doorway for a moment and then abruptly walked out. My mother's body yearned to run to her husband, wanting to continue the unfinished conversation. But she cast her eyes downward and returned to rolling and twisting her cookies.

"The Evil Eye will curse you and your money!" Irini chanted in Greek.

Irini turned over her demitasse coffee cup and watched the thick black coffee grounds run down the curved insides of the white porcelain cup. She looked into the cup and whispered harshly and slowly, as if reincarnating the soothsayer Cassandra whose prophecies of doom were never believed.

"New restaurant! I — smell — burn!"

My mother's eyes widened and she hurried to the oven. Her forgotten cookies had turned black and gray smoke seeped from the oven.

"The Evil Eye has a good nose too. *Voíthisé meh.* Help me with this," my mother mumbled absently. Usually she was patient with Irini, finding sympathy for this old outcast. But today her tolerance had run dry. "Enough for today. *Ftani!*"

My mother stared at the door that my father had stridently shut behind him. Yet another set of doors for my mother. Should she chase after my father and sit by his side at the bank, loyally endorsing what she believed to be a chancy business proposition? Or should she stay glued to her wooden chair? This was the first true rupture she had experienced with my father since they arrived together in America. She could feel the fabric of their union rip ever so slightly — with a little more pressure there could be two pieces where there was now one.

My mother did not rely on Evil Eyes or calamitous predictions. This was unfamiliar territory and she begged St. Sophia for another piece of well-timed good advice. She attempted to gauge how she could preserve what she had believed to be her indestructible bond with my father and, at the same time, not lose everything they had worked for. With one hand holding on to what she and my father had created, and one hand wanting to roll the dice for my father's sake, my mother decided she would wait to see what happened. She made the sign of the cross and hoped St. Sophia approved.

SEVENTEEN

"You got all my receipts? How much tax I pay?" My father interrogated my brother like a detective in the movies.

"Yeah, Pop. Got 'em all. Not quite done yet," Demo patiently replied.

His long legs were crammed beneath the disheveled office desk in the back of The Classic Grill. My brother worked intently over ledgers and papers that were stacked high while my father peeked over his shoulder, reaching into the stack from time to time to snatch a few documents. He couldn't read, but he scanned them and tossed them back again.

I circumnavigated my broom around the tax zone, sweeping behind my father's footsteps. I wanted to help with the taxes. I wanted to know everything about running The Classic Grill.

I also wanted to run interference for Demo. I wanted to throw myself over the grenade of my father's temper to protect Demo from a possible explosion that seemed to erupt more often these days when my father and Demo were together. Sort of a blow-up protection plan for my brother, although I wasn't much of a shield. One thing was certain about my father: any obstruction to his new restaurant plan was his flashpoint. And Demo was the centerpiece of his plan. And that was just the *mezé*, the appetizer, for the rest of my father's tirade. What subject would it be today?

"For this reason, I give you education. To help our new business."

"Sure, Pop. Sign right here." Demo muttered, finishing his tax calculations. "They changed a few rules this year."

"Ach!" My father slapped his forehead. "How much more I pay?"

"Not much more than last year, Pop."

Putting aside the taxes, Demo ushered my father by the elbow, past me, into the immense walk-in refrigerator, the only private conference room at The Classic Grill. He left the door ajar.

"Pop, I need to talk to you."

"Talk no make money. We finish taxes now." My father's eyes darted around the refrigerator shelves, deciding if he should add eggs to his grocery order.

"Pop, it's important! I can't work here anymore."

Still in the office, I stifled a gasp.

"I spend all my time here. I have a few other things I want — I need to do," Demo explained. "There is a play at school, and they practice after class — I need the time."

I inched closer to the walk-in, my stomach twisting. Demo had never stood his ground like this before. My father seemed to stare at my brother, not really seeing him. As if Demo's honest revelation was simply water dripping off the roof after the first downpour of the season, trickling down the drain, seeping into the earth, insignificant.

Then, unexpectedly, he cupped his hands around Demo's face.

"Demo, you are my brains!" My father whispered, his voice raspy with desperation. "I no read. You need to help me always. Do our family business! Nothing else important!"

He marched out of the walk-in as if he had spent the last few weeks practicing with the infantry. Disappointment on his face, Demo walked quickly behind my father.

Of course, I thought I could solve the problem. I would volunteer my education to my father. I could read and write. I would again offer my interest in menus and cooking. I would again serve up my vision of how our family could run The Classic Grill and give it new life with new menu items to entice new customers. And Demo could be free.

Pushing my broom, I kept my head bent toward the floor. "Pop, I can help!" I offered weakly as my father passed me by.

"No, George. You no bother Demo. He my businessman."

Demo clamped a hand on my father's shoulder and spun him around.

"Pop, listen! I can't work here anymore!"

"My first son take over! The Greek way!" My father wildly waved off Demo's words. "Demo, you got work to do. George, you too."

I stashed the broom and disappeared behind the dishwashing sink, submerging my hurt into the soapy suds. From my station in the back, I watched Demo consider his next move. He looked up as if hoping for one last chance with my father. Then he simply bundled the taxes and straightened the desk like it was his last day on the job. I was amazed at how tranquil he appeared, almost happy. While my father left the kitchen to work in the dining room, Demo licked a stamp and applied it to the envelope for the taxes and hung up his apron. He pulled on his jacket and headed for the backdoor, giving me a nod to follow. I quickly dropped my scrub brush.

"You stay on and help Pop," Demo whispered in my ear. "He's gonna need it and you'll do great. You're smart and you love the restaurant."

Demo slapped my back gently. It was like the first time I had dressed in a suit or what old-timers used to call "a suit of clothes" instead of my worn school shirts or cook's pants. At that moment years ago, Demo overflowed with compliments and again, he made me feel grown up and worthy.

I felt closer to Demo than ever, as we both were imprisoned by our father's fossilized ideas of how to live our lives. Demo wanted out and I wanted in. My father could have it all. At the time, it never occurred to me that my father might have been afraid of adjusting his ironclad vision. He might have been terrified that a loosened grip on the leash would bring pandemonium to his team of horses, when, in truth, the animals would perform better if given the lead.

Demo suddenly seemed to be an adult. "I guess it's Athens versus Sparta around here. I'm not ready for war but sometimes you have to fight."

My brother wrestled a small book from his jacket pocket and flipped through the pages. I saw he had scribbled notes everywhere in red ink.

"The secret of happiness is freedom. The secret of freedom is courage." Demo read out loud in his best dramatic voice. He looked up and smiled becoming my teenage brother again.

"Might be time to stand up to Sparta!" Demo gave me a bear hug and then ambled down the alley to who knows where. Alone, I watched Demo — whose heart knew mine better than anyone's — step away from our family's restaurant. I knew that wherever Demo went in the future, I would miss him as much as I did at that moment.

EIGHTEEN

The place smelled like bundles of old greenbacks stacked in towers within a cavernous steel vault. At least that's the way it seemed to my father as he impatiently fidgeted while seated in the lobby at the San Francisco National Bank in downtown Vallejo. He looked across the sea of men in white shirts and bulky wool suits each navigating a desk in front of them, appearing to carry out important financial matters. None of them could last a day as a fry cook, he calculated.

My father was certain this meeting was a formality before the final papers were drawn up. "I borrow money, they make interest. I borrow more, they make more profit." His logic was simple. Wasn't everyone out to make as much money as they could in this town?

A petite brunette motioned to my father to follow and she escorted him to a sturdy, polished wooden chair. Walking behind her, my father assessed that she was too skinny and should eat more. They probably don't pay her enough to buy good food, he assumed. He briefly flashed on Daphne but quickly put that sweet thought aside. He didn't want to mix pleasure with business, even if only in his mind.

My father proudly planted himself across the desk from a bland, rotund banker nesting behind an enormous desk that seemed to confine the banker's girth. Looking at him, my father was reminded of a large bowl of Cream of Wheat. The banker checked the paperwork my father had submitted.

"Your request for twenty thousand dollars, for..." he flipped the paperwork, "...a new restaurant. And your collateral for this?"

"Yes. Collateral." My father rolled his r's hoping that the banker didn't take notice of his foreign pronunciation. "I own a restaurant. The Classic Grill on Georgia Street. For twenty-two years. And my house here in Vallejo on Virginia Street."

My father sat back, waiting for a word of praise. Perhaps this banker had even come to the restaurant a few times and was impressed. One truth my father lived by: no one who had eaten at The Classic Grill walked away unsatisfied. And this man definitely looked like he was no stranger to good eating.

"And you want to make another restaurant?" The banker queried, with his small reading glasses pinched on his fleshy nose as he looked down on my father.

My father lit up with his vision of the new restaurant.

"Yes! I make bigger, better!" My father could hardly contain his enthusiasm. He could picture the marble floor buffed to a high gloss. He imagined his cooks, adorned with their stiff white toques, sautéing delicate fillet of sole in a rich butter sauce and roasting meats in a wood-fired oven. My father could see the crisp black and white menu printed in elegant script listing entrees with French names. The picture was softened by golden lights from chandeliers hanging low from the ceiling.

"I'm sorry." The banker rose from his chair to tower over my father.

In an instant, the banker's words cut off my father's movie like a projector that suddenly lost power in the middle of a feature film. The fantasy whirred to a halt. With two words, the banker brought my father back to reality in Vallejo, California, 1942.

"Our Chamber of Commerce has directed our downtown to feature fewer, uh...ethnic businesses. And with that emphasis, we think your restaurant would not succeed."

My father's thick eyebrows clouded low over his eyes. His anger raged, his body was ready to punch and defend at the same time. He could smell it coming.

"What is this...uh...ethnic?" In his gut he already knew.

"The tenor in our business community is to foster legitimate enterprises that will last." The banker spoke these words as if he had proudly nailed the final board on the fence to keep out intruders, maintaining the neighborhood sanctity and protecting the community from immigrant ruffians.

My father paused only for a moment. The words *ethnic* and *legitimate* reverberated in his brain as if they had been hurled at his head from a speeding car, squarely hitting their target.

"This new restaurant is not a safe investment for us." The banker calmly pressed his fingertips together. His idle hands signaled they had nothing more to do, no paperwork to fill out. No adding machine to punch. The banker patiently waited for the moment my father would exit the bank.

"Twenty-two years is not to last?" my father shot back, unashamed that his voice had increased in volume, well past the approved hushed mutterings of the other bankers and borrowers. "I understand how your bank work. Sorry I no part of your club!"

My father stood up and spoke in a loud voice that was like the ear splitting air horn blasting the morning and afternoon work call at the Mare Island Shipyard. Everyone in town could hear that whistle signaling all workers to clock-in or clock-out. Now all necks twisted to see the local fireworks that were unfamiliar in a bank that was usually as lively as McDonald's Funeral Home on Virginia Street.

"I no want your money. I no need it!" My father's baritone bellowed across the bank. Again, he was insulted in this town where he had once belonged, was once part of the revered old guard of businessmen. My father collected his hat and angrily marched to the exit. All eyes were uncompromisingly locked on this older immigrant man. He reached the oversized mahogany door and turned to fire one more shot across the bow.

"Be sure you tell your mayor!"

My father crashed the mahogany and prism glass door behind him. I know this because, although he never saw me, I had slipped into the bank earlier and then I waited for him outside.

NINETEEN

"Well, what the heck happened?" Zach wanted to know. He refilled sodas at the self-serve bar for himself and his kids. "Did he make the restaurant? The one he wanted?"

Aman and Mariam sat shoulder to shoulder, uniform to uniform waiting for the next chapter of the Pappayannis family odyssey.

At that moment I truly ached for my family to surround me, wishing they were all here to tell their stories from their own points of view. I chuckled to myself imagining the scene — everyone jabbering at once, hands waving passionately in the air, for emphasis of course. My father would have carefully examined the fast-food menu hanging above the cash register and certainly would have pulled aside the manager to suggest improvements. New signage. Perhaps tableside service. My mother would have scrubbed down every table and thoroughly swept the floor — and probably would have tucked some homemade pastry into the plexiglass cookie case. Theo Vasili and Taki would have sipped coffee all day long and happily taken advantage of their senior discounts — even if they were underage.

TWENTY

The streets of Vallejo were slick with residue from the low morning fog. I watched as my father quickly walked past the downtown storefronts whose colors were faded by the grey curtain of mist. His thick soled kitchen shoes squished a little as he hurried past Greene's Cigar and Liquor Store.

Theo Vasili popped out of Greene's, precisely on schedule, stogie hanging from his lips. He fell in step with my father as they quickly walked past Medico Drugs, then the Florsheim Shoe Store, towards what they used to call the seedy end of town known as Lower Georgia. Most of the storefronts were bare-bones bars with a few cafés, stores and barber shops mixed in. They walked past the second-story whorehouses with which my uncle had reasonable familiarity. Theo Vasili snuck a look up at the window of the Hotel Portland, his favorite. He hoped to catch a glimpse of a certain evening companion but was disappointed. Apparently late night work didn't allow for early morning rising.

As they neared the waterfront my father and Theo Vasili picked up the pace. They had little time to complete their mission before the morning cooks arrived at the restaurant and the breakfast crowd settled in for ham and eggs or my father's signature hotcakes.

My uncle, for once, took the lead, his gangly arms swinging at his side to increase his speed. Suddenly he cut left, down a narrow alley used for small garbage trucks, and then took a sharp right to find a storefront on the alleyway. My uncle and father stooped to walk under the low doorway of Charlie's Bakery. A long, empty pastry display case with a lazy fly buzzing inside was only a prop to shield the action in the back. My father and Theo Vasili looked around. Neither Charlie nor a bakery was to be found anywhere. Familiar with the landscape, my uncle took a breath and calmly walked behind the empty pastry case. He pushed open a thin plywood door that squeaked open to expose a room foggy from the haze of cigarettes, cigars and another herbal odor my father recognized as hashish. Back in the village, his family had cultivated a small amount to sell to those who had the money for luxuries, but the young boys in his family were forbidden to use it. Hashish clouded the brain his mother warned. Makes you lazy, and work will be only a dream, she cautioned. My father had sampled the cannabis resin as a young boy but his ferocity to escape his meager surroundings made hashish seem like a plaything for the rich, and my father had no time for playthings. His stomach turned at the thought of lying about in a daze when an opportunity to catapult out of a lifetime of settling for scraps might present itself. He would not miss out.

A dozen tables teemed with men, Chinese and Caucasian rolling dice, mulling over cards and calling bluffs. Right at home, Theo Vasili stood waiting at the back of the room. A few gamblers raised an eyebrow or nodded recognition in my uncle's direction. My father, who controlled everything in his own life, was uncomfortable in this atmosphere, especially with his mercurial cousin in charge of his fate. But my father knew his new restaurant was on life support and this was its last opportunity for a plasma transfusion.

They waited for a moment. A short Chinese man herded them with quick steps into a dark room where one narrow dusty shaft of sunlight streamed in from a tiny window facing the alley. They approached a figure in a slightly out of date suit and tie who sat behind a low table covered with tall stacks of handwritten ledgers. He reminded my father of the Greek and Turkish moneylenders in his village who always seemed to be present, and at the same time, hidden from the public.

My uncle whispered a few words in a low tone and a hefty envelope was placed in his waiting open hand. My uncle passed the envelope, which was gorged with cash, to my father. At that moment my father's dream of a grand restaurant was born — with a not-so-legal birth certificate.

TWENTY-ONE

Later that day I was running. Running through the same downtown streets of Vallejo my father and uncle had trod just hours ago. By mid-day, the sun had burned though the morning mist and the landscape had dialed into vibrant color.

I zipped past Levy's department store, past what we called the Alibi clock, an elaborate freestanding clock that originally told time in San Francisco until it was put out to pasture on Georgia Street in our little Navy town. I was desperate to find Demo and I could only hope he was not on a ferry scooting across the bay in search of a poetry reading.

When I reached our house, I took the stairs two at a time. I was thin, ran track at school and at that moment was scared out of my wits about my father and the future of The Classic Grill. I dashed through our wooden sunporch, scanned the living room and peeked into our shared bedroom. Then I turned towards the bathroom where the door was half-closed.

I shoved the door open. Time stopped for just a second. Demo stood there in full make-up, his face painted a Kabuki white, his eyebrows drawn together as if they were one. A thin gold ribbon encircled his head. Instead of being plastered down with hair tonic, his dark curls were soft and feminine around his face. I noticed a photo taped to the mirror of a woman's face with dark curly hair and white makeup. My first thought was to shield Demo from my father's sight, even though I knew my father was working at the restaurant a few blocks from our home. I was certain my father had a Cyclops eye, watching everyone and everything in our house.

I needed Demo to listen. As I yanked him close to whisper in his ear, I was startled to see my mother's small gold earring hanging from his lobe. I tossed him a towel, hoping he'd get the idea to rub the thick white make-up off his face. Then we sped away to The Classic Grill and my father.

We burst through the back door and then quietly crept to the front of the restaurant where the regulars, Theo Vasili, Taki and now Daphne, were seated at the counter. In front of the counter stood my father, apron on, as if making excuses in front of a firing squad.

"It is written here in plain English!" An unfamiliar white-haired man held up a document dense with text. I could see the word "Lease" printed at the top. He wore a fashionable grey wool suit and tightly gripped an expensive leather briefcase. This bureaucrat was not a friend.

My father took a proud step forward and yanked the paper from him like he was pulling a shirt off a clothesline. Chin held high, he quickly scanned the lease, pretending to take in the printed words.

"Paragraph two, section one. Read it!" sneered the official.

"Read it, Vasili!" my father called to my uncle, buying time.

Reaching for the lease from my father in slow motion, Theo Vasili sluggishly passed it to Taki who was our ace in the hole. He could read enough to make sense of the daily newspaper.

"*Diavasé toh!* Read it!" My uncle gave Taki a lukewarm command.

Taki reached for the lease. Suddenly Demo stepped forward and snatched the paper from Taki. My throat tightened as I realized Demo had not removed all his makeup. His brows were still dramatically dark and patches of white paint had stuck to his face.

"Lessee The Classic Grill," Demo read aloud, "will pay ten percent of the monthly gross to Landlords Grey and Finch at the end of each month. Failure to comply will result in automatic eviction."

Demo looked up and lowered the lease. My father stared at the lease, not at my brother.

"But Mr. Grey was in here three months ago. He said he would never enforce it," Demo argued. "He shook hands with my father!"

"And he like our meat loaf. Remember, Taki?" Theo Vasili recalled.

Taki sipped his coffee and nodded in agreement.

"I cannot pay extra!" my father cried out. "You want to rob me!"

The official in the suit set down his briefcase and gracefully slipped onto a stool at the counter. He scanned the menu.

"Roast beef on white. Extra gravy," he spat out as if my father was his personal servant. "Coffee, cream. Custard pie."

My brother immediately ushered my father into the kitchen.

"Gimme a minute with him, Pop," Demo whispered softly. Narrowing his eyes at the official, my father reluctantly walked away.

"What do you really want?" Demo demanded like a fierce prosecuting attorney in a courtroom. I watched my brother at work.

"I'm Finch's attorney. Finch bought out Grey and we're enforcing the ten percent on the gross. Every month." He spread a napkin meticulously on his lap.

"Gonna raise the rent too?" Demo pressed.

"Come June first. Just like a clock." He did not bother to look at Demo. A few long seconds ticked by.

"Your old man's a fresh-off-the-boat bumpkin," the official added impatiently. "Doesn't know anything about business. Never will play the big time. We're going to change this town."

"My father created this business from nothing!" Demo retorted. I sensed my brother attempting to fling his cape of protection around my father. "He's a good, honest man."

The official pushed his face close to Demo.

"Kid, let me make it simple for you: Finch is in line to be mayor next year and he can finish the clean up in this town. No more two-bit immigrant businesses. We own this town. We'll be ready for the boom when this war is done."

With perfect timing, my father swung through the kitchen doors with plates loaded with the official's lunch order. Tetsuya and Mr. Chris meekly peeked out from the kitchen.

Demo never broke his gaze from the official's cold stare. "Pop, don't serve him! We don't need his business!"

The official threw his napkin on the counter, slid off his stool and swept up his briefcase.

"I'll get a veal steak at the place across the street. The Restaurant St. Charles." With disdain dripping from his words, he looked over the platters of hot food my father held. For a moment I thought he might reconsider.

"Their veal is only beef. I see them beat it!" Theo Vasili's remark slid off the official like oil on a slippery fish that was ready for roasting.

"Afternoon, all!"

We watched him click out of our restaurant in his expensive black wingtips with hard soles. At the door he nonchalantly tipped his hat.

"He thinks we're idiots," Demo said darkly.

"Idiots to stay here. The mayor and his friends! *Kléftes!* They are thieves!" My father threw his hands in the air.

Customers began flooding The Classic Grill for dinner and we were forced back to our workstations. Demo hurried to the office with the lease and I read it over his shoulder as he walked. Was there a loophole I could spot? I wanted to help my father too. One thing was for sure — I was amazed how Demo, a 17-year-old kid, had stared down that official. We Greeks called Demo's power *dýnami* — dynamic strength. His performance art wasn't bad either.

Just then, Demo turned to me, the five-page lease between us.

"How can I leave him? He needs me." Demo was talking more to himself than to me. His look was a mirror of his tug-of-war between loyalty to my father and his desire to break free.

I wandered to the front of the restaurant to find my father. What would happen to this restaurant that I loved, that was my true home? I desperately wanted to save it, especially from the jaws of the official bigots that ran the town. I quietly walked into the dining room to find my father lost in thought, vigorously wiping down the bar, his strokes brisk and angry. Unlike Demo, I didn't have the right words. In fact, I searched my brain for any words at all that would soothe my father. Instead, Daphne's musical voice floated up to our ears.

"I think it will be wonderful."

My father's head jerked up, waking from his tangled thoughts of anger, revenge and financial calculations.

"The new restaurant. *Your* new restaurant," Daphne breathed, taking a slow sip of her coffee. Her gaze was glued on my father.

"Achilles the brave Greek warrior can do anything! Make your dream!" Daphne sat back on her stool, waiting for my father's response.

A fire ignited in my father's eyes and landed on Daphne. My ears did not want to hear his next words.

"And you will be in it," he spoke softly. "You no left behind."

Daphne radiated femininity, little girl sweetness and something else too. I paused a moment to identify just what it was. I could feel Daphne needed a rock to tether her small wooden rowboat in the uncertain waters of this port town of Vallejo. I looked at Daphne and my father and felt the heat between them rise twenty degrees. Now, I truly did not have the right words.

TWENTY-TWO

A few days later, Tetsuya, Theo Vasili and I worked in the kitchen between the lunch and dinner rush. Tetsuya peeled cucumbers and my uncle sipped wine while resting on a kitchen stool. I had my father's big cookbook open. Tetsuya's experienced hands prepared tall mounds of vegetables.

"I told Pop to put Lamb Fricassee on the menu, like he used to make." I spooned a bit of the Fricassee on a saucer for both Tetsuya and Theo Vasili to taste. "Here, try!"

Tetsuya sampled a bite.

"Vasili, this boy is not a cook, he is a chef!" Tetsuya proclaimed. Theo Vasili slurped a spoonful. I was certain Tetsuya was put on earth to fill the emotional gaps, the holes where my father lacked tenderness and loving care — which was almost every day.

"*Neh!* Yes! This Fricassee is better than your father's!" Theo Vasili chuckled. "But you no tell him!"

I beamed with pride. Theo Vasili took another sip of the rough homemade white wine he and my father purchased from a small country town north of Vallejo. Napa was just a crossroads, really.

"*You* tell Pop, Tetsuya," I answered. "He never listens to me."

I stirred my Fricassee and added white pepper, the perfect ingredient, I decided. Tetsuya smiled softly.

"I am number two son like you. My father had no place for me. I leave Japan to make my own life."

Tetsuya put his arm around my long-limbed frame in a fatherly hug as he spoke. Theo Vasili poured out another glass of wine in his small tumbler glass. He always drank to the half-full mark, then filled his glass again. Harder to count glasses that way. From his stool, my uncle watched me attend to my Fricassee and observed Tetsuya peel and chop.

"Achilles, your father, my cousin, is first son in the old country." Theo Vasili sat back, remembering. "Your father's brother, second son, stay back in the village to plow rocks for nothing. Best thing for Achilles is stay here and send money for three dowries for the sisters. They depend for him."

He summarized my father's life by the amount of money he could earn and send back to Greece. Another sip.

"Did you send money too, Theo Vasili?" My Fricassee was just about done and perfectly well-seasoned, if I said so myself.

"No, I lose too much." My uncle looked down at his shoes, embarrassed, a little tipsy.

Tetsuya wiped his hands on his apron. With uncharacteristic dramatic flair, he sat down and began to hunt and peck on the typewriter.

"My day to make the menu. What we put on? Ah! Lamb Fricassee is good today." Tetsuya smiled.

"Pop might get mad!"

"The customers will order. He is never angry when he make money," Tetsuya assured me. No wonder he was the only person other than the Pappayannis family to hold the keys to The Classic Grill.

TWENTY-THREE

"Tetsuya sounds like he was a good man." Aman's dark eyes surrounded by fringy lashes darted to the door to keep watch for customers.

That story took me back to the day when Tetsuya featured my new recipe on the menu. A glorious day for me.

"Tetsuya was my teacher — or as they say today, my mentor. Although I didn't know what that was at the time. I trusted him like a father. Loved him like I should have loved my father. We were both second sons. I was trying to be noticed. And in Tetsuya's case, he had only wanted a comfortable place within his family back in Japan."

"Fathers," pronounced Aman, with a disgruntled snort. "They just don't know. They need lessons."

TWENTY THREE

TWENTY-FOUR

All this pulled me back to how our family got to know Tetsuya. I always thought of Tetsuya as "mine," but as jealous lovers say, someone else saw him first. And that someone was my father.

Tetsuya had immigrated to San Francisco around 1906, just before The Gentlemen's Agreement was employed around 1908, cutting off all immigration from Japan — even after Japan agreed in 1900 to deny passports to workers seeking to enter the U.S. mainland. He arranged for papers to move first to Hawaii, and from there, to San Francisco. He expected to encounter a difficult new Western world, but he was not ready for a nearly impossible one. San Francisco had not been a welcoming place.

Growing up in the tiny mountain village of Ainokura in the Gokayama region of northwestern Japan, Tetsuya had planned to take his place in the Togami family silk manufacturing business. Tetsuya loved the sweet, cool mountain air in summer and the spectacular snowstorms that covered his country homestead in silvery, serene beauty in winter. He could not imagine living anywhere else but in Japan among his parents, four brothers and three sisters who all participated in the silk business. His mother and sisters cared for the *bombyx mori*, the mulberry silkmoths that would develop into hungry caterpillars. The women made sure they were able to offer an abundance of mulberry leaves for the perpetually ravenous silkworms. His sisters Chieko, Fumiko and Eiko became expert weavers and extracted the long, silken thread from the cocoon by dissolving it in boiling water. Later the sisters mastered the family dyeing technique. The males in the family supervised the weaving, and Tetsuya's father, Mitsuo, traveled the countryside selling the silk which had earned an excellent reputation. The Togami family silk was delicate and did not tear easily, and the luminescent color of seaglass blue became the signature color of the Togami looms.

Tetsuya's family had lived in the village of Ainokura for over four hundred years and he had no reason to believe he would break the tradition. His father had slowly saved enough to modernize and purchase one mechanized silk loom to keep the business competitive — but he had plans for more. There would still be the need for a great amount of family labor, especially from the women, as the nurturing of the silkworms was vital to the industry. Naturally, his family always maintained a small plot for rice farming to supplement the silk trade.

The delicate yet relentless snowfall in the small village of Ainokura was the subject for painters and poets. The steep thatched A-shaped roofs of the Gassho-style houses were tilted at 60-degree angles to allow the snow and sleet to slide downward, keeping weight off the roof. The tented rooflines stamped the village with a quaint look, like a Japanese Innsbruck. In his younger days, Tetsuya welcomed the mountain snows, as he knew the frozen landscape would soon lead to the greenest hillsides a child could imagine as a playground or the best spot for lying back and contemplating clouds.

As a boy, Tetsuya intensely studied the lives of the individual silkworms, wanting to understand which exact conditions led the pupa to spin a cocoon of one long silk fiber. What could make the silk thread stronger? The young Tetsuya began his personal research on which worms produced the finest, strongest silk fibers in their cocoons and how the weaving process could be improved. He envisioned himself someday pursuing advanced studies in science and mechanics, and later bringing his newfound knowledge back to his home village.

Taller and more physically imposing than his brothers, the young Tetsuya was happily certain that his sincere enthusiasm would help propel the family business to a new level of success and prosperity that every member of the family could enjoy. Although he was born into the thankless second son position, Tetsuya's future vision for himself was like the bolts of the silken blue magic his family had created — strong, unending and tranquilly beautiful.

Gentle in his manner, Tetsuya became his mother Hisako's favorite child. Hisako often spilled her private stories of her husband's cruelty to Tetsuya who listened patiently. But he was terrified to say a word against his father who rarely showed his children anything but a ready lash for disobedience.

As Tetsuya grew, his father increasingly disliked him, and soon his siblings — even his sisters — shunned the second son who was at ease chatting with the elders in Ainokura, the Buddhist priest or the occasional visitor who wandered through the mountain village. His older brother Kiyoshi, smaller than his father who was barely five feet tall, seethed with envy at Tetsuya who excelled in all sports. The tension finally exploded when the family nest egg, hidden in the sacred place under the gnarled roots of three cedar trees, was inexplicably stolen.

To rid himself once and for all of his younger brother, Kiyoshi concocted several damning details as to how and when Tetsuya had stolen the money. Like a long silken thread from the finest cocoon, Kiyoshi spun the tale with the soul-consuming envy he felt in his heart for his younger brother. Tetsuya's father swiftly blamed his wife's favorite child and allowed the tough, twisted silken thread of lies to strangle Tetsuya's lifeline to his family.

Mitsuo immediately banished Tetsuya from the family home, with no possibility of return. The news dealt a punishing blow to his mother. Hisako relentlessly pleaded for her son, blurting out that the number one son, Kiyoshi, had actually stolen the family funds. But this only earned her a harsh beating that ended with Mitsuo's words *"Kare wa mo modoranai."* They were the last words Tetsuya heard from his father: "He will go away forever."

And he did.

Tetsuya's father and brother saw to it that he was removed from his family home. With a resume of silkworm-watching and planting in the rice paddies, he slowly trudged the long muddy path to the waiting train, head down, feeling an unbearable rage wrack his body and a profound pain that his young heart had never experienced. He attempted to collect his raging anger to use it someday for fuel to avenge his brother. But even at his youthful age, Tetsuya felt this burden was too great for him.

His knew his spirit was destined to move forward, not to reel backwards into the black poison of retaliation. As he plodded his way out of town, Tetsuya understood the quick glance over his shoulder at the charming peaked roofs of his village would be his last look at his mountain home. Alone and knowing the miniscule amount of money in his pocket would not sustain him for long, Tetsuya vowed he would never become either his brother or his father. He would make it his life's work to keep bitterness from his heart. A difficult job for a fifteen-year-old boy with his worldly belongings on his back, a bit of money in his pocket smuggled to him by his mother and worn straw sandals on his feet.

TWENTY-FIVE

"Ok, that's what he did *before* he got to America." Jason was obviously anxious to hear more details. He stood up to stretch his legs and placed hands on the back of the plastic seats as if he were in a courtroom in cross-examination. "So how did Tetsuya meet your dad?"

"Hold up!" Mariam cut in, her immigrant pride irked, defensive. "It's important to know what the old-school generation did before they got here. Everyone thinks foreigners are just laborers! My father—he went to university in Cairo and was an engineer in Eritrea. Here, he works at Quick-Frames downtown! Yes, I want to know everything Tetsuya went through."

She looked around the fast-food restaurant and then added in a quiet voice, "We're not all meant to work here."

"Well, if he were here now, Tetsuya would have told you he just wanted to move forward, but he really didn't have a blueprint," I replied. "That generation was optimistic because they had no other choice. But I will leap forward a few years in Tetsuya's life."

TWENTY-SIX

Tetsuya found himself in Hawaii, the island of Oahu, to be exact. He saved nearly every dollar from his soul crushing, excruciating labor in the sugar cane fields. Smoke and fumes from the practice of burning cane fields before harvest were toxic to Tetsuya's system and he counted the months, weeks, then days before he could sail away. While harvesting the cane fields covered with heavy black clouds of ash, Tetsuya imagined breathing in the crisp ocean air in San Francisco that was fabled among his co-workers. Some of his fellow Japanese transplants embraced the idea of permanent roots in Hawaii. Many began sending their photos to matchmakers back in Japan with the desire to snag a "picture bride." To marry and set up housekeeping in Hawaii.

Tetsuya watched as the would-be grooms located photos of themselves taken when they were at least ten years younger to attract a young wife. They posed near expensive automobiles and luxurious homes to appear prosperous in the single photo they would mail away to potential brides back home. Of course, their true profession in Hawaii was backbreaking, slave-like labor in the sugar cane fields—but that information was not revealed until the picture brides arrived and were herded into group marriage ceremonies on the docks. The expensive cars and posh homes never materialized, and the wives often worked the same exhausting hours as their husbands—with babies strapped to their backs—just to make ends meet.

Wanting no part of lying to a woman simply to acquire a wife, Tetsuya reasoned he was too young for marriage anyway. By the time he applied to work on the mainland, he was slightly over twenty years old. He would take his chances for marriage in America, a wedding being secondary to his own day-to-day survival. To be sure, there were fewer Japanese women on the mainland, but Tetsuya was determined to avoid an unhappy union like the one his mother endured. At the least, he would marry someone pleasant and strong, with whom he could brave this new world. He would not lie, cheat or force his future wife into a marriage with a false bottom. His vision of his life — as strong, unending and quietly beautiful Japanese silk — had not died. It simply had become transformed from blue-green silk to indigo and white cotton patchwork with Sashiko — traditional Japanese country-style stitching — thick and durable for years of hard work. And then decades more.

Tetsuya was both blessed and cursed upon entering San Francisco in 1908. Having lived in Hawaii he knew his face would be reviled simply for being Japanese — appearing exotic at best, malicious at worst. Conversant only with a few English words he had learned in Hawaii, Tetsuya was fortunate to arrive after the traumatic San Francisco earthquake which caused eighty percent of the city to burst into an urban fireball that raged for four terrifying days.

When Tetsuya set his feet on the mainland, San Francisco was in the midst of an energetic rebuilding phase and opportunities for work developed before his eyes. After the quake and fire, much of the city's Japanese population had moved west of Nob Hill to the area that was annexed by the city of San Francisco, and then aptly dubbed the Western Addition. Later, a small Japantown sprang up there, offering vibrant stores, baths, florists, restaurants, Buddhist temples and even Methodist and Presbyterian churches.

Strolling through Japantown, Tetsuya slowly exhaled while the sweet, familiar Japanese language filled his ears instead of the harsh-sounding English he encountered every day in San Francisco. He allowed himself to recall a few joyful memories of his mother when he inhaled the smell of miso soup, steamy sticky rice and fried tempura vegetables drifting to the street from open windows two stories above. Each day as he walked down Post Street near the Usui-Shota Grocery, Tetsuya passed a flat where a piano teacher's open door faced the street. His ears slowly became accustomed to the western scale. The music of one composer in particular, Tchaikovsky, moved Tetsuya to tears. It was Tchaikovsky's dramatic, stormy, seductive music that was a bridge for Tetsuya to this new culture, this new land. Tetsuya felt the music expressed his inner feelings that he, himself, could barely identify.

After he first arrived, before moving to Japantown, Tetsuya worked the small fishing ships on the waterfront near the Southern Pacific Railroad terminal. Through word of mouth from his fellow workers, he rented a room within walking distance to the docks, next door to the lovely Eimoto Hotel on South Park Street. He felt a bit more at home in this enclave, home to people who looked like him. Yet something inside Tetsuya was incessantly curious to venture out of the Japanese world, to inculcate himself into the excitement of this vibrant metropolis of San Francisco.

TWENTY-SEVEN

Several weeks had passed since the expensive lawyer haunted our restaurant announcing the extra payment and an increase in the rent. In another part of Vallejo, my father, Theo Vasili and a small wiry real estate man in a three-piece suit slowly strolled through a spacious warehouse with miles of cement floors and a twenty-foot ceiling. I timidly trailed behind my father and uncle, not daring to peep a word. This empty, dilapidated warehouse seemed hostile and a million miles away from The Classic Grill, the warm and friendly mainstay in the bustling downtown commerce district.

My ears were filled with the yammering of the real estate man who was a nonstop talker. He pointed out every possible benefit including the leaky roof (an opportunity for a roof light), the noisy neighbors (the feeling you're in the heart of town), and most of all, the barn-like atmosphere (the chance to create a unique ambiance). My father soaked it all up and seemed to weigh the features and benefits against the monthly rent.

"How about the gas for kitchen?" Theo Vasili asked. I saw my father's look of amazement when my uncle actually focused on a functional detail. My mother, his usual partner in business affairs, had emotionally not signed onto this project. My father muttered under his breath that it was just a matter of time until she saw that financial success would come. I knew my father did not want my mother to prove him wrong. But most of all, he could not lose her trust, stretching the elastic of her faith until there was no more. We had heard my father's simple logic a thousand times. "We make one good business, now we make another." In his mind, the only outcome could be an overwhelmingly successful restaurant.

My uncle and the real estate man had vanished into the alley outside of the soon-to-be kitchen, their footsteps resounding in the vast hollow space. My father and I were now alone.

"Classic Grill easy to make. But here…"

I was hoping he aimed his words for me, but as usual, my father was only talking to himself. I knew that to establish The Classic Grill, he had taken over the space that another bar and restaurant had occupied before he plunked down the substantial treasury saved from his dishwashing and my mother's pastry baking. Ike's Place, they used to say, was a speakeasy where illegal backroom booze attracted the well-heeled and naughty residents of Vallejo and a few wealthy Central Valley ranchers who could afford to travel. After the cops busted Ike's Place, my father's restaurant which offered good food at good prices was just what the city leaders wanted. Now that page had turned.

Staring high into the rafters, hands locked behind his back, my father slowly paced across the entire floor. I stepped in his footprints. Scanning the dusty girders, I could see the spiders had been at work, leaving webbed doilies on the sturdy wooden crossbeams. I knew my father's eyes could only see richly polished wood planks from which glorious chandeliers hung, softly illuminating the restaurant as if by candlelight. A small, shabby platform high above the main floor that was stuffed with old crates and boxes would become, in my father's mind, an upstairs dining area for the well-to-do customers who dined with long white gloves and shiny bracelets. The dozen or so rough, upright redwood girders sustaining the building's structure became decorated with the rich glow of gold leaf arranged in an ancient Greek geometric design. Excitement bubbled up in me too. I could almost imagine the polished marble floor with rivulets of cocoa brown and gold under my feet.

My father's eyes glistened as he looked across the warehouse. I knew he could see gleaming stainless steel ovens and twenty wrought iron burners housed within a modern kitchen, sparkling in the morning light. I was certain, because I could envision them too.

Theo Vasili and the real estate man returned and my father reeled himself back from the restaurant-palace of his imagination. A chunk of the borrowed cash carefully wrapped with brown paper was passed from my father's hand into the open, expectant palm of the real estate man. Briefcase closed, hands shaken, heads nodded and the deal was done.

One might say there was no turning back. But my father later admitted to me that once my uncle and I were out the door, he did indeed turn back to stare at the empty warehouse one last time. He saw every table packed with well-dressed patrons, waiters in white coats and stiff bow ties, bustling everywhere in an atmosphere of graceful, elegant details.

I heard my father let out a small sigh of satisfaction, knowing the restaurant of his dreams was finally within his grasp.

"*Téleios!* Perfect!" he whispered and shut the back door of the warehouse that needed a hearty tug to close properly.

TWENTY-EIGHT

For no man ever proves himself a
good man in war unless he can endure
to face the blood and the slaughter,
go close against the enemy and
fight with his hands.

I had listened for weeks as Demo practiced these lines. I anticipated he would perform that evening with his natural talent — I never worried about that. But I certainly was worried about what might follow.

One evening in late October, when leaves the color of pumpkins lined the streets, my mother and I eagerly located our hard, wooden pull-down seats. We sat in the high school auditorium which was constructed by the WPA during the Great Depression. To be honest, it felt more like a disturbing haunted castle. I kept watch for my father, looking to wave him down, as I had saved him a seat. I was miffed that he would not come with us as a family to see Demo. Was he afraid Demo would forget his lines and reflect poorly on the Pappayannis name? Maybe he was worried about the same thing I was.

On stage, a trio of sixteen-year-old girls were doing their best impression of the swinging Andrew Sisters, crooning *Apple Blossom Time* in three-part harmony. With curly tufts of hair peeking from beneath their caps like poodles, they sported Army shirts and skirts and had worked out military-inspired choreography. The trio muscled through the awkward harmonies. While we gratefully applauded their exit, I looked for my father again, his seat glaringly empty in the sellout crowd.

I was breathing heavily now, having chewed my nails until they bled. I knew what was coming and there was no foxhole to jump into for the fallout. The student master of ceremonies clumsily walked onto center stage and unenthusiastically read from his card. It was Demo's turn to be introduced. He flipped through his note cards and studied them, his lips silently moving.

"We have Demo Pappa... Pappa YAWN eez reciting the poem *Courage* by Try... Tyrtaeus of Sparta."

The dark blue velvet curtain pulled back to reveal Demo. A leafy green laurel wreath crowned his curly dark head. He was draped in the white and red robes of ancient Greece, and my stomach tightened to see his face painted with the same make-up he tested out in our bathroom. A single spotlight illuminated his gleaming dark eyes.

> Here is courage, mankind's finest possession,
> here is the noblest prize that a young man can
> endeavor to win, and it is a good thing his polis
> and all the people share with him when a man
> plants his feet and stands in the foremost spears relentlessly...

My mother's eyes were magnetically fixed on her adored first son. She clutched my hand in her excitement at seeing Demo on stage. The jittery girls twitching to leave for the dance afterwards were suddenly quiet. The bookworms, the stodgy faculty members and the ordinary neighborhood kids who just wanted to see their friends on stage seemed captured by Demo's spell. I was too. Demo was in command.

I turned in my seat to find my father had slipped into the back of the auditorium to observe my brother. Even from this distance, I could see my father's dark eyebrows knit together. Demo hid nothing.

> And he who so falls among the champions and
> loses his sweet life, so blesses with honor his polis, his father,
> and all his people, with wounds in his chest,
> where the spear that he was facing has transfixed
> that massive guard of his shield,
> and gone through his breastplate as well...

The audience started to titter, but Demo took a breath and continued proud and strong. I could see shiny crystals of sweat forming on his thick white makeup.

> Why, such a man is lamented alike by the young

and the elders, and all his polis goes into mourning
and grieves for his loss…

The titter became a chatter. From my seat, I could see Demo's upper lip twitch — but he persisted.

His tomb is pointed out with pride,
and so are his children, and his children's children,
and afterwards all the race that is his.

An older boy's voice ripped through the crowd.
"Beat it, Shirley!"
I swiveled in my seat toward the back of the hall. Standing there, my father had seen enough. He pulled open the heavy auditorium doors and swiftly disappeared into the darkness.

Thus a man should endeavor to reach this high place
of courage with all his heart, and, so trying,
never be backward in war.

Demo's forehead was slick with sweat now. His voice was strong, but I could tell it was a little higher, a little tighter than usual. Demo kept his eyes focused straight ahead. Upon the last word of his Tyrtaeus poem, Demo bowed and walked off the stage to scattered applause which quickly became jeering whistles and ferocious catcalls.
"Pansy!"
"What the hell was that?"
"Go home you fruit!"
As my mother and I applauded loudly, I was struck with fear. Demo had unleashed his homosexual self at this school where the senior-class boys ran the place like longshore bosses.
I left my mother in the front foyer and rushed to find Demo backstage among the tap dancers, baton twirlers and a barbershop quartet. His hands were trembling as he untied the knot of his outer red velvet robe.
"How'd you like it?" Looking up from his costume he seemed unsure of my reaction. As he slowly removed his thick copper bracelets, Demo let out a long sigh. After seeing his many performances presented only to me, an audience of one in our bedroom, I temporarily erased the hecklers from my mind.

"You were great."

As usual, I could not say what was in my heart. He had spoken about courage while standing in front of the entire school, revealing his authentic self. And I couldn't even tell him he was brilliant—beyond anything I could imagine. My silent tongue betrayed my brimming heart.

Suddenly, from a dark corner backstage, two boys I recognized as seniors walked swiftly towards Demo, hands at their sides. One took his place between Demo and me as the other swung his man-sized fist swiftly into my brother's gut. He let another powerful fist fly into Demo's chest and my brother doubled over, his laurel crown spinning onto the dirty backstage floor. As an afterthought, the second boy shoved Demo to the ground and kicked him squarely in the ribs. I stood there frozen, not knowing what to do. Should I find the principal? My mother? Terrified, my feet were glued in place while my injured brother laid on the ground, attempting to rise. He was ready to fight, but couldn't.

I watched the savage who punched my brother calmly walk away with his cohort, laughing. He took a few swings in the air, probably re-telling the story of his power over a "fruit."

But I did nothing.

I should have run and tackled them and beat them to the ground. But I didn't. Rage boiled in my heart, but I stood with my arms at my sides, my face hanging out. Demo seemed woozy on the floor and I bent down to help him.

"Let 'em go, George." Demo attempted to find his balance and stand. That was my brother, worrying about my feelings when he was hurt. "You don't have to do anything."

Snapping out of my fearful trance, I slowly helped Demo to his feet and gingerly guided his arms into his coat over his costume. I was ashamed I did not fight for my brother—no matter what he revealed to the school.

Together we hobbled slowly toward my mother. Demo, the actor, arranged his face into a weak smile and talked about everything else but his aching gut and ribs. My mother smothered my brother with praise and loving words. Both seemed stronger and surer of themselves than I could ever be. Demo had the courage to stand up in front the school and show the part of himself that he kept hidden most of the time. My mother always stood her ground and spoke her truth. Had she been aware of Demo's beating, I am certain she would have stood face-to-face with her son's assaulters. I wished I could develop the courage of Demo, Tyrtaeus and my mother, but I didn't know where to start.

TWENTY-NINE

Years later, my father told me that Demo's "drama," as he called it, sent him into a frenzy. That night, before we three could return home, my father beat us to it. He quickly stomped to the back of our house and flung open the door to Demo's and my room. He was determined to get to the bottom of Demo's disturbing performance. He could not simply write off the presentation to ancient Greek drama, especially the performance overtones my father had just witnessed. He knew better. His son didn't seem to care if people might ridicule him or gossip about the family. But my father had spent most of his life trying to fit into American society. He could not comprehend such an enormous display of "different" to the public at large. Why would his first offspring reveal that unsettling side of himself to the world?

My father attempted to reason that perhaps his ears had heard English words they did not fully understand. Maybe Demo was not actually "like that" — but my father set out to find the truth. He feverishly needed to find nothing suspicious in Demo's belongings and put this night behind him, smothering any forbidden notion.

He scanned our bedroom. A homemade lyre lay on Demo's bed accompanied by a pandouris and a drum decorated with the ancient Greek key design. My father walked further into the room and examined flowing robes and wreaths of woven flowers hanging on a nail.

He looked into a mirror and his attention was seized by the back of the closet door which displayed a collection of colorful artwork. He slowly made his way to the door, then stopped short. A haphazard collage of photos and drawings of ancient Greek ruins, statues, sculpture and pottery was displayed on the door. This visual collection appeared to have been torn from magazines, clipped from books and drawn by hand. Ceramics revealed half animal-half human beings frolicking with humans. Men and women wearing animal skins tantalized as they tempted each other around the belly of a terra cotta vase. Women dressed in ancient costumes were entwined with other women and naked men reclined with each other on the artwork affixed to the door.

Gasping for breath, my father slammed the door on this disturbing alternative universe he had exposed. Despite this revelation, my father clung to the knowledge that Demo possessed the natural charisma that was perfect for American business that he, himself, could never conjure up. My father's mind exploded with frightening possibilities, those sharp, icy glaciers that lurked far beneath the ocean's surface. At any moment, those dangerous edges could tear the hull and capsize my father's plans.

Attempting to calm himself, my father vowed he would not let this unexpected, uncomfortable, should-have-been-hidden information alter his course. He would make sure those glaciers remained in the distant waters and steer his Greek ship through the choppy, treacherous waves to reach the lucrative American shore.

THIRTY

"So, was he really gay?" Mariam wanted to know. Her large soda cup was empty and her straw made a dry, scraping sound as she hit the bottom. She made Demo's being gay sound easy.

"Gay. Straight. Our family didn't know those words at that time," I answered, thinking it would have been easier to have the right words to describe the way people lived. "My mother and I loved everything about Demo but my father could not open his heart — not even a little — to let Demo in."

"Too bad. So hard for your brother." Aman looked down at the table, reassessing my family. "What did Demo do then?"

"What *could* he do?" answered Mariam. "He was stuck in your father's life. And your father in his."

"Parents like ours — they will never understand their American kids," Jesús added. "I know about that, believe me."

He slid from his seat and walked quickly to the kitchen for a cup of coffee and it seemed a moment to collect himself. I was secretly pleased when Jesús returned to our group, steaming cardboard cup in hand. He sipped his coffee, staring upward at me.

"So, like, what *did* happen to your brother? To Demo?"

THIRTY-ONE

Another performance by Demo.

This time, Demo's audience was just those of us in the restaurant dining room after the lunch rush. Theo Vasili, Taki, Mr. Chris, Tetsuya and, of course, his most loyal fan club — my mother and me — encircled Demo with an invisible net of adoration. My father was meeting with the workmen at what we now called "the new restaurant," so we felt safe.

Demo held a mask to his face that he must have sculpted himself. With its mouth gaping and eyes hollowed out, the painted mask of Pan, a god with goat horns and a devilish human face, unsettled me more than a little. I was just a teenage kid accustomed to watching Jimmy Cagney, Gene Autry and Gary Cooper at the movie houses in downtown Vallejo. I could barely keep up with Demo's ancient Greek dramas and myths. But I desperately tried.

He stood on a bentwood chair with us, his audience, standing in a crowd around him. He was wearing one of my mother's bedsheets — Demo's version of a toga. Although they were Euripides' lines, Demo spoke as if each word was his own.

> Let no one think of me that I am humble
> or weak or passive; let them understand
> I am of a different kind: dangerous to
> my enemies, loyal to my friends…

From across the room, a noise from the back kitchen caught my attention and fear squeezed my heart. My father was a dark specter in the doorway. His eyes registered incomprehension, then quickly disgust.

Demo must have heard the back door creak open, yet he carried on undeterred.

> To such a life glory belongs!

My father bolted threateningly towards Demo, throwing aside his paper sack of French bread loaves.

"This is *my* restaurant!" he roared at Demo — at all of us.

Theo Vasili forcefully threw out his arms to protect Demo's lean but strong body. Like ants to an ant hill, we all huddled to surround Demo.

"*Áfise ton!* Leave him alone!" shouted Theo Vasili, unbelievably standing strong against my father. "I will not let you crush him like you crush me."

That comment chilled me but I had no time to question it. A rift, even a cross word, between my father and uncle was unthinkable.

"He must obey! I am his father!"

"Then be one!"

"You shame your family," my father fired at Demo, glaring at his older son, clutching the goat-devil mask. So far from the hardworking young man in an apron, clutching a clipboard that he desperately needed to see. So far from a businessman in a classy suit that would one day lead the family enterprise. The image of Demo in a feminine-looking toga darkened the picture for my father and he wasn't sure if he should slap Demo, whip him or swing a two-by-four at him. People like his son were supposed to hide their tendencies, not celebrate them.

"Pop, I want to be an actor. This is who I am!" Demo's voice was shaky but his spirit was strong.

My father took a step nearer. Their faces were hot, close together.

"Help me with my restaurant! Our family depend for you! My plans, they are big!"

Was that a bleat of pleading?

"My plans are bigger!" Demo cried out, moving dangerously closer to my father. His words exploded at my father who staggered from our circle as if wounded. My brother was more than disobedient. My father's path to success had been clear — pennies to nickels to dollars, to a lifetime of making money, never wavering, always forward. He had no experience in the journey Demo seemed determined to embark upon, and no taste for it.

Demo hurried to my father in the back of the kitchen.

"I will be an actor. I quit school."

My father was stunned into silence.

"I will be—I am—an actor!" My brother breathed heavily. I quietly stole behind Demo thinking my protection might be required. But my useless hands were motionless at my side, terrified to throw a punch.

Like a prizefighter reeling from the first solid blow, my father began to regain his focus. He surveyed Demo, from the wreath in his hair to his leather strapped sandals.

"You *will* work with me! I hear nothing else!" He turned his face away and clenched his fist, his jaw tight, teeth gnashing. "The first son ever to get education and *you*—you quit your school?"

"Listen, Pop, for once in your life!" my brother demanded. "Listen!"

My father grabbed Demo and pulled him further back into the kitchen, to his tiny office.

"You will study business at big university in Berkeley. Like we plan!" My father's voice filled the kitchen and spilled into the dining room.

"To cook chops and fries all my life?" Demo fired back.

I knew my father had never before heard such defiance. Such ungratefulness. Absurdity. This could not be his kin. His first-born son.

"Cooking *make* my life! And yours!"

Demo said nothing but met my father's eyes, waiting for his next move.

My father forcefully planted his work-worn hands on Demo's thin, bedsheet-draped shoulders. He was breathing harder than when he trudged up the steep Virginia Street hill to our house after his usual sixteen-hour day. For an instant, I believe my father remembered how he painfully ached to attend school, piecing together a crude version of the Greek alphabet out of necessity. The university was an unimaginable privilege that his peasant class could only dream of. Printed words had only been hieroglyphic symbols to him.

"Demo, you don't know. To look at a paper and no understand is a terrible thing!" he cried out, thinking of the deep-rooted envy he felt for the well-off boys in their uniforms who traveled afar to attend school.

"George loves to cook, he loves this business—send him!"

"I need my first son. The smart one," he growled.

This time, it was me, the second, lesser son who felt the sting from my father's words.

"Pop, didn't you ever believe that you were fated to do something big?" Demo's voice was raw. "Something that is in your *psyché*—your soul?"

My father pushed Demo toward the poster of Roosevelt's Four Freedoms he had tacked on the wall. The poster showed images of Freedom of Speech, Freedom of Worship, Freedom from Want, Freedom from Fear.

"Our president say no want — no more. With new restaurant, our family never want no more. Never!"

"Pop, I can't do it!"

"You never know to be hungry! You never know what I give to make good for this family!"

Demo stretched his arms out toward my father.

"Pop! I want your blessing!"

Turning away from Demo my father reached for his coat.

"If you no go to school," he rumbled low like a dog ready to bite, "you will leave our house."

It was Demo's turn to feel the jagged words sink in and cut deep.

"You want me to — leave home? But I have nowhere..."

"We make restaurant business. Not drama business! You are part of the Pappayannis family dream. Or you are not."

My father studied his son, then jerked the long, soiled string controlling the light bulb in the windowless office. In one click, my father left Demo and me alone in the darkness.

The blackness in that little room struck terror in my teenage heart. In one conversation, the planets in the Pappayannis universe had fallen from their orbit, and our attraction for each other, which kept us suspended in the heavens, had been destroyed. My father was to blame. He was our self-appointed sun, the center of our system. I suppose we secretly craved a god who gracefully guided his chariot across the sky, reliably bringing the rays of sunlight to the despair of night. Instead, my father was the temperamental and vengeful Zeus, who dictated how the sun, moon and stars should behave around him. If only we could have written our own mythos that controlled our family's universe.

THIRTY-TWO

I quickly ran back to the front of the restaurant to find my mother. She assumed this argument was another of my father's rants and knew her presence would only inflame the situation — as if we all stood against my father. I whispered to her and we dashed to the little office to soothe my brother, but the back door to the restaurant swung open in the breeze.

I thought I had memorized every street, alley, empty lot and bus stop in Vallejo, but Demo knew them just as well. After countless sweaty hours of running through the streets, I stopped at the backdoor of The Classic Grill — without a brother.

The restaurant was closed now and I shoved my key into the back door lock. I looked to the side of the building where a crumpled figure was slumped in the alleyway. Theo Vasili, his hat tilted forward on his head, clutched a bottle of Canadian Club whisky in his tight fist. Seeing me, he tried to stand up but stumbled back down to his original flopped position.

I ushered my uncle inside through the little office to a kitchen stool. A few cups of coffee later, Theo Vasili, my free-spirited, bon vivant uncle, the southeast to my father's true north, began to softly weep. But then, when I did not expect it, his anger flared.

"Again he does this!" Theo Vasili was as angry as I'd ever seen him. "He will not crush Demo — like me."

He threw down the half-empty bottle of whisky. I poured another cup of coffee and rushed to toast thick French bread slices and slather on his favorite marmalade. Slowly my uncle relaxed enough to allow his secret, kept for decades, to trickle from his heart.

"Your father not the man you know. When he young, he play the mandolin good," my uncle said, as if it was a well-known fact. "But me! I was best in our village!"

I was shocked at my uncle's bravado. He never spoke highly of himself. But then again, he never spoke of anything personal, as if he was ashamed of his life's meager outcome. He had always trod behind my father, occasionally wandering among the daisies. But he always dutifully found his way back to the path my father had doggedly carved out for our family. My father made room for my uncle's drift, and in turn, my uncle relinquished the rest of his life to my father's heavy hand, which guided his destiny. I always thought it was a perfect match.

"We play together. *Oi dyo mas* — the two of us — cousins together. We young but in our village, we grown up. But I the best. I learn by my own practice. I play from my *kardia*." He touched his heart dramatically, aided by the whisky.

Thoughts of my father and uncle harboring artistic souls intoxicated my brain. And now, my father, a would-be musician, had deported my brother, a would-be actor. It didn't make sense, but nothing did that night.

"He fourteen years and me thirteen. The people they love the music from our mandolins." My uncle sank his teeth into the toast and crumbs stuck to his mustache.

"Then, our sisters getting older and we need dowry for them. Two sisters in my family. Three for Achilles' family. Your father decide he go to America and make money for the dowries. But I want to play! But *oxi*, no, is not enough for your father."

He sighed heavily.

"A teacher say I go to music school with my mandolin. He pay! Imagine a boy like me to go for music school and *no pay!* But two nights before your father leave for America, he come to my school and find me. He have *two* tickets for America. I say *oxi!* No!"

I was silent, thinking any word from me would cause my uncle's history, of which I had never heard a word, to squeak to a halt.

"He say our family was — *stis plátes mas* — on our backs to carry. He say we have no time for nothing but make money. He depend for me. What could I do?" My uncle shrugged, his eyes closed and his eyebrows raised.

"Didn't you resent him, Theo Vasili? How did you forgive him?"

"Your father, he save his money. Then he pay dowry for Voula, then the other sisters. Then, he pay for *my* sisters. He pay for houses for his parents, my parents. He pay for everyone. They all heavy on his *plati*, his back. He work for all of us."

My uncle thumped his fist on his chest. "I hear no more my mandolin music here, no more."

With that, Theo Vasili untangled his long arms and legs from his stool and slowly shuffled toward the door. He stopped to give me a man-to-man Greek body-hug and then he cupped his large, dry, calloused hands around my face.

"You and Demo are my sons," he whispered. "But now Demo need to hear his music. He need to make his dream."

THIRTY-THREE

After hearing Theo Vasili's story, I hurried home hoping maybe Demo had defied my father and slipped into the house — even if only for the night.

Our house was not big, but I found it just right for our family and an occasional three-month stay by Theo Vasili or a cousin traveling to and from San Francisco for a dishwashing stint. The redwood interior of our house reminded me of a farmhouse. The rooms were large and sunny and hardwood floors graced the entire house. My favorite part of the place was the sunporch that was built outside of our weighty, varnished oak front door with large windows everywhere. Outside the porch stood twelve steep red steps that visitors often whined about after they had climbed the Virginia Street hill to get there.

As I turned the corner, I saw no lights in any window. Maybe my mother and father had found common ground and were now asleep. But once inside, I saw the glow from a lamp in their room through the transom high above their bedroom door.

"My son will not live on the street!" The bedsprings cried out in agreement as my mother leaped from bed and began to pace the creaky wooden floor. I couldn't quite hear everything so I snuck closer in the darkness of the spacious kitchen. I could see only a little, as their door was left open a crack.

"He want to live in *to théatro* — the theatre," my father retorted. "Let him!"

"He is only a child! My child!" My mother angrily wrapped a bathrobe around herself and turned her back on my father who was sitting up in bed, feigning to be in command of the situation. They must have been at it for hours.

"I come here when I fourteen. I not a child then. Demo seventeen now!"

"He want something different than you! For this — you leave him on the street?" My mother's voice was hoarse but defiant.

"You think he die? He can read!"

115

My mother stormed from the bedroom and swept through the house, switching on every light until the house was ablaze. When she saw me in the kitchen, I knew it was the time to slide into the conversation.

"Demo didn't come home?" I whispered to my mother, hoping she would hear me and not be frightened. Above all, I did not want to ratchet up my father's anger.

"Your father has a dream." My mother spat out her words, hands on hips, eyes fast on my father. "Your brother another. General Achilles' dream more important than our family! *Ach!*"

"My dream is for strong family. You promise me this — but now you want to destroy!" My mother stared down my father, with a look that took him back to that evening when he negotiated a marriage deal with the beautiful young folk singer.

I lifted the heavy receiver of our black telephone and quietly spun the dial. Speaking in whispers, I prayed my father was too involved in his attack and defense to listen.

I was wrong again.

"*Ftani!* Enough!" my father shouted at me. "Everybody got to know the Pappayannis family business?"

My parents stood very close, their eyes burning.

"A father sends away his child?"

"Demo does not love what we love."

"*Achilléas*, get my son and bring him home now! *Tóra!* Now!"

I was in awe. I had never heard my mother order my father to do anything.

My mother later told me she had observed that pride and anger had glued my father's feet to the Greek rug her own mother had woven in what seemed like centuries ago. She flashed back to the night her mother risked everything to protect her from her father's drunken threat. The holes in my father's armor seemed larger than ever, and my mother seriously questioned her future with him.

That night, she struggled to pull her camel hair coat over her robe, shoved her feet into her worn gardening shoes and spun around with one last attempt.

"Is your ego bigger than your heart? You bring him home. Now!"

My father said nothing, his mouth held tight in a straight line. Astonished that a wall continued to barricade my father's heart, my mother strode to the front door and forcefully twisted the crystal doorknob. She quickly glanced back one last time making sure my father had not opened one last portal of hope. Seeing none, she pulled the massive oak front door behind her with all her might. Fear of my father paralyzed my tongue, and I did not argue for Demo like I wanted to. Like I should have. I quietly crept out the back door to avoid my father's poisonous bite.

Through the window I could see my father, still shamefully standing in his pajamas. Now, without a companion, without reinforcements in this battle, my father stood motionless as my mother rushed from the house, away from him.

THIRTY-FOUR

This time, Jason spoke up. I assessed he was about Demo's age at that time. He attempted to stir his chocolate milkshake with a straw but the gelatinous whatever-it-was in the cup wasn't budging. At our restaurant, we used to whip up milkshakes with fresh whole milk, real hand-made ice cream and dark, rich chocolate syrup from Ghirardelli in San Francisco. I wondered what corporate recipe was in fashion now.

"Couldn't your dad see that he was breaking up the family?" Jason asked, his uniform the most untidy of the bunch. His buttons were pressed into maximum duty by his tummy which had enjoyed a few too many burgers from the kitchen. He reminded me of a few cooks at The Classic Grill.

"Why didn't your dad just turn to you?" Jason deducted logically — something my father never could have conceived. "You were the one!"

"That was not my father. He was stuck in the dream where Demo would run the show. I was, well, second choice." I smiled to myself that this teenager could pick up on our family dynamics, but my father in his fifties could not. Looking back, I couldn't place all the blame on my father.

"I just didn't know how to ask for it," I confessed. "It was safe for me to stand in Demo's shadow and hide behind my mother's strength."

Jason shook his head, not understanding my father's logic. "That's what I want. To be a cook in a *real* restaurant someday," he said looking around. "You know, someplace good."

I felt sympathy for him wrench in my body. I knew his plight.

"You will, son," I said softly, knowingly. "I'm sure you will."

"He sounds like *my* father!" Aman interrupted. "They just don't understand what we go through. What we want. We're in America. They need to let us go."

Aman looked alarmed that she had leaked out a little more information than she planned to say about her own family and quickly changed the subject.

"Your father really sent him away?" she asked.

I was embarrassed that my throat was tight and my eyes had misted.

"Yes, but first we had to say goodbye," I remembered. "And that wasn't easy."

THIRTY-FIVE

I spotted Demo from a distance and ran to him through the late night mist. He looked up and seemed relieved it was only me. Standing on the dock, Demo buried his hands into his padded navy coat. The black water chopped at the dock and the fog lamps looming over the pier cast an eerie orange glow on the water.

"Want me to come with you?" I stood next to him, searching my mind about how to comfort my brother.

"Nah," Demo said blandly, purposefully holding back his pain. Wasn't he fearful of suddenly leaving home? I was worried sick for him. He had not even packed a duffle bag.

"Want to come home with me, Demo?" Perhaps our mother and I could create a neutral zone, a fantasy cocoon, protected from my father, where Demo could live undisturbed, sublimely pursuing his ancient Greek arts.

Demo shook his head. "Can't. Won't. But thanks."

My brother was set on leaving and I could hardly keep my balance.

"Pop is so hard-headed." I hoped Demo might just accept the usual explanation of my father's rage and just come home.

"George, he doesn't like who I am." He shrugged and turned away.

I had no answer for this. But like most Pappayannis men, when befuddled, I turned to money to fix things. I shoved a wad of bills at Demo. The entire lifetime savings of my sixteen years.

"Thanks, George, but…"

I shook my head firmly and rammed the bills in his coat pocket.

"Watch over Mom." He looked at me but his mind was somewhere past the waterfront. "The Grill is a good restaurant and you'll be great taking it over some day. I just don't want to die there."

At that moment heavy footsteps and a rustling of clothing brought Theo Vasili forward. He hurried to Demo and embraced him with a giant six-foot-four hug. He pressed a handful of cash into Demo's hand. "You will need."

Then Tetsuya appeared from the darkness. He thrust his fistful of money forward at Demo.

"Be safe." I could tell he was trying to hold back tears. "*Musuko yo.* My son."

Taki made his way through the crowd.

"Here, take!" Taki blurted, his tears dampening the money in his hand.

Parting the men like a steamship at top speed, my mother rushed to her son. "*O gyios mou!* My son!" she cried. "You will not leave!" She swept Demo into her arms, to keep him safe forever.

"Don't worry, Ma." Demo was distant, distracted. "It will be okay."

The ferry chugged to its customary landing spot and the ferrymen noisily lowered the gangplank, metal scraping on the wood dock. Demo whispered so only my mother could hear.

"He doesn't want me."

"He want only you!" my mother roared. "Do not leave us, Demo *mou*, my son!"

She buried her face in the harsh wool of his coat. Kissing her forehead, Demo turned away. With long strides, he walked purposefully aboard the ferry. He did not turn around to wave. I knew if he did, Demo might have jumped from the ferry and returned to us. All ropes had been untied now. Unfettered, the ferry and Demo became distant lights in the night that now seemed much colder to me.

THIRTY-SIX

The next morning the warm sunlight illuminated The Classic Grill which was packed with customers. The kitchen crew worked silently. No chatter among the cooks and dishwashers, no radio, all eyes cast downward. Tetsuya and I worked slicing zucchini and shelling peas. The waiters flipped the kitchen door, rushing in with lunch orders and rushing out with trays heavy with the daily special — a hot turkey sandwich with fluffy mashed potatoes and cranberry sauce. Demo's favorite. Tetsuya had typed up the menu and had uncharacteristically sent a stinging message to my father who worked at his desk, nervously twitching in a silence he could cut with his butcher's knife.

"What is wrong?" he screamed at the crew. "Even the damn violin is quiet!"

Wearing oversized yellow rubber gloves, Mr. Chris stepped away from his suds and towers of stainless steel pots to meet my father's gaze. He dramatically stripped off his gloves, one finger at a time and scooped up his violin. His bow rang out a slow, plaintive Greek folk tune that could have been written 300 years ago in the mountains of Asia Minor.

"Enough! You are fired, Christos!" my father cried, hands waving wildly. "Get out!"

Mr. Chris continued his mournful folk song with his feet planted. Aggravated, my father walked out to the dining room. The lunch customers gobbled their entrees and sipped their coffee. The door opened and Taki strolled in with his customary newspaper.

"Ach, Taki!" My father was relieved to see his friend and raconteur. "What is the news?"

Taki took a seat at the counter and quickly unfolded his newspaper. He held it up as a shield between my father and himself and said nothing. Theo Vasili soon arrived and dropped onto the stool next to Taki. He shot a dark look at my father.

"Long night, cousin." Ice crystals formed on my uncle's words, allowing his eyes to linger accusingly on my father.

"I pray to God Nikko safe in England. This war, it go on forever!" Taki sighed.

My father filled a cup of coffee for his friend while Taki leafed through the paper, holding it between them, his message to my father.

"Never let your son go far away, Achilles," Taki shot at my father from behind the World News section. "It hurt too much."

I watched as my father ignored this and worked his way down the counter with his polishing rag. His face brightened considerably as Daphne ambled through the doorway. For my father, the vision of Daphne was a joyful harbor in the stormy and unsettling chain of events from the night before. He steadfastly clung to the thought that he was justified in cutting off Demo. After all, a son's duty was to dedicate himself to his family as he had done from an early age. The first son was destined to steer the ship. His family soon would realize this as the new restaurant took shape. And Demo would come back. Yes, Demo will return — I heard my father repeat this to himself that day, attempting to believe his own words. But I believe somehow he knew Demo was just as resolute as he was.

And there was the matter of my mother's telling absence at work that day. My father's anxiety began when she was not completely on board with the new restaurant, and now Demo was gone. To make matters worse, she would blame him for their son's welfare from this day forward. My father blocked out this unfathomable burden for now. He could not deny that my mother was the graceful fulcrum that balanced his world. It was as if my mother was unconsciously able to design their lives together and equalize the parts, so his life felt satisfying and whole.

But before my father could contemplate my mother's silence and the tipping — or crashing — of scales he had caused last night, he heard that melodious voice that melted him like a schoolboy.

"Achilles! How's every little thing?" Daphne made herself comfortable on a stool, placing her purse on the counter. She looked around to see which regular customers were in attendance today.

"Better now I see you," my father said mostly to himself, grateful for a brief respite from the emotional vortex of Demo's absence. He noted Daphne appeared much more relaxed and sure of herself at his restaurant.

Maybe she was beginning to feel at home, which meant she would come in every day.

"Achilles, I got the job! Down at Mare Island!" she beamed. "And thanks for the twenty to get me through!"

Daphne placed her hand lightly over my father's hand, which rested on the counter.

"Thank you," she said without embellishment.

"I want only to help you." He looked deeply into her eyes, not quite sure what he was searching for — or what he would find.

A swarm of businessmen wearing fedoras and double-breasted suits rushed into The Classic Grill. They hovered over a table and landed, buzzing about the anticipated housing boom after the war. The boisterous chatter from the businessmen's table annoyed my father who was hoping to prolong his conversation with Daphne.

"Achilles, you lucky today," Theo Vasili cracked from behind the counter as he poured himself a cup of coffee with his own hand. My uncle knew that when Daphne was in the restaurant, he had to fend for himself. "The mayor come to eat your food."

The mayor, sporting a suit of charcoal wool pinstripe, sauntered to the counter close to Daphne. Everything about the mayor was smooth. His greying hair was styled perfectly into a soft pompadour. The dazzling red silk tie seemed carefully selected to match the handkerchief in his breast pocket. His shoes must have been polished by the professional shoeshine man on Georgia Street, not the kid on the corner. The mayor had no hard edges. All soft and manicured. Most of all, rich.

"Six scotch and sodas," the mayor commanded to my father, who was planted behind the counter and, for the first time, felt woefully underdressed in this match up with the mayor. His apron with "The Classic Grill" embroidered on the pocket branded him as "the help." My father bolstered himself by remembering he was the owner of this restaurant, not a waiter. And he had the new palace-of-a-restaurant in the wings.

My father reluctantly turned his back to mix the drinks, with a side glance to the mayor whose eyes, as my father expected, lit on Daphne. The mayor extended his hand and my father noted it was pale and smooth. Hands that pushed a fountain pen, my father grumbled to himself. The mayor had never put in a real day's work in his life.

"I'm Richard Millard, Mayor of Vallejo. Home of the oldest navy ship-yard on the West Coast. Founded in 1853." The mayor's eyes could only focus on Daphne. I looked through the doors from the back kitchen to catch the mayor in action. His slow look began at Daphne's strapped navy blue shoes and slipped up over her thighs, breasts and then, reluctantly, moved to her eyes.

Daphne didn't seem to take offense from this kind of attention. Maybe she was accustomed to men glomming on to her. Or maybe she didn't care. Daphne offered her hand and spoke with her customary charm.

"My pleasure. I'm Daphne." She held out her hand to meet the mayor's.

"We could use your lovely company at our table!"

The mayor clasped Daphne's hand to help her descend from her perch at the counter. At the same time, my father approached with the tray of drinks.

"Daphne, I make your lunch." My father sounded a little more fatherly than he intended.

"Thanks, Achilles. I'm going to sit with Mr., uh…"

She cast her peaches-and-honey smile to cover her gaffe of forgetting his name.

"…Mr. Mayor for a while. Thanks, Achilles!" The two walked away, the mayor leading Daphne with his fingertips against her back.

"Bring that tray to our table!" the mayor barked orders at my father. He and Daphne moved to the table that was crowded with the dark-suited businessmen.

My father, holding the tray of golden scotch and sodas sparkling with ice cubes, watched as his little lamb seated herself comfortably in the midst of the pack of wolves in pinstripe suits. My father suppressed his raging jealousy and told himself he only wanted to protect Daphne from the rav-enous takers in this community, whose outward motivation was usually a scam, concealing their true intentions.

In the back of the kitchen, my mother entered through the rear door and unloaded her pastries in the quiet kitchen. Deflated from last night's events, I knew my mother would not work in the dining room today. She would not hand out menus and portray the happy, welcoming face of The Classic Grill as she often did. She would leave that masquerade to my father.

After we returned home from the dock the night before, I heard my mother pacing the floor and rustling in the kitchen. Never one to shirk her duties, my mother began baking cakes for the restaurant at two in the morning. She couldn't sleep and certainly was not about to crawl into bed and lie next to my father. And I don't think she minded clanging bowls and beaters in the middle of the night to signal her boiling discontent to my father who had banished her beloved Demo.

Now, in the restaurant, in no mood to chat with the kitchen crew, my mother set about her work, placing cakes on pedestals and touching up the frosting on a perfectly delicious-looking German chocolate layer cake. I watched her work with admiration. My mother's face wore the mask of calm and serenity but I knew she was bleeding inside from Demo's absence. I knew because I was too, only I couldn't hide the pain and disappointment on my face.

Out in the restaurant dining room, my father, unaware of my mother's presence, continued to linger near the table of the mayor and his cronies. He locked onto the mayor's every move. He hoped to protect Daphne from the mayoral advances that my father was not sure she would rebuff. Maybe she didn't know how to protect herself, my father considered. She had lived in smaller towns and hadn't been around much. Did Daphne have experience with selfish men like the mayor who could effortlessly consume anything or anyone?

After the first few rounds of drinks, my father struggled to serve the orders of fried chicken, roast beef sandwiches and filet of flounder to the table of distracted men who had pressed in tight around Daphne. The crowd opened up just enough for my father to set down the plates loaded with food. Then the jaws snapped tight with my father on the outside again.

With no other remedy to get proximity to Daphne, my father found reasons to serve the table — offering more bread, then salt and pepper and later fresh napkins. When he ran out of reasons to hover, he loitered only a few steps away.

From the kitchen, my mother's eyes were fixed on my father, attempting to detect the degree of hold Daphne had on him. Reading my mother's face, I could see that this performance was almost too much. First Demo. Now this.

The rowdy table roared with the laughter of a three-Scotch lunch. Watching my father, my mother paced in the kitchen. Behind my mother, I was doing my own foot patrol, worrying about my family's future. Daphne was the odd puzzle piece in our family's one thousand-piece dilemma. Never intended to fit, Daphne's curved edges, once shoved in place, could rearrange the outcome of the scene our family was destined to complete, frame and hang on the wall. I resented this woman's intrusion into our family picture, especially because it now was in more disarray than ever.

As if on cue, Mr. Chris once again picked up his violin and began an exotic *Zeibekiko*, a slow and sensual tune in a minor key to accompany this zigzag dance of pursuit and jealousy. My father watched Daphne and her admiring wolf pack. My mother watched my father and I observed it all from my place in the back, wondering if the weight of my family in transition would burst the stitches that held it together.

Suddenly I saw my mother quickly move and the back door crashed to a close. She had seen enough and left our restaurant for what I hoped would only be the day.

THIRTY-SEVEN

The Classic Grill was almost empty, only dirty dishes remained. Waiting for the table of men to finish their last round of scotch, my father sat near the mayor's table like a guard dog.

Finally, the mayor signaled for the check. As if hearing a silent command, the group of men quickly rose and prepared to leave. They dumped a few extra coins on the table as a tip for my father, another jabbing insult. The mayor turned to a more-than-tipsy Daphne. Her less than perfect hair-do only added a wild look to her beauty. The mayor flicked his card from his pocket and tossed it on the table.

"If you're lonely." The mayor then hurried out of the restaurant, not looking back.

From the back of the kitchen, Theo Vasili and I watched my father run to Daphne.

"My Daphne! Sit over here!"

He pulled out a chair for Daphne in the back of the dining room, far from the mayor's table which was still crowded with dirty plates and empty scotch glasses.

"The mayor said he might get me a job!" Daphne purred, walking slowly to the waiting seat.

"You got one! A good one!" My father was howling now, pleading her to dial back to reality.

"Great pay! Lots of trips!" Daphne leaned close to him, slightly slurring her words. "He has lots of money." Listening hard from the kitchen, I could hear the drunken wistfulness in her voice.

"Stay away from him!" My father sounded jealous, not protective.

Realizing that his paternal warning was not penetrating the scotch-soaked Daphne, my father poured her a cup of strong coffee and sat down next to her, assessing the damage.

"You're good to me, Achilles. I don't have a home anymore since Mama died. I need you." Daphne looked around The Classic Grill. "I need — this."

My father took a long, slow breath while he weighed his next words.

"A man need to help. A man need to…protect."

I watched his hand move to lightly touch the tips of Daphne's fingers, her hand resting on the table.

"Daphne, always I will help you. Do not forget this. My…"

Daphne looked up, waiting for his next words. So was I.

"…friend."

Fetching her jacket, my father gently placed it over her slender shoulders. She smiled up at him like a child, basking in his care and the security of The Classic Grill.

THIRTY-EIGHT

"And then things changed. Again." I dreaded even the memory of what I was about to reveal. Maybe these kids had read about it in their history books. Then again, who knows what the schools teach nowadays.

"What this time?" Mariam asked seriously. Her chestnut eyes were wide with concern. "Did you run away?"

I raised my eyebrows in surprise but said nothing. I could not imagine that I, the soft-spoken, hesitant second son of a hard-boiled father with a determined actor-brother, could ever contemplate a breakaway. I was too busy sweeping up the fragments of our shattered Grecian family vase and attempting to glue it back together. The terra cotta figures that once joined hands to form an intricate design of unity were now each stranded on their own rough-edged piece of pottery — each was its own island, scattered on the floor. I felt responsible to mend this family, that I hoped would be admired for generations, with only a few cracks displayed to the world.

"I desperately wanted our family to return to the way it had been," I recalled. "And couldn't accept it never would be."

I almost avoided talking about the wound I often skipped over in my own mind. But I just had to tell my little group the rest of the story, painful as it was. I dove right in.

THIRTY-NINE

As if things couldn't get any worse for our family, one small piece of paper suddenly materialized and represented the hacking of another healthy limb from our family tree. Only the blood on our hands and the scars on our hearts would remain for years. For the second time, another family member would be snatched from our grasp — for no good reason.

February 19, 1942. That was the day that, for me, lived in infamy. At least, that's the way I remember it.

That chilly Thursday morning, my father and I were clanging pots and frying pans in the restaurant kitchen early before school started. We were the only cooks on duty before the doors opened at six o'clock. The back door to the kitchen squeaked open and Tetsuya, bundled in a warm coat and fedora, stepped in and stood quietly waiting. He slid his hat from his balding head, waiting for my father to notice him.

My father set down his twelve-inch knife next to the tall pile of raw yellow onions he had chopped fine for the chili he would cook up for the lunch menu. He preferred to tackle the onions first and then wash away the pungent odor so it would not taint the rest of the food we would cook that day. He stared uneasily at Tetsuya.

"You early, Tetsuya. Coffee is ready." My father nodded to the coffee urn near the front counter.

Tetsuya's feet remained planted.

My father gingerly approached Tetsuya who was not preparing to work. My father inspected him carefully, sensing darkness.

"You no work?"

My father wiped his hands on his apron and studied Tetsuya closely.

Tetsuya's voice was low.

"We are leaving soon."

My father drew closer, breathing more quickly.

"Who leaves?"

"This is war. I am Japanese. They take us away. My family. All of us. I do not know where to."

My father stepped back and observed Tetsuya.

"Where you go? Who is taking you? You do nothing for this!"

My father began revving up for a rant. "We live in God's country!"

"Achilles, your God is sleeping."

"This is a trick of the mayor! I go to City Hall! We fight!"

"This is the order of the President of the United States, Franklin Roosevelt," Tetsuya interrupted.

"*My* President Roosevelt? This cannot be!" My father rushed to his beat up desk and pulled a tin box from the lower drawer. He opened it to reveal his rainy day fund. It was known only to us immediate family members and, of course, to Tetsuya.

He clasped Tetsuya's hands emotionally. "I pay who I need to pay! You will stay!"

Tetsuya gently pulled away. "Achilles, you are like me. We work hard to make better for our families. That is all we want. Now, we are different forever." Tetsuya's voice was heavy with regret. He shook his head.

"God's country." Tetsuya turned to leave. "I come back later to work. Now, I need my wife, my sons."

He then took a step closer to my father. "Achilles, war is a very bad thing. Too much pain already. Keep your family together." He stared unwaveringly at my father. "Bring Demo home. War change everything, Achilles. Love him while you can."

My father stood frozen. Tetsuya popped his hat on his head and walked towards the back door. Then he spun around and crossed in front of my father to give me a hug that fathers give their sons. He released me from his grasp and walked again toward the door.

"I be back to cook. Until I have to go."

I watched Tetsuya leave and my need for him flooded my body. I wanted to run to him. I wanted to hide him safely away, protected from my father's president. But I couldn't find my voice and my feet were cemented to the concrete kitchen floor. And so, in my usual style, I did nothing. The United States government had crushed my family pottery to smithereens under its thick, black, Army-issued boot. I sighed. More shattered pieces for me to mend, but this time I didn't have the stomach to try.

FORTY

For once, my father was silent when the first cooks came on duty that morning. He ripped off his apron and found his heavy wool coat. As I jumped on my bicycle heading for school, my father quickly walked in the opposite direction towards the waterfront. Adrift in his thoughts, he never considered taking a moment to comfort me.

The bonds holding together my father and Tetsuya seemed unbreakable. Now, the strings that connected them were tangled and complicated. It took the government and the president — the one who promised Freedom from Fear to all citizens — to pull them apart. As my father paced the waterfront along the Mare Island Strait, he probably remembered the first thread that connected his life with the person that would become his indispensable right-hand man and lifelong friend. I remembered my father's story about his first meeting with Tetsuya.

Before my father and Tetsuya coincidentally met, Tetsuya had transferred the newfound knowledge he acquired on the fishing boats to a less taxing job at the Tokyo Fish Market on Fisherman's Wharf in San Francisco. His duties required him to set the newly hooked fish in orderly rows on their icy beds and politely serve customers from the first light of day to long after dark. He placed the selected glossy fish bodies on waxy white paper, heads facing in the same direction, and wrapped them tight for the cooks and housewives who were always hungry for fresh fish. Tetsuya's mastery of English and knowledge of the ways of San Francisco society slowly improved. He observed that a small bowing gesture was perceived as subservient and Tetsuya would not be second-class in his new home, if he could help it. He learned to look a man in the eye, but being Japanese, not too threateningly. When a man's hand was extended, he learned to shake it, but not use his full strength.

On a particularly cold and foggy Friday in San Francisco, the wind cut through Tetsuya's shabby coat, patched on the front and sides for more insulation. As he stood behind the outdoor fish counter, he attempted to keep warm while serving dozens of customers crowding the counter to purchase tuna, cod, halibut, sturgeon or king salmon.

One of his regulars, a Greek man — my father — caught Tetsuya's attention. He had come to recognize this customer named Achilles, whose coal-black hair and large, droopy mustache were easily identifiable in a world where most Caucasian men looked alike to him.

My father purchased fish each week on Monday, Wednesday and Friday for The Old Clam House, located far from the center of town. He was tight with his fish budget and never bought the most expensive variety, yet never the cheapest. Why my father had briefly introduced himself weeks ago had always been unclear to Tetsuya. Did he expect a lower price? Was my father searching for a friendly face, although Tetsuya's was from the Far East? Or maybe it was that Tetsuya never pressed his thumb on the scale, like many of his co-workers, to add an extra two or three pennies to the tab.

Years later, Tetsuya learned that Kosmos, my father's favorite relative, was of some undetermined Asian descent and had a faint resemblance to Tetsuya. They shared the same gentle, good-natured manner. People of Asian, Turkish and Middle Eastern descent were not uncommon as occasional travelers drifted through my father's part of Greece. It pleased my father, who had lived in America less than a decade, to do business with Tetsuya, as this gentle Japanese man somehow made him feel a little more at home. My father's dealings with Tetsuya were brief but warm and kindly. Immigrant to immigrant. With only his cousin Vasili who occasionally accompanied him to market, my father, like Tetsuya, was alone in the new world.

On that day, when the fog cut like a blade through all coats and scarves, an insignificant yet momentous incident occurred. It would not disrupt world affairs but would cement my family with Tetsuya forever. It was a simple act, one that occurred hundreds of times a day on the wharf, where people traded money for fresh fish and seafood. With the intention of scooping up his regular fish order and quickly returning to the restaurant for the lunch trade, my father hurried to the Tokyo Fish Market and waited impatiently in line. Tetsuya briefly greeted my father and stooped over to pull up a box filled with the Friday order for The Old Clam House.

As my father reached over the counter to receive the box, a thin, slippery hand stretched into his pocket and swiftly, silently pulled out his wallet which was lodged inside his coat pocket. From his post behind the orderly display of cold fish, Tetsuya caught sight of his younger co-worker, Toshio, lifting this Greek cook's wallet. While my father searched his pocket to pay with the money entrusted to him by the restaurant, Tetsuya had already whipped around the counter, jumped on Toshio's bony frame and pinned his sticky-fingered co-worker to the ground, a firm grip on his neck. Tetsuya, almost always bigger than his fellow Japanese, overpowered the small Toshio and punched him only once, with no more force than was necessary. He wrestled the wallet from Toshio's tight fist and staggered to stand, feeling he had defended the integrity of Tokyo Fish Market from a bad reputation. Straightening his coat and apron, Tetsuya was surprised at the immediate surge of anger rising from his heart — an emotion he did not know he harbored.

My father watched with surprise as the tall Japanese fish market man, slightly younger than himself, returned his wallet stuffed with bills. Before my father could thank Tetsuya, the enraged owner of the market rushed to stand between Tetsuya and Toshio. A tiny man in comparison to his young, healthy workers, the owner screamed at both men. My father did not understand the words but the owner's emotions were easily conveyed in the universal language of livid upper management. With the fuming owner's stubby finger pointing in the direction away from the fish stand, Tetsuya and Toshio were both fired on the spot and sent away from the Tokyo Fish Market, never again to harm its reputation.

Later that evening, as the sun slipped below the fleecy grey fog line hovering over the Pacific Ocean, my father circled back to the waterfront looking for Tetsuya. My father later revealed he was unsettled knowing that Tetsuya's job had been ripped away from him that day only because he avenged dishonesty in my father's favor. My father also knew it would be difficult for Tetsuya to find a job in the cruel, racist San Francisco employment circles. The Japanese were known as solid, faithful workers so white laborers worried they had to defend their jobs, which could be snatched by those whose faces and culture seemed so very different from their own.

My father trolled the piers and docks familiar to him and finally found Tetsuya near Pier 29. Darkness had nearly cloaked the city in blues and grays. Only a few lights reflecting off the water allowed my father to recognize Tetsuya's silhouette. He sat on a dock, staring at the small, family-owned fishing boats running to the outer reaches of the bay for a good catch.

My father stood close to Tetsuya who did not look up.

"You help me today." My father's words were simple. He didn't know exactly how much English Tetsuya understood and he wasn't fluent in English himself.

Tetsuya looked up, taking a moment to identify this figure standing in the shadows, a person he only encountered during the day at the fish market.

"Yes," Tetsuya replied.

"I thank you," my father added. "You have no job now?"

Tetsuya clearly understood the words "no job." He nodded.

"Help we need at my restaurant. The Old Clam House. I work there. I cook there."

My father hoped Tetsuya understood his choppy, jumbled English. Earlier that day, he had asked the owner, Mr. Coil, if Tetsuya could wash dishes at least for a few weeks to see how it worked out. My father had no real knowledge of Tetsuya's character or if he was a skillful worker. But he wanted to correct a wrong for a man who had risked his own safety to help — especially when he could have taken the side of his countryman. He realized Tetsuya had jumped in because he was honest. And honesty went a long way with my father, especially when money was concerned.

"You want to work? We need dishwasher."

Tetsuya said nothing, and my father waited for an answer. Actually, Tetsuya was not comfortable with a white man offering him something. He also had no idea where The Old Clam House was located and why he would want to wash dishes there.

My father began to feel foolish for trudging along the waterfront to offer up a miserable dishwashing job. He was now convinced he had insulted this Japanese man who had saved his wallet and his reputation back at The Old Clam House. My father paused and reached into his pocket.

"The restaurant is here." He passed Tetsuya a slip of paper upon which the owner had scribbled the address. "We make fish good and you eat there too."

Letting those words sink in, my father waited another moment. He hoped Tetsuya understood he could eat for free and get paid to work. My father always looked for those restaurant jobs that came with generous meals for the help. His motto was "always work in a restaurant and you will never starve." And my father would never starve.

He waited a few more uncomfortable long seconds after handing the slip of paper to Tetsuya. Not knowing what else to do, he turned and walked away, back to his room at the boarding house on Seventh Street, south of Market Street.

My father didn't know that Tetsuya understood his words and Tetsuya was amazed that this *gaijin*, this foreigner, would come to find him, to help him. He looked at the scrap of paper and shoved it in his pocket contemplating his next move. Until that point, he had only worked for Japanese employers and was hesitant to break out of the Japanese world in San Francisco. Then, again, he considered the effort this Greek man made to locate him, attempting to make things right.

The next morning at seven o'clock, Tetsuya appeared at the shabby screened back door of The Old Clam House, about four and a half miles south of the Ferry Building. He knocked but no one answered — and he dared not enter. After a few minutes, my father walked into the kitchen, saw Tetsuya behind the screen and slowly opened the door. Without words, he showed Tetsuya the rags, sponges and steel wool he would need for his new job. Together they worked side by side that day, one scrubbing, one cooking. Neither man was to know that a lifelong relationship had been just been forged. Two immigrants who had turned their backs on their home countries and who now seized opportunity — and honesty — wherever they could find it.

Tetsuya soon elevated himself at The Old Clam House from a dishwasher to fry cook. Tetsuya and my father went on to work together in restaurants throughout San Francisco — a breakfast and lunch eatery on Market Street, and a steak house in the Mission District. And they both back-filled their wages by working as the night clean up crew at The Tadich Grill, or The Original Cold Day Restaurant, as the Tadich was called at the time, on Clay Street. Several years later, the duo drifted apart when my father went to Greece and returned with his wife, my mother. But when my parents saved enough money to open The Classic Grill, my father ensured the success of his new enterprise by making one call. And Tetsuya answered it.

And now, it seemed the union with our Japanese family member was forbidden and he would soon be ripped away from our heart and our restaurant.

FORTY-ONE

The sun attempted to slice through another foggy morning in downtown San Francisco. Despite his heavy coat, Demo was chilled, tired and a little stiff as he picked his way down the docks with no obvious destination. He hoped that a brisk walk would keep him warm until the sun decided to make a half-hearted, mid-day appearance as was customary in the city. The ferry anchored near the Ferry Building on the murky, rough waters of the San Francisco harbor. Demo had made the most of his ferry ticket, stowing away his seventeen-year-old body on the ship all night, sleeping on a bench, out of view. He crawled off the ferry when the sun faintly lit the foggy sky in pale shades of pink and gray. The drowsy mist clung to Demo's dark hair and he pulled his coat tighter to protect himself against the winds that whipped the bay.

If Demo didn't reflect too long, the day after the emotional hailstorm with his father almost felt like any other day. After all, he was completely at home in downtown San Francisco as he had been for years, sneaking visits to see live theatre in his adopted hometown. He always sensed he would end up living somewhere in this city. It was just a matter of time. Demo was both terrified and relieved that he was free, although his departure was much earlier than he expected. The seed of theatre had been planted in his heart long ago, involuntarily, as part of his being. That vital spore would either blossom and infuse him with beauty and result in an artful life, or if not allowed to develop, that kernel would swell and grow dense with malicious branches that would strangle him, cutting off all oxygen and hope.

But now Demo had been expelled by our father from the Greek world, which was stillborn by generations of tradition rooted in the Middle Ages and someone else's expectations. My brother had been jettisoned from our family home to live on the untamed streets of San Francisco.

My brother admitted to me that he knew he was different—always had. He was harangued at school and over the years had described horrible beatings he had taken and later disguised for my mother's sake. With all his might, he pretended that the violence was repelled from his skin as if he were drenched in the finest Greek olive oil while attempting to hide the hurt. I was the only one who truly knew his pain. Demo said he tried to focus on the ancient spirit that ran through his body like electricity. And he knew that spirit and his sexual self were fused together as one. Like an embryo that grew to become a chick too large and energetic for its shell, Demo ruptured the delicate casing that had protected him in his youth. He brazenly cracked it open to unleash the dramatic arts of Dionysus to the world around him, whether that world was prepared or not. And most of the time, it wasn't.

Demo adopted the idea of destiny, and the three white-robed Fates, the sisters who supposedly determined one's life. He would not look back on his comfortable existence at home, clearly understanding that his psyche and passion could never squeeze into the narrow confines of 1942 Vallejo during a world at war. His soul required the space and breathing room that San Francisco offered. Demo wished our father could see himself as a jailer who tightened the chains until his son could accept the role of the restaurant executive that he had created in his own imagination. Demo knew he and our father were too much alike — yet lived a bay and a world apart.

As a warm-up for his new life in San Francisco, this time a permanent resident without an address, Demo worked his way past the busy piers along the Embarcadero. With the war at full speed on both the German and Japanese fronts, the docks were lively with cargo booms swinging crates and palettes while sailors unloaded supplies from railroad cars to waiting ships. Swarms of sailors in their work shirts and bell-bottom pants hurried past him to the grueling work that awaited them for the day.

Demo turned down Market Street and briskly walked toward the heart of town, feeling the need to begin making a life — or at least a day. He promised himself he would move ahead independently, never to become one of those men who wandered by the back door of our house during the Depression and years afterwards. They said nothing, looking down at their more-than-worn shoes, hat in hand. Without fail, our mother cooked up a skillet of fried eggs and bacon to offer them. The word "bum" was often used in our neighborhood, but our mother would correct us and call them *atychís*, unfortunate or unlucky. She knew they were actually good men who had fallen on hard times which was easy to do in America. Demo knew it was our mother who taught us, her sons, to keep our hearts for open extended hours — breakfast, lunch and dinner — just like The Classic Grill.

Demo moved down Market Street and decided to take a tour of the larger department stores near Union Square. Although they weren't open, he lingered near the facades of Roos Brothers, City of Paris and Ransohoff's which offered colorful store windows where he could kill time. He swung past the expensive Shreve & Company and Gump's to watch the attendants precisely position the sparkling jewels in the window show-cases before opening their doors. Demo then zipped to the Golden Gate Theatre on lower Taylor Street for the first vaudeville show of the day. He settled back in his seat and was pleased that a few of his favorite acts were on the bill.

After the warm-up juggling act, Think A Drink Hoffman took the stage with his pitcher of water and empty glasses. With a restrained flourish and the graceful hands of a magician, Think A Drink Hoffman took random drink orders from the audience and, from his pitcher of water, poured out the requested drink. After shouting out, "Martini!" the lady next to Demo trotted to the stage to taste her Martini, freshly poured into a triangular Martini glass. Next, the man in the second row requested, "tomato juice!" and was summoned to the stage to claim his drink, as requested, which was served in a tall glass tumbler. Demo marveled at the showmanship and applauded heartily with the mystified audience after each drink revelation.

Next was super magician John Calvert, the striking mustachioed gentleman in a debonair tux who began his act with a baritone message, "I am here to fool you. If I don't fool you, you will be fooled." With ease and grace, Calvert levitated a shapely woman wearing lavender chiffon, waving brass hoops around her body to prove he used no strings. Next, with his signature elegance, John Calvert produced twenty dancing handkerchiefs that undulated in thin air. Then he sawed a woman in half with a handsaw, only to produce a whole person moments later.

The show cast a calming influence on Demo and for a time, he was distracted from his impending homelessness. When the curtain came down on the last act, he drifted to the Curran Theatre to investigate the play-bill for the evening, unsure if he could afford such a luxury quite yet. Just another day in San Francisco, he told himself. The difference was he had nowhere to sleep that night. Finally, about five-thirty in the afternoon, Demo decided to eat, the first time he was hungry since my father had commanded him to leave our home.

Demo walked down Geary Street to the busy Foster's Cafeteria and peered through the large glass restaurant window. Cooks, busboys and waiters were engaged in preparation for the dinner rush. A cook hoisted a roasted turkey onto the steam table, ready for carving. With that, Demo pulled open the heavy glass door to a home away from home.

Demo sat at a long cafeteria table savoring his favorite: roasted turkey, mashed potatoes and cranberry with a side of peas and carrots and a green salad. He had to admit his father's version was more tender and Tetsuya's vegetables were more flavorful. But this luncheon fare filled his immediate hunger and he was grateful to find affordable food. Demo figured a once-a-day eating plan might get him through until he could cook up his own regular income. He looked around Foster's and assessed that, if absolutely necessary, he could inquire about a job, having plenty of experience. Then he quickly nixed that notion as he had promised himself that he would always move forward. His father taught him that much. But the thought of having nowhere to sleep kept nipping away at the momentary pleasure of a hot lunch.

Halfway between the salad and turkey courses, Demo sensed a nearby presence. He looked up to see a very tall woman in her late forties. Her dramatic makeup and long jet-black hair were theatrical—or borderline freakish. Her black dress and long jacket could have been found in a vaude-ville trunk or at the swankiest store on Union Square, Demo was not sure which. In his many excursions around San Francisco he had seen people wearing the all-black look hanging around San Francisco, mostly poets and playwrights in bookstores. And old Italian and Greek widows.

This woman placed her tray opposite Demo and fell into her seat. Demo looked up but continued to eat, uncomfortable with a stranger in such close proximity. Now the large woman began eating her sandwich and slurping coffee.

"I've seen you at the Curran Theatre."

She munched on her tuna on rye. Demo looked up and immediately slid the change he had offhandedly tossed on his lunch tray into his pocket. Could never be too careful around strangers.

"I've seen you plenty of times." She pronounced her words between large bites.

Alarms screamed in Demo's brain. He said nothing, shoveling down the last of his turkey, gravy and mashed potatoes. Demo wanted to finish his meal and get his money's worth before he hurried out of the cafeteria. He was annoyed that he was forced to be on guard while enjoying his only meal of the day.

"I'm an usher at the Curran — that's how I've seen you." She searched out Demo's eyes but Demo was wary, not returning the warm enthusiasm. "But I do it all."

She slid her slice of custard pie onto Demo's tray.

"Here — for a growing boy." Her brilliant crimson lips smiled broadly and disarmed Demo just a little. He snatched the dessert and summoned enough trust to sink his fork into the creamy slice.

"Thanks," Demo offered, eagerly downing the pie. "Just like my family's restaurant."

She sipped her coffee and sat back into her chair. Demo relaxed enough to study her face, theatrical makeup and gestures — and to size up her motives.

"Daddy and Mama were cellists with the New York Symphony. Boris and Raisa Goldshein," she stated with pride. "And I'm a founder of the Pacific Coast Repertory Theatre. Kind of defunct now, but when it was hot — it was somethin'!"

The woman in black offered her hand across the table. Her powerful handshake gripped Demo's slender hand.

"Natalya Gold. My stage name."

Demo shook her hand tentatively, still reserving judgment.

"Actress?"

"Since I was five. A little off-Broadway. A little on. Sing, dance, act — the old triple threat. Headlined almost every club around here. Know every actor in New York and San Francisco...that's worth knowing that is."

Natalya dug in her giant purse and pulled out a bundle of photos.

"John Garfield. Martha Graham. Paul Muni. Helen Tamiris, Alfred Lunt, Lynn Fontanne. Did a bit with Eleanor Powell. Worked with them all." She proudly popped a stick of Clark's Teaberry gum into her mouth.

Her big grin revealed Natalya's more-than-transparent personality — over-sized and optimistic.

Demo leaned toward Natalya, dropping his guard at least for the moment. Something about her offhanded chattering relaxed Demo.

"I am an actor. Well, I'm working on it." He gave Natalya a long, steady look, dismissing her oddity. "Tell me how you did it."

As the sun slowly disappeared into the evening bank of fog and the soft afternoon air was displaced by the chilly wind off the Pacific, the oddly matched pair — the young, lanky Demo and the dramatic, bulky Nata-lya — trekked the hills of San Francisco. They strode past the restaurants, bars, derelicts, theatres, plentiful movie houses and women of the evening. They ambled through North Beach, passing signs for dancing, cocktails and entertainment that reflected the district's remnants of the Barbary Coast. Natalya pointed out more saloons and secret hide-a-way bars than Demo knew existed. They hiked up the vertical incline of Nob Hill and wandered through the lavish Fairmont and St. Francis hotels. Finally, they strolled along fishing docks, Natalya talking nonstop. And Demo, desperate for her stories, her decades on or behind the stage, inhaled every one.

FORTY-TWO

"So how'd that work for Demo?" Mariam asked.

"Who *was* that woman?" Aman looked uncomfortable and worried. "Your mama, she go crazy when your brother gone. No cell phones."

"Woman? Man?" Jason said, getting to the point. "Who or what was Natalya, anyway?"

"A little of each, I think, looking back on it now. Demo was learning everything that San Francisco had to offer."

Aman and Mariam looked up to see a family of fidgety children and bossy parents who were ready to order. They jumped up to dash behind the counter.

"Wait for us!" Mariam whispered as she passed me. "I want to know what happened to Demo. To all of you!"

I sat back and took a sip of my now-cold coffee, but I didn't mind. I was happy to soak up the vitality and curiosity of these kids who, like me, seemingly had perfected the art of how to live in two worlds: your parents' circle of traditions from the old country that you were required to follow, and your own version, the world you were inventing as you went along. Sketching it in as you matured, while educating your parents at the same time.

Looking at these young people, I could see they were just beginning, with all hope and anticipation, to expand their lives and expected everything good that America could represent. Like our family, I know they were on guard against the constant and sometimes barefaced antagonism against being foreign. But youth has a way of dismissing the worst and hoping for the best. That was me back then. And that was Demo too. We expected everything. And expected that everything would be good.

FORTY-THREE

After Tetsuya's notice, the war seemed somewhere far away from Vallejo. But soon World War II reported for duty — front and center — at The Classic Grill.

I watched from the kitchen as Taki pushed the door open with his foot. His hands were burdened with a large 1930s-style radio. Theo Vasili trailed behind, holding the radio's electric cord so Taki would not trip and fall. Taki carefully placed the radio on the counter and after plugging it in, quickly began an intense search for a news station. My father appeared baffled at the large radio in his restaurant. Whatever was going on with Taki, he did not approve.

"I need to know where is Nikko," Taki worried. "The newspaper is not enough."

"Taki, this is restaurant — not USO." My father sternly folded his arms in front of his apron.

"Taki want to keep *his* son close," Theo Vasili thornily tossed in.

Ignoring the jab, my father poured coffee to soothe emotions and keep the peace. Taki turned the dial of the wood-cased Zenith model, with its rounded corners and fabric-covered speakers, in search of news from the European war front.

I saw my father motion to Theo Vasili. "*Ella*, Vasili, come!" My father nodded to his cousin and hustled him to the back of the kitchen.

"Where is Daphne?" I overheard my father demand.

Theo Vasili shrugged.

"So, she no come for a couple of days. No worry, she come back. She like it here!"

"Six and a half days!" my father corrected. "I worry!"

Pulling out a cigar from his worn jacket, Theo Vasili slowly placed it between his lips. Before he could strike a match, my father ripped it from his mouth.

"You go find her!" he screamed without raising his voice above a whisper. "You know I cannot leave!"

He was right. My father could not leave the restaurant and run around town looking for the whereabouts of an unmarried, beautiful woman. He dare not do that to my mother, who was hardly speaking to him anyway. And with the new restaurant in the nascent stage, he could not risk a bad reputation when he was already on the outs with the mayor and his brother.

Just as Theo Vasili turned to leave, Tetsuya entered, ready to work the lunch rush. The front door of The Classic Grill again creaked open and Daphne hurried inside, dressed in a sea-blue, long-sleeved dress, more striking than ever.

"Mmmmm! Something smells good!" she said cheerily, as if she were returning home from summer camp. My father nearly jumped over the counter to greet her. Sensing all eyes on him, he pulled back the reins, keeping his cool. Theo Vasili smiled gently to welcome Daphne, helping to cover my father's anxiety.

"How you do today, Miss Daphne?" my uncle offered nonchalantly. My father drafted off Theo Vasili's opener and blurted out a calm greeting.

"Hello, Daphne. You gone long time," my father interrupted in quiet tones. "We miss. We worry."

I watched him pour Daphne a cup of black coffee while attempting to examine her face. Had she been in an accident? Lost her job? A rendezvous with a paramour?

"Tetsuya!" my father shouted to the kitchen. "Make her favorite!"

Tetsuya nodded and pulled a copper-bottom frying pan from the overhead hooks. In the kitchen I watched as he cracked eggs against the ceramic bowl and soon the decadent aroma of eggs bubbling in a lake of golden-brown butter tantalized our noses.

"So where you go?" I could tell he was attempting to sound conversational, unpossessive, chatty.

"Oh, a little trip up North. Took care of a few things." Daphne inhaled the aroma of her coffee.

"Boyfriend?" My father polished the counter, looking down.

She didn't reach for her customary cigarette and nervously kept her purse in her lap, as if she would leap off her stool at any moment. Daphne motioned for him to move closer. She nervously checked her watch.

"Remember you told me that you'd help me?" Her soft, whispered words pulled my father's face very close to hers. "No matter what?"

My father's eyes were glued to her face, his body motionless.

Daphne leaned into my father. "I need you!"

Later, my father told me those words tightened his stomach. He was conscious of wading in farther, sinking deeper. He had ignored his latitude and longitude and, with his next words, he threw away his compass.

"Yes. Yes, Daphne," he blurted out without his better judgment — or any judgment at all. "I do anything. To help you."

Daphne immediately broke away, jumping off her stool and ran out the front door. My father, Theo Vasili and Taki looked at each other. I pushed through the swinging doors of the kitchen to the dining room, my arms loaded with platters of hotcakes, fried eggs, toast and bacon for Daphne. I didn't know if I should set them down or wrap the food for her to take away.

Daphne rushed back inside, leading a small boy by the hand. She pulled him to the counter and he crawled onto the stool next to hers using his hands and knees like an agile little monkey. Then he plopped straight-faced into a sitting position.

"Achilles, this is Alex." Daphne rested her hands in her lap as if she was presenting her most prized possession.

My father slowly nodded to the child, waiting for Daphne's next clue.

"My son!" Beaming, Daphne pulled Alex close to her. "My one and only. Four years and six months."

All of us stood there frozen. This woman, rather, this mother was no longer just a pretty girl in my mind. She was responsible for someone else, not just for her stylish clothes or a boozy afternoon. She had taken on weighty responsibility. She was the touchstone for another small being which was, in my Greek-American mind of a 1940s teenager, the most important thing a woman could be. Or maybe I was just blinded by my own mother's endless love. I heard my father react first.

"Uh, welcome to The Classic Grill." My father nodded respectfully to the boy, as if addressing the president. "This is my restaurant."

Darkness clouded Daphne's eyes. She checked her watch again and looked at my father and back at Alex.

"Achilles, I have no one to care for Alex today and I'm going to be late for work."

Alex glanced up at my father with his dark, chocolate-colored eyes. He could have been a refugee child from war-torn Greece. Alex was a statue, not daring to move. He probably had been through this before, even at his tender age. I instantly felt sorry for him and wanted to tell him everything would be okay, although I was unclear how it would be.

"So you see my problem, Achilles?" Daphne checked her watch again. "I don't trust anyone in town but you." Gracefully she slid off her stool. "Just for today...and maybe tomorrow?"

Daphne's lips seemed to tremble despite her brave smile. Finally, my father imperceptibly nodded, not knowing how else to respond.

"I was sure I could count on you. Thank you so much, Achilles." Daphne turned to small Alex who remained expressionless.

"It's just like home — you'll see." Daphne kissed her son on the top of his head and swept out the front door. Eyes wide, Alex stared at my father. My father stared back feeling the weight of this new responsibility he did not ask for.

I set down the platters of Daphne's hot breakfast food in front of Alex. My father slowly walked around the counter to the boy and looked him over, from his little legs that were miles away from touching the black and white tile floor to his dark eyes and long eyelashes. Alex had not inherited Daphne's lighter, more refined features. He looked more like my family — dark, but not swarthy.

My father sighed and then, as many Greek fathers would have done, he unfolded a cloth napkin with "The Classic Grill" embroidered on it and tucked it under Alex's chin. He turned the child's stool so he faced the three platters of breakfast awaiting him on the counter.

"You eat good, my son."

We watched incredulously as the four-year-old wolfed down a tall stack of hot cakes and quickly moved on to the fried eggs.

Those words "my son" rankled me. I found it unconscionable that just as my father sent Demo away, he quickly agreed to take in another boy. I could only picture Demo across the bay, perhaps with no home, nothing to eat. But I couldn't be angry with this child. He was another boy looking for a home, a place where he could finally relax and be himself. I decided at that moment that I should open my heart to little Alex. And go back to cook him up another plate of hotcakes.

A half-hour later, my father paced around our kitchen table at home, waiting for my mother to arrive. I sat next to Alex, waiting. We could hear her sweetly humming a Greek folksong as she drew nearer. I could see her through the screen door, carrying a small basket of oregano and basil she had harvested from her garden for the evening meal and the restaurant's soups and roasts. As my mother's voice became louder and her footsteps got closer, my father uneasily shifted in his seat.

The screen door squeaked open and my mother stepped in, slightly out of breath and damp with perspiration from her garden work. As was my mother's way, her nails showed a little temporary dirt from contact with the soil and plants she nurtured to feel connected with her personal universe.

She slowly set down her basket and looked at the three of us — three generations of males who depended on her strength. Her eyes lit on Alex but looked away, not wanting to be rude to a boy she did not know.

As always when in a difficult situation, in the presence of a non-Greek we quickly switched to our native language, the secret code that few understood. The Chinese and Italians were not so lucky, as more people in our community understood their mother tongue. Greek was our secret language. The faster the better.

"Who is this?" my mother asked in Greek.

"The son of one of our customers." My father offered few words.

My mother looked squarely at him.

"*Opoíos?*" she asked point blank. "Who?"

"A new customer."

My mother motioned for my father to move away to the service porch. I was searching the kitchen drawers for a toy that Demo and I might have left behind years before. But I could hear my parents.

"It is that blond woman! Why she no take care of her child?" My mother demanded, her hawk eyes searching for truth from my father.

"She got a job. There is nowhere for the boy." As long as my mother did not ask about his attraction for Daphne, he hoped to be on solid ground.

My mother and father looked at little Alex, silently sitting at the kitchen table, perhaps waiting to see what these new adults surrounding him would do with his life.

"Why you do this to me, *Achilléas*?" I saw my mother search his face.

Looking at the child, then at my mother, my father shrugged helplessly. "I do not know what to do with a boy."

"You prove this with your own. With Demo. And now I should care for the son of that woman?" my mother demanded.

"You no understand, Chrisoula." My father searched for the right words to soften her reaction, filling in the seconds somehow until this conversation might be over.

"I understand everything, *Achilléas.*"

My mother crossed back into the kitchen and took Alex by the hand. She led him to the small, worn sofa in the kitchen area sitting down next to him. She clasped Alex's small chubby hand in her soft, strong palm.

"What is your name, my child?"

"Alex. Alexander," he said flatly, his eyes straight ahead.

My mother gasped and looked at Alex with a warmhearted smile.

"*Alexandros!* That is the best Greek name. Alexander the Great! A king! Do you know his story?"

Alex vigorously shook his head and settled back to listen to the tale my mother began to weave. I could read my father's face as he took a step back from my mother and Alex. I knew he marveled at my mother's ability to provide a loving place for all lost souls, because I certainly did.

FORTY-FOUR

In Greek tradition, the child among adults always takes the main stage and wins the heart. Children have always been the centerpiece of any Greek family and at The Classic Grill it was no different. The routine went something like this: every workday Daphne dropped off Alex at the restaurant. We cooked up his customary big breakfast and after a week or two, he began to wander into the kitchen and investigate. For awhile, my father led Alex by the hand to our home. But soon, on my way to school, I led Alex a few blocks to our family home where my mother expected him and offered *koulourakia* cookies and milk. On the way, we'd have rock throwing contests in an empty lot near our house and I usually would let Alex win. Sometimes we'd play tag and run most of the way to our house. He became my little brother, and I treated him the way Demo kindly treated me.

If I couldn't escort him, Theo Vasili, who helped raise Demo and me, could be counted on to walk Alex up the hill. My uncle always dug into his pocket for candy money and the pair often stopped at Greene's Cigar & Liquor Store, always open for the early morning trade. A cigar for my uncle, licorice for Alex.

Taki also volunteered for "Alex duty." Their routine included a stop on a bench near the waterfront to scour the funny papers, and a few reading lessons for Alex. Mr. Chris, of course, showed Alex how to hold the violin. For once, my father did not discourage music lessons in his kitchen. Tetsuya wrote Alex's name in Japanese and showed him how to meticulously shell peas.

During this time, I learned more about my mother than I ever imagined. My mother focused on the child and his needs, never on the fact that his mother was an attractive young woman whom she thought my father fancied. My mother would not let a child in her purview languish from lack of attention. It didn't take long until she greeted Alex with her warm hugs and a waterfall of conversation in English and soon Greek. Alex was another flower thriving in her garden of love.

FORTY-FIVE

My little group was back together after supplying the hungry new customers with their trays of burgers, fries and soft drinks. The soccer family that was the first to hear my story was finishing their ice cream course. The kids were listening, while licking the drips from their soft-serve vanilla cones with the chocolate shell dip.

"You had to babysit? You were just a kid yourself!" Zach said with a touch of sympathy. He now seemed relaxed and engaged, happy to have story time for his kids. He checked his mobile phone and looked up at me.

"It was my job to make sure Alex made it to so-called daycare. But we didn't call it that in those days." I remembered. "I took him from the restaurant to our house nearly five days a week."

"Didn't your family go find Demo?" Jason asked. He had long ago set aside his cleaning tools and rested his head on his two fists which were tucked under his chin.

I sat back, ready to tell Demo's story. I wished Demo were here to speak about his own life and exactly what he felt. But I was always happy to talk about my brother. I felt a little closer to him when I did.

FORTY-SIX

Caring for Alex might have distracted my mother, but she desperately wanted to know where Demo was living. Theo Vasili, the restaurant crew and I did too. After a few days, Demo called home when he knew my father would be at the restaurant. He told us he'd found a room at the downtown Army Navy YMCA. It was a safe, clean place for cheap. Demo promised my mother he would call once a week, a big expense on his limited budget.

Demo later told me that about a week after he landed in San Francisco, he found himself at ground-zero of the bustling backstage action of costumes, stage managers, makeup and pre-performance energy at the Curran Theatre. One evening's bill featured *Pal Joey* with the stars of the day, Gene Kelly and Vivienne Segal. Natalya fulfilled her ticket-taking duties at the front entrance and encouraged Demo to wander through the theatre and soak up the intoxicating behind-the-scenes atmosphere.

Demo observed the stagehands as they pulled the painted scenery flats into place, ready for the backstage cues and scenery changes. He walked past the dressing rooms and viewed both male and female actors in various stages of dress or undress — they didn't seem to care. He took note of the stagehands as they adjusted the footlights while they cursed a demanding actress who required a special lighting setup. The curtain puller was reviewing his cues from a crumpled piece of paper. Demo couldn't wait to tell me he got a glimpse of Gene Kelly himself and he watched the play from a ninth row center seat that Natalya arranged for him because of a no-show.

At intermission, Demo had spotted the tall Natalya in her usher uniform. Like a giant palm tree hovering over the sandy beach below her, she good-naturedly observed the chaos as the audience mingled. Chewing gum in her back teeth, she answered questions for patrons and checked ticket stubs. Demo pressed his way through the crowd and stood next to her to observe the intermission confusion.

Natalya then led him backstage and allowed him to linger for a few additional moments during the frenzy of intermission. A voluptuous young actress in heavy makeup, probably all of seventeen, drifted past and gave Demo a seductive glance that looked odd on her chubby face. A handsome male actor with wavy dark hair and full makeup projected an equally sensual, lingering look and pantomimed a kiss to Demo.

"Demosthenes," Natalya spoke with dramatic emphasis in low tones. "These are your people!" Demo smiled and observed the scene like a starved man seated in front of a lavish feast.

Parting ways with Natalya for the evening, Demo caught the Geary streetcar, heading west, hoping to spend a few minutes at Ocean Beach. At home in Vallejo, he strolled along the waterfront whenever he had an opportunity. Here in San Francisco, he could envision a sliver of platinum light on his horizon as he looked down Geary Street towards the end of the streetcar line. He contemplated his new situation but admitted that the stomach pangs that plagued him each morning were not hunger, as he had become accustomed to his once-a-day eating schedule. Demo honestly admitted that he profoundly missed us, his family. However, the wall constructed by our own father preventing Demo's return was unscalable. Demo would have appreciated a swinging door in and out of Vallejo — a hall pass to visit with his mother and family whenever he wanted. But he also was sure he would never again permanently return home, especially because my father could not accept him for who he was. His senses had been ignited and there was no stomping out the spark. He was open and ready to see where this new life would take him.

Demo emphatically decided he could never turn his back on his family, including our father. That burden would be a hefty weight to bear forever in his heart when he needed to be without bounds. Demo had no safety net but sensed he would learn to fly on a trapeze with a little coaching from below. He would learn the tricks of survival that he could from Natalya. He would keep his gaze up, perfecting his performance and never, ever look down.

FORTY-SEVEN

Demo had been gone for several weeks. As much as my mother and I prayed it only would be temporary, his absence was clearly becoming permanent. Though Alex was a sweet distraction, my mother had created her own prayer center with Demo's photo lovingly placed among crosses, candles and icons displayed on the familiar crocheted doily. Each morning and evening she prayed passionately to St. Sophia. "Let Demo come home! My son should come home!" She made sure my father heard her prayers — loud and clear. A cloud of sadness hovered over her and our home. Nothing seemed right without my brother nearby. If my father sensed the empty space that Demo's bright spirit had inhabited, he said nothing.

One afternoon, I stopped at home before reporting to the restaurant after school. I checked on Alex as he napped on Demo's bed. I didn't think Demo would mind, in fact I imagined he would enjoy Alex. And I was certain Alex would love the plays and make-believe wonderland that Demo conjured up. My boyhood sparkled with memories of Demo and our fantasy adventures that began when he sprinkled magic dust on my shoulders. Demo could not come home soon enough — in my book, that is.

In the kitchen, I found my mother at her stove pensively stirring the rice pudding that would soon complement the stable of desserts that filled the mirrored case at The Classic Grill. I hovered over her shoulder attempting to judge her mood more than the pudding. I sank into a bentwood chair at our kitchen table and stretched out my gangly legs in front of me. I assumed her thoughts were in San Francisco with Demo.

"I will ask him one time again."

She was talking to herself more than to me. My mother mixed the milky liquid with a worn wooden spoon and added a handful of raisins to the bubbling pudding.

"Your father, he love Demo in his *cardia*, his heart. I know this. I will remind him and then Demo, he come home."

Looking up over her cooking, my mother caught my look of disbelief. How could she be so sure my father would allow my brother to come home? I hadn't noticed love pumping from my father's heart towards Demo, or me either, for that matter.

"Your father, he always need to show he *dynatós*, the strong one, for our family. But I always remember your father a very good man."

My mother explained she would change her tactics. She would not be a rock wall that stood parallel to my father's opposing wall, both steadfast, neither yielding, always space between. She would construct a bridge to connect the walls and help my father's side crumble just a little, enough to find the love she was certain he still held in his heart for Demo.

Joining me at the table, my mother cradled a china teacup and saucer in her hands. She took a moment to sip the comforting tea brewed from the chamomile flowers she hand-picked from her garden. A little flame in my heart glowed when she confided only in me — especially about my brother.

"When Demo young like Alex, your father go to church to show him off to everyone. 'My son so smart!' he say. 'He talk early! He know everything! First Pappayannis boy that go to school!'"

"Always your father and your brother. *Mazi*, together!" My mother used the hem of her apron to dry a tear in the corner of her eye. "When your brother nine years, we both catch *pnevmonía*, the pneumonia. Your father he go crazy for this."

How could I forget? I was nearly eight years old and for weeks my father and I were unsure if my mother and brother would survive. Their breathing was labored and all the steam pots and mustard poultice recipes from the herb-gathering Greek women of Vallejo were useless. My father and I — his miniature first assistant — were attentive to their every sip of *avgolemono* soup, Greek lemon-chicken soup and weak tea. My father bathed my mother and Demo's brows with cool water and reeled in Theo Vasili from Reno to cover the restaurant duties so he could fulfill my mother's and brother's every need.

"That's the only time he brought toys home." I remembered desperately wanting to lay my small hands on the wooden train set that my father brought home for Demo — not for me. I was healthy, afterall. "I guess Pop wanted to keep Demo interested in living."

Finally, my mother and brother gained strength and graduated from soup to my father's boiled chicken with lemon sauce, and later, his steak and pan-fried potatoes. My father celebrated their recovery but fretted over his first son if he stayed out too long in the cold air or ate too little at breakfast.

My mother scooted back her chair on the kitchen floor, stood up for a moment and aimlessly began buffing her white tile countertops with a fresh kitchen towel.

"Demo always a good boy. He always work hard at the restaurant, but that not enough for your father." She walked towards me and her gentle hand touched my cheek. "Just like you, *Giorgi*. You try to make your father happy."

By the time we were in junior high, that truth was as plain to me as the white toast we served every day for the breakfast crowd. Writing plays, acting the roles, discovering Greek poets and playwrights, making believe, dressing up. These were the interests that magnetically attracted Demo's heart and mind. The Classic Grill was the theatre I chose, but my father's eyes could only fixate on each step of Demo's development.

"And Demo, he like to be free. He make up his own life." My mother turned to me when she said this. "Because he is *omofylófilos*, homosexual."

I was shocked into silence when she boldly admitted out loud that she sensed that Demo was a man who liked men — something that proper Greek mothers never talked about in the baklava-making circles. I was relieved to know she, like me, was fully aware of who Demo was. My mother told me she considered it early on, but that only intensified her love for Demo. She could see he was brilliant, gifted, and loving. What mother could turn her back on such a son? She believed Demo would need her strength and support to weather a future that would undoubtedly be filled with cruelty, ridicule or much worse.

"But never I think your father to make life so hard for Demo." I saw her shudder as she took in a long slow breath. "Now it is on my *plati*, my back to carry."

My mother returned to her rice pudding, pouring it into small glass dishes. "Your father want to make business for all the Pappayannis family. He cannot do when we all cry for Demo, for our family."

She told me that if my father was the master architect for the family plan, she certainly could lay the foundation for a family where each member was immersed in love and security. If her own immediate Pappayannis family was not bound together by love for each other, what chance did future generations have? Those unnamed babies would grow up to be selfish and unforgiving of each other.

"Without love, without *sevasmós*, respect, this family have no chance." My mother was quite certain our family could not survive even one generation without it.

She quickly moved her hand to make the sign of the cross tapping her fingers first on her forehead, then her chest, then the right and left shoulders. "My St. Sophia. I hope she give me words for your father's ears. He need to love Demo."

I knew my mother would need St. Sophia and any other saint who happened to be listening, to find a chink in my father's impenetrable heart and help bring my brother home.

FORTY-EIGHT

A few weeks after my father sent Demo away, my mother sat at the bar in the restaurant polishing glasses in the late afternoon. With no customers in the dining room, I worked in the back kitchen, cleaning the stove with a metal brush and bucket of soapy water, which always seemed to be my job. The swinging doors were open and I had a view of the bar.

My father approached my mother, an uncharacteristic bottle of wine in his hand. Usually this was the time he compiled his to-do list for the next day: an order for the butcher shop, a bread delivery, the waiters' schedule. He kept all of that in his head.

Today he shuffled to the bar in his white apron and cook's pants, after an exceptionally busy breakfast and lunch service. We all knew Tetsuya's impending departure weighed heavily on him as it did on all of us. But he seemed unusually drained of his usual freight train of energy.

He sat next to my mother and poured wine in one of the glasses she had just polished to sparkling. Still polishing, my mother smiled gently at him.

"In Sparta you played your mandolin, and for a few drachmas I sing, remember?"

She hummed a bit of *Miserlou*. I was astonished when I heard my father's low voice quickly join in.

> Misirlou mou, i glikia sou i matia
> floga mou 'hei anapsei mes stin kardia

I imagined that my father remembered the moment he picked up another musician's idle mandolin as he courted my mother at the club where she sang. My father's face softened a bit, probably remembering the short duet with the fetching, fiery woman who was my mother.

"That was a long time ago." My mother's face reflected his look of sweet remembrance.

"For a moment, I think I should not marry you," she teased. My father quickly glanced up at her. "But I saw your soul was strong!"

She squeezed his arm with affection.

"Your strength make all this for us!" Her sweeping gesture took in my father and all of The Classic Grill. My father seemed momentarily content with this praise.

"But it is time to change."

I dropped my scrub brush. I could see my father's face instantly darken. Although they were spoken softly, sweetly, my mother's words were sharp daggers hanging in the air. I could feel his cold, steel barrier of self-survival shoot up and his drawbridge pull in. He took a slug of wine.

"In Sparta, you promise me strong family. Remember this?" She searched his face, looking for a crack where love might pour through.

"You need to love your son!" My mother's voice could not hide her pleading. "I cannot live when our family not together."

"He shame our family, Chrisoula!"

"Where is your courage, *Achilléas*?" My mother would not accept my father's barrier, her desperation streaming to the surface. "Make room in your heart for your boy. I need this from you now. Demo must come home. To our family that love him. *Achilléas,* I need my son!"

"I need a *real man* to help my restaurant."

With that, my mother's love for Demo flashed into flames.

"*Your* restaurant, *your* plans, *your* life! Always *you*! Demo is your *son*. *Achilléas*, love him!"

My father signaled the Greek look of "no," chin up, nose slightly in the air. He remained silent, stony, impenetrable.

"This is courage?" My mother jumped to her feet, throwing aside her polishing rag. Like the Furies of ancient Greece defending justice, her fire suddenly detonated and she launched it directly at my father. She was a Greek woman warrior who would die for her cause, her son.

"I need a real man too!"

Scorched by her heat, my father was shocked more than I was. She would not accept an *oxi*, a "no," from her husband on this matter.

"He should want what this family want!" My father slammed his glass on the bar.

An earsplitting crash of breaking glass caused my gut to wrench. I doubled over. My mother's fist struck a stack of glasses that smashed into glittering splinters on the floor.

"You say no to Demo — you say no to me!" Now she roared at my father.

She took a step away but spun around facing him eye to eye. With all the majesty of her being, she put a hatchet to this conversation with words that no proper, dutiful Greek wife would even think of murmuring to her husband.

"A sto' diávolos!" she hurled, in her loud, clear voice.

My mother had just told my father to go to hell.

Was that enough to move this resolute mountain? I could only hope her scorching words would bring my brother home.

FORTY-NINE

"What did your father do when your mother spoke to him like that?" Mariam fidgeted with the napkins, straw wrappers, her soda cup. This latest installment in the Pappayannis story seemed a little too much for her. Aman leaped up to serve another customer, as did Jesús.

"My father would not allow this talk from my mother," Mariam added after a few awkward moments. "He would be very angry. It would be bad for all of us."

I could not comment on that one. From experience, I knew that families were private circles and, in most old-world clans, the father ruled the roost. I could only offer a lifeline of understanding.

"I actually believe my father was stunned," I said, thinking back about how my mother relayed the story to me years after. "He also knew my mother was fighting for her son. Family situations are always complicated."

Mariam gave me a weak smile and I thought for a moment she might reveal more. But then Zach broke in.

"I can't imagine my seventeen-year old-kid out there — somewhere and not knowing." He patted his daughter gently on her shoulder.

"Parents were different in those days," I said, but quickly reconsidered. "No, it was my father who was different. He was stubborn and only wanted to build his dream."

FIFTY

The ferry from Vallejo delivered me to San Francisco early in the day, hours before Demo's performance. I decided to save the streetcar fare and soak in a little of the city as I strolled to the Victoria Theatre. With every visit to San Francisco, I was overwhelmed by the shapes and sizes of cars and oddly decorated trucks delivering dry-cleaning, groceries, milk and drugstore items to businesses and housewives' doorsteps. The streets were packed with vehicles peeling off in every direction with little room between them to see the worn asphalt below.

Market Street crawled with long, gray, green-topped San Francisco Municipal Railway streetcars battling for space with red-topped Market Street Railway streetcars. An elongated trolley pole planted on the roof of each one sucked power from the electric lines above. The streetcars were locked bumper to bumper while automobiles and overloaded trucks angled for space on the main thoroughfare. The jammed streetcars nearly burst with people riding on the stairs and bulging from the fenders in the rear. One brave driver crammed new riders onto his streetcar by pressing the existing riders back with his bare hands, like they were clothes in an over-crowded suitcase that needed to be zipped.

As I ambled down Market Street I passed a familiar landmark: The Emporium, the lavish department store where my mother, Demo and I occasionally shopped for school clothes after my brother and I would inevitably shoot up and render last year's corduroy pants useless. On Mission Street, the pool halls, office supply stores, drugstores, a variety of local banks, loan offices, tailors, rooms for rent and lunch counters jammed the street, each with its own blazing neon sign or hand-painted insignia.

Behind the enormous plate glass windows of bakeries, the Italians proudly displayed their chocolate and pistachio biscotti while the Irish exhibited their soda bread and seedcake loaf and the Danish their delightful bite-sized cookies pressed into classic geometric shapes. The shops were mostly run by pop and supplied by mom — just like our restaurant.

I passed the Armory on 14th and Mission Streets which looked more like a gloomy medieval citadel than a sports complex. I smiled remembering when Theo Vasili had escorted Demo and me there to watch a prizefight and observe my uncle bet his week's wages. In his early days in California, Theo Vasili had boxed as a prizefighter for extra cash, so we discussed each fighter's technique and where he had gone wrong — or victoriously right. On the way home, there was always an ice cream for us boys and a quick shot for Theo Vasili.

San Francisco was overshadowed by World War II which hung over San Francisco like a dark fog that the morning sun could not dissolve. Navy blue sailors' uniforms darkened the Embarcadero and Army privates, dressed in their "suntans," spilled to the streets and bars. The Army officers usually stayed out of trouble in their officers' club within the scenic eucalyptus-lined Presidio, which offered Army's top brass the best views in the city and occasional relief from the pressures of war.

My mother did not come with me on this trip to San Francisco. She reasoned her leaving Vallejo at this point to visit Demo would only add another sharp edge to our family's broken mirror that lay on the floor waiting for repair.

That afternoon I sat through *A Midsummer Night's Dream* and tried to make sense of it. When Demo lived at home, he was available to answer my questions about the meaning of an ancient text, the essence of a poem or his own handwritten plays. This time, I was a little confused as to why William Shakespeare wrote about noblemen, fairies, kings and a talking wall — all in one play. Wasn't Shakespeare supposed to be about grand matters of the human condition?

When Demo spoke his lines — or words, actually — I nearly jumped up from my seat and applauded every one. Demo portrayed the character Mustardseed, a fairy ordered by Queen Titania in the play. My brother was actually speaking words in a Shakespeare play — and getting paid for it! And I remembered them all:

"And I!"

"Hail!"

"Mustardseed."

"Ready."

And then — *three* words in one sentence!

"What's your Will?"

My heart brimmed with delight, like root beer flowing over a glass of fresh-made vanilla ice cream — all anticipation and sweetness. And I was ecstatic that he had escaped my father's handcuffs for Shakespeare's dream even if I did not completely understand this mid-summer version. After the play, I loitered near the stage door in the small alley next to the Victoria. When the back door opened I ran to Demo and embraced him for his bravery and his eight words of Shakespeare.

We enjoyed a hot roast beef sandwich in a dark, old-world hofbrau on Market and Fourth Street — my treat. Then Demo and I ambled along the Embarcadero waterfront. For once, I felt optimistic. Surely there was a chance we could again become the strong, solid family we used to be. Once Demo established himself as an actor, he could come home to live and work in San Francisco. If Demo was getting paid for his acting work, how could my father argue? Wasn't making money full validation in his business world? Couldn't he pretend to ignore that Demo did not want to live like everyone else?

Looking back, that idea was naive and, I'll admit, selfish. I was the youngest in the family and, honestly, I required the constant security my older brother offered to me while growing up. We spent long hours talking in our dark bedroom, with only our disembodied voices exposing our most inner thoughts. Demo assured me I would become a fine cook and envisioned the grand day I would take over our family's restaurant. He was a born actor, but Demo's great talent was seeing the good in people and believing they had a choice, that their spirit was a flame that simply needed a little breeze to ignite. Demo's strength was transferable to people like me — small closed buds that just might be brave enough to someday slowly crack open and reveal a dazzling sunflower. I missed his optimistic countenance and certainly his American-born view of the world. Most of all, I missed my best friend.

"God, I love it!" Demo was beaming now. "Every minute of it!"

On one side of us, small lights glowed softly from the fishing boats bobbing in their berths. On the inland side, the brightly lit neon signs of the bars, restaurants and dance halls beckoned. We walked, hands in pockets, bracing against the stiff waterfront wind.

"And Natalya is seeing about another part for me when this show is over. She's the friend I was telling you about. She knows everyone in town."

"Pop still talks about your coming back to help him at the new restaurant. And Mom will do anything to get you back home."

Demo stopped walking and faced me. "Pop will burn inside until he gets what he wants. And I know just how it feels!" He took a breath, reflecting. "But now, I'm over here."

Demo looked across the bay and spoke the words that cemented our family's future. "I'm home now."

I sensed my brother's newfound confidence and felt the tide pulling back the sand under my feet. It was clear that Demo would not return — he had found his place in the world. That was the way it would be.

FIFTY-ONE

An hour later, we were in another dark room in San Francisco. I had never been in a place like this. Not in Vallejo. Not anywhere.

Demo's friend Natalya had caught up with us and I met the person who had helped my brother with his acting career. My view of the world was stretched to the maximum when I was introduced to Natalya. From my inexperienced outlook, my brother's friend was big, tall and mannish. Was she a mannish woman or a genteel man? None of this seemed to bother Demo who protectively put his arm around me, helping me ease into the unfamiliar surroundings. As I wasn't sure how to perceive Natalya and exactly what my reaction was supposed to be, I quickly pushed aside my unformed thoughts about her and pretended I didn't notice. Like always, I took my cue from Demo who chatted about his performance at the Victoria and the other actors with whom he shared the stage. Natalya asked him questions with almost motherly interest and concern. Her wide, warm smile, painted a ruby-red, invited me in and I relaxed a little. I liked her and the fact that she seemed to protect Demo.

The moment we walked into Mona's 440 Club on Broadway my eyes and ears began to live a new life. No one asked my age and Natalya obviously knew everyone in the dark club with its noisy bar and small stage. The first thing I noticed — no, the first thing I felt — was the music rumbling in my body. A stout, energetic woman the color of rich cocoa sat at an upright piano and pounded the keys so fast that the lyrics didn't seem to fit the timing of her music — until I realized her syncopated phrasing was absolutely perfect. Gladys Bentley mesmerized everyone in the place with her enticing, growly voice as she coaxed boogie-woogie and the blues from the back of her throat. She was impeccably dressed in a white tuxedo and her black, straight hair was slicked-back and smooth. Her beguiling smile and songs of naughty mischief brought the audience in closer and closer until she held all of us in her fast-moving hands. Gladys rolled out musical stories of bittersweet trysts and misbehaving lovers. Her voice was as confident as her solid presence on the piano bench rolling out song after song. Gladys' fingers feathered the keyboard lightning-fast and her voice scatted like a rusty trumpet.

I'd never seen anyone more sure of themselves. The crowd soaked up Gladys' power and raw, playful sexuality. When her music erupted, everyone in the club couldn't help but stomp, clap, whoop or break out into instant applause — and I was right there with them.

I took note of the small posters around the room that advertised, "Gladys Bentley The Brown Bomber of Sophisticated Songs" and "America's Greatest Sepia Artist." Demo had brought me here for a reason. He was giving me a taste of the best music San Francisco had to offer. He wanted to show me another person whose artistic soul was so enormous that it burst from her heart for all to witness. I realized some people, like Gladys Bentley, and in my opinion, my brother, were simply forces of nature and required the opportunity to find an appreciative audience.

When Gladys took a break, I glanced at Demo and Natalya and realized that I had taken a leap into this new world. I was uninitiated — I had never even kissed a girl. But no one seemed to pay attention to me and my own embryonic sexuality. I happily became invisible and simply observed everyone else. Looking over my shoulder I realized that in my old world at home, we dared not even speak the word "sex." Now, I was in the company of people that not only sang about it, but they celebrated it — strictly within the confines of the club, that is.

I had a lot to think about that night riding back on the ferry to Vallejo. The roller shade of my consciousness had just been snapped upward revealing people and lives outside the safe world of The Classic Grill. I would not dare relay a word of this to my family, especially my father. I would be ridiculed by him, my school friends and everyone I knew, for that matter. So I kept quiet. But I kept thinking about Demo and what might be next for him in a world so different from ours at The Classic Grill.

FIFTY-TWO

Jesús the cook looked shocked by my story.

"Your brother, he took you to a lesbian bar?" Jesús asked incredulously. "When you were sixteen — in 1942? *¡Ay! Que cosa!*"

"Yeah, and the funny thing was, I didn't seem to mind," I answered. "In fact, I think I understood my brother a little better. Watching Gladys Bentley, I witnessed a true original — and I was positive Demo had the same artistic spirit in him."

Aman looked down at her hands placed carefully on the laminated fast-food table. Her fingernails painted shiny black were short and evenly filed. It was obvious she had applied the lacquer herself. No fancy manicure for this young woman. Aman had taken my family story to heart.

"I didn't know people showed they were gay to outsiders in those days," Aman spoke softly. "In my culture, in my family, you can never do this. Never."

She hung her head. I sensed this young woman had troubles weighing on her slight frame that she could never share with a stranger or anyone. Her dark eyes misted. "Go on. Tell us. Your family — did they survive? What about Demo? Did he ever come home?"

"Did your old man ever build that new restaurant?" Jason eagerly asked. "Did your father get to make *his* art?"

FIFTY-THREE

My father's tall, black work shoes crunched through the sawdust and over discarded screws and nails as he slowly picked his way across the expansive cement floor. He avoided the large stacks of lumber and wheelbarrows holding cement bags that awaited mixing in days to come. He had wanted to inspect the premises with care and reflection and not bring my uncle or the contractor.

Having stepped away from The Classic Grill during the afternoon lull, my father thoughtfully observed the construction. He had pressed so hard to begin the building phase, dangerously close to destroying his relationship with my mother, that it nearly came as a surprise to him when workers arrived and hammers began to swing, transforming his fantasy into marble floors and plaster walls.

At The Classic Grill, my father was familiar with every scratch on the black and white floor tiles, the missing pieces of the Greek key mosaic at the entryway, the misbehaving back burner in the kitchen, the high-pitched ring of the cash register and the distinguishable squeaks of the front and back doors. My father's first restaurant was a well-fitting coat that he could wear in any weather — and yes — classic in every way. The dependable Classic Grill was, when unbuttoned and open wide, welcoming to family, friends and strangers and offered warm comfort, stability — and when he was alone inside it — a tranquil refuge.

My father remembered his days assembling The Classic Grill in the space Ike's Place had occupied over twenty-two years earlier. He worked as a cook twelve hours a day at another restaurant. In his off-hours, with my mother working by his side, he thoroughly steam-cleaned the kitchen, scrubbed and waxed the floor, amassed second-hand cookware and began recruiting other restaurant-working Greeks in the area to staff the new place. In his heart, he was sure The Classic Grill would not fail — it could not. Too many lives depended on its success, both in Greece and here in America. This restaurant was my father's ticket.

My mother worked in two delicatessens as a pastry baker — every penny of her paycheck was saved for the new restaurant. To her, baking pies and cakes seemed more like a pleasurable hobby compared to the grueling housekeeping of her childhood in the village without the aid of electric beaters or reliable ovens. When she gave birth to Demo, she continued baking from home and brought Demo, and later me, to the restaurant, to play in the corner of the kitchen or sit at a back table while she greeted customers as the charming host at The Classic Grill.

Our restaurant was truly Demo's and my first home, and it seemed to me, our little house on Virginia Street was simply the place where we slept at night. The Classic Grill was not just our home — it was our heart. Building the new restaurant seemed like jilting a beautiful and gracious wife for a more glamorous woman whose future was a question mark. I wondered if the new restaurant would be our gold mine, or a sorrowful regret we would be forced to live with. I wasn't sure how our lives would change, but the relationship with the new flame had begun.

My father could not see me in the back of the new restaurant as he inspected the progress. I believed if I witnessed the nails pounded into the lathe and plaster walls, squares of marble laid down in their place, the chandeliers carefully hung, that I would be more in touch with the new restaurant, from the studs to the ceiling. I wanted to know every inch of it before we opened the doors and greeted our first customers.

I told my father that we should stop calling it "the new restaurant." I felt as if our family was having a baby and would not give the child a name until the christening six months after the birth. I suggested the name The Symposium, assuming my father would like the Greek twist. After a little research in our high school library, I found that most symposiums were drinking gatherings for upper-class Greek men. In Plato's text, *The Symposium,* Socrates, the Athenian general Alcibiades, the playwright Aristophanes and other men had consumed a fine meal and had drunk their fill when their host challenged them to say something about the meaning of Eros, sensual love. I figured that if people today still pored over Plato's literature, then I had picked a solid, maybe even classic name that would last for years to come.

So without the fanfare of the ancient Greeks, the new restaurant became The Symposium. Good enough for Plato, good enough for Vallejo. My father never acknowledged my contribution on naming the new baby, but the name The Symposium would proudly brand everything — from the sign hanging in front of the restaurant to the plates to the napkins. I had finally made my mark in the restaurant world where I happily envisioned my future. I warmed myself with the thought that my father would have no choice but to someday depend on me.

From the back of what would be the kitchen, I watched my father observe the craftsman sanding down the length of the mahogany bar as a radio faintly played a Benny Goodman tune in the background. The workers toiled in silence. This was just another workday for them. But to me, every brush stroke or beam nailed in place was one step closer to the new higher standard of business we would be required to meet. This restaurant would be more than a challenge. My father had catapulted us from our familiar surroundings at The Classic Grill to this new uncharted territory for which, in my opinion, Demo had been sacrificed.

My father stopped to scrutinize an artisan straddling a high scaffold, painstakingly applying gold leaf to a column near the ceiling. He made the sign of the cross in front of his body as he estimated the fall if the worker stretched a bit too far to reach his can of adhesive glue. Better not to look, my father thought, as he calculated that he had not yet insured the new restaurant, saving a few dollars until it opened, only a month or two away. Instead, he walked to the center of the large space and soaked up everything — the dark wood paneling, the rich marble floor and the stainless steel kitchen gleaming from afar. My father pulled an old chair from the corner and placed it in the middle of the dining area to observe his dream slowly evolving into a reality. He sat backwards on the chair and leaned on his arms. Tears streamed down his rough face.

I wanted to run to my father and tell him that I had been here every day — even when he was not. Before and after school, when he was occupied at The Classic Grill, I came to inspect the slow and steady progress. I would graduate from high school in less than two years and I could manage the place. Maybe now was the perfect moment for us to become more than father and son.

I walked quietly from the kitchen area, closer to my father.

"Pop," I said quietly.

My father was lost in thought and did not react.

"Pop, got a minute?" I repeated, louder, a little less enthusiastically.

"Pop!" This time I was certain he heard my words, but I did not exist for him.

I slammed out the back door. I was furious at myself for thinking that my father might hear my voice in that empty warehouse that would become — with or without me — the next level of our family business. I could only hope we were ready for it.

FIFTY-FOUR

The door to The Classic Grill squeaked open and Taki shuffled in under a cloud of dark despair. He slid onto his customary stool, pulled out the wood-paneled radio from a shelf and set it on the counter. My father had relented and not only allowed Taki to play his radio during business hours but also to store the large device behind the counter near the stack of clean coffee cups and saucers.

Taki was one of the few customers in the restaurant between the lunchtime and dinner crowds. He flipped open his newspaper and the headlines jumped out from the front page.

"THOUSANDS OF CASUALTIES IN EUROPEAN BATTLES"

My father energetically wiped down the counter while Theo Vasili circulated with his cup of coffee. My uncle settled on a stool next to Taki.

"Still no letter," Taki painfully moaned.

My father appeared sympathetic and moved the radio a little closer to Taki.

"You no worry. Nikko is strong," he advised with his most comforting voice. "He come home to you."

Taki's face showed the deep furrows from sleepless nights. World War II was still new to America. Families wore anxiety long on their faces from daily worry and nightly wakefulness, imagining what could befall their cherished sons, fathers and brothers. At home, my father anguished about his family in Greece. Since the Italian invasion in 1940, the war had raged in Greece. In the months following, he received no communication from the relatives and wondered if his monthly stipends were unexpectedly shortstopped by the constant graft within the Greek government and financial institutions. During that time, my father shuffled through the few photos of his parents and sisters when he believed he was alone in the back office. He never spoke a word of his family or their peril during the war — but faithfully sent their monthly allowance.

"This is war! Nobody safe!" Taki cried loudly. "Every day I worry!" He motioned for my father to lean in closely.

"Be good to your son while he is here," he whispered harshly.

"Demo—he want to leave us! He want to quit school!" my father spouted back.

Taki arched one eyebrow indicating he didn't buy my father's story. He then pointed to me in the kitchen.

"And that one?"

Taki let his question hang in the air.

My father felt the sting and considered the question to be invading his family's business. He quickly determined no response was best. After all, Taki's only son was at war.

At that very moment, Tetsuya and I enthusiastically rushed out of the kitchen with a plate of beautifully arranged food, if I do say so myself.

"Achilles! Georgie, he make phyllo-wrapped chicken! Best dish we make!" Tetsuya cried. "You must taste!"

Tetsuya appeared to be happy for the first time in weeks since he heard the news of the impending Japanese internment. He gave me a sturdy push toward my father. With more than a bit of pride I offered the number-one judge and jury a taste of my new creation. I tempted him with a forkful of tender chicken breast rolled in Parmesan cheese, wrapped with crispy butter-drenched phyllo. I had gently pan-fried the chicken and added a subtle sprinkling of rosemary and a hint of garlic before I rolled it in the phyllo. Of course, I added a generous dash of butter before I baked it in the oven until the phyllo was crispy and golden brown.

I looked up, waiting for my father's reaction. But when would I ever learn? My father waved me off as if I was offering him yesterday's smelly leftovers.

"Americans no want phyllo for nothing!" He pushed away the fork as he walked to the cash register to assess the day's take. "Phyllo for peasants! And no more you waste my butter rations!"

Enough! I had enough of my father for today, perhaps for the rest of my life. I spun around and flew to the kitchen with Tetsuya in retreat behind me. Tetsuya looked over his shoulder and then gave a mighty slam to the swinging doors leading to the kitchen as he disappeared from the dining room.

"Cousin, you never know what is good." I heard Theo Vasili mutter as he sipped his coffee. He looked up and sent a louder message to my father's ears. "You will only know what is good when it is gone!"

Then, customers wandered in for the dinner rush and The Classic Grill crew took their places. Waiters appeared and cooks stepped to their stations. As the well-orchestrated commotion began, Mr. Chris tuned the strings of his violin.

Tetsuya marched into the kitchen and scraped the plate of food into the trash barrel. I had never seen him this angry. Not even when we lost electricity and his entire refrigerator of prepared vegetables rotted. Pounds of his precise vegetable handiwork were sold to the pig farmer that brought his dilapidated truck to collect the spoilage.

"Fathers and second sons!" Tetsuya yelled to the kitchen staff. He looked at Mr. Chris and snapped at him as if his kitchen-mate were someone else. "Why you never play Tchaikovsky for me?"

Mr. Chris hurriedly packed his violin and bow into the purple velvet-lined case and bashed it shut as the restaurant filled with customers. In the dining room, a young woman held out a small handmade sign reading, "Change for the USO." She strolled through the dining room, waving a can for donations. Customers searched their pockets for a nickel or a dime with hopes that their donation might somehow send comfort to their own homesick soldier across the seas. The war had taken full hold of this Navy town and dark blue military uniforms colored the restaurant. The unofficial civilian garb looked anemic in comparison.

Suddenly the mayor and his posse spilled into The Classic Grill. They appropriated a large table for the seven men who were outfitted in dark suits, crisp white shirts and fedoras. The business garb of these small-town tycoons in a sea of military uniforms to me felt unpatriotic and out of touch, as if they were ungrateful for the soldiers who risked life and limb overseas and at home.

Standing near the cash register my father motioned to Theo Vasili to pass out menus to the mayor's table.

"Get them out — *grígora!* Quickly!" My uncle, not as agile as our regular waiters, limped to the table, menus in hand.

He immediately circled back to my father.

"They want to see you!" my uncle warned my father in a low tone. *"Pigaínete me machaíri sta dóntia sas, xáderfo!* Go with a knife in your teeth, cousin!"

I felt like my family was still fighting invaders. Come to think of it, maybe my uncle was right. These foreign-looking men had come to our Greek-American island of commerce to damage us. I think it was genetic, but we Greeks would not be told what to do by anyone. *Oxi!* No! Just over two years ago, when asked if Greece would surrender to Italy, Greek Prime Minister Metaxas indignantly answered, no — *OXI!* We were defenders of democracy. Heck, I'd like to think we Greeks practically *invented* democracy. We would live without oppression from these business types. My father would not surrender his pride or his restaurant.

My father purposefully headed to the table, desperately wanting these men out of his restaurant. He was nervous, but only projected strength.

The mayor greeted my father as if they were somehow friends.

"Ah, Achilles! Sit down... you Greek!" He indicated an open chair next to him.

The other men smirked at the ethnic crack, but my father stood regally, unsmiling, poised to take their order. His long white apron, once again, screamed that my father was working class. But my father showed no shame in his status. He had created something tangible and positive for this town. He nourished people and made them happy, which was more than he could say for the gaggle of bankers, politicians and Chamber of Commerce officials.

"Meatloaf good today. Mashed potatoes too!"

The men scoured the menu and I could see my father shifting his weight foot to foot, awaiting their decisions between the meatloaf, steak and potatoes or the fried chicken. At that moment, Daphne entered The Classic Grill. I could see terror creep across my father's face. I remembered what happened last time Daphne and the mayor met. I watched as this semi-truck and sleek sports car raced towards each other at 60 mph at our restaurant's intersection and waited for the crash and the clean up.

"Your order?" My father sneaked a look at the mayor, hoping he had not noticed Daphne. Although not a revealing outfit, her simple black skirt and white blouse unquestionably skimmed her body's curves.

"There's that bombshell!" The mayor bellowed, noticing Daphne the second she arrived. Clutching her black leather handbag in front of her, Daphne smiled when her eyes met his. She began to walk to the open seat at the table.

"Daphne!" my father shouted, a little too loudly. "You sit at the counter! Over there!"

He pointed to the stool the farthest from the mayor's table. Always able to quickly assess a tricky situation, Theo Vasili stepped towards Daphne. He gently took her elbow and politely steered her away from the table, towards the counter.

The mayor narrowed his eyes at my father. He glanced at Daphne and then hurled his words with a truckload of contempt.

"You her moral advisor?"

My father saw Daphne's eyes cast a net on the mayor.

"She is a good girl! She stay that way! *Your order?*"

The mayor had plenty of experience in public speaking. Tonight he would make the most of the audience in our own restaurant. The mayor stood up and faced my father.

"Greek! You're in my way!" The mayor proclaimed as if he were on a campaign stop.

Shoving his pad and pencil into his apron pocket, my father took a step toward the mayor. Like an elite Evzone soldier standing guard outside the presidential palace in Athens, he would proudly fight.

"I do nothing to you!" he retorted angrily. Louder than I had ever heard him speak in front of customers in his own restaurant. The mayor took a step back and positioned himself to better address my father and all the customers dining in The Classic Grill.

"You people take our good American dollars. You fill up our schools and pray to your gods — whoever they are. You speak your language. You don't mix in. You send all your money back home. Get it straight! You are not wanted here!"

"You no own this town!" my father boomed.

"Stick with dishwashing and running crummy cafés like this. Something you people know how to do!"

"Leave!" My father pointed to the door. "Leave my restaurant! Now!"

Grabbing their hats and scraping their chairs on the tile floor, the mayor's followers began filing out the door. The mayor lagged behind, hovering near Daphne.

"You need a breath of fresh air." He tossed out the bait. "Someplace new. Got a couple of C-notes in my pocket. The party's on me!"

My father stared at Daphne, bracing himself for her response. By this time, the fiery exchange had drawn me out of the kitchen, near the counter, watching tempers blaze. The triangle of the mayor, Daphne and my father was tight with tension for what seemed like an hour.

If the mayor made a move towards Daphne I knew my father would attack him. I had to protect my father. The customers returned their attention to their plates, consuming the daily special. I watched the waiters go back to work as the buzz of the restaurant continued. I had to help my father save face.

An earsplitting crash of glass to crack the high tension was all I could think of. Standing near the counter, I stared down at the glimmering shards around my feet from the water glasses I had purposely dropped from a tray. A graveyard of dismembered goblets on the floor.

For just that second, my father turned his back to Daphne. He did not see her hesitate, glance at him, then slide off her stool. She took the mayor's waiting hand.

"Well, just one quick drink," she squeaked in a small voice, as if it were any kind of excuse. They quickly whisked out of the restaurant into the night. Stunned, my uncle and my father stood near the open front door. As the sound of the motor became a whisper, I found the broom and dustpan and clanked through my clean up.

"If women know how the men think…" my uncle shook his head, "…no woman ever walk alone."

Daphne had just left my father standing up to his knees in a thick slurry of ethnic insults and disdain. After everything my father had done for her — lending her money, cooking up free meals, arranging childcare for her son — Daphne turned her back on him.

But then I took a moment to reconsider my opinion of her. Yes, she was only thinking of herself but she did not grow up in this restaurant. And it was obvious Daphne was struggling to get by. I don't think she quite grasped the stinging lash of the mayor's hatred of our family and Greek culture. Daphne blended into the "American" world and had never experienced what it was to be an "other." She wasn't what we now call a hyphenated American: Italian-American, Japanese-American, African-American, Chinese-American, Mexican-American. Those hurtful words the mayor felt comfortable spewing out were supposed to make us feel inferior and leave our town.

By the way, didn't he know that we Greeks didn't believe in the playful gods of Mount Olympus anymore? No matter. I couldn't blame Daphne for wanting to have a good time with someone who could easily pay for a glamorous evening on the town. She was young, closer to my generation than my parents'. At the same time, I knew her evening out with the devious mayor would come to no good. He wanted our family out of this town that was — and would be — our home.

Would our family leave?

Oxi!

FIFTY-FIVE

"Dude!" Jesús gasped and looked wide-eyed at me. "That mayor said *that* to your *father? In his own restaurant?*"

Before I could answer, Jason piped up, shaking his head. "And your father, he didn't punch that jerk? I woulda…"

Zach looked up and broke in.

"He knew better," he said. "Your father didn't want to escalate the bad will in his own restaurant."

I nodded and found I needed a refresh on my cup of coffee. I started to move my old bones for a refill, but Aman snatched my cup and quickly returned with a fresh steamy one.

"I don't get it," Aman pondered. "And you Greeks are white, right? So like what was the mayor's problem with your family?"

"Competition!" Zach chimed in. "Your restaurant was cooking along and from what you say, the mayor's brother's restaurant — the Restaurant St. Charles — was lagging behind."

"Exactly!" I responded, appreciative of his business overview. "The mayor simply wanted us out. He couldn't believe we lowly immigrants were running a better business than his brother. Looking back, he really despised us Greeks, Greek-Americans that is. But there was more."

I was sorry I sounded as if I were lecturing in a history class to these young people, but I had to give it to them straight.

"In those days, anyone different was an outsider." I looked at the beautiful faces of my group. "The mayor's problem was not only about skin color. An accent helped to send you down the river. Those families that came a generation or so before ours thought they owned the town. Some of them and their parents even went to college and they felt like they held great knowledge and we did not."

Jason sunk his teeth into a cheeseburger. He had worked up an appetite as my story had gone on longer than any of us expected. He looked around the fast-food place to make sure no new customers had slipped in.

"And they knew how to control things," I filled in. "They'd finagle a seat on the city council or board-of-something, find out where the opportunities lie, get in early and make a pile of money, In most towns they wanted to control everything and wanted us to keep to ourselves — or go away."

"And they criticize you for keeping to yourselves," Mariam tossed in, frowning. "Yeah, I know that line."

"We looked the same, but people like the mayor kept pointing to our differences," I added, stirring my coffee that Aman had gently set in front of me. "And with Demo and me — we were American but the mayor and the rest thought of us as different. Lower."

Aman's young face fell, seriously troubled by this part of my tale.

"So how did your family put up with it? Your father? You?" she asked.

"And what happened to Daphne?" Mariam asked. "Her little boy?"

"And Demo. Where'd he go?" Jesús asked.

I looked around to make sure my young group would not get in trouble for listening to my story. No new customers. On with the Pappayannis family tale.

FIFTY-SIX

For once, there was no important job left for my father to do at The Classic Grill. And for once, he had no energy left to do it. The mayor's blistering outburst and Daphne's ungrateful exit was about as much as my father could take for one evening. He puttered aimlessly, polishing tables he had already scrubbed, sweeping the floors to which he already had applied the worn broom. Back in the kitchen, the ever-loyal Theo Vasili and I were unsure how to help my father after the mayor's speech which scorched a layer of skin from my father's Greek body.

Around ten o'clock, I snuck out the kitchen back door to quickly run home and alert my mother that she would need to keep Alex overnight. It seemed that no one was looking out for the child that night, except my mother and me. It was my duty to inform my mother that the woman whom my dad found attractive and for whom my mother herself provided loving childcare each workday — unpaid — would not come home that evening.

I opened the door to the sunporch of our home and crept into the kitchen where she sat alone at the table, nervously stirring a cup of untouched chamomile tea placed carefully on her hand-embroidered table-cloth. My mother raced to me and pulled me close.

"Where your father?" she whispered harshly. "Why he not home? Why no one come for Alex? Where his mother?"

My mother was a mind reader and had already put Alex to bed in my room. She made sure his door was tugged closed and then switched into rapid-fire Greek.

"Your father is with *that* woman? What do they do so late? Do I need to go to the restaurant?" Somehow it sounded worse in our native tongue.

My mother glared at me with the frustration of taking extraordinary care of a little boy whose mother now proved to be as reliable as the bread man whose deliveries we could never count on at the restaurant. A woman younger, more beautiful and unquestionably more American than she. And

Panagia, Mother of God—a woman liable to lure her once-faithful husband to who-knows-what. She sensed the high voltage current that flowed under my father's skin when Daphne's strawberry blond hair made its way into the restaurant.

Yet my mother had grown quite fond of Alex. Her heart softened when he sat at her table or when she could feel his warm breath on her arm while he listened to her village fairy tales. Little Alex had been almost left to her care in a basket on her front door. She could not—and would not—turn her back on this little boy.

I wanted to quickly deliver the facts and get back to the restaurant. The fewer words, the better.

"Daphne is not at the restaurant. She's with the mayor." My voice was flat. "Probably for the night."

"And your father?" my mother demanded.

"Uh, I think, well, he's still at the restaurant." I could not meet her eyes. "I think, uh, he's waiting." I did not add, "for her."

My usually unflappable mother exploded with hot, spikey outrage. But it was not my father or Daphne she ranted about—it was Alex.

"What so important that this child's mother leave her *agapiméno gio*, her beloved son? All night!"

She paced across her kitchen, absently collecting Alex's jacket and small toys. She tossed them on a kitchen chair with frustration.

"How Alex to grow strong and be happy? He a good child. And no father. If his mother no here for him, Alex no feel she love him. He should not be *város*, a burden!"

I was monumentally relieved that my mother turned the conversation to Alex's well-being and did not focus on my father's behavior. I nodded in solidarity, gave my mother a tight hug and swiftly raced to the restaurant.

On my return trip, I considered my mother's brilliance. Just as she was protecting Alex from harsh words about his mother, she had protected me from the haranguing she could have unleashed about my father. She left that crate of dynamite untouched and gingerly walked around it, avoiding the explosion we would endure if she rattled the box or opened a wooden slat—just a crack. She could only imagine the dangerous contents of my father's box of ballistic missiles and prayed they would remain nailed shut in the dark forever. Once again, my mother was thinking five steps ahead so as not to disturb what was left of our family. She would tiptoe away from a standoff about Daphne — at least for now.

Back at the restaurant, I cooked up a plain omelet for my father, a dish that clearly was becoming one of my specialties. I often daydreamed about opening a restaurant that specialized in omelets, with all the variations a creative chef could concoct. Make that an omelet and waffle shop. Open at six, close at three. I tucked away that idea while I finished off my omelet with a final flip in the buttery pan — fluffy, hot, perfect. I placed my work of art in front of my father who sipped black coffee at a table in the back. This time, I didn't expect him to notice my work. He didn't. But he ate the omelet anyway.

Another nervous hour crawled by.

Around midnight Theo Vasili gave up on Daphne's return after "one quick drink." He popped his battered hat on his head. Looking at me, he was in truth addressing my father.

"I have one drink. I have *quick* drink. But never I have one quick drink with woman like that. *Megálo próvlima*, big trouble."

My father said nothing. My uncle glided through the front door into the chilly night toward his tiny rented room on Marin Street, two blocks away.

My father spent the rest of the night at The Classic Grill. Waiting. Hoping. I kept myself busy by leafing through cookbooks and sipping the coffee that I normally didn't drink. Luckily, it was Saturday night — now Sunday morning — and I had no school, and certainly no church for me that day. I stayed put because I didn't know what my father's reaction might be when Daphne crept back to the safe haven of our restaurant. Someone might need my protection.

In the early morning, my father suddenly let out a little snore, lifting his heavy head from his folded arms. As the clock nudged four-thirty in the morning, he pushed back his chair and walked to the kitchen, splashed cool water on his face over the stainless steel sink and dried it with a dishtowel.

My father looked up to see me uncharacteristically sipping coffee behind *A Guide to Modern Cookery*, where August Escoffier was just getting to the five mother sauces. I was wide-awake reading about Béchamel sauce and thankfully Mr. Escoffier meticulously discussed the technique for a young cook such as myself.

My father dragged a comb through his wild, wavy hair and silently tied on a fresh apron. He began the morning ritual of cracking eggs into a large ceramic bowl, setting it in the refrigerator for the morning rush, several painful hours away. He looked at the big clock in the back kitchen and sighed. It would be a long day for all of us.

FIFTY-SEVEN

The sun rose across the bay through the fog in Vallejo. Little Alex toddled into my mother's kitchen, hair rumpled from his night in Demo's bed. He made his way to a wooden kitchen chair and patiently waited as my mother cooked him a breakfast of eggs, hotcakes and bacon.

Below the surface, my mother's engines worked overtime. She was caring for the son of a woman she sensed had designs on her husband. For the first time, she truly could not identify my father's romantic intentions. But she believed he was inches away from shattering her first marital requirement of absolute faithfulness.

Alex's eyes lit on an impeccably ironed navy-blue jacket, pants, crisp white dress shirt and tie just his size. The clothes hung like inflated balloons from hangers that were carefully balanced on the doorframes in the kitchen. No wrinkle could hide from my mother's ironing obsession as she used the techniques she learned from Andromache in the village.

"It is Sunday today. Together we go to church." She set Alex's large breakfast plate in front of him and pointed to the new clothes. "These all for you."

My mother lovingly raked a comb through Alex's dark, shiny four-year-old head of hair while remembering her previous evening of intense prayers and all-night pacing on the hardwood floor of her bedroom.

"Eat, *chrisos mou*, my dear. After church, we go to your mother."

"Where is she?" Alex sailed his bacon strip through the ocean of maple syrup on his plate.

My mother bit her lip. "She have extra work to do for her job." She walked to the back porch and revealed to Alex a pair of small, gleaming black dress shoes.

"These for you, Alex *mou*." Her voice was honeyed with affection. "You a good boy!"

"*Efharistoh.*" His jaws still worked on a mouthful of pancakes. "Thank you."

Alex's eyes were as dark as Kalamata olives. My mother impulsively hugged this small boy who earnestly cleaned his breakfast plate.

"My smart boy! You learn so quick!"

After the syrup was washed from Alex's sticky hands and face, my mother plunged him into the new clothes. She clutched his hand as they carefully walked through the alley on Napa Street to the entrance of the Ascension Episcopal Church.

Now, I must take a moment to say that most people assumed that we Greeks automatically attended the local Greek Orthodox Church, but at that time, we had none in our little town of Vallejo. When we wanted to experience the complicated Byzantine world of Greek Orthodoxy with our treasured mysterious icons and gold leaf frames, we had to pay for a bus ticket to San Francisco or Oakland and travel an hour each way. That was in addition to the hour and a half Liturgy. And the coffee hour. And the lunch of roasted chicken, pilaf and baklava in the church hall.

Although my parents did not often attend church because of their long hours at the restaurant, Demo and I — and the rest of the Greek-American youth of Vallejo — did not escape Sunday services. The Greeks second-handedly picked up the knowledge that the Episcopal community did not seem to actively recruit the young people for a lifetime of membership. This lore was the incentive my parents needed to send Demo and me to the Episcopal Church most Sundays. We were merely on loan to the Episcopals, as the Greek parents naturally expected their children would meld back into the Orthodox religion when a local church was someday built. And the Episcopals did not disappoint them.

Demo and I served as acolytes for the solemn, well-mannered congregation. I think Demo liked the costuming and pageantry of our soft, white, gathered cotton frocks with dark long robes beneath. Demo, older than the rest of us, had the privilege of carrying the large wood and brass cross down the center aisle and was allowed to wear snappy white gloves to do the job.

As my mother looked through the doors of the Episcopal Church, she wished with all her heart that she had been introducing young Alex to a Greek Orthodox church. She would have loved to point out the priest, in his gold brocade robes, who would have been hypnotizing the congregation with the exotic incense smoke. The *psalti* would have chanted a low, painfully mournful tone, stretching out a low gravelly note for what could seem like minutes.

My mother directed Alex's attention to the simple wooden cross displayed front and center in the nave of the Episcopal church. The dark wood paneling behind the altar gave the feel of a small cozy cabin. My mother was always caught a little off guard when parishioners seated in pews sang from the hymnals, with the organ joining in. In the Greek church, the congregation was allowed to simply listen to the choir sing in doleful tones. In the Episcopal church, the congregation was part of the show.

My mother had made her peace with this church that was sweet in its simplicity.

"Say a prayer," she whispered.

"For Mama!" Alex chirped.

"And I will pray for my big boy, Demo."

Holding my mother's hand, Alex lasted through the entire church service. When the outer doors finally swung open and parishioners milled about, Alex spied a few other boys running among the adults and looked up to my mother. My mother nodded and, for once, Alex ran to play with children his own age.

A bony, ancient, Greek-immigrant woman wearing a hat layered with pheasant feathers and a short black veil approached my mother. She surveyed Alex and began the Greek inquisition that could quickly kindle a spicy round of gossip.

"A new boy?" she asked in Greek, trolling for tidbits. "A relative? And where are your own *paidiá*, your sons, this Sunday?"

My mother, well-rehearsed in dodging gossip with the ease of a politician, smiled warmly. "He's a very good boy." She looked to see Alex happily playing in the sun. "*San na eínai dikó mou.* He almost feels like my own."

FIFTY-EIGHT

Luckily, the church crowd had not yet dribbled into The Classic Grill. My father had not staffed up the cook line and worked it himself until noon. Sometime after ten o'clock, Daphne quietly crept in. Her windblown hair was not combed to its usual fluffy confection. Without a dollop of makeup, her bleary eyes and yesterday's clothes could not hide her all night entertainment. Only Theo Vasili was on duty at the restaurant — and me, of course. I had not left the kitchen knowing my father would need me. Daphne walked to her customary place at the counter.

"Good morning." She breathed her greeting softly, like a dove's call. She did not meet my uncle's eyes.

Theo Vasili had brewed two pots of coffee, assuming gallons would be consumed this morning. He poured a cup for Daphne without her asking.

"Where's Achilles?" Her voice was small.

"Bread man no come. He get more." He began wiping down the counter and flashed a look at Daphne.

"You have good time? See 'Frisco?"

Daphne stirred her coffee and looked up.

"Yeah, 'guess I did."

"Achilles want to protect you. But you run away. With the mayor."

He pronounced the last words with more than a ladleful of distaste. Theo Vasili set out a plate of small bran muffins.

"Drinks, dinner — the mayor never even looked at the check!"

Pouring himself a hot cup of coffee, my uncle sat next to Daphne at the counter. He sighed, probably reflecting on hundreds of worn-out Sunday mornings, regretting most memories and maybe treasuring a sacred few.

"A good time is what you want. This is something I know!" he admitted.

Daphne spun her stool to face him directly. Her face had suddenly turned red and her eyes took aim at my uncle.

"No—no you don't! At home, we always had to worry about money!" Her dam was broken, the floodwaters surging ankle deep.

"Mama was a waitress in a restaurant just like this!" Daphne's brow was tight with pain. "We lived upstairs and had next to nothing. Always leftovers from the restaurant where she worked. What other people took home for the dog. No heat in winter. No new clothes. School was the only place to go. And thank God it was free!"

She slammed down her cup.

"I don't blame Mama—but that one-room flat upstairs is also where she died. No doctors! No help from anyone!" Hot, angry tears rolled down her cheek. "I can't end up like Mama—I won't!"

She held my uncle's gaze for several uncomfortable seconds. He nodded and handed her a napkin to dab her eyes. Back in the kitchen, even I opened my heart just a little. Daphne was a person stumbling her way through life. Not so unlike me, I figured, or the rest of my family.

"Ach, I know, Daphne." My uncle took a slow sip of his coffee. "I always no have money in this country. But Achilles, he love big. He never give up on me. So I never give up."

The loud squeak of the front door jolted us out of Daphne's past. My mother briskly walked in, leading little Alex by one hand and carrying a small leather satchel in the other. Alex was still in his Sunday clothes, a little rumpled now.

"Here is your son." My mother's eyes would not offer Daphne a glance.

"Mama!" Alex reached to give his mother a hug. Daphne immediately slipped down from her stool and hugged her little boy, her eyes taking in the Sunday clothes. My mother addressed Alex in rapid Greek.

"My child, take off your coat and George will give you something to eat in the kitchen."

"Yes, Thea Chrisoula," Alex replied. My mother pointed the way to the kitchen. I opened the swinging doors wide and led Alex to a safe place to sit. My uncle and I watched in awe.

"When did he learn that?" Daphne gasped.

"Some people forget to love their son," my mother shot out.

The front door squeaked opened again. My father emerged carrying a box of long, thin loaves of French bread. As he approached, the scene of my mother standing near to Daphne came into focus. My father's mouth gaped open. No commanding words leaped from this throat. My mother, the heart of his life and family, had planted herself directly across from the woman who, from my point of view, tempted my father beyond any reason or good sense. My father could only brace himself for the explosion when my mother and Daphne connected. If a flak jacket were available, he would have pulled it on in a hurry.

Eyes glowering at my father, my mother opened the satchel and handed Daphne a stack of children's picture books.

"Here are books for my — " she corrected herself frostily, " — the child." My mother's words sent a cold wind whipping around my father's heart. He had never heard my mother speak with no emotion. Was this the first clue to my mother's detachment — and perhaps more?

With nothing else to communicate, my mother exited through the kitchen, giving Alex and me hugs.

"Be a good boy for your mother!" Her Greek words were loud enough for my father, Daphne and my uncle to hear. With a forced smile to Alex, she swept out the kitchen door.

Out in the dining room my uncle refilled his cup and Daphne's too.

"What is it that Chrisoula cannot do?" Theo Vasili asked, not expecting an answer.

"Absolutely nothing." My father stared at the space my mother had inhabited.

"I find George." My uncle gently moved away from my father, leaving him to walk behind the counter and face Daphne. In the kitchen, my uncle and I anxiously craned to hear my father and Daphne's next words.

"Daphne! I worry for you! I stay here all night! You no come!"

Taking a few nervous sips of coffee, Daphne hurriedly gathered her things. She stopped for a moment, her voice was hushed, almost mumbling.

"He made me feel like a princess." She dropped her eyes but my father moved in closer. He touched her chin to raise her face so their eyes locked.

"A princess with a child!" he exploded. "How do you leave your son?"

Daphne began to weep and The Classic Grill napkin did little to stop the flow of tears. Feminine tears had always been a deal breaker for my father. My mother never cried in front of him as she always wanted to stand on equal terms.

Now my father spoke more gently.

"I see you are a child too." He walked around the counter and stood near her but avoided a homecoming embrace.

"How much he give you last night?" He asked so quietly I could barely hear him. She pulled the money from her purse and inhaled a sob.

"You look at me, Daphne. You listen to me now." My father spoke with genuine kindness, sounding more like a father than I had ever heard him.

"Daphne. Never, never take a man's money like that. Make your own. Money is freedom." My father straightened up and stood tall, believing with all his might the words that would follow. "And always — every day — you must fight for your freedom. Make your own way in this country."

He placed a heavy hand on Daphne's shoulders.

"Now take your son home. Be with him."

Daphne wiped the remaining tears from her face and collected herself while my father slowly entered the kitchen. He found Alex finishing the last of the thick turkey sandwich on sourdough that I had constructed for him. If there is something we Greeks know how to do, it's feed children. Four square meals a day, at least.

After Alex left with Daphne, I remained over the dishwashing sink all day, not wanting to see my father's face. I was jealous of this woman that I only knew through glances from the back of the kitchen. Neither Demo nor I had experienced this type of fatherly advice — ever. Like an angry dictator, my father had banished my brother, but now, he somehow found a warm, hospitable place in his heart for another boy and his mother. My face felt slapped when he easily dispensed his paternal wisdom to this woman, this intruder.

Where was *my* dose of paternal wisdom? I knew that my father only saw me as a silent, stupid workhorse to plow his fields. As I washed a coffee cup lost in the suds, I imagined it slathered with Greek coffee grounds, the future hidden in the oozy black residue. Staring into the hollow of the cup, I wondered what the devious Irini might predict for what seemed to be our family's muddled future.

FIFTY-NINE

"What kind of mother just leave her little boy for the night?" Jesús' eyes were irate at Daphne's behavior—decades after the event.

"I certainly was unhappy about my father's attention toward her. Now I can see that raising a child alone was a hard job." I was remembering Vallejo back the 1940s. "Back then, single mothers were not well looked upon."

"Your mother was a saint!" Mariam announced, more opinionated than she had been. "To put up with your dad sending Demo away and then taking care of the boy—for that Daphne! Your mother—that's a real woman."

"That's what women do," Aman murmured.

"You're forgetting your brother." Jason leaned forward in his plastic seat. "Where was Demo in all this? Was the dude all right?"

Zach and his children had left us just before I told of Daphne and the mayor's escapade in San Francisco. It seemed he needed to drop off his kids elsewhere but, amazing to me, he quickly returned. Aman jumped to take his order at the counter and gave him a free cup of coffee. Soon Zach was back with our group and sat closer to us than before.

"I'm not sure what I missed, but wasn't your mother upset after not seeing her son for weeks?" Zach pulled the tab on the small, plastic, fake-cream dispenser and dumped the thick, white substance into his coffee. I shuddered to watch him drink it. We never would have served substitute food at our restaurant.

"Like my uncle said at the restaurant that day, what couldn't my mother do?" I contemplated my mother's character. "I think her best quality was she desperately tried to understand people and their motives, forgive them and move on. But I'm getting ahead of myself."

I stirred my own coffee, without fake cream, and remembered how I felt with Demo absent for so long.

"After Demo was gone for weeks, my mother was far from forgiving my father. The longer Demo was away, the more resentful she became. Personally, I didn't see why my brother couldn't do his acting and live at home. But my father would never open his heart to Demo. I kept in touch with my brother as much as I could. I needed him — probably more than he needed me."

SIXTY

Demo stood in the center of a dark stage with only one bare light bulb illuminating his curly head, reflecting the luminosity of his olive skin, his youthful face, his hopeful expression. That image of my brother Demo would always be with me. Always expecting the best from himself. From other people, from the world.

Natalya and I arrived to watch Demo's audition in a tiny theatre in downtown San Francisco, south of Market Street. When he was sure my father was not at home, Demo had called me to ask if I was interested in attending. Interested? I was already there in my mind. As we walked in, Natalya shook a few hands and had a laugh with a man who seemed important. She and I found seats in the second row of chairs. I attentively watched Natalya smooth the way for Demo as he auditioned for a part in a play that I was unfamiliar with — which was most plays written in the English language.

We settled in and waited a long moment. Looking back, I sensed we all felt something powerful was about to occur, like the still moment before an earthquake or the precious seconds before lovers declare their heart-to-heart devotion. The words tumbling from Demo's throat told the story of his life.

> From all I did and all I said
> let no one try to find out who I was.
> An obstacle was there distorting
> the actions and the manner of my life.
> An obstacle was often there
> to stop me when I'd begin to speak.

Demo had told me he would speak the words of Greek poet *Constantine P. Cavafy*. And he spoke with all the sincerity and tenderness that had taken residence in his heart. He said that Cavafy's words were the feelings that existed on the dark ocean floor of his heart, only to dart to the surface when they sensed light and a portal to the world. Demo, like Cavafy, longed to be free from the emotional tangle of what was acceptable to our father and to the world.

Demo continued:

> From my most unnoticed actions,
> my most veiled writing —
> from these alone will I be understood.
> But maybe it isn't worth so much concern,
> so much effort to discover who I really am.
> Later, in a more perfect society,
> someone else made just like me
> is certain to appear and act freely.

Demo finished his words and slowly looked up, his eyes glowing with emotion. I felt his spirit at that moment become profoundly lighter. The important-looking man in the first row allowed a smile to slowly creep across his face. Heads nodded and pencils scribbled in notebooks.

"Okay. Demo...what? Pappaya...Pappas? Great. Make sure your information is with our production manager."

Natalya immediately jumped to the stage and hugged Demo. I hung back, just watching my brother, who only a few months ago was frustrated to the point of bursting. Demo had transformed himself into a person with a voice, even a person who could appear and act freely. Or at least a little more freely than the author of those words.

Demo shook hands and Natalya hovered over him, proud of Demo's audition. With motherly attention, Natalya steered us out the back door of the audition hall, toward the nearest bar, ready for a long evening of drinking and planning Demo's brilliant future.

SIXTY-ONE

The Classic Grill kitchen was quiet and dark in the very early hours, long before opening. The morning was unusually chilly, a special day. I quietly crept through the back door, went straight to Tetsuya and sat down beside him.

On this heartless gray morning, Tetsuya was a shadow occupying a seat at the counter. He wore a heavy black boiled-wool overcoat and kept his plaid fedora on his head to keep warm. I watched as Tetsuya sat motionless at the counter in the early stillness. I knew it was the day he would be taken from us. From me.

To my surprise, he smiled softly and put his hand over mine.

"I just wanted to see how it feels out here," he said quietly.

My love for Tetsuya pushed tears down my cheeks. I poured him a hot cup of coffee and toasted some bread. He had served me since I was born. All I could do was serve him now.

"My family is ready. But I have to be here today. I want to remember everything. Everyone."

Suddenly, my father appeared and hovered near the counter, unable to find words to soften this thorny moment. To this point, their lives, native Greek and Japanese, were folk tunes played harmoniously, hand over hand on the keyboard — a melody which somehow worked behind the swinging kitchen doors. Each life was made better and steadied by the other's presence during the sweaty hours over a blistering stove where they eked out a living. But today that would end.

Avoiding the cloister of his cramped office where he could have hidden, my father shadowed Tetsuya. He wanted to drink in Tetsuya until there was no more. We all did.

That day, the cooks turned out the eggs and bacon breakfasts for the morning customers without words. Later, Daphne swept in, dropped off little Alex and Theo Vasili walked the child to my mother's house. He returned carrying three large tins of *koulourakia* for Tetsuya's journey. My mother had already said her personal goodbyes to Tetsuya the day before, when Daphne was not at the restaurant.

As the lunch crowd scurried back to their jobs of supporting the war efforts on Mare Island, Tetsuya sat at the counter. I swept up the last bits in the kitchen, head down, my mouth in a tight line. I had never seen Tetsuya drink, but today my father poured him a shot. Then another. He easily knocked them back, yet seemed unfazed. Then I heard a tentative knock at the door. The time had come. My head felt pushed deep under water and I struggled to pull it out, gasping for breath. I gingerly walked over to Tetsuya and stood in front of him.

"They're here." I needed every last second with him.

Tetsuya slowly rose from the counter and made his way through the kitchen. As he passed, he touched a shiny stainless steel ladle and the knife on which he had nicked himself so many times paring vegetables. He traced his fingers over the worn cutting board. He and I had secretly carved our initials there one slow afternoon, when my father's attention was focused on why Demo again was not at the restaurant.

I heard Tetsuya take a breath. He turned to face us.

"Goodbye, my friends." He slowly fished the keys to The Classic Grill from his pocket. He had held them until the very last minute.

Tetsuya's middle-aged wife Kimiko and their three sons stood at the back door. They were dressed in their traveling clothes and carried a few mismatched suitcases. Tetsuya's sons, slightly older than Demo, wore the strain of their expulsion on their young, handsome faces.

I couldn't help it. I ran to hug Tetsuya, my true father. Theo Vasili held up his tumbler of wine in a silent salute. My father's fingers fumbled with something in his pocket and he pulled out a small knife covered by a brown leather sheath.

"Take, Tetsuya! You might need!"

Tetsuya slowly shook his head.

"They will think I am dangerous. A traitor to my country." Tetsuya pushed away the knife. "I had American dream like you, Achilles. Now it is broken."

Tetsuya placed his keys to The Classic Grill in my father's hands and turned his back to us. He and his family then slogged down the dusky alley out of sight.

SIXTY-TWO

The next day, I was sick for the first time in years. Sick at heart. I skipped school and avoided the restaurant. I had a vague hope that my father might come to me and share his sorrow, but I quickly shoved that thought aside.

I later learned that after Tetsuya left, my father and Theo Vasili sat on a curb near the waterfront for hours in the dark. My uncle sipped on his customary bottle hidden in a crumpled brown bag. He reported my father could only repeat, "My president do this? My American president?" My uncle had no answers and sipped from his bottle.

They drank in silence, feeling the pain of watching a friend, a family, a culture unfairly plucked from society and carelessly tossed into the waste bin. After an hour, my father took the bottle from my uncle and rose to leave. My uncle offered his final words on the subject.

"We only can wait for him now."

"I no like to wait. For nothing!" My father drank from my uncle's bottle and walked on.

Lying on my bed that day, my stomach wrenched and my mother's chamomile tea did nothing to help the pain. I wondered how I could stand in Tetsuya's place in the restaurant kitchen. My true father was taken away for no reason — and I had offered him no comfort besides hot coffee and toasted bread. I knew I should stand up for Tetsuya and his family — but I had no idea how to stand against Uncle Sam during wartime and demand Tetsuya's return. For that matter, I had not defended Demo to my father when it counted. I was a fool to lurk in the shadows and allow the strong winds of power to blow down the lives of the two men I loved most. My silence — my weakness — kept me from helping them. That hung heavily around my neck, and would, for all my years to come.

SIXTY-THREE

"So you think that can happen again?" Mariam asked softly, almost whispering.

"It happens all the time!" Jesús walked away from the table, grumbling. "Immigrants getting busted everywhere."

"But so many were taken away all at once!" Mariam chewed her straw, considering the facts.

I had few soothing words to speak or happy endings to paint. These kids lived the reality every day.

"Now-days, you'd better have your papers straight," Jesús added.

"In Tetsuya's case, he did have his papers straight," I remembered. "And his children were citizens."

Aman sat on her hands and looked down. She was brooding over what had happened to Tetsuya.

I thought they had learned about the U.S. government's concentration camps where Japanese-Americans were forced to live, but their school had nearly skipped those shameful events of World War II. I had to tell my young audience that Tetsuya and his family were sent to Tanforan Racetrack to live in a horse stall and clean out the droppings before they could attempt to live in the small space. They were later shipped to Tule Lake, a stark, frigid region of northern California near the Oregon border where they were forced to build their own small rooms in which to live. The guns that were mounted on the elevated guard towers pointed into the camp — instead of out.

My story about Tetsuya was interrupted as the four young restaurant workers, now my friends, looked up, checking for customers. Zach checked too. I was growing fond of Zach who had made himself comfortable in a group of immigrants, soaking up a story about immigrants a generation or two ago in history.

Luckily no customers appeared at the counter so the kids relaxed. I figured I could sneak in a bit more of my story before my audience ran to make milkshakes whipped with candy bars and burgers packed with three meat patties loaded with bacon and piles of avocado. My father would have been distraught that customers had drifted so far away from the tasty, fresh food he had served. His theory was that customers didn't need to stuff their stomachs. His food would satisfy their souls.

SIXTY-FOUR

My mother's footprints in the muddy earth served as stepping-stones for Alex's small feet as he tiptoed behind her. My mother's gardening shoes consisted of her old black leather loafers, the backs squashed down at the heel. She tromped through her garden while holding a large basket and shears, a detective in search of the first beans, tomatoes or nectarines of the season. The branches of her lemon tree were laden with bright, tangy fruit most months of the year. She often clipped small branches of shiny green lemon leaves and starry white blossoms to decorate our kitchen. In the Greek folk tradition, my mother sometimes slipped a few lemon leaves under our pillows to make for sweet dreams. If we hadn't been Greek Orthodox, I'd swear we would have built a temple to Lemos, the ancient Greek God of Lemons, if such a god existed.

Alex followed my mother, never letting her out of his sight. My mother slowly had become the reliable metronome in Alex's life, her daily routine counting out a happily predictable rhythm with Alex's welfare in mind. The day started at our house with a cup of hot chocolate and a Greek cookie for Alex to top off the breakfast he had consumed earlier at The Classic Grill. Next came wondrous garden time where together they identified beetles and bugs, ripe fruit and vegetables. Later came pastry making where Alex was commander of a small bowl, imitating my mother's mixing and beating. And Alex accompanied my mother to The Classic Grill when she worked as host. The cooks hovered over the boy, offering bottle caps to toss into a coffee can or an old-fashioned eggbeater to twirl. The safety experts of today might cringe, but we closely watched our cherished Alex. In our restaurant kitchen, he had taken the place that young Demo and I occupied years ago.

My mother took a rest on a small bench overlooking her vibrant garden which shouted out with bursts of color as the season progressed. She leaned forward and snipped an aromatic sprig of rosemary, then handed it to Alex.

He inhaled the herb and sat back on the bench, legs swinging, content to take in the sun.

"*Alexandros*, we take a trip today."

"To where?" Alex asked, jumping off the bench to pull out a handful of spearmint leaves and breathe in their lively fragrance.

"To see my big boy, Demo, in San Francisco." My mother wrapped her arm around the boy once he settled on the bench.

"Even if mothers do not see their sons, they are always loved," she said, more to herself than to Alex.

Standing in the distance, shielded behind a neighbor's knobby pine tree, Daphne silently observed my mother and Alex peacefully contemplating the garden scenery, adding another gauzy layer to their accidental mother-and-son connection. Neither my mother nor Alex had noticed Daphne's presence as she observed her son thriving in my mother's garden. After watching Alex for several minutes, Daphne quickly began the long walk back to work in her black office pumps, tears in her eyes.

SIXTY-FIVE

My mother pulled Alex by his small, moist hand and helped him safely climb the tall stairs at the entrance of a Victorian house on Central Street, left off Haight Street. Walking behind her, I noted that the cream-colored paint on the siding had peeled and the wobbly wooden stairs leading to the front door could use some shoring up. On the ferryboat ride to San Francisco with Alex, I told my mother that Demo had moved out of the YMCA and into Natalya's house. The rent was free in exchange for Demo taking over the cooking detail. Demo told me he didn't mind whipping up a few meals that were second nature to him as Natalya had introduced him to everyone in her dramatic circles and had asked for nothing else in return.

My mother overflowed with frothy anxiety as she worried what Demo truly was forced to surrender in exchange for free rent. She crossed herself, thinking of what Demo might have endured and how she could possibly save her son.

At the top of the stairs, the door slowly opened before we could ring the bell. I stood behind my mother and Alex, carrying the bundles and sacks filled with *dolmathes*, chicken and rice, feta cheese, *koulourakia* and a giant chocolate cake my mother had created to celebrate her precious oldest son. Her cooking frenzy nearly depleted our sugar rations until our next "sugar book" issued by the U.S. Office of Price Administration would become available.

Natalya's smiling face at the door met my mother who was bundled in her camel hair coat and paisley peasant scarf knotted under her chin. Natalya's lipstick, as always, was bold and outlined her wide, perpetual smile. Before Natalya could open her mouth, my mother burst out.

"I am Demo's mother." She quickly took in all of six-foot Natalya. "This is Alex. I think you know my boy George. I come to see Demo, my son."

My mother twisted her body around Natalya's bulky frame for a glimpse of Demo. She needed to see her son immediately.

"Of course!" Natalya cried out, pulling the door back. "Demo! Your mother and brothers are here!"

"And I…" She introduced herself as if she were giving a dramatic reading, slowly pressing a hand on her heart. "…am Natalya!"

Natalya swept her arms around my mother who felt an instant jolt from the past, as if Andromache's arms were encircling her. *Tis ídies doníseis,* the same vibrations. I could tell that my mother was madly piecing together Demo's new life picture: a handmade collage of people, places and sexuality that did not include his mother or her nurturing ways.

Demo rushed out from a small adjoining room wearing a garland of flowers on his head and an ancient Greek costume over his street clothes. He was adjusting the shoulder on the costume with a safety pin.

"Ma! You made it!"

Demo's arms surrounded my mother and held her tightly. I think I heard my mother's heart beating against Demo's chest. Demo released her, clasped my shoulders with both hands and then looked at Alex who was wearing his Sunday suit of clothes.

"You're all here!" My brother was delighted. "I thought it was only George who was coming to see me perform." He looked down at the child whose eyes took in the colorful décor in the unfamiliar San Francisco flat. "And you must be Alex. Do you like make-believe?" Demo placed his crown of flowers on Alex's head.

"I am four." The child mumbled quietly and held up four small digits for Demo's inspection.

"Then you must love make-believe!" My brother's eyes sparkled. For a moment I was back in our bedroom where Demo's network of scarves, pixie dust, plays and songs enchanted my life on a daily basis.

My mother had busied herself by untying the protective cloths surrounding the glass-covered casserole dishes, plates and shoeboxes filled with Greek delicacies. "You no eat good. And today your birthday." She looked at Alex. "My big boy eighteen!"

"Thank you, Ma. I love everything but we really don't have time for that right now. Maybe after the show? My call time is five o'clock."

My mother pushed him into a small side room that she assumed was out of earshot.

"Who is this woman? She do things to you?"

"Natalya's great, Ma. She's an actress herself. She believes in me."

"I always believe for you!" My mother whispered with a drop of jealousy coating her words. Of course, Natalya, Alex and I heard everything that was said in the living room of Natalya's small home. "You come home!"

"Pop doesn't want me," Demo stated with cool acceptance. "I don't belong at home. Not anymore. You know that."

"I make him understand!" She spoke with the desperation of wanting to make it so.

Then my mother became silent. In this new atmosphere — Demo's world — it became obvious her son never would return home. She no longer was Artemis the protector with the power to fuse together the pieces of our family. Another door had opened. And this time it was Demo who had taken a heroic leap forward. It was clear my mother needed to dissolve the bonds of her old world and accept that Demo was free.

"I am so proud of you, Demo *mou*." She searched his eyes to connect with her son. Joy engulfed Demo's face.

"Ma! The San Francisco Opera! Just an extra behind the chorus. But the San Francisco Opera!"

My mother could not hold back her tears as she embraced her son and his new life. I watched as Natalya lingered outside the doorway, wistfully observing the profound connection between my mother and Demo — one that could only be temporarily hers.

SIXTY-SIX

Natalya reported that the director had taken one look at my brother and immediately cast him as one of the heavenly souls of the Elysian Fields in his opera. He would not add much to the vocals, but his looks were perfect for the role.

My mother plowed through the crowd to find our seats, a simple sparrow among a pandemonium of tropical parrots, unashamed that we were dressed like kitchen help among these patrons of the arts. I felt glaringly out of place in my brown corduroy pants amid the rustling of long satin dresses, the clanking of pendulous jewelry and old men in over-starched tuxedos. I was fully aware that I stood apart from the rest — a Vallejo hillbilly in the swarm of San Francisco glitterati. These fears did not occur to my mother, who was oblivious to worries about a cloth coat in the midst of silver fox stoles and authentic pearls.

My mother, Alex, Natalya and I positioned ourselves on our cushy velour seats in the gilded War Memorial Opera House on Van Ness Street in outer downtown San Francisco. I was grateful Natalya could arrange tickets for all of us. I couldn't quite get over the opulent gold leaf carvings above the stage area. Just for a moment, I imagined that this is where my father drew inspiration to create the gold leaf décor on the pillars at The Symposium. I quickly dismissed that thought, knowing my father would never waste money on frivolous entertainment when he could, for the same amount, buy a week's supply of chicken for the restaurant.

I dared to stare upward, revealing to the world that I was a newcomer in this 24-carat crowd. I studied the weighty chandelier that seemed like frozen water splashed from a giant bucket high above in the balcony, twinkling before it melted. I counted the years since the '06 San Francisco earthquake and hoped we had a little more time until the next big one.

I'd never attended an opera and could not understand a word of the Italian lyrics, but I was captivated by the beauty and spectacle of *Orfeo* ed Euridice — *Orpheus and Eurydice*. My mother attentively absorbed the drama on stage. I felt she completely understood the story: the opportunity to again love the person that was thought to be forever lost. Alex quietly sat beside my mother, taking in the magic of the music and performances, never dozing off once, although it was late for him. I wondered if, years later, Alex would look back and believe he was hurled into the midst of the Pappayannis clan with the task of observing our family, each one blind as Oedipus, groping our way through our own operatic story toward an unknown ending. But for now, Alex was content to sit sandwiched in safety between my mother and me.

The sweet melodies of Christoph Gluck were a kind of music I had never heard — not even in my music appreciation class at our high school. My mother craned her neck to locate Demo, dressed in his ethereal finery, standing in the back part of the stage. He was fully immersed in his role, welcoming Orfeo through the heavenly gates as he attempted to locate his precious wife, Euridice. In my eyes, Demo was an angel up there on stage, glowing, weightless. I watched my mother take it all in. At the final note, she sprang from her seat, emotion bursting from her soul, and applauded her brilliant son, the actor. It was clear, my mother completely accepted her boy and the important work they both knew Demo was destined to do.

"Bravo! Bravo, Demo *mou!*" My mother could see that Demo had become the ancient Greek actor who had lived in his soul since birth.

The rest of the audience broke into hoorahs and hearty applause. Most people probably thought my mother, the only person standing in ovation, was applauding the lead singers. I saw Demo's eyes searching the audience, looking for my mother and her reaction. Their eyes locked and I believe my mother's heart now overflowed with all the joy a Greek mother could possibly conceive. And as for Demo, he took his bows with the extras and chorus and then nearly floated from the stage along with Orfeo and Euridice.

We celebrated both Demo's performance and his birthday in a restaurant near the ferry building so the three of us could easily catch the very last ferry of the night. My mother paid the tab with her secret stash of one dollar bills she had squirreled away deep in her coat pocket. Demo, engaged and talkative, radiated satisfaction that I could sense across the table. My brother seemed to have absorbed the music of *Orfeo ed Euridice* through his skin. Just sitting near Demo, I could feel his happiness seeping from his pores.

SIXTY-SEVEN

"So, like, your dad never saw Demo perform?" Mariam asked. "He never watched his own son on the stage?"

I took a sip of coffee, finding this memory difficult to reconcile, even after seventy-five years or so.

"Nope, never did. Didn't want to see him get a foothold on his new life. Didn't want to see him 'that way.'"

"Just like my brother." Aman breathed the words into the safe atmosphere of our little group. "He can't tell anybody. Just me. My father would send him away. Forever. Probably worse."

Just when I thought society had progressed in my nine decades on the planet, I was quickly reminded that change was slow. Our old family fears were now Aman's weight to carry on her *plati*, her back.

I paused, then slowly resumed my story. But it was not going to make my new friends happy.

SIXTY-EIGHT

On a fogless Monday morning in June, Theo Vasili lingered over a cup of coffee at the counter when Taki bolted into The Classic Grill. Instead of tuning up his radio, he paced behind my uncle, perched on a stool, then paced again, then threw his folded newspaper on the counter.

"*Katseh*, sit down, Taki." My uncle stirred his coffee. "Tell us the news."

From behind the counter, he poured coffee for Taki.

"I meet Nikko in San Francisco next Wednesday. Nikko comes home!" Taki was almost shouting. I looked up from my cutting board where I was chopping mounds of onions for the beef stew on the dinner menu. My uncle swung open the kitchen door and yelled.

"*Achilléas!* Nikko comes home! Cousin! Nikko comes home next week!"

My father raced to the counter and I followed right behind him. Taki unplugged his radio, wrapping the cord around it.

"Then we make party!" My father beamed with happiness for Taki. Nikko had been serving in the Army when the United States joined the war. His company was one of the first to land in Europe.

But Taki's face was a puzzle — no happiness where it should have been.

"*Chorís toh pódi!* Without the leg!" Taki screamed as if we could absorb his pain.

Suddenly the air was too thick to breathe. My hands were cold and limp at my side.

"A bomb goes off in London! He loses the leg!"

Tears washed Taki's face. "They cut it off! The right one. It is gone!"

Taki crumpled as if he was shot in the heart. As if he, a parent, had somehow failed to protect the body of his only child.

Nikko had always been kind to me. Although he was about seven or eight years older, he included Demo and me in his circle of friends during name day celebrations. While our fathers told endless stories and consumed gallons of Greek coffee, our mothers occupied our house rolling out phyllo dough, laying the paper-like sheets on sofas and beds to dry and Nikko let us younger boys play street ball with him and his friends. He was by far the best athlete I knew. To me, good looking, gregarious Nikko effortlessly straddled two worlds — keeping his Greek parents happy and living his own American life.

Taki marched to my father, his words hot in my father's face.

"How I help my Nikko now? In ten years, everyone forget this war. But my Nikko, still he have no leg!"

My father's face was white, motionless. My uncle stared into space over his coffee cup. My heart had suspended its beats. Just last week at the restaurant, we served lunch to a soldier with a stump where a well-formed leg had once grown. I was sickened to imagine that Nikko would attract the same glances of pity.

Taki made the sign of the cross from shoulder to shoulder and swept up his bulky radio in his short arms. He began to trudge out of The Classic Grill with his radio but stopped before walking out to the street.

"This war? For what?" His rage rang out through the restaurant.

I had never heard him raise his voice before. Ever.

SIXTY-NINE

The next afternoon, I paced the brown marble floors of The Symposium. I was jumpy, unsoothed, restless. With the unspeakable seizure of Tetsuya from our restaurant kitchen, the agony of Nikko's severed limb and the ache of Demo's absence, my spirit was battered like the bloody beef my father butchered in the kitchen. Looking for a distraction, I forced myself to walk around the new restaurant, brooding over the future I would be forced to share with my father.

The week before, I attempted to discuss the first week's menu with him and also the cleaning regimes for the new equipment at The Symposium. I was bursting with ideas for our new restaurant. But my enthusiastic words only clattered to the ground, unheard, around my father's feet. If Demo wanted to discuss something, he would have dragged my father to a corner and confronted him eyeball-to-eyeball with his important concerns. My sensitive skin had already been singed by my father's caustic words in recent weeks and I didn't have the stomach to open myself up for another burn. So I lived with ideas crawling out of my head and no home to give them. Did I have to break away — like my brother — to cut my own path in the restaurant world? Maybe I somehow could find the words to make my father see me as an equal. Or at least as a son who deserved respect.

I heard my father turn the key to the front door. Striking heavily on the newly polished floors, his policeman's shoes stomped from the entry to the main dining room.

He didn't see me standing there with my broom surrounded by the fine dust piles left by the carpenters. I watched him slowly inspect the final gold leaf trim on the pillars, the rich beauty of the marble floors. He scrutinized the mahogany tables and matching chairs, running his hand over a scratch. He worked his way to the kitchen and office area, straightening the red glass votive candle he kept lit on his makeshift altar — just as he had at The Classic Grill.

I decided this was the time to let my father know that I was his "restaurant man," his future partner. Sweeping closer to my father, I cleared my throat to break my father's contemplation.

"Just getting a feel for the place." I stepped forward enthusiastically, a smile plastered on my face. "Pop, when should we have the grand opening? I was thinking maybe an unofficial opening with our family and friends first."

My father said nothing. His eyes seemed to flicker in my direction, but then drifted away. Maybe he was lost in the past, or the future. He certainly was not talking to me. He quickly stood up and walked away.

"Pop, what do you think?" I insisted, following him with my broom, the smile sliding off my face.

"Your mother and you see Demo in San Francisco!" He whipped around to face me, snarling. "You bring him home to help me! I depend for him."

I could read his mind. Without Demo, his bright and able first son — and with no more Tetsuya — he had only me to count on. Me, the *pedi*, the kid who never spoke his mind. The young one he would not allow to calculate his taxes. The weak son who was good for potato peeling but empty-headed for more. Suddenly my spirit exploded into a firestorm. I wanted my words to burn. It was my turn to rage.

"Well I miss Demo too! He thinks I should go to college. He thinks I should run this restaurant. He thinks that I'm pretty damn good! I'm a great cook! One day you'll miss me too!"

I wanted him to yell at me, to attack me. I waited for his cascade of cruel remarks so that for once, I could stand up for myself and fight back.

Instead, my father stared up at the ceiling. Lost in endless dreams of Demo.

"George, you tell you' brother — "

I felt something crack between us.

"Why don't you?"

I threw down the handle of the broom and it clattered on my father's treasured marble floor which was dearer to him than I was.

At that moment, I missed Tetsuya's warm, comforting presence. I vanished out the back, slamming the door with the sticky latch, which was — except for me — the only flaw in my father's perfect restaurant.

SEVENTY

"How'd you put up with that?" Jason asked, shaking his head. "There you were, right under your father's nose! The son he needed."

"Well, I was young and not ready to leave home, but I didn't speak to my father for days. I'm not even sure he noticed."

"All fathers are like that," Aman whispered — from experience I was beginning to learn. "I think he hates my brother. He suspects him. My brother is gay."

She looked down at her hands resting in her lap. "My father will kill him." She looked back at me. "Seriously."

Mariam had taken a moment to wipe down a few tables with a wet rag. Few customers occupied the restaurant, so it was a quick swipe and she was done, back now with our little group.

"You ever have kids?" Mariam asked me. "You nicer to them than your father?"

I was about to admit to these young people, full of hope, that I did not have children. If the world cracked open and laid out its treasures, the one I would have plucked from the riches would have been rocking an infant daughter to sleep in my arms. Or surrounding myself in the sweet chaos of unruly toddlers running through the house. Or a Greek Orthodox christening when my child was dunked into a giant brass tureen and splashed with heavenly blessings and later dressed in new white clothes reflecting the purity of the child's newly blessed soul. Helping another Pappayannis — girl or boy — navigate this world would have been much more satisfying to me than any new restaurant. I would have tenderly listened to my child's every word, no matter how wild his thoughts or how unattainable her dreams.

"No, I did not have children." I did not want to reveal much more. "Married for a short time. A wonderful woman. The very best."

They did not ask anymore, assuming I had suffered a painful divorce, as one would expect in today's world. What I did not offer was that the best

Greek-American woman in the world, Lula, chose me to be her husband when I was twenty-eight years old. She said I was the warm fire she knew she needed forever in her heart. I loved her more than anything. As a nurse, she commuted from Vallejo to Oakland every day, working at Providence Hospital on what they called "Pill Hill," The location where most of the hospitals in Oakland were crowded together. After nine of the most glorious years of my life, Lula's bus crashed on her way to work in Oakland where she died.

Just as we had consecrated our marriage in the Greek Orthodox Church of St. Constantine and Helen in Vallejo, I said goodbye to the only woman I would ever love in that same church. With a tender kiss on her forehead, I placed a large silver cross alongside her uninhabited body. As the priest pronounced the final words, "May her spirit be eternal," over her coffin at the cemetery, I promised Lula that I was hers alone. I believed in one true love and would never remarry. I could never do better than Lula who had chosen me, a young, unsophisticated cook in a small Navy town.

I was lost in my thoughts of laying Lula to rest at the Sunrise Memorial Cemetery on Sacramento Street, the closest cemetery to my home. I realized that my eyes had misted behind my glasses and hoped the kids hadn't noticed. I slid the glasses off my nose to wipe them and lighten the mood of our conversation.

At that moment, small fingers lightly touched my ancient, spotted hand. Aman's black nail polish came into my blurry view.

"It's OK, *Dādā*." She spoke for all the kids. "She must have been a good woman."

These kids perceived more than I could imagine. I looked up at my group who all wore sympathy plainly on their faces. Jason brought me a cup of tea instead of my bottomless cup of coffee.

I took a long breath. They had not yet heard everything about Demo's new life in San Francisco. And what I thought about it. And everything that was to come for our Pappayannis family which was not so sure of its direction anymore.

SEVENTY-ONE

Although The Symposium was scheduled to open in a few weeks, I decided I needed a change of scenery, especially after the conversation with my father — or lack of it. I knew Demo was always thrilled to see me and I could use his brotherly counsel. He did not have a performance on the weekend I chose to visit. After Mr. Chris agreed to fill in for me at the restaurant, I quickly jumped a Greyhound bus to San Francisco late on a Friday. The farther from my father the better.

Natalya opened her arms to me and my weekend duffle bag. My mother insisted I bring Natalya an icon as a gift — a St. Sophia icon, to be exact. I believe my mother somehow reasoned that since St. Sophia had successfully watched over her and Andromache in Greece, her personal saint should have acquired enough experience for the task of protecting Natalya and Demo. When I presented her with the icon, Natalya clasped it in her hands and sincerely said she would treasure it forever. A sign, I think, that she was pleased that my mother accepted her in Demo's life. Of course, Demo skipped over telling my mother that Natalya had introduced him to the clubs and bars of San Francisco — merely an insignificant detail.

On Saturday night, Demo, Natalya and I sat in a dimly lit bar where no one seemed to care about Demo's age, or mine, for that matter. We had just slipped out of The Old Crow on Market Street and Natalya said we should pay a visit to her friends at The Silver Rail, a new bar that had recently opened on Market Street near Fifth. I was nervous, not knowing what kind of new people I would be asked to meet. My stomach was jittery, but I trusted that Demo would not lead me to an experience that I couldn't handle.

Since we last visited Mona's 440 Club with Natalya, I sensed that Demo had matured in ways I'm not sure that I completely understood. Natalya didn't seem to be interested in Demo "that way," but that didn't mean Demo's beauty went unnoticed by San Francisco's men and women.

Demo was drinking a shot and a beer and seemed to handle it well. I didn't want to push my luck any farther, so I stuck with a soda and sat back to observe the patrons of this bar. Each was a unique combination of masculine and feminine, and all of them were just working folks. I watched as men approached — more like swarmed — Demo. I felt like my brother was a movie star and, perhaps in their eyes, he was. Demo introduced me to a fellow fledgling actor in his early twenties and an older man who would be singing at the Black Cat Café on Montgomery Street later that night.

I observed Demo closely to assess if his San Francisco life had transformed him or if he remained the same big brother that had sailed from the Vallejo dock that night. You may not believe this, but I think Demo *was* that same brother. He laughed, made small talk, and patiently listened to each person's desire for respect. Demo, at his young age, gracefully held court for this friendly, colorful crowd. He could see the extraordinary in each person. It was a lifeline when he saw it in me.

Demo kept me close to him that night. After an hour, he signaled to the bartender for another drink. I had just begun to relax in this, the third official adult bar that I had occupied in my young life. The front door suddenly bashed open and a swarm of policemen, cocooned in dark blue wool uniforms, carrying shields and waving batons, crashed into the place. A police whistle let out an earsplitting shriek in the shadowy bar and someone screamed, "Raid!"

Instantly, men and women sprang up to push their way out of the building. I felt panic ricochet off every corner of the bar. Bodies and drinks flew in all directions. Demo grabbed my arm like a tourniquet and attempted to pull me toward the front door. My eyes were horrified to watch batons crashing down on skulls, backs and shoulders. Blood spurted from eyes and cheeks as the bar patrons attempted to push their way through the wall of police blue and stagger out the main entrance. Darting in haphazard directions, some men held napkins on their wounds, attempting to help each other get out of the club. As we three pressed toward the entrance on Market Street, another horde of police entirely blocked our escape. Demo and I spun around, looking for a back door exit. We spotted Natalya across the room at the very moment a fist planted itself on her jaw and a baton cracked her back. "God damn faggot!" I heard the policeman growl. Demo dropped my arm and hurried to Natalya's large, limp body in a pile on the floor.

Crack!

I was standing only a few feet away as I looked up to see a baton landing in slow motion across Demo's face.

"Fuckin' fruit!"

I was separated from my brother by men and women attempting to escape the flying batons. A shock ran through my body as I realized I was one of the few left standing. I looked to see Natalya's substantial frame still lying dazed, like a wounded doe on the forest floor.

A bartender tugged at my sleeve. Through the din, I thought I heard, "Over here, kid." I pulled at Demo who was woozy, and we both helped Natalya to her feet. The bartender dragged us to the small back kitchen and opened a door. Just before he pushed us toward a black hole, which I assumed was a secret exit, two policemen shoved all three of us outside the front door swinging their billy clubs. They herded us into a worn out paddy wagon that smelled like beer, stale urine and sweat.

We silently bumped our way to the Hall of Justice on Kearny Street. I glanced up at Natalya's wide, gentle face that looked like the raw scraps of beef that my father pushed through his meat grinder. Demo's beautiful curls were mashed with blood and dirt and I could tell that the skin under his eye would be black for weeks.

Hours later, Natalya had enough money to bail us all out of jail but we didn't need it. Since Demo and I were underage, the police dismissed our charges, saying something about being influenced by bad morals and that our parents should watch out for the kind of people we associated with. The police had halfheartedly threatened to call our parents, but they were busy processing many older bar patrons. I felt a giant rush of relief, as I could not fathom my outraged father taking two buses to the Hall of Justice to bail me out for being caught in a bar while underage, or perhaps a graver charge that I didn't even want to imagine. And I didn't want to contemplate what my father would do to Demo.

Natalya did not fare as well. She was charged with lewd conduct, although she was only enjoying her scotch on the rocks when she looked up to see the police burst in, batons swinging. Sitting on a curb, Demo and I nervously waited for Natalya outside the police station, and just before dawn, she was released. Too bruised and bloody to travel home on a late night streetcar, Natalya asked us to hail a cab to drive us directly to her flat in the Haight district. We rode home in silence, wanting only a safe place where we could all exhale.

Natalya's place was quiet that early Sunday afternoon. I ministered to Demo and Natalya by making a breakfast of omelets, toast and coffee that I hoped would both strengthen and calm them — and me too. I set out plates and went to roust Demo and Natalya before it was time to catch my bus back to Vallejo. I snuck into Demo's room. It was quite plain, in comparison to the festoons of ancient Greek decorations he had proudly displayed in the room we shared. Demo heard me creak into his room and managed to open the eye that looked swollen and purple, like a small eggplant. I brought him another round of ice wrapped in a towel and a few wet tea bags that my mother often swore helped reduce swelling.

"How's the eye?" I asked gently, sitting down on the bed next to my brother's thin body.

"Two weeks before my next performance." He groaned as I placed the ice to his face. "I'll be okay."

I assessed my beautiful brother huddled under three wool blankets and a bundle of ice cubes. Perhaps this new life was too much for him. I foresaw that he would have to take great risks to live the life he wanted so badly. I wondered how strong my brother needed to be, how many more beatings and how much more ridicule would be dished out to him in the future. I contemplated Natalya's courage to live her life with as few pretenses as possible. I now understood that Natalya saw Demo as prey for this cruel, unfair world and had offered him a safe harbor while he figured things out for himself.

Demo read my mind, I'm sure. He smiled up at me, the same confident, impish smile as when he performed a line of some ancient Greek play he had just memorized in our bedroom.

"I'll be fine, George." Demo shifted in his bed and winced a little. "And you will be better."

I was forced to take him at his word because my bus was leaving soon. Having laid out food for Demo and Natalya, I dug into my duffle bag and handed Demo a small bundle of mail addressed to him that had come to our family home. I also unloaded my mother's *melomakarouna*, Greek honey macaroons, as well a three-pound shoebox of *koulourakia*, the universal care package of cookies manufactured by devoted Greek mothers.

I peeked in on Natalya who was fast asleep in her room, bandages everywhere. Without her scarlet lipstick and bouffant hairdo, which I now could see was a wig, her face looked angular, with a strong jaw, her hair short and thin against her head. I desperately hoped she would quickly recover, since I wouldn't be around to help. I guess St. Sophia on the icon near Natalya's bed had turned her head and clasped two hands over her eyes the night of the beatings.

I popped back into Demo's room to say goodbye. He was intently reading a letter and he did not move until he heard me walk in.

"Don't worry about my eye, George." Demo's good eye stared ahead, not blinking. "Guess I have another job to do before I go back to the stage."

I dashed to him and snatched his letter. Once glance was all I needed.

ORDER TO REPORT FOR INDUCTION

President of the United States

Greeting: Having submitted yourself to a local board composed of your neighbors for the purpose of determining your availability for training and service in the land or naval forces of the United States, you are hereby notified that you have now been selected for training and service therein.

You will, therefore, report to the local board named above...

A deep chill flooded my body and my hands were suddenly numb. I never imagined my brother being drafted, suited in Army green, marching in an inhospitable foreign land, perhaps firing a rifle. Demo had lived in the spirit of fantasy and love since my young eyes could focus on my big brother, and now he might be forced to kill a man. Not Demo! I wanted to scream. Not my brother!

Demo had just landed a role that would require a different kind of bravery. But I was not so courageous. I felt the floor give way with my panic. My brother would be plucked away like Tetsuya or maimed like Nikko, for a war whose violent tentacles were everywhere, seemingly on every continent, strangling families that just wanted to live a decent, peaceful life. I threw my bag next to Demo's bed, sat down near my brother, planted my head in my hands and did not leave Demo's room for much of the day. The hour for my departure seemed insignificant and I missed my bus. I would stay in San Francisco that day and maybe the next. I needed to tend to both Demo's and Natalya's wounds. And now to my own.

SEVENTY-TWO

Later that day, I boiled up a batch of what I hoped would be therapeutic chicken and rice soup and considered life with Demo far away in the Army. As I ladled out two bowls for my patients, I decided I would wear a brave face for my brother, who I assumed, was wearing one for me. After setting the soup on Natalya's night table, I swung into Demo's room with his own steaming bowl and a hunk of hot, spongy French bread on a bamboo tray. He sat up for the first time that day and sipped the soup, using the bread to wipe his bowl clean. I was thrilled to see him eating, with a tiny spark of life in his good eye.

I watched my brother and attempted to memorize everything about him before he would be transformed into an Army private, his curly hair buzzed off into a harsh crew cut, only a shadow remaining on his scalp. Because it was now summer vacation from school, I decided I would be near Demo every day that I possibly could. Like the bread in Demo's bowl, I desperately needed to soak up as much of my brother, my life-giving force, as I could.

Life was not much better at home in Vallejo, where our wounds bled from a place no bandages or balm could touch. Visiting Demo in San Francisco, my mother said she had been momentarily uplifted when she saw with her own eyes that her son had achieved a morsel of satisfaction on stage. His dreams were aloft, like a colorful Chinese kite with a long, whippy tail, expecting to rise to greater heights. When I gently informed my mother about Demo's notice for a Selective Service physical exam, she asked if he would be shipped off to Europe as Nikko had been. She prayed Demo would be stationed stateside, perhaps in a position dispensing blankets and Army-issue boots, or a job as a cook in a massive, protected fort somewhere on the East Coast. Anything safe until the war was over. Unfortunately, the German and Japanese forces seemed invincible, and none of us could foresee the moment when — or if — Hitler and Hirohito would be crushed.

Of course, I never told my mother about the vicious police raid or Demo and Natalya's gruesome, painful gashes that marked them for weeks as victims. I reasoned that the thought of Demo's bashed and bloodied face was more weight than my mother could carry. I also omitted discussing my worries for Demo's safety in the Army, if anyone suspected he liked anything except girls. I feared it could be more disastrous to him than the scene at the Silver Rail, but I shielded my mother from possibilities we could not control.

My mother grinded away on her own set of worries, in addition to Demo's draft. From the hallway in our home, my eyes followed her staring at a suitcase yawning open, empty on her bed. Years later, my mother told me more about the suitcase and the day she packed it.

My father bought her the tattered beige fabric and leather suitcase with a scuffed wooden handle shortly after they were married in a small chapel in the Castella District of Piraeus. My parents' wedding ceremony, with flowered crowns connecting the bride and groom, transformed them from two wandering and wanting souls, and instantly seared their futures together with one purpose, one reason for being, always one direction. An hour before they sailed to America, my father purchased for his new bride what he considered to be a trousseau — three towels, two handker-chiefs and, as he turned his head in modesty, a few pairs of soft, pink silk underwear, one of which she wore on her wedding night. He presumed his bride required an appropriate suitcase in which to carry her posses-sions that would christen her life with him in a new country. In a few years' time, that became our family suitcase, which we cheerfully shared in happier times.

Later my mother revealed to me that my parents' early years had become blurred in her recollection. In those days, when my father treated her with loving attention, their future was painted in clear, primary colors, straight lines and above all, honest intentions. Now, the blues, reds and yellows had faded behind a mist for her — as if that had been someone else's life. She reviewed my father's banishment of Demo, his continual dismissal of me, the introduction of Daphne into my father's workaholic days and sleepless nights and the weight of the soon-to-be-christened Symposium restaurant. My mother felt she had been herded behind a barbed wire fence and kept apart from my father while he made his own plans. She was not accustomed to passively observing from afar, unable to cross the prickly boundaries my father had created.

She had reached the end of her days as my father's silent supporter. She would not become an understudy for the leading role in her own marriage. She would not be replaced or directed out of her own story. She was resolute that my father would not nip away small fragments of her self-respect. It was unheard of for a Greek wife to walk out on her family, but my father's promises had collapsed under his weighty ego, which she mistook for strength in the early years of her marriage.

She quickly placed her rough cotton underwear, a few dresses and thick beige stockings into the worn, empty suitcase that held so much promise decades ago. She folded a black dress and added it to her portable belongings because one never knew when respectable funeral attire would be needed. She tucked in a few aprons, as she was not afraid to earn her living by baking and restaurant work, as she had done for years. The only things left to do were to return Alex to the full-time care of his mother and invite me, her son, to join her. Then she would break the news to my father. She was leaving him for good.

Breathing hard with hot tears in her eyes and an unfamiliar feverish feeling, she once again longed for her own mother's sound advice. My mother truly had no one but St. Sophia upon whom she could rely. She reached up to her small altar shelf and pulled down the icon of her favorite saint, dusted off St. Sophia's dark, brooding face and lovingly set her at the top of her pile of clothes, ready to be swallowed up by the suitcase. She prayed that a female saint could comprehend that, although she was a wife and mother, she could never again accept disrespectful treatment from a man — especially her husband.

Pressing down on the suitcase to click the latches, my mother heard a small shuffle of feet and the creaking sound of the hardwood floors. Bleary eyed, Alex trundled into her room, dragging a small blanket, although it was early afternoon. She looked closer. The skin on Alex's arms and legs appeared translucent, his purple veins tracing an intricate map of his vascular system. All motherly intuition in her body abruptly stood at attention. Alarms in her brain shrieked a warning signal. He crawled onto her bed, dark hair matted to his forehead and collapsed next to the suitcase. Although his face was bright with color, Alex shivered as if he had been slapped on both cheeks. My mother slid her cool palm onto his burning forehead and scanned Alex's small, limp body for clues. Her eyes lit on a fine, red rash covering the boy's face and limbs as if he was coated in scarlet freckles.

My mother jolted into action. She snapped her suitcase shut and quickly slid it off the bed, hiding it out of sight. After fetching a cold towel for Alex's head, she dialed the doctor, who had tended to Demo and me as small children. She raised an eyebrow to St. Sophia in the heavens, who seemed to say that my mother had more work to accomplish at home before she could finally walk away. My mother would have to dig for all the strength in her heart, ignoring her own sense of dignity, to help this small boy — a child who was not even her own.

SEVENTY-THREE

Jason was the one who fidgeted nervously with his paper cup.

"I've got a little brother that age." He had finally revealed something about his life, his family. He shook his head. "They get sick fast. Like, we almost lost him to the flu last year. I didn't think anyone died from that anymore."

I was happy that Jason didn't lose a family member, especially a young one. A loss like that could stain your memory forever and never blot out.

"Just like you, Jason, we were worried about Alex who slowly had become our little brother. But he's not the only one who was ill, although we didn't know it yet."

Aman seemed alarmed. I could feel her big heart opening up, sympathetic to our family drama that had played out decades ago.

"Did you get sick too?"

I looked down into my coffee cup and assessed that I would need a refill for this part of the story.

"No, but it got more complicated."

SEVENTY-FOUR

Dr. Winston removed his spectacles and wiped his balding head with his handkerchief. Standing behind him, watching his every motion, my mother wrung her hands and patted an embroidered handkerchief on her own forehead. Alex was a small mound under the sheet, surrounded by fluffy pillows and cold towels. He was still feverish, listless, covered in a light spray of red rash. I stood behind them, anticipating what would be needed next — medicine from the drug store, blankets, hot chocolate. I hung onto the doctor's words.

Dr. Winston turned to gravely face my mother. "Mrs. Pappayannis, the child has contracted scarlet fever. Hit hard."

He gazed over his glasses and stepped closer to my mother. With his thumb on her chin, he slowly lowered her jaw and examined the dark tunnel of her throat. He exhaled as his look of concern quickly transformed to worry.

"You're worse, Mrs. Pappayannis. Bed rest for you too."

Only then did I realize the ruby-red rash had cannibalized my mother's skin, her body seemingly turning scarlet before my eyes.

"But my — the child!" my mother protested. "He must — "

The doctor stepped past my mother and spoke only to me.

"They need to be quarantined from the rest of the family for at least ten days. We don't need an epidemic, especially now."

After Dr. Winston left, I ran for my high school textbook, *Modern Health and Hygiene,* which said I should wash my hands and face every chance I could. The doctor had no medicines for this malady, but I could keep Alex and my mother swimming in warm soup and press cold towels against their heads and wrists.

In Greece, my Yiayiá had taught my mother that sliced raw potatoes slipped onto the soles of the feet, held in place by clean socks, had the ability to reduce a fever — and quickly too. It always worked like a charm when

Demo and I were hot with fever. My mother and Alex lay propped up in the twin beds, sipping my famous chicken broth served at a warm — but not hot — temperature. It might as well have been garlic soup as I had added two handfuls of tangy cloves because of their supernatural healing properties. After a few hours, I replaced the potatoes with a fresh slice on each foot. Maybe the grandmother I had never met could help me outsmart this treacherous disease.

While they slept, I scrubbed my hands and face, collected some clean clothes for my father and rushed down to The Classic Grill. I walked into a wild dinner service with the counter crowded with workers and tables packed everywhere — not an open seat in the place. Customers crowded the entryway, impatiently waiting to be seated. This was unheard of in our restaurant. I felt the gentle tug-of-war between serving our loyal customers and needing to hurry back to care for my mother and the boy who was becoming my kid brother.

"Pop!" I stepped between Panos, the new vegetable man, and Mr. Chris who was a mad dishwashing machine when the restaurant got this busy. I found my father wearing his suit jacket and tie, cleaning up a spill of marinara sauce on the cement floor when he should have been greeting guests and handing out menus. I had to give him the news.

"George!" My father looked up from the pool of red sauce and rags. "Get the mop! People waiting in front! Where your mother? She come soon to help me?"

I waved him off so he could seat the customers. While I cleaned up the mess, I struggled with how to tell him that my mother and I would not be helping him at the restaurant for ten days or more. And that he could not enter our home for nearly two weeks. I knew my father would abide by the rules, as he would never expose our customers and crew to scarlet fever.

I swabbed the red ocean of marinara off the kitchen floor and cut through the cooks to the dining room. I caught my father's arm before he could seat the next group of customers.

"Pop! Mom's sick. Alex too!"

"George, what you saying?"

"Scarlet fever!"

My father turned to me with panic in his eyes.

"Your mother? Where is she?" His eyes narrowed, eyebrows low and heavy. "How she get this?"

I explained that my mother and Alex were resting now, but since they were under my watchful care, I had to get back to the house quickly. And because of the quarantine, my father should sleep at the restaurant. I reassured him that I was carefully following the directions given to me by the doctor. My father was silent, ruminating the news. For once, he could not make a plan to remedy the situation — besides pay the doctor's bill. This was one of the few times that I was in control, delivering to him the crucial news as I was living it. He gave me a direct, steady look.

"Tell you mother... *ó, ti chreiázetai*, whatever she need." Those words slipped out of his mouth as he dashed to the kitchen and shoved a box of Cream of Wheat and a loaf of bread into my arms. "Remember, with fever she need to drink water."

I turned to rush back to my patients.

"Call me with *ta néa*, the news," he muttered, almost to himself.

As I hurried out of the restaurant, Daphne, handbag over her wrist and cheery expression on her face, entered The Classic Grill. It was the end of her workday and I cruelly assumed she was there for another free dinner. I decided to let my father tell her about Alex. But for now I had to get back to the Pappayannis medical clinic. I was "on assignment."

SEVENTY-FIVE

As I swiftly walked home, I remembered my father telling us about his self-survival kit for the flu here in America, a lifetime ago, before he traveled back to Greece and met my mother. Feeling sick and feverish, with no family to comfort him and entire neighborhoods falling to the pandemic, he continuously drank strong chamomile tea and honey, fashioned a necklace out of fragrant garlic bulbs, chewed a handful of potent garlic cloves and crawled into bed. He woke only to shoot a jigger of whisky down his throat that would knock him out as he slept for hours. One morning, after a week of the ritual of tea, whisky shots and the mighty force field of garlic, my father sat up in bed. Feeling energetic, he pulled on his clothes and lumbered to work, hoping the odor of garlic emanating from his body would not be permanent. The old-time Greek remedy had put the flu behind him and he felt a renewed sense of appreciation for the ability to walk down the street, feel the warmth of the sun, breathe the marine air and lift his eyes to the future.

Years later, he revealed to me that after he heard the news about scarlet fever, a curious feeling had swept over him — he felt cut off and apart from our family. In earlier days, my mother, Demo and I swarmed him, seeking his grand paternal knowledge and experience about the way life was lived in this country. He preached that education was the key to our future success — and his own. Now, one son had drifted to another universe and my mother and I had concealed ourselves behind dark clouds and purposefully avoided his powerful command.

He also told me that after I had broken the news about the scarlet fever, Theo Vasili had popped into The Classic Grill, observed the chaos, swept up menus and began to seat the customers crowding the entryway. My father breathed a shallow sigh of relief. He could at least depend on my uncle for moral support, although his assistance was erratic and would never be financial.

Having a moment of reprieve, my father spotted Daphne searching for a seat at the crowded counter, but not locating one. He watched as his cousin, menus in hand, walked her to a table while the eyes of the single and not-so-single men followed her. From afar, he observed Daphne scan the menu. He would explain Alex's and my mother's illness to her. She should be slightly comforted that an experienced doctor — at no charge to her — was treating her son.

Gazing at Daphne from behind the counter, he could not articulate her power over him — more like a soft, silken net over his consciousness. He tried to make sense of it. Beautiful women had come and gone in his restaurant, but this woman was magnetic in her everyday manner. And my father also felt an unusual desire to protect her. No matter how he fit the pieces together, he knew any situation with Daphne would do more damage to his life than World War I and World War II combined. The carnage would be unbearable and he would never again enjoy a guilt-free moment. He briefly dared to wonder if the scene had changed at home with his family drifting like untethered rowboats to the point that they could manage without him. He imagined them floating far away, which would then allow the opportunity for him to discover what life with Daphne might be like.

Slap!

My uncle shattered my father's gauzy daydream by smacking him with a stack of menus across the chest.

"Wake up, cousin!" My uncle strolled past my father on his path to lay out silverware for waiting tables. "Watch out — maybe you give her the Evil Eye!"

Like a hungry dog called away from his vigilant watch of juicy steak slowly being wrapped at the butcher shop, my father was suddenly conscious of his intense staring at a single woman. He quickly seated two Navy officers in a booth. Then he slowly walked to Daphne's table, sat down across from her and delivered the painful news about the health of her young son.

SEVENTY-SIX

"So you had your mother *and* Daphne's son to care for? And how old were you? Only a teenager?" Aman's eyes were wide, disbelieving.

"I watched my brothers since I was eight," Mariam offered with a shrug. "Healthy or sick. Every day."

"Scarlet fever? What did they do for it anyway?" Jason asked. "In those days …"

"Well, antibiotics had been invented, but not widely used," I recalled. "So I was really on my own. And I used every trick I heard my mother talk about. Just lucky for me they worked."

"Maybe we put one of your soups on our menu," Jesús smiled. "During flu season!"

Mariam rolled her eyes. "They make our menus in a laboratory somewhere in Chicago — not a kitchen!" She rose to greet two teenage girls at the counter who were deciding between the Guacamole Burger and the BBQ-Ranch Burger. "I'll be back. Don't go on without me!"

We waited patiently, but I couldn't help but fill in the silence.

"I've got to say that my *avgolemono* soup started my mother and Alex on the path to healing. Our Greek penicillin."

My little group all raised their cups in unison to the health of my family, who had been suffering and bedridden so long ago.

SEVENTY-SEVEN

I had never worked harder in my life. Not when I washed a restaurant full of dirty dishes. Or scrubbed the black and white tile floor until it glowed. Or when I hauled the heavy garbage cans out to the alley. My shoulders felt leaden with the weight of my mother and Alex's precarious health. They teetered between good and bad, like the scales the druggist used to measure sulfa powder. During those days, I felt a kinship with mothers of newborn babies. I slept on the floor, listening to both of my patients breathe — my mother's breath light and fluttery and Alex's more like a little snore from a Chihuahua napping in the sun. I was terrified I might overlook a cough, a change in the scarlet rash or a sudden spike in temperature. I could not — and would not — miss a crucial clue. I fluffed their pillows, changed their sheets daily, fed them my *avgolemono* soup one spoonful at a time. I surprised Alex with a variety of ice cream flavors and cheered when he swallowed sips of water or finished a few tablespoons of my special rice pudding with cinnamon on top. Never would I let my mother perish for lack of care or our precious four-year-old want for anything. He had a place in our family forever, healthy or not.

After a week, I walked into the bedroom, now the hospital ward and was delighted to see Alex lying on his bed, playing with a small toy fire engine, rolling it over the make-believe mountains of his pillow. Too weak to lift her arms just days ago, my mother was slowly brushing her hair. No longer harsh crimson, their bodies were now a light pink color. For the first time in a week, life stirred in the room.

"*Kali mera*, everyone! Looks like a good morning!" I was surprised at this happy turn of events. My mother's eyes glimmered vaguely with well-being, as if her scale had finally tipped toward health.

"And your breakfast order?" I pretended to write down Alex's choice in my make-believe waiter's book.

"Hotcakes!"

His favorite breakfast! Those were the sweetest words that could have penetrated my ears. I was ready to dash off to cook for my charges.

"You take care of us good. The best." My mother's voice had not yet gained back its usual vigor. "You are a wonderful man."

I stopped and smiled. "Thanks, Ma. Tell that to Pop."

In the kitchen, I began sifting out the flour for Alex's hotcakes. It didn't matter what my father thought about me now. My mother and Alex were alive! I had succeeded in that important mission. And I felt honored to do it.

The routine had changed without my mother and me to help at the restaurant. My father was relegated to buy the pies and cakes from the German bakery down the street, much to the disappointment of our customers. To replace my second set of hands in every department — from mopping the floor to operating the deep fryer — my father took on Panos' thirty-year old nephew, Lefteri. He had never worked in a restaurant — or at any other job — for more than a week. Lefteri sulked his way through the chores. Theo Vasili would re-do his work until my father mercifully relieved the nephew from duty.

Walking in circles as if one of his wings was severed and he was unable to take flight, my father had no appetite and barely kept the restaurant going. My uncle never left his side. Each night, they rolled out blankets on the restaurant floor to sleep. They washed their faces in the back sink and bathed every other day in the shared bathroom at my uncle's rental. After the restaurant closed, they sat for hours playing cards, sipping wine. They shared the latest news about my mother and Alex's health and decided from afar what I should do to speed up the recovery effort.

My father telephoned home several times a day and was relieved when the news of good health cracked his dark, anxious gloom. The tightness in my father's chest released its grip and he was finally able to eat a full meal.

Years later, my uncle revealed to me his conversation that night. My father and he once again pushed back the chairs in the restaurant to make room for their bedrolls. Theo Vasili chuckled softly as he spread out a scratchy brown wool blanket he had transported from Greece.

"Cousin! Remember we sleep in the kitchens? Yuba City, Marysville, Redding, Sacramento. We save rent money."

My father cracked a smile. "Yes, until they catch us and throw us out. Then we sleep in the alley with the dogs. So young. We know nothing!"

My uncle sat on his bed on the floor and sipped his wine.

"Ha! One hundred ten degrees every day in Redding. And in the kitchen — who know how hot?" My uncle chuckled. "And you tell us to eat only bananas and milk to save the food money. Always saving the money."

My father poured a glass of wine for himself, sipped it, looking out the front door of The Classic Grill.

"Now we make The Symposium. My restaurant — it beautiful!"

"Symposium better than Le Central in New York!" My uncle compared our new restaurant to his vague memory of the most opulent restaurant he could recall. "Remember we shine shoes in front? How old we then?" My uncle topped off his glass to the brim. "How we do all this — with no mother and father?"

Sloshing with wine, my uncle then changed the subject.

"*Achilléas*, when you let Demo come home? He get the draft now. He leave soon!"

"He is lost to me." My father frowned. "In the Army, he clear his head and know what important for our family. Then he come back — and he do the work he need to do!"

My uncle shook his head.

"Demo is American. He is now soldier. He leave soon — who know to where? Talk to him. *Achilléas*, tell him goodbye."

"*Poté!* Never!" My father turned away from my uncle.

"Just say goodbye to your boy." My uncle prodded a little more. "Do it and your heart feel better. We all feel better."

My uncle took another slug of wine and turned to my father.

"And the girl?"

"Daphne?" my father asked, as if another existed.

"Who else?" My uncle looked out the window, waiting for an answer.

My father rose from his blankets that lay on the floor. He poured himself another glass of wine and gulped down half.

"I am crazy when she not here. I am old — but she need me."

My father heaved a long sigh. Theo Vasili stood up and pulled the string on a small incandescent bulb overhead. They sat in the darkness on the bed rolls that were spread out on the hard floor.

"Maybe she marry and you forget this girl." My uncle sighed wearily, as his old bones attempted to find a comfortable position. My father let out a grunt in the dark.

"As long as it not the mayor!"

SEVENTY-EIGHT

Dr. Winston visited the Pappayannis hospital ward once again and assessed that my patients were indeed recovering. But he sternly warned they should not attempt activity too quickly. With this happy news, I escalated my kitchen game with lemon-basted chicken and potatoes. Just to encourage their appetites, I also cooked up a fluffy batch of egg custard with a caramel glaze. Twice a day, I stretched the curly phone cord, black as licorice, to the edge of Alex's bed and he happily breathed into the receiver listening to his mother's voice. Although they shared a room, my mother pretended not to overhear the child's conversations with Daphne, with whom she had not exchanged words in weeks.

Earlier, during the most crucial days of the quarantine, I knew my mother would want St. Sophia on her bedside table. The saint had vanished from her customary spot, front and center, sitting on the shelf between *Pangaea*, the Virgin Mary, and a small carved wooden cross that once belonged to my Yiayiá in Greece. While my patients slept, I searched for St. Sophia who also seemed to be quarantined. One afternoon while I attempted to coax a spoonful of broth past my mother's unmotivated lips, I dared to ask.

"Did you give away St. Sophia? I can't find her anywhere."

She quickly spun her head towards me and spit the words out of her mouth as if I had heated the soup to boiling.

"Never! She is mine!" She took a breath. *"Valítsa*, suitcase!"

I spotted the family suitcase partially hidden behind my mother's lacy bedroom curtains and I flipped open the latches. St. Sophia lay on top, waiting to be resuscitated with fresh air and daylight. She needed to get back to her saintly activities in a proper location. The bedside table was ready for her, neatly decorated with an elaborately crocheted doily. Embroidery was the Greek woman's Good Housekeeping seal of quality — the more handmade *kéntima* doilies, the more she was a *nekokira*, a five-star housekeeper.

But why had my mother packed her suitcase? Was my mother actually prepared to leave my father? I stared at her slight figure, lying in bed, eyes closed, still fighting off the wicked fever. At that moment, I felt the crushing burden she shouldered, thanks to my father. Maybe St. Sophia, posing innocently by my mother's bed, had wanted her to remain at home and make a stand against him. Or — just maybe — my mother had stayed to protect me.

SEVENTY-NINE

What happened next affected us for all our years to come. Our family's direction turned like a PT boat abruptly changing course in the Pacific, a white foamy stripe in its wake. I later talked to every member — just to get their version of the story — which I wove together to become my own.

The evening before the quarantine was lifted at our home, my father once again carefully inspected The Symposium. He admitted he pensively examined the tables outfitted with sparkling white cloths, napkins folded in the shape of stiff white birds ready to take flight and the twinkling chandeliers hanging from dark wooden beams high above. My father had inhaled the scene with pride. This sophistication was authentic. The Vallejo version of the Fairmont Hotel. His version. As my father promised, The Symposium was indeed a palace for Athena, a creation forged by his own hands without his family's support. He reminisced, wishing his mother who cooked almost every meal over an open hearth in her stony hut in Greece was alive to experience his Symposium. She would have burst with pride for her son, who had nothing but courage and determination when stepping onto American shores with newspaper wrapped around his feet.

My father was angry but secretly perplexed about how to deal with my brother, should he want to visit our family before leaving for the military. He bitterly surmised that Demo would be too preoccupied with his elaborate acting roles and his own grand achievements to be impressed with The Symposium. He seethed with anger and weighty despair, needing emotional reinforcement — here — now at the new restaurant. Instead, he stood in his new restaurant, alone, sharing it with no one except the new tables and chairs that would soon seat his customers.

His gaze lovingly rested on the frying pans dangling from a rack above the white marble work area in the center of the kitchen. His eyes caressed the stainless steel stock pots and sauté pans as gleaming works of art — well-crafted and useful. Walking into his new office, my father prided himself on the glossy desk he bought cheap at a second-hand store. He had determined this office would be his main center of operations, as The Classic Grill practically ran itself.

My father had swiped a few of his good luck charms from his office at The Classic Grill and arranged them on a small shelf above the desk. He positioned the pounded gold St. Nicholas who lay imprisoned on an icon in a glass frame. He brought along used thumbtacks to mount Roosevelt's Four Freedoms poster, but the "freedom from fear" message felt deceptive to him now. He swiftly folded the poster and shoved it into the bottom desk drawer. Days before, he had positioned the red glass votive holder he brought from The Classic Grill on the shelf, and since then, had kept the candle lit. Examining his display, my father crossed himself, just to be on the right side of any observant saint. This new restaurant deserved a good blessing, family support or not.

He took one last look around The Symposium which he proudly built by himself. If his family, namely my mother, was not ready to move forward with him, he forced himself to consider the unpleasant concept of operating this enterprise — and everything else — on his own, without her. Shoving that distasteful possibility aside, my father located his keys and walked out the back door. He closed the door but jiggled the latch before finally bashing it shut and turning the key in the lock. My father walked into the unusually blustery night, making a mental note to repair the unruly back door latch before the kitchen crew's comings and goings made it worse.

Just as my father disappeared into the darkness, across the bay, Demo walked onto the dimly lit deck on the ferry, seeming years older and confident. The bright flare from a match as he lit his cigarette was the only sign of life on the ferry that night. Demo paced the upper deck, and burrowed into his navy coat, just as he had during every trip across the bay. He was accustomed to the feeling of elation when he rode the ferry away from his Vallejo home, anticipating exploratory days and entertaining nights in San Francisco. But sailing in the opposite direction that night, returning home, he was tense, his breath coming quickly. He knew this would be his last visit before he reported for basic training at Fort Ord, situated on the cold, foggy Monterey peninsula. Even more worrisome, our mother, the eternal marble pillar of strength in our family temple, had temporarily fallen to illness and could not help Demo when he needed her unwavering support.

EIGHTY

That evening, my father flipped up his coat lapels as he cut a path against the fierce wind from The Symposium to The Classic Grill. This was his last night away from his quarantined home. He swept the floor between the tables while he sorted out his re-entry to our home the next day. He knew my uncle would arrive soon for one more hard night on the floor.

The door to The Classic Grill creaked open and Daphne slowly crept across the black and white tile floor into the dining room of the restaurant. My father did not hear her quiet footsteps and was startled to see she had appeared in his restaurant at night. A place she should not be.

"Achilles." Daphne whispered, not taking a seat. "I walked by The Symposium today. You're nearly finished. I knew it would be beautiful."

My father rushed to her and pulled a chair away from the table to seat her, scraping the floor, not sure whether he should serve her, talk to her — or exactly what she had in mind.

"You no here yesterday. Or day before." My father finally had the opportunity to search her eyes for a hint of her emotional whereabouts. He wanted to speak his heart, except his feelings were as clear as the hash he ground for yesterday's lunch menu.

"With Alex under quarantine, I took a couple of days to get the last of my things in Redding." Daphne walked to the bar and poured a glass of wine.

My father watched her move about his restaurant with familiarity and wondered what would happen next. She was drinking. They were alone. He had made Vallejo as homey as he could to encourage her to stay — but maybe his actions expressed too much. Or was it too little? His heart beat so loudly he was certain Daphne could hear the bass drum in his chest. He could not predict if this were the beginning or the end of their story together.

"I'm settling in." She found a chair and sipped her wine from a small tumbler glass, a habit she had picked up from Theo Vasili. My father attempted to remain calm, speak nonchalantly. Fatherly.

"Then, you stay in Vallejo?" He was buying time, as he did not want to forego this opportunity to understand Daphne's mind. With eyes locked on her, he slowly picked his way along the edge of the cliff. With one more step, the earth might give way. The long fall would be treacherous, sending him crashing into the bottomless ocean that would sweep him far from the life he had methodically built.

"Yes, Vallejo. I love it here. Alex does too." Daphne looked into her wine glass as if she was finding her words in the bottom of the tumbler. "Thanks to you."

My father took a seat near Daphne. The Greek Orthodox church ladies would have said it was too close for a Greek married man and an unmarried woman.

"Daphne, I must tell you…"

My father did not know exactly what he must tell this young, beautiful woman who seemed to idolize him, depend on him.

"I know what you're going to say. Achilles, I —"

"Finally I make my new restaurant. And you believe for me…" My father filled in, buying a few seconds which he could measure with a yardstick.

He moved closer to Daphne, his heart appropriating his brain. This was his moment to lay his feelings at her feet, like a bouquet of fragrant lavender from the high mountains of Greece. He let the words tumble from his heart to his mouth.

"I need to — to protect you, Daphne. Always."

"Achilles, I know exactly what you want to say." She spoke with the girlish honesty he found so familiar, so magnetic.

Daphne reached across the table and gently placed her hands on either side of my father's rough face. She inspected his worn skin, his salt and pepper mustache, the small scars from a few fistfights and the strong jaw that always pointed forward. His thick, waxy skin was a rough map of the decades of backbreaking work in the restaurants, kitchens and bars.

At the same moment, outside, the strange, fierce wind ripped through the vacant streets as Demo quickly strode up the Georgia Street hill. Out of habit, he directed his feet to pass by The Classic Grill on his way to our family home on Virginia Street.

Seeing a light softly glowing in the back of the restaurant, Demo placed his hand on the all too familiar door handle and set his feet on the welcome mat outside the door. Looking through the window, past the hand-painted lettering on the door, Demo saw Daphne's hands gently cupping my father's face, like petals on a flower, leaning in too close, her crimson lips moving, their energies engaged at high voltage. He immediately spun around and walked double-time, then sprinted up the steep hill.

Demo burst into the sick room, but seeing my mother lying in bed, he immediately reined back his energy. He gently sat near her on the twin bed that had been his for nearly eighteen years. I walked in and gave Demo a hug as it had been weeks since I attended to his wounds in San Francisco. Demo seemed thrilled to see me, but quickly turned his attention to our mother.

"Better now, Ma?" Demo asked her in a low tone.

Hearing Demo's voice, my mother's eyes fluttered open.

"Demo *mou*. You come back!" She spoke with more strength than I had heard from her in the last week and a half.

"For a little while..." he mumbled imperceptibly. "Until I..."

Abandoning talk of reporting for duty, Demo looked at Alex who was sitting up, playing with small, colorful farm animals I had surprised him with from the downtown Woolworth's.

"Well, he looks pretty good!" Demo observed.

"Nursed him back to health myself," I reported proudly. "Me and my *avgolemono* soup!"

Unlike me, Demo never avoided a conflict and now, head down, he rammed his horns into the question of the evening.

"So what's Pop doing with that blond woman down at the restaurant?" he whispered, leaning toward me.

My mother shot up from bed, feet in motion before they hit the floor. She had heard every word.

"Ma!" Demo called after her. I knew he believed his words would cause a relapse to our mother who had hardly recovered in the first place. "Come back! I'll handle it!"

But my mother was already out the door in her nightgown and had sped halfway across Napa Street, a torpedo seeking its target. Demo ran after her, but I was concerned for Alex's welfare and, for the first time in weeks, I was left alone with no idea what to do next. I secretly did not want to witness the destruction of what was left of our family, but I needed to throw my body over the explosion that would surely come.

At the back of the restaurant, Daphne kept her eyes on my father. "I knew when I saw you that we belonged together." She lowered her eyes, searching for the words to continue.

My father, one step from falling into the dark universe with no gravity, no center, just more space, measured every second, every breath between them.

"I was going through a few of my mother's things." Daphne's voice was hushed. "And I found this."

Dipping into her purse, Daphne quickly held up a tattered black and white snapshot. There on the creased photo, a young Achilles stood next to a vibrant blond woman with free-spirited curly hair. Her arms snaked around him in an enthusiastic embrace of young love.

"The waitress at The Redding Hotel. Gloria! Remember?"

She held her breath, waiting for my father's reaction.

"The Redding Hotel!"

Daphne pulled my father close to her.

"When I first walked in, you seemed familiar, and I thought you were mine." Daphne stated plainly. "Now I know — you are my father."

The earth stopped its revolution, the stars were frozen in their astral path and time screeched to a stop.

"What you saying?" My father was unsure if the universe had played its celestial music too loudly and distorted her words.

He snapped the photo from her hands and brought it closer to his eyes. The Redding Hotel filled the background as it had on the photo with Theo Vasili and himself that sat on his shelf in the back kitchen.

"It's my mother. Gloria! The waitress? At the hotel? Remember? The Redding Hotel?"

My father did not breathe. He frantically rewound the filmstrip of his memory, restaurants, kitchens, bars and women flashing past, as he attempted to focus on one woman in one location he had drifted from and discarded as unnecessary history decades ago.

"You were gone before you knew about me. Mama always called you Johnny. Johnny the Greek. So I came down here looking for Johnny, a Greek dishwasher. And I finally found you!"

Daphne wore a brave smile, waiting for my father's reaction. Her eyes took in the restaurant, the empty tables, the quiet kitchen.

"I'm here! I found my home!" She was like a small child, reunited with her father after being lost for a long afternoon at the county fair. My father scrutinized the photo, then studied Daphne, who quite certainly resembled her mother. He pulled back to study her carefully and allowed more space between them that befitted a father and a daughter.

"Your mother, Gloria. You say she is gone?"

"Yes. Two years now." Daphne's face darkened, unsure of his reaction.

"I did not know..." My father sputtered now. "About you. About a baby."

"Mama said you and your brother left for another job. Guess that was Vasili." Daphne tied up the details as if my father was unable to piece them together himself.

Daphne threw her arms around my father — now her father.

"I found you!" Then, more seriously she whispered, "I found you."

"Then Alex..." My father broke away, calculating on his own.

"You're his — "

"Papou...his grandfather."

My father spoke the word reverently, as if he were the grandfather to the Christ child himself. His eyes scanned Daphne's face closely while madly recomputing his passion and digesting his surprise.

"A daughter..." he whispered to himself. "I have daughter."

The phone began to ring in the kitchen but neither my father nor Daphne noticed the shrill, persistent interruption.

"I'm sorry, but here I am!" Daphne hugged my father again.

At that moment, my mother swung open the front door and slammed it shut almost in the same motion. The glass rattled with her rage and indignation. Demo stood behind her, closely watching everyone, eyes fixed on my father, in the wake of my mother's power.

"*Yannis Achilléas Gregori Pappayannis!* What you are doing? To me!" she roared.

The phone continued its piercing ring, screaming for someone to answer.

"Chrisoula!"

My father was immediately stricken by the supremely uncomfortable timing the events had taken on. He was caught in guilty circumstances, when with this new truth revealed, he was in fact innocent. Only his mind was guilty of wandering too far.

"I know you love her!" My mother charged forward to my father.

"I want to tell you…" Daphne began her explanation like a wispy breeze against a gale-force tempest.

"You I do not listen to!" My mother dismissed her as she stared down my father.

"*Achilléas*, I am not your wife — I am your life!"

At that moment, I arrived at the front door of The Classic Grill with little Alex thrown over my shoulder, wrapped in a heavy quilt. My uncle stepped in behind me, overnight bag in hand, ready for his sleepover with my father. He could hardly keep his footing in the wild, windy night, trying to make sense of our family's gathering at this odd hour.

All I could do was scream at all of them.

"I called a million times! The Symposium! Come *now*!"

As a young immigrant arriving after the 1906 earthquake and city-wide fire, my father had learned how the earth shook for sixty agonizing seconds, leaving thousands living in tents, their homes and business incinerated, their lives plunged into misery. But those tales did nothing to prepare him for that evening. The Symposium, my father's entire world, was ablaze in a giant orange inferno. The glaring heat infused by the relentless gale-force wind kept us at a distance. My father's marble floors, his expensive gold leaf columns, his graceful chandeliers and the dark wood tables he had lovingly selected, ignited and burned before he had seated his first customer.

My father's carefully nurtured dream, the palace he promised the goddess Athena, had turned on us and had become a hostile, threatening creature, a monster of nature. The Symposium raged at our family, a two-story fireball, as if it intended to hurt all of us. The restaurant had been consumed by evil gods who wanted revenge from a crime that I could only identify as my father's stubborn pride. Feeling the intense heat from the fire a block away, I was certain that pride was not offense enough to warrant a punishment like this. Three modern fire engines attempted to extinguish the blaze but appeared to be as useful as Alex's toy fire truck rolling across his pillow.

My father stood on the sidewalk across the street from the fire in silent shock, knowing there was nothing he could do but endure seeing his dream melt before his eyes. My mother was planted by his side while the rest of us stood huddled nearby like an aimless choir that had forgotten the words to their song. I held Alex tightly, but I soon walked back about a block from the fire so that he would not breathe the thick, gray smoke. I observed my family as a group, a black silhouette against the angry red and yellow flames of pain and evil. They watched The Symposium expire that night, as if they were holding the hand of a dying relative with whom they had never really become acquainted. As the dark, wicked smoke overtook the glaring light of the fire, my mother slowly crumpled against my father and fell onto the dirt.

In years past, Demo and I had always relied on my parents to fix things large and small, believing that their optimism and hard work would piece together a solution. But this time, my father and mother, together as a team, could do nothing to bandage this blistering wound that I knew would sear a brand on our family for decades to come.

EIGHTY-ONE

"Whoa! Like the whole thing burned down?" Jason gasped. "Your dad — how did he take that?"

My little group of listeners was devastated to learn that my father's dream restaurant had burned to a pile of metal and ash.

"Did your mother leave him?" Mariam pressed. "He was such a fool!"

"The fire started in the kitchen, near the back door — that's what the fire captain told our family. Of course, my father's little candle was the only thing that was lit back there." I sighed and shook my head. "And he hadn't activated the fire insurance on The Symposium. He was waiting until the grand opening two weeks later, trying to save money."

"After how hard your folks worked…" Zach reflected on the situation. He sat back, crumpling his paper cup into shapes and looked up. "So I guess your dad learned his lesson."

I smiled and shook my head. Yannis Achilléas Gregori Pappayannis never learned anything easy.

EIGHTY-TWO

My mother slept most of the afternoon while my father paced the room, wearing out a path on the Greek hand-woven rug and the hardwood floors. Early that morning, Daphne whisked Alex to her apartment and Theo Vasili volunteered to take charge of The Classic Grill for the next few days. Demo spent the night with Theo Vasili, then left for San Francisco the next morning, knowing there was nothing else to be done for The Symposium.

That left my father to hover over his life, his love, my mother. I split my time between cooking soup at home for my mother and then hurrying to The Classic Grill to help out in the kitchen. The tension between my parents was raw and wounded and frankly, I was happy to escape. I felt like the wrung out dishrag we used to wipe the counters. My hands craved only the simple rhythm of chopping an avalanche of vegetables, tossing them in a frying pan of hot olive oil. I wanted to hide my devastation in the bottom of our giant gravy saucepan. After all, The Symposium was not only my father's dream. It could have been my future, my place in the world. But none of that mattered. It was all gone before it began.

Much later, my mother told me what had transpired between them that day. My father, weary of pacing, sat down near her on the bed. He urgently needed my mother to wake from her slumber — not only to determine if she was well after her illness and fainting episode, but also to establish her emotional state. Had he pulled so far away on his tether that my mother already had cut him off? My father, who liked to wait for nothing, grew increasingly uncomfortable while contemplating his past actions. Sitting on the bed, feet nervously tapping, he took stock of his new situation: No restaurant. No insurance. A new adult daughter. A grandson. But now all that seemed unimportant to him as my father could only worry if he still possessed the most important thing in his life — the respect and love of my mother.

An hour later, my father brought in a cup of chamomile tea and set it near my sleeping mother. She stirred in bed and opened her eyes as my father hurried to her side.

"Chrisoula." My father spoke gently. "You come back. To me."

My mother raised herself on one arm and attempted to sit up.

"Where are the boys?" Her words were faint. "They eat?"

"Alex, he feel good now." He offered her the cup of tea. "He with his mother. With Daphne."

"Your *thygatéra*, your daughter."

My father, stepped away from her bed, avoiding her direct gaze.

"And your daughter — her mother? Where she now?" My mother released her arrow, aimed at the heart of the matter.

"Gone now. Daphne say she die two years ago." He rushed the words out of his mouth so he could hurry back to her side. He sat close to her now, taking her hand as he did the night in Sparta when he proposed marriage. "I just stupid dishwasher. I know this woman a month. Maybe two. Before I go to Greece and I meet you."

My mother's eyes narrowed, attempting to sort out the facts that had suddenly blown in like the destructive wind from the night before.

"You know about this daughter?" My mother slowly found strength in her voice. "You know you have *koritsi* — a baby girl?"

My father's fingers inched toward her wedding band. He seemed relieved she had not taken it off.

"Daphne, her mother. Her name Gloria. She write to me in San Francisco, before I leave to Greece. I no come back to Redding. To her. I could not read...the letter. I throw it away."

My father suddenly needed air. He walked to the window that was open a crack. "I never read this letter."

"You love her? Daphne's mother?" My mother waded into the dense, dark swamp that most wives would let lie quietly, forever holding secrets.

"She was a good girl, I think. American pretty girl who like me. I no remember her so much. I am sorry for this." He hung his head and stared at the floor.

My mother was not sure if my father was sorry for not remembering Daphne's mother, for engaging in a romance with her, or because he ignored a letter that he assumed confirmed his paternity — and who knew what else? My father returned to sit near my mother who was regaining her strength — and her practicality — by the minute.

"Now we have two leases, no insurance money, bills from the construction, new daughter, new grandson and son who go to war. Demo, he leave soon."

With this, my mother slowly pulled her legs out of bed, swung them to the floor and walked away from my father, staring at St. Sophia high on her shelf.

"What we do now?" My father looked up meekly.

"Cook. Work at the restaurant. Pay the bills." She looked up at my father, her voice a flat monotone. "I will wait for *my* son to come home."

My father rushed to my mother and embraced her as he had on their honeymoon, when they had sailed to their new home. He pressed himself around her thin frame, hoping her goodness and honesty might become absorbed by his body and soul.

"Chrisoula." He searched her hazel eyes that had not changed since the day he saw her at the nightclub. "Will you still take me?"

"I have to," she sighed. "I love your grandson."

EIGHTY-THREE

Most families would have broken up and drifted apart, without much care about what happened next. Each member of the Pappayannis family, however, possessed one thing in common that fused us together, the thread that never snapped. Our restaurant was the safety net that held us together. It was our livelihood, our pastime and somehow, after the twelve- or fourteen-hour days, it remained our love.

After the devastating fire at The Symposium, we invented new ways to pull in a few more dollars every day. Juggling food shortages, we attracted new customers while keeping the old ones. We invented The Homefront Special of the Day: Gluten meatballs with spaghetti sauce renamed Patriots' Delight. Our Victory Lasagna was meatless, featuring the vegetables from my mother's garden. We began to feature "loafs" as we had never done before: our Stars and Stripes Loaf was in truth a loaf of soybeans with a tomato glaze. The most popular of all, our Mare Island Meatloaf, utilized ground tripe, kidneys, tongue, heart, liver — all cheap parts of the cow. Of course, mounds of sautéed onions and garlic made it delicious. The only extravagance my mother allowed each week was to pass me a few quarters, so that I could slip into the movies at The Hanlon or The Empress, both theatres on Virginia Street. It was my small reward for caring for her and Alex and for my enthusiastic labor every day at the restaurant before and after school, often long into the night. My father worked non-stop, saying little, head down. He never discussed his failure with me and certainly did not speak of Demo. Only once, after he learned that an untended candle had started the blaze, I heard him whisper, "What have I done?"

EIGHTY-FOUR

"How could he still be so stubborn?" Aman asked, passing out mini-cheeseburgers to everyone. I slid her a ten-dollar bill to pay for them all, not wanting her to cover our snacks. After all, my new young friends had listened to my story much longer than I had imagined.

"He wasn't humbled by all of this?" asked Zach, possibly picking up a few lessons about humility as a father.

"That's what my father would do," Aman grumbled. "He would pretend he is still king of the house."

"For sure." Jesús sunk his teeth into his cheeseburger and nodded knowingly, as if an arrogant father ruled his family too.

"But there was one thing we hadn't taken care of that was more difficult than rebuilding our restaurant business."

I suspected they already knew.

EIGHTY-FIVE

I appeared on Natalya's doorstep the night before my brother was scheduled to leave for basic training. Demo thought it was better if I came alone to see him off at the bus station, telling my mother on the phone that he would be allowed to come home to Vallejo before he was shipped off for active duty. Demo didn't want her to worry at that point, saying he would only be gone for six weeks of basic training. My mother was not happy with this arrangement but honored Demo's wishes.

Of course, I brought him the obligatory shoeboxes of *koulourakia* she had prepared. But Demo, attempting to avoid attention of any kind, left them behind. The evening before he would board the bus to report for duty at the windswept, desolate Fort Ord Army base, Natalya invited their friends to her home for a farewell gathering. I cooked up a rich, flavorful vegetable stew and corn bread with baked apples for dessert and Natalya bought a case of cold beer for their show business friends. Demo did not talk about being anxious to start a new life in the United States Army, but his eyes were dark sockets and he appeared even thinner, if that was possible.

At the Greyhound bus station on Seventh and Market streets, I waited for my brother to stow his small overnight bundle in the luggage compartment. He embraced Natalya and then stood looking at me, hands at his side.

In one more second the giant hand of the U.S. government would swipe my beautiful brother in its palm and squeeze tightly. When the hand again opened, a soldier would appear, identical to all other soldiers, designed to kill, destined for injuries, bravery demanded, fear expected and ignored.

"Do a good job on Pop's taxes." Demo flashed me a wry smile. "Write if you can. Let me know how things are going."

I hugged Demo tighter than I ever thought possible. I wanted to enlist, go with him and never be torn away from him again. My lips quivered, but Demo was already showing his courage.

"Take care of The Grill — it's all we got now." He managed a little grin and then looked toward Natalya who had given us a private moment. "And keep in touch with her. She might need a Pappayannis around."

With one more hug, Demo stepped up into the bulky, worn out bus, the driver munching a fat sandwich like it was any ordinary day. The folding doors squeaked to a close and the bus roared away. My heart felt as if it was ripped from my body, trailing along after the bus, like shoes tied to a newlyweds' car, but leaving bloody streaks behind instead of streamers of happiness. Natalya asked if I wanted her to wait until my bus departed to Vallejo, but I just shook my head. I sat alone on my outdoor bench, waiting for the Number Five to take me home.

I was thinking about what life would be like without knowing that Demo was only a ferry or bus ride away. A paper cup of hot chocolate came into my view and I looked up to see Natalya holding the cup, smiling.

"It's not your chicken soup, but it will make you feel better." Natalya sat down next to me after all. "He'll be back after the six weeks. And then back after his active duty. He has to be."

Sipping my hot chocolate, I knew exactly what she meant.

EIGHTY-SIX

I propped up a large paper calendar on the kitchen shelf, in place of the incinerated St. Nicholas icon and the reverential red candle, both disastrously relocated to The Symposium. I crossed off each day Demo served in basic training on that big calendar, every day closer to his return.

I was not much of a letter writer, but I took on that job for our family, since I was the only one who could actually write in English. I did not have exciting news for Demo, but I tried to embellish the goings-on at The Classic Grill: how our mother and Alex were gaining strength every day, whether my new Toffee Pudding with Maple Sauce — sweetened with dates, not sugar — was a hit, and news from Natalya whom I called each week. Demo's days were occupied with marching, climbing, eating and assembling and re-assembling a rifle. In a short letter he wrote that because he was lithe and rangy, he had no problem keeping up with his unit with no physical complaints. But the food was less than spectacular, he wrote, and the Army mess hall could take a lesson from The Classic Grill kitchen. He offered no mention of his dreams of acting on stage, but I was sure he thought the Army was just a detour demanded of him, not a destination. The theatre remained his reality.

Six exhausting weeks later, my brother arrived in his uniform at the waterfront in Vallejo to say his goodbyes to our family before he left for active duty. He arrived on the ferry in full uniform, looking quite dashing, I will admit, with his Army cap jauntily set to one side. A new costume for my brother, the actor.

We walked side-by-side back to the restaurant so that Demo could say his goodbyes. Happily matching my brother's pace, I pretended we were walking home from school without a care in the world. But in fact, I was terrified for him. Demo would leave us this time for more training and then be shipped overseas on a tour to Europe or the Pacific. Looking at his uniform, I was reminded that the harsh world had intruded on my brother's life and that of every other able-bodied man of his age and older. They had to push aside their dreams, their lovers, their children to do this job they never asked for.

We walked straight to The Classic Grill, a neutral place — not our home. That evening, my mother had closed the restaurant an hour early so we could concentrate on Demo's farewell. My father's goodbye could be simple and short. Instinctively we headed up the alley to the back door of the restaurant. It just felt like the right thing to do.

I watched Demo's face as he pulled open the screen door. Not a pan or a pot had changed since he left for basic training. My brother's eyes softened as he gazed at the kitchen in which he and I had spent many long afternoons, so many endless evenings. Mr. Chris was up to his elbows in suds, Petros sautéed onions for tomorrow's loaf special and Panos shelled peas into a wide stainless steel bowl. My mother and Theo Vasili's faces lit up at the sight of my brother. The crew rushed out of the doorway and covered Demo in a layer of embraces and talk, talk, talk.

Except my father.

After five minutes of chatter, my brother glanced at his watch. Time had run out. Everyone filtered inside except my mother and my uncle. Theo Vasili surrounded Demo in his long and loving arms and then slapped him on the back, man-to-man.

"Show them Greeks can fight!" Long tears rolled down his face. "*Deíxte tis dynámeis su*. Show them your strength!"

He turned away, as my mother clasped Demo tightly. She crossed herself, mumbling in Greek and pulled a large silver cross from her coat pocket. In one long breath, syllables fused together, she exhaled a prayer.

Lord, please protect my son! Panagia, protect my son! Bring him back to us. In the Name of the Father, and the Son, and the Holy Spirit. Amen.

As if it was an enormous magnet attracting divine energy from the universe, my mother lifted the weighty Greek cross on its long silver chain high in the air.

"Take! For your protection!" She shoved the cross into Demo's hand — the only defense she could offer him against the Germans or the Japanese. She clutched him again, I thought, to imprint his molecules on her skin. Then she turned to face the back door.

"*Achilléas! Ella!* Come! Say goodbye to your son!" Her voice was a deep, mournful cry.

We waited.

"*Achilléas!* He is leaving!" She called louder, bleeding for my father's attention.

Still, we did not hear my father's heavy shoes shuffle to the back door.

With a nearly imperceptible shake of his head, Demo turned toward the Greyhound bus station and his new life as a soldier in the U.S. Army. I followed, impulsively hooking my arm in his to keep him close to me — or simply to keep my footing, I didn't know.

My mother, however, would not accept my father's petrified heart and calcified spirit.

"*Achilléas!* Your son! He is leaving!" She was screaming it now.

Demo and I proceeded toward the bus station while my mother begged my father. We left her calling for the response that would never come.

Inside, my father remained seated at his prized bar made of nickel, listening as my mother's pleadings ran down his own impermeable iron surface, pooling around his ankles. Tears thick in his eyes, rooted in his seat, my father could not move his legs or his arms as he tried to suck breath into his chest. Months ago, he would not give his son a blessing to become an actor, destined to pursue an unconventional life in San Francisco, without participation in his own grand plans for a restaurant. Now my father had allowed his first-born son, an eighteen-year-old, fresh-faced American boy, to head into the black bog of war without a light — or a blessing.

EIGHTY-SEVEN

My little group had no words. They were uncomfortably quiet and I realized they thought my father was a monster. Finally, Zach, a father himself, cleared his throat.

"Uh, how did Demo take it?" he asked solemnly.

"Perhaps he might have expected it, but I don't think so." I tilted my head to one side and shrugged, like the gesture Theo Vasili made when he was unsure. "We both assumed my father would at least come to say goodbye."

Jason was the first of the group to react.

"How did your mother take *that* bullshit?" He called out my father's action for what it was.

That was a more complicated story.

EIGHTY-EIGHT

For weeks my mother removed herself from my father's presence, as she had little to say, her emotions had run dry. She consulted a Greek Orthodox priest about a new selection of icons, as she could make no mistakes in a perilous situation like war. She replaced St. Nicholas with golden-winged Holy Archangel Michael clutching a staff in one hand and balancing a silver orb in the other. She invited St. George, who stood victorious over a slithery, fire-breathing dragon to join the watch over Demo, as well as St. Christopher who unknowingly carried the Christ child safely across a river. And my mother lovingly placed a photo of Demo, handsome in his Army uniform, on the shelf among his holy watchdogs.

I occupied my time with school and extra hours at the restaurant. Working side-by-side with my father, I only spoke to him to learn which cleaning duties were mine, when I would type the daily menu and which of us would pick up the bread order. My mother, however, took it upon herself to invent ways to generate income. I jumped at the opportunity to help. Together we doubled the vegetable and fruit production in her garden, using much of her produce in our cooking at The Classic Grill. I sold lettuce, zucchini, carrots and tomatoes from a cart as my father had done decades ago in San Francisco. My mother created pastries with honey, molasses, maple syrup — ingredients that were not rationed — and sold them to customers thrilled to enjoy sweet desserts and pretend — just for a moment — it was not wartime.

We learned from Demo's letters that he had been sent overseas to Italy after additional training at Camp Roberts in the central part of California. My mother and I agreed that these new business ventures kept us from fixating on my brother's welfare and my father's iron-clad stubbornness.

She later told me that the grand idea came to her during an afternoon of cake production in her kitchen. As she folded flour into her *karidopita* cake batter, the dessert we advertised as Sweet Freedom Cake, she contemplated the future of the Pappayannis family. My father had valued his feelings miles above her simple and honest desires and had not apologized. My mother said she realized she could singlehandedly pour venomous ink into the clear water of our family's future and poison any chances of making a clean start for all of us. But she would not emulate her own father back home in the village who had harbored bitter resentment, always reminding her of her shortcomings and severing communication like the twisted head of a chicken.

While pouring the *karidopita* batter into the pan, she revealed to me that she had noticed my father was quieter, more dutiful than ever, working at The Classic Grill before dawn and well after closing. In the early morning hours, she once caught a glimpse of him silently sitting on Demo's bed, and she wondered if my father needed to wipe clean his conscience just like he scrubbed the counters in the restaurant kitchen. She later told me that while sliding her walnut cake into the hot oven, she knew that she alone could help my father open his heart to Demo. And as she poured the sweet hot syrup on her cooled cake, the idea burst open in her mind, nearly blinding her. Jolted by the revelation, my mother's hands sloshed the syrup onto the kitchen table but for the first time in weeks a smile tugged at the corners of her mouth.

The next day, my mother and I prepared every dish in her Greek village repertoire of recipes and I hauled them all down to The Classic Grill: *pastitso*, Greek lasagna; *dolmathes*, stuffed grape leaves; *fasolikia*, stewed green beans in tomato sauce; *skourdalia*, garlic sauce; and *marides*, small white fish sautéed in olive oil and lemon. In the kitchen, Theo Vasili cooked up every meat our ration books could afford: tender lamb with lemon and oregano, mouthwatering roasted chicken with lemon and rosemary, *plaki*, swordfish baked with mounds of tomato and onions and roasted zucchini stuffed with rice, currants and spices. We laid out our delicacies on the back tables in the dining room and announced to our friends, favorite customers and a few local cousins that the Pappayannis family was welcoming two new members to our family.

My mother again closed the doors to our restaurant for the afternoon. Instead of hiding my father's relationship with another woman in his early life, my mother was one step ahead of the evil darts aimed by the town gossips. With an open heart, she would celebrate Daphne and her adored, wide-eyed Alex, now taller by two inches. And for the first time in months, we enjoyed one happy afternoon that was truly a feast for the gods. My mother was careful that the most wicked tongues in the community — both American and Greek — came early to our family circle to witness that Daphne and Alex were loved and welcomed by us, their new family. Theo Vasili played Dionysus to our group of fifty guests and made sure his cheap Napa wine flowed from the heavy ceramic jug all afternoon.

After our mouths were jammed with stuffed grape leaves and feta cheese, my mother, taking the role of the patriarch of the family, raised her glass toward Daphne and Alex. Daphne was seated next to my father, and Alex happily sat at the counter inhaling an ice cream sundae. My mother made sure I was by her side.

"Today we bring two new people to our Pappayannis family. Achilles' daughter — now our daughter — and grandson. Daphne and Alexandros." Their names rolled off her tongue in their original Greek and she held her glass high in the air, her hazel eyes bright. "And now they belong to all of us! And Alex is five years old today, his birthday! *Yámas!* To all of us!"

The hearty chorus of "*Yámas!*" resounded from the crowd, filling the room, filling my heart.

I had only known Daphne for less than a year, but I could see that my mother's generosity deeply touched my new half-sister. Because of my parents, this wildflower that grew unruly in the field had transformed into a lovely rose, poised with newfound confidence. Daphne now had a place in the world — one that unconditionally welcomed her and her son. They were home now.

Suddenly, my father took the floor. Dressed in his worn suit, he gently slipped his arm around my mother's waist.

"For this woman I love. *Ee zoí mou*, my life. Her heart big enough for all of us. Most of all, me. *Efharistoh*, thank you, Chrisoula." He sipped humbly from his glass and pulled my mother's small, sturdy body close to his. I thought I saw him lean on her, just a little.

Later, my mother told me that at that precise moment, she felt the rusty hinges of the door to my father's heart creak open and saw the narrowest sliver of light emanating from within. Her mission was to pry open that door and allow love to flow from his heart, the love she was certain was dammed behind high, solid walls. She would prepare my father's heart for

Demo's return from the war, when our family could be whole and happy again. It was just a matter of time.

I slowly made my way to the back of the restaurant dining room, in awe of my mother. She understood each person's needs just as she carefully tended the plants in her garden — the roses, zucchini, onions, potatoes, oregano, basil, the dahlias. Watching her elegantly move across the room to warmly greet each guest, I wasn't so sure she needed to pray to St. Sophia for guidance any longer. She had knitted our remaining family together — without saintly interference.

EIGHTY-NINE

"So your mother, she be holding it together for your family," Jesús summarized. "And she never complain?"

I didn't want to tell my group that after Demo left, my mother often slipped away to bed with a massive headache. The pain had marched forward in pointy black combat boots and surrounded her brain. I spared my little group from the memory of her anguish — and my distress as I watched her writhe on clammy sheets, her face ashen.

"Bad headaches," I minimized the truth. "But no, she never complained. In those days my family did not know what a migraine was — or even how to pronounce it. All I could do was bring cold towels for her head and strong chamomile tea for her stomach."

"So what happened to the restaurant?" asked Jason, leaning forward, wanting more.

"And to Demo?" from Jesús who seemed to take a liking to my brother.

"And your father?" Zach asked, maybe because he was a father.

Aman looked at me and placed her small hand over mine, black nail polish like tiny chips of coal on her fingertips. "And, tell us, *Dādā*...just what happened to you?"

NINETY

For a kid who didn't much like English composition class, I became a librarian of letters. Every few weeks, one from Demo appeared in our mailbox, and occasionally Tetsuya's family sent a letter on Army-issued paper. Demo and Tetsuya were scout bees exiled from our hive, sending word home to the colony to which they belonged. When we received a letter from Demo, I quickly read it out loud to my mother and later to the kitchen staff. Tetsuya's short, factual letters were obviously dictated to someone else to write. I sang his words into the ears of the kitchen crew as they were starved for news from their treasured friend, team member and vegetable expert. The postman also delivered an avalanche of notifications from the bill collectors to my father's outstretched hand every morning at The Classic Grill.

On the other side of town, Theo Vasili's creditors in the Chinese gambling parlor in Lower Georgia unfortunately demanded payback. According to my father's plan, The Symposium should have been floating in money by this time. We were forced to secure a second loan on The Classic Grill to pay for The Symposium, now just a sorrowful, smoky memory. However, World War II had provided one positive side effect — a meteoric increase in the daily income of The Classic Grill. Mare Island was jumping because of the long hours at the The Yard which during World War II, produced seventeen submarines, four submarine tenders, thirty-one destroyer escorts, thirty-three small craft and more than 300 landing craft.

As the first rays of dawn broke through the fog that was thick as gray meringue, a line of hungry customers lined up outside our restaurant. In the evening, we kept the bar open for those sailors who wanted one more drink before they headed off for a staggeringly drunken evening in Lower Georgia that usually ended in a brawl on the street.

But we were not denied that second loan at the bank. Before the bank meeting, I suggested to my father that we ask a frequent customer and real estate agent, Mr. Robert Jameson, to accompany him to do the talking.

He was a breakfast regular who sported a three-piece suit, his heavy gold pocket watch hanging on a substantial chain. Mr. Jameson had no foreign accent, olive complexion or bristly mustache to deter him from clinching a deal. He became our family's bridge to the established banking world, quickly smoothing over any questions of our legitimacy as an "ethnic business." With his help and our restaurant's spectacular balance sheet, we were granted the loan. Every week after that, Mr. Jameson received a freshly baked apple pie from my mother's kitchen, with our heartfelt thanks.

Soon after, Theo Vasili carried a fat stack of cash to the dank gambling den where, months ago, he had collected it in the first place. Later that day, I saw my uncle slowly drag his feet back inside The Classic Grill. He sipped coffee at the counter, after drinking a full bottle of wine in Lower Georgia on his way to the restaurant. He sat at the counter that long afternoon, unusually silent, never taking off his coat, wounded.

"I want to help your father. But I no help him." The Symposium was another dream unachieved for my uncle.

With all the added restaurant duties, I could hardly keep up with my studies at school, scurrying to the restaurant after the last bell in the hallway shrieked our release at three o'clock. Few classmates bore this weight, and my friendships with other students deteriorated due to lack of use, like the rusty old mixer sitting in the back of our restaurant. I belonged to my family.

Even during wartime, students participated in after-school sports, clubs and plays, as Demo wanted to do. They pretended their lives were normal, without the tension of Hitler, Hirohito, blackouts and the looming threat that older boys would soon be swallowed up by the military, their futures suddenly uncertain. Only Gus, another fellow Greek-American classmate, struggled with the burden of working after school and into the evening at his father's small wooden-floor grocery store located in Lower Georgia, near the Mare Island entrance. He sold liquor to sailors and bread and fresh produce to the rest of us. Occasionally a sailor would appear at the store with a satchel full of butter, hinting around to see what the black market would bear for his bounty. I had given Gus and his father precise instructions that I was good for ten dollars whenever butter mysteriously materialized on the scene, never requiring a history of the contraband that was bound for pastry in my mother's kitchen.

NINETY-ONE

Taki sat on his customary stool at our restaurant and sipped his usual black coffee. But his spirit had crumpled and his energy did not reach the outer edges of his body to lift his limbs. Taki sat there as limp as the mop I used for the nightly cleaning.

My father was out of the restaurant and Theo Vasili and I were working the counter and handing out menus. We kept Taki's cup full, as we knew he was exhausted from his weekly visit to Nikko.

Each day, Taki spent money on a Greyhound bus ticket to get to San Francisco. He walked to Van Ness Avenue, then spent seven cents more to catch the H Line, then transfer to the D Line and walk to Letterman Hospital. There Nikko struggled with the stump, all that remained of his leg that had once propelled him to become the star running back in Vallejo Senior High School football games. Taki spent the same amount of time and money on the return trip back to his small home, four blocks away from ours. After a week or two of the daily commute, Nikko mercifully insisted that his father take Saturday and Sunday off to stay home and rest.

I toasted bread and served it to Taki with butter and jam. Hoping to cheer him, I waved off his ten cents to pay for it.

"How Nikko is feeling?" My uncle warmed Taki's coffee. "He no have pain?"

"Hrumph! He no got a leg. Who want him now?" Taki looked into his cup, nearly falling into it from exhaustion. "And a Greek girl wanna marry man with no leg? Maria Kotsakis? Tina Dimitriou? Tassi Stratos? They no want husband with one leg."

Nikko was the most handsome and good-natured charmer I had met in our Greek community, yet I had no answers as to how a missing leg might affect his marriage possibilities. Taki dropped his head onto his arms which were resting on the table and dragged his face along his long cotton shirt sleeves. "God help him when I am gone."

I gently pushed a few letters from Demo and Tetsuya near his coffee cup, hoping to distract him from Nikko's tragedy. He lifted his head, wiped his glasses and proceeded to slowly read with one finger tracing beneath each word.

I worked my polishing rag in vigorous circles while contemplating the war, Nikko, his leg and my father. I often wondered what my father would do if Demo came back injured. Would my father travel two-and-a-half-hours each way to visit my brother in San Francisco? I was doubtful that he would sacrifice his energy — mental or physical — to help Demo feel whole again. I realized he would be unable to inspire a son with a missing limb, encouraging him every day to try harder, that a good life could be his. At that moment, I vowed I would never be like my father. I would never give up on anyone in my family — including him.

NINETY-TWO

A few weeks later, during a rollicking Saturday night in the restaurant, we served fifty Mare Island Meatloaf Specials and filled battalions of glasses brimming with amber scotch and fizzy soda. I closed down the restaurant and lingered in the kitchen long after my father and mother had trudged home for the evening. At ten o'clock, I observed that my parents were drained of moneymaking energy. I volunteered to stay until the two remaining barflies sucked the last drops of liquor from their glasses and thumped them on the bar for a final percussion to their evening's drinking. At my age, I was not able to serve liquor, but I could make sure no one fell off a barstool.

Around midnight, I good-naturedly escorted a Navy officer and his date who was wearing a cheap fox stole and rhinestone earrings, towards the door and bid them a cheerful farewell. After all, for them, a late-night drinking binge was a blissful distraction from duty at Mare Island. But to our family, their merriment translated to ten-and-a-half extra dollars of profit.

Alone in the dim kitchen, I sorted out my thoughts as if I was reaching into a brown paper sack, evaluating the juicy lemons from the over-ripe. I shuffled aimlessly in the kitchen and decided to stand in Tetsuya's customary place, behind the vegetable station. I was hoping to calm my unruly feelings about this war that, to my seventeen-year-old self, seemed to have no end. Standing in Tetsuya's place, I realized I had never for a minute allowed him out of my mind or away from my heart. At his vegetable station, I tightly gripped his favorite kitchen cutlery. I ran my finger over the Japanese hiragana symbols representing his name that he had carved into the wooden handle of his treasured knife. てつや — Tetsuya.

Occupying Tetsuya's space, I felt like a child, wishing the unwishable, wanting Tetsuya to come back to me. I deeply missed our daily chats, like a forlorn dog searches for his absent master, desperately seeking a gentle touch or an encouraging word. My imagination drifted to Tetsuya enduring what the government called "internment camps," the happy-face word slapped onto the jail camps. All I knew was that a six-hour car ride to the northern border of California, a barbed wire fence and big guns lodged in tall, wooden towers on stilts kept me apart from Tetsuya. His simple letters stated only facts. He worked as a camp mess hall cook and had taken charge of preparing the daily meals. He, his sons and wife were getting along. He hoped we were all well. I understood his impersonal letters told nothing, revealed nothing, because all communication from the camp was heavily censored.

But none of that mattered now. Every day at the concentration camp pushed Tetsuya and his family further away from their former American lives, and further cracked any trust in the country they believed to be their home. My second father would never know that I had desperately wanted to help him. But I did not stand up for him when he was swept away to the concentration camp. And after he was gone, I simply planted my feet behind his vegetable station where the floor was worn from his steps. I didn't know what else to do.

I decided to scrub our menagerie of well-worn stainless steel and aluminum pots and pans until late into the night, avoiding sleepless hours alone in my twin bed. Demo was gone, Tetsuya gone. The lack of information from both of my heroes was a constant twisting in my gut. I wanted to set the clock forward to my next birthday, when I would turn eighteen and be eligible to strut down to the Draft Board, pull my bony shoulders back and enlist. Admittedly, I was terrified to fight the mighty German army or be shipped to a south seas atoll to fight in bloody hand-to-hand combat. But at that point, I was willing to take the chance that my meager efforts overseas would somehow help bring Demo and Tetsuya home.

I worked through my thoughts as I scrubbed the soup cauldrons, frying pans, double boilers and stock pots while the new light of day kissed the kitchen window with a special delivery of optimism. It worked magic, at least temporarily. Maybe today would be different. Maybe today we would hear good news about Tetsuya or Demo. As I finished drying the last gleaming sauté pan, I realized my world was built on maybes, each day a playing card that might flip over to reveal a winning ace or a miserable two. I only hoped that my midnight meditation on two of the people I loved most would push good fate in their direction, and keep away the Evil Eye — which, of course, I did not believe in — but wanted to placate anyway.

NINETY-THREE

The faces of Aman, Mariam, Jesús and Jason stared at me, perplexed, as if they could not make sense of my story. Zach, obviously much older than the rest, wore a gloomy, knowing look. Had my young listeners been taught next to nothing about these concentration camps? I did not forget that the U.S. government's official name for these places was internment camps, in an attempt to sanitize the image of the confined jails that held Japanese-American citizens against their will, their rights stripped away with no appeal. A four-year sentence without a trial.

"You didn't read about this in school?"

"We studied it for a few hours in eighth grade," Mariam shrugged. "We saw some pictures on the Internet."

"It happened forever ago — and the photos weren't in color." Jason stirred his soda with a straw. "Like it won't really happen again, so...."

I told them we — the non-Japanese — did not want Tetsuya, his family or any of the kids in school to be hauled off to who-knows-where. But we stood aside, as if we had no voices, like everyone else in our community while our friends and neighbors walked toward trains to take them away.

"We knew our friends were not traitors. But no one dared stand up to the government, after bombing raids shredded Pearl Harbor and over two thousand people died." I guess I was rationalizing now. "No one cared what we thought — we were just a bunch of immigrants ourselves."

I pushed myself back from the small table and shuffled a few steps away. The remorse of having done nothing for Tetsuya still haunted me, more than seventy years later. I pulled off my glasses and wiped the dampness from the lenses.

When I returned to the table to forge ahead with my story, I wanted to take a moment and explain to my group the Loyalty Questionnaire that Tetsuya, his family and Japanese concentration camp prisoners seventeen years-and-older were forced to complete.

Their blank expressions told me they had learned none of this history.

"The older generation, the Issei, was not permitted to become citizens because of the anti-alien land laws created back in the early 1900s. The American people, the government, were terrified of a different race," I explained. "Different looks, different language and a new group of smart, hard workers who many Caucasians believed would take over their jobs, their world."

The kids nodded. That painful reality was familiar to all of us second-generation immigrants. A dark, knowing smirk from Mariam.

"Tetsuya was not allowed to become a citizen, but his kids, the Nisei generation born in America, were legal citizens. Then came World War II, concentration camps and the Loyalty Questionnaire, with the infamous questions 27 and 28."

I laid out for them all the knowledge I had stored up since the war.

"All people of Japanese ancestry over seventeen-years-old were asked to swear unqualified allegiance to the United States and swear off any form of fidelity to the Emperor of Japan. If a person like Tetsuya, who was not allowed U.S. citizenship, denounced the Emperor of Japan, he would be left without a country. But unless he swore allegiance to the United States, he would be seen as a traitor and thought of as the enemy."

On the same questionnaire, the Japanese were asked if they would be willing to serve in combat duty wherever ordered. Most young people were torn, not wanting to split up their strong families. Some Nisei eagerly enlisted because they were American and wanted to prove their loyalty. Many did serve in the military, but their units were segregated.

"Tetsuya decided his sons should swear loyalty to the United States, their home. Each son — Ken, Mike and Ted — volunteered for the U.S. Army. Tetsuya and his wife, who renounced the Emperor, were moved to another part of the Tule Lake Camp. By responding 'yes' to questions 27 and 28, Tetsuya and his wife were then truly without a country. They were separated from the so-called insurgents who answered 'no-no' to questions 27 and 28. Those Japanese-Americans, who became known as the No-No Boys, were seen as traitors, placed in a jail within the camp and separated from their families."

"Years after Tetsuya and his family were released, I wanted to see where the government imprisoned Tetsuya. I drove the six hours to see Tule Lake with my own eyes." I revealed to the group my interest in the camp — or maybe it was my guilt. "A godforsaken part of California."

"Everyone thinks Japanese have no problems." Jesús casually shrugged, bringing me back to the present. "The Japanese kids I know are smart — always get into college. UC Berkeley, no sweat. Didn't know they *had* worries."

Jesús broke away from the tension at the table and ambled to the soda dispenser on the far side of the dining room. He filled his co-workers' cups, one by one, with their favorite soda, plugging plastic straws in plastic cups, like plunging small daggers into scabbards. He made a special trip to bring me a fresh hot cup of coffee, carrying it with two hands.

The young workers contemplated the wrenching of the Japanese — citizens or not — from their home, shoved into prison behind barbed wire fences, guarded by guns. In the twentieth century. In the United States of America.

"How did they get so many people to move so quickly?" Mariam attempted to sort out the logistics, her mind working overtime.

"I didn't know at the time, but the government acted so quickly, they were just winging it as they went along," I replied. "Most Japanese families were given just a few weeks to arrange their affairs which usually meant selling their land, crops or store goods at a fraction of the market price. Then 'All Persons of Japanese Descent,' as the posters plastered everywhere stated, were herded like livestock to 'assembly centers' which were racetracks or the local fairgrounds."

The injustices Japanese-Americans endured were almost too many to list, but I thought the kids should learn what I knew about this history.

"Many were forced to set up housekeeping with their families in smelly horse stalls, with few toilets, horrible food and excruciatingly long lines for everything. They were prisoners in their own country."

"I learned something in school — and I'm an accountant for God's sake," Zach unexpectedly jumped in with his knowledge of that traumatic time. "The Japanese businesses, houses, farms — everything was taken. Their bank accounts were frozen. Even when neighbors said they would guard their farms and stores, most things had been stolen by the time the Japanese families were finally released from the camps. They returned to nothing and began again. With nothing."

"If it was me, I would be madder than hell," Jason interrupted, finally drawn into the conversation, feeling the truckload of injustice that had been dumped onto the Japanese. "Why didn't they protest? Stand up for themselves."

These kids just did not get it. They'd never experienced anything like a nation at war. Just babies during the 911 attack.

I looked at Aman's almond eyes, her thick black lashes revealing her Middle Eastern background. Jesús was tall, brown, burly. If he did not wear his constant, pleasant grin, he could be seen as intimidating to those who did not know him. Mariam's skin was a glowing dusky brown and she wore her hair in tight rows of braids, the lower half of her mane flaring out in puffy ponytails. Jason's pockmarked pink skin and rotund middle section exposed his flaws, but his dark ginger colored hair and soft, brown-speckled eyes gave him the appearance of being slightly older and tougher than his years.

My new friends were magnificent, their youth vibrating through their skin, eyes bright and hopeful for the future. But I suppose after listening to Tetsuya's story, each person in our group was wondering if, sometime not so far in the future, a U.S. government concentration camp could snatch away their precious years and supposed inalienable rights in the country they — at the moment — believed was their home.

NINETY-FOUR

He came to me softly, dressed in filmy white robes. A crown of flowers peeked out from his thick dark curls as he lay down beside me in his twin bed, lovingly, playfully staring at me until I opened my eyes. I turned to see my brother smiling at me. I gasped in surprise, not expecting Demo anywhere near the North American continent or our home. Where was his Army uniform? Had I slept through his homecoming? What was that knowing look on his face?

"I am safe." He smiled again as the morning light cracked through the fog and blasted into our room, shining a floodlight onto our twin beds. I wasn't sure if the light was coming from my brother or the glow I felt from his being home, his proper place.

I bolted up and reached out for him—but Demo's bed was heaped with a giant snowball of clean aprons that I was to fold and return to the restaurant that morning. No crown of flowers, no robes. No homecoming. No Demo.

I had overslept! I hurried down the Georgia Street hill so I could set up for the lunch rush—no time to fold aprons. And I was late for my job of whipping up buckets of gravy for our Hot Turkey Sandwich Special—using cornstarch, instead of rationed butter. The idea that Demo had come back to our family—to me—if only in a dream, was a hot water bottle I pressed close to my heart as I quickly walked to work.

As I pulled back the brass handle on the front door of the restaurant, I was immediately swept into a soft cloud of safety that surrounded my body. I relaxed. Like a favorite grandparent who understood everything, The Classic Grill never failed to soothe my senses: The rich, dark scent of freshly brewed coffee kept warm in the giant metal urn. Garlic floating in a sea of golden olive oil awaiting its companions of onions and celery for a quick sauté. The screech of the metal rack loaded down with a giant roasted turkey pulled from the hot oven cavern, white meat soft and steamy.

I contemplated my satisfaction when I extended comfort to our hungry customers with the food I had created with my own hands. This restaurant, The Classic Grill, was my home — the place where I belonged. It was the serious work I was meant to do in this world.

In the kitchen that day, I contemplated my dream and how I had almost touched Demo. While I ate a quick lunch of tomato-basil soup with giant hunks of French bread, I reread the letter he had written several weeks ago. He had addressed the letter only to me, probably not wanting my mother worrying that he would soon see combat. I chose to think he just wanted to talk to me, like we used to do, lying in the dark, our bodies too long for our beds.

I slowly deciphered Demo's scrawly handwriting telling me he was happy to leave Camp Roberts north of San Luis Obispo. He hated the hot inland weather and the relentless nightly battle with a squadron of mosquitoes. He was assigned Kitchen Patrol, seen as the lowest-rung duty among his fellow soldiers. Although the heat in the kitchen was fierce, my brother reported he was in familiar surroundings. Stirring deep caldrons of spaghetti sauce, peeling potatoes, slicing canned hams thin as paper — Demo performed well and the head cook was pleased to assign tasks to his experienced hands. Just like in our restaurant, the moment breakfast was served, the lunch preparation had already begun. In addition to KP, the U.S. Army trained Demo for artillery duty, in charge of feeding monster machine guns with heavy carpets of live ammunition. Of course my brother, like everyone else in the Army, practiced with a rifle for field combat.

I imagined him lying on his bunk, writing the letter as the Seventh Army destroyer steamed towards the Mediterranean — Italy, precisely. Never having traveled farther south than San Francisco or farther north than Boy Scout camp in Mendocino County, Demo admitted he was homesick, despite being crammed on a ship with hundreds of men. He became accustomed to the rigid commands barked by his officers but allowed his own made-up stories to spike from his brain like fresh, green shoots poking through his combat helmet. He secretly envisioned each officer as a lead character wearing his own brightly painted ceramic mask. His sergeant wore his hair coiled heavy and serpent-like around his head with his flaring nostrils setting off his wide flat nose. The commanding officer's beard was a braided herringbone weave. The head cook wore a gaping smile from ear to ear. Demo pretended each day was another performance with his commanding officers acting as directors. While his body obediently performed duties in the U.S. Army, Demo's mind ran free, secretly keeping his imaginary world alive.

Demo hinted that he kept up enough fraternal chatter to avoid unwanted suspicion about his sexuality. My brother, the actor, occasionally referred to girlfriends back home, or of the sweet potential of linking up with women while on leave. He made friends with a few soldiers in his unit, especially those on KP. Another Greek-American, Pete Knossos, took a liking to my brother, as a fellow countryman looking out for one of his own. Pete teased Demo about his last name, saying it was too long and would never fit on the official U.S. Army forms. A little older, Pete was a tough, streetwise guy from Chicago where his parents owned two restaurants — a diner and a high-class steak house. They had made their real money distributing booze during Prohibition, as the police looked away while trucks ran white lightning from stills in the countryside to Chicago's back-alley clubs and bars. His parents also waited for their son to return and operate the family restaurants. But Pete was another soul who was not sure that standing behind a deep fryer and slicing roast beef would be his life story. He had taken to the strict regimen of Army life and hoped to make a career of living on Army bases and traveling to foreign countries — or at least to states far from home. Looking back, Demo wrote more about Pete than he did about himself. I was happy Demo had a big brother looking out for him as they pushed their way to Italy for God-knows-what.

But lately Demo's letters had become as rare as a cup of unrationed granulated sugar. We had not heard from him in weeks. I told my mother he was too busy with KP to write, but I secretly calculated his every move. By now he should have landed in Europe. By now he should have started whatever mission they were assigned. By now he should be stationed securely in Italy. By now his company should be ousting Germans at every turn. By now it was autumn of 1943, and the U.S. and Britain had just invaded southern Italy. I could not rely on the newsreels at the movie theatre to report events a week after they actually happened. Instead, every night I tuned in the evening news broadcast on Taki's abandoned radio as I swept up after closing. I waited. We waited. The world waited.

I knew it when the doorbell sang out its cheerful notes the first thing that grey drizzling morning. The finger pressing the bell belonged to a young man wearing a leather bag slung over his shoulder. Not usually at home at this hour, my father was lingering on our sunporch, waiting for a roof repairman. I was just leaving for school and my mother was in Napa Junction at another Greek's family farm in search of eggplants for her moussaka, or "Liberty Lasagna." As the messenger handed my father the telegram envelope, he mumbled the word "sorry," with his eyes glued to my father's shoes. Frosty icicles replaced the space my wildly pumping heart normally occupied. I watched from the sunporch as the messenger cast a quick glance of pity toward our house, jumped on his bike and jetted away, down the Virginia Street hill.

My father stood there with his hand on the doorknob, his lips parted, no voice coming from his throat. He dropped the official envelope and it fluttered to the floor. I scooped it up and tore it open.

THE SECRETARY OF WAR DESIRES ME TO EXPRESS HIS DEEPEST REGRET THAT YOUR SON...

I didn't need to read the rest to understand. My father's dry rasp repeated what I already knew.

"He is gone." My father softly exhaled the words, and I gave him the slightest nod.

I wasn't sure if someone had pulled the oxygen from the sunporch as a horrible prank—I couldn't breathe. My hand reached out to find something on which to steady myself before I dissolved into a chair. Maybe they had taken the wrong serial number. Demo might only be wounded. My mind reached out for a living Demo, but my hopes smacked against a stone wall and dropped to the gravel below. The black letters on the telegram floated on the page. Killed in action. I studied the words but could not allow the sharp blade of truth into my heart. It would not fit.

My father, his hand frozen on the doorknob, stared out at the street or somewhere far beyond. I could not drill past my father's glassy eyes into his mind. Later, he told me he recalled moments with Demo, before their defiant confrontations began: covering his infant son with a soft blanket. Demo's precocious reading ability—the first Pappayannis in family history to read. Demo's loving spirit entwining both my father and mother when it was time for bed. His elaborate stories that entertained my parents when they had worn out their village folk tales. My father's mental photo album of happy moments suddenly snapped shut. He later told me the thought of Demo's last seconds at the restaurant, dressed in his Army uniform, felt like a boulder under which he was pinned. My father knew his son deserved a farewell embrace before he marched to war. But he did not — could not — go to his first-born.

Demo was everywhere in my father's mind — and now, nowhere. Demo was dead, never again to stand up and demand to live his life as he planned it, not the version my father prescribed. Never again to insist on living his life without apology, without fear. At that moment, my father realized he himself had been Demo's enemy — warring against his son at every turn. My father lifted his eyes and looked at me, but gazed through me. I followed him as he, without a word, walked into his room and for the first time in his life laid crosswise, face down, on his perfectly made bed.

I held that telegram as if it were gossamer. Until his body arrived, it was the last memento from Demo. Like my brother, my father had always been transparent, unable to hide his feelings. I knew that guilt, dressed in its dark, prickly coat, crawled around his room, tugging at the hem of his pants, gnawing at his fingertips, lying heavily on his back. He had not said goodbye to my brother. My father crept into Demo's grave before my brother was even lowered into the ground. I knew of nothing that could save him. I slowly walked back to the sunporch, holding the official document, proof that Demo would never return.

While my father disintegrated in the bedroom, I was left to tell my mother. Officially, reluctantly, I became the parent. For the moment, I put aside my grief for my brother, my hero, to take care of my family. My dismal consolation prize was that I had loved Demo every moment and I absolutely had no regrets, as my father did. In fact, I wondered if Demo had come to say goodbye in my dream, sending a message across the universe of space between our twin beds.

When she arrived home holding six shiny amethyst eggplants in a small wooden crate, my mother saw that my eyes were like the black, empty sockets of Demo's ancient masks. My body occupied a chair on the sunporch, limp and unmoving. My thoughts stretched from the Pacific coast across the Atlantic and landed in Italy, searching to relive Demo's last moments with him, my mind aching to give my brother a signal, a sign. Seeing my mother walk through the door, my body went through the motions of turning to her and my mouth attempted to form the words.

Her eyes whisked to the telegram and she read the horror on my blank face.

"Demo *mou?*" She knew.

Dropping her crate of eggplants, she sat down next to me, breathing hard. Eyes closed, she crossed herself again and again as if her prayers might make this terror only a dream. Paralyzed, before the tears could begin, she dispatched her spirit to survey the universe, searching for Demo's soul that, in her mind, was seeking hers. Even in his death, my mother was desperate to locate and protect her child. She needed to cradle her son's curly head from impact, his body from danger. Her powerful maternal shield of protection could not reach the end of the universe, not even to the Germans in Italy.

After a moment my mother took my hand and kissed it to seal her devotion to her two sons. "How will we live with this?" She was shifting from shock to horror. "Tell me how..."

That phrase comforted me more than she knew. She included me as the solid, reliable member of her personal congregation. A pillar of strength she could trust. I stood in our family's emotional ruins, where my father's feet should have been planted.

"I will go to the restaurant and let them know." I attempted to form some sort of plan on how to proceed, still sleepwalking in this strange land without my brother, a land I never wanted to navigate. I was always Demo's wingman, never the leader. Now I was thrust into the driver's seat in our family chariot, the position a first-born was destined to occupy. But I wasn't ready to take the reins.

My mother attempted to gather her strength for me. "Yes, my son." She pronounced "son" with a kiss in her voice. "Help them understand this at the restaurant. I will go to your father."

She already knew that he was incapable of helping anyone. She and I stood on the edge of the dark sinkhole, staring into the depths we could not understand. My father had surrendered and immediately leaped into the blackness. My mother would be forced to heave a lifeline to my father and then use every muscle in her body and the last fragment of understanding in her heart to pull him back to the surface. Or maybe she just needed to be near my father because they had created Demo together. Someone who was there at the beginning. And now, the end.

I was nearly at the corner of Virginia and Napa streets when I heard a deep, wounded cry coming from a strange wild animal. I quickly twisted around to see my mother at my bedroom window that faced the street. She stared towards the east, unfathomable anguish on her face, her scream muffled by glass. My mother had lost her firstborn and she let loose the shrill, devastating cry of so many mothers over so many centuries whose sorrow did not have a body to touch, to love, to grieve. Each could only wait on a distant continent, heart ripped to bleeding, preparing to bury her son.

NINETY-FIVE

My young group of listeners had few words after they listened to my story about the telegram. Now, I almost felt as if I was reliving my announcement to the kitchen crew that Demo had died in the war.

"How did you manage? You were only seventeen!" Aman asked, a mist clouding her dark eyes.

"Your father was a bastard!" Mariam shot out. "Making you do a man's work. Where was he for you to cry to? What an ass!"

I had to agree with her, but arrangements had to be made, and I — the only English reader and writer in the group — was thrust to the front of the line. We were contacted later by the Army about the shipment of my dear brother's remains. I learned that if fifty percent of a soldier's body was recovered, the Army would send it home to the family. Otherwise, the solider would be buried overseas. We were lucky Demo would be sent home to us, but I doubted that seeing a coffin would make his absence any easier to digest.

I did not want to burden these lovely young people with my sadness. But it seemed they cared about Demo these many years later. And I know my brother would have loved them back.

NINETY-SIX

I was only seventeen. But my job was to inform Theo Vasili, Taki, the cooks and the waiters that Demo would not be coming home. One burden at a time, I told myself. I walked to the restaurant, a path Demo and I had taken a million times. I could see us in our younger days, rolling up to the restaurant door on our bikes in search of a juicy turkey sandwich and a chocolate milkshake. I felt a knife twisting in my stomach.

I whispered the news to the cooks and waiters who then went about their work in silence, heads down, attempting to make fact out of what seemed to be fiction. Mr. Chris' violin remained in its velvet-lined case, his tears rolling into the suds as he slowly washed stacks of dishes to keep his hands busy. Theo Vasili was still outside in the alley, kitchen screen door propped open, smoking a cigar to start his day. Seconds after I told him, my uncle dropped onto a shallow cement curb, his brittle bones crashing hard on the cement. Demo and I were his children. His fatherly concern poured out for me, the younger son left on the home front, alive — just barely. He pulled me down next to him, hugging me sideways, his rangy arm around my shoulders.

"How you do, my son?" Theo Vasili asked, tears trickling down his leathery face. "You no go to school, no work today. You go home, I take care of it."

He took in a breath, attempting to hold back his sobs — but it was no use.

"*O kyménos* Demo. My poor Demo." Sobs seeped from the cracks in his body. He leaned into me, as if I too might slip away. Taking my face in his hands as he had done with Demo over the years, he touched his weathered, freckled forehead to mine.

"My boys…"

The long afternoon hours melted into the evening and then into the night as I wandered the streets, now without a brother. I saw no use in going home to agonize over my father's crushing grief. Frankly, I was weary of my father's weight, exhausted by his emotional needs.

I lumbered down to the waterfront and stood across the channel from the Mare Island shipyard, where, it seemed, subs and ships were turned out by the hour. How many men would board those vessels and climb out whole when their mission was completed? And how many would be left behind, buried in soggy graves, their bodies separated from their families? What type of ship was transporting Demo across the Atlantic to us? I wondered where Demo's spirit was now.

I walked to the ferryboat dock, Demo's favorite place in Vallejo, his springboard to adventure. I don't know how long I sat on the concrete, my back against a telephone pole like a vagrant. Under the moonless, starless heaven, I became chilled, as if I had napped in our restaurant's walk-in refrigerator. I felt a tapping on my foot. Laboring to open my eyes, I wanted Demo to be standing there, grinning like a devil. I lifted one eyelid to see the slight figure of my mother, bundled in her old camel hair coat, scarf around her head like a village peasant. The tapping became more vigorous.

"*Giorgi mou.*" She spoke solemnly.

In the darkness, I could almost make out the exhaustion she wore on her face. Was it possible for someone to age ten years in a day?

I knew I should return home with my mother, to spare her more worry. As we slowly walked home, I glanced at the long filigree hands on The Alibi clock standing proudly on Georgia Street. One-thirty in the morning brought on another tidal wave of sadness. Yesterday, at least part of the day, Demo was alive for me. Now the earth had revolved around the sun and I would forever refer to Demo in the past tense. I would never understand the reasoning behind any war where young men came home dead for old men's battles.

Later at home, as the sun began to crack the darkness, I pulled up the covers over my exhausted body. I glanced at the empty bed beside me. I lamented that our room — now my room — would never again overflow with wondrous ancient Greek tales told by a young actor-warrior to his most admiring listener.

Weeks later, we still awaited Demo's body. I watched the flesh melt off my mother's bones as she became too despondent to cry. She often frantically worked wall-to-wall hours, dawn until midnight, canning sweet tomato sauce in sterile jars, mopping our wooden floors as if they needed it, cracking walnuts into tall piles like sand dunes.

Other days, she sent word to my father that she would stay home. She spent hours haunting our kitchen, absently swallowing chamomile tea down her dry throat. She wandered aimlessly about the garden she had previously tended so carefully, harvesting nothing, drifting through the towering weeds. My father ignored me, keeping to himself, disappearing at four in the morning for the restaurant. Demo's death was the end of our family-style meal with the crew in the evening. Our home and the restaurant kitchen were nearly silent, except for the necessary exchange of words. I welcomed visits from little Alex. I never mentioned it to anyone, but I thought Alex resembled Demo around his eyes. It made me feel good to think that maybe a little piece of Demo was floating around in Alex's blood and flesh.

We received a telegram saying Demo's remains would be sent home in a week. My mother began to plan a funeral for my brother — the last possible act she could perform for him. She repeatedly reached for the heavy black telephone to call the Greek Orthodox priest, but then quickly hung up. She could not face making Demo's *kollyva*, the large rectangular pillow of boiled wheat dressed in snowy powdered sugar that appeared at the memorial ceremony forty-days after the funeral. That would mean the page had turned, and life would go on without Demo. Every moment waiting for his body crushed my chest until I could hardly breathe.

Then the letter came that explained everything. We had wanted any news to be our own pillow of powdered sugar sprinkled over what was an intolerable dish. Our souls had been dragged through dirt, stones, cut glass and pounding waves that nearly drowned us. Unfortunately, there was more to come.

The letter delivered to our tiny black metal mailbox destroyed the notion that Demo's last breathing moments had been peaceful or dream-like. Demo's buddy Pete had written the letter, his handwriting small, tight and childlike. I swiftly and fiercely decoded every word — I needed to drown myself in every detail about my brother.

They were in the same unit as they landed in Sicily and moved to Messina with the Fifth Army. Pete wrote that marching north, they did not see much action. Their unit was later transported to the mainland, at the toe of

Italy's boot, across the Strait of Messina. From there, they marched north again, burrowing into the outer part of Salerno, where cover was hard to find. Most villagers had secreted themselves away in the nearby hills, abandoning their homes and possessions. Pete and Demo were assigned to a small stone house, with their commanders making plans to take possession of the entire village soon. Dirt floors, crumbling stone walls, a deserted hearth for cooking family meals. The house probably resembled my parents' own one-room homes in Greece. Pete wrote that they often heard the crack of distant bullets and grenades blasting in the distance. For three days they saw no action. Pete and Demo were informed that the enemy had moved on and that they would soon be called to safe ground. Eating rations only once a day, Demo and Pete were parched for water and felt woozy for lack of fresh air. Most of the time, Pete wrote, he and Demo waited in silence, expecting an "all clear" sign at any moment.

The third night of their occupation, Pete moved outside the house to patrol their assigned area. Demo, finished with his guard duty, stepped inside at the moment a grenade blasted the house. A fallen wood roof beam protected Pete from flying stones and debris as the explosion erupted into flames. Knocked back and bloodied, he attempted to locate Demo amid the smoke, stones, and burning wood. At daybreak, Pete and other men from his unit located parts of Demo's body — but he did not say which parts. Demo's identification tags and a small, bent photo were scattered near his body. Pete slipped the photo into his pocket and then into an envelope addressed to our family.

The photo was now in my hands, special delivery from Demo.

My eyes rested on the crinkled, hand-worn photo of our family and The Classic Grill crew that victorious day when we festooned our restaurant window with all-American décor. Theo Vasili stood tall behind the red-haired crewcut of Mr. Chris and the other cooks. Tetsuya beamed from the middle of the crew. Taki had taken his place in the front row, months before he assumed his exhausting duty to console his war-maimed son. In the center, my father stood close to my mother, his arm around her shoulder, a couple, a team. Demo had carried us with him as he fought and died. He loved us enough to take us with him.

I stifled a cry from my throat. The photo accidentally slipped from my fingers and fluttered to the hardwood floor, landing on the fringe of my mother's carpet. As the photo with creased corners came to rest face down, I noticed a drop of blood on the back. It was Demo's blood, I was sure. I greedily pressed the photo to my heart. I would carry it everywhere for the rest of my life.

NINETY-SEVEN

Five pair of eyes stared at the worn out photo of The Classic Grill crew that I had laid out in the center of the table. I could not determine if my group was surprised that I still carried that photo with me, or if they were hesitant to touch it. About twenty years ago, I had the photo laminated, causing the faces to be less discernable, softened, while living for decades flattened in my wallet. There for all to see were images of my proud parents, Theo Vasili, Taki, the kitchen crew—and surprisingly of most interest to my group—me.

At that moment, as in most restaurants, the dinner rush began in the little fast-food place. A swarm of young children pushed open the glass door. They were followed by two sets of overprotective parents walking while transfixed by their cell phone screens. Aman and Mariam leaped from their seats to dash behind the counter, fingers poised, ready to take orders. Jesús immediately appeared behind his grill and turned up the gas, scraping the grill with a metal spatula like the cooks at The Classic Grill.

The chattering kids exploded with exuberant energy into the empty restaurant while their parents attempted to find healthy choices on the carnivorous menu, requesting garden burgers and inquiring about non-hydrogenated oils. Thank God we did not have to contend with that nonsense at The Classic Grill, where a hamburger steak was juicy with fat and the hand-cut potatoes were sunk into the deep fryer twice—once to cook and again later for flavor. And who knew what hydrogenated was anyway?

Twenty minutes later, the sun began to soften in the sky. One-by-one, my group slipped back into the seats they had occupied before leaving to serve their hungry customers.

"Regulars," Mariam said watching through the plate glass window as the family loaded the last child into their enormous minivan. "Without them, some of our dinners would be super-slow."

"Yeah," Aman chimed in. "It's empty some nights. I hope they don't lay off any of us. I need the money."

Jason had been silent through the last part of my story. Now that he had returned to his seat, his chubby fingers were the only ones to reach out to touch my family snapshot, still in the middle of the table. He slowly turned it over to see the spot of Demo's blood, now faded and brown with age.

"There he is." Jason ran his finger over the spot. "Now I've touched Demo."

Aman chewed on her black nails, her brow creased in contemplation.

"So how did your family get along? And you?" She stared at the photo and back at me, her eyes assessing my crinkled face, my ears too long, my olive skin darkened with the years.

"And the restaurant?" Jesús interrupted. "The Classic Grill?"

I smiled. Jesús rolled the 'r' in the word "Grill" just like my father did.

NINETY-EIGHT

I made short work of talking about my brother's funeral. The kids, not surprisingly, wanted to hear about how we lived, not about how we buried our dead. I quickly explained that my brother's body parts were buried and prayed over. Demo's photo was centered on a table surrounded by a dozen platters of hot food at the post-funeral lunch held in our restaurant. My mother sang the Greek funeral song before we all drank shots of Metaxá brandy. Frankly, I think Demo would have arranged something more dramatic, like a funeral pyre, with a chorus chanting ancient Greek poems. Or the erection of a stone beehive dome, like the Tomb of Agamemnon, to house his remains. Or maybe a coin placed in his mouth for payment to Charon, the ferryman who floated souls from the land of the living to the dark world of the dead. But none of these burials were available during wartime in humble Vallejo, California. The hour-long incense-laden Greek Orthodox ceremony in the Episcopal Church was our traditional memorial for my brother. My mother wouldn't have it any other way.

Natalya appeared at my brother's funeral, dressed sedately in her long black wool coat, her dark gray scarf knotted under her chin. At the ceremony, my father asked who was the *xéni*, this stranger. I told him Natalya was a friend who had been very kind to Demo in San Francisco. He nodded his head and did not question her presence. He set his eyes forward and kept to himself the rest of the day. After the funeral, Natalya disappeared into the fog. I hoped life would be bearable for this loving soul who took my brother in when he needed guidance in his new world.

But Jesús' question hung in the air. What happened to The Classic Grill? Why wasn't it still an active restaurant on Georgia Street, lively with fourth-generation family members, re-invented with new menu items and updated décor?

"The truth is, The Classic Grill had always been *my* restaurant, *my* place in the world. And when Demo was gone, it was my everything." I shrugged and slid the family photo back into my wallet. "But what happened next was completely unexpected by everyone. Most of all, me."

NINETY-NINE

On an early Sunday morning, I saw my father walking to the restaurant, pulling little Alex by the hand. My father opened his worn-out hand and offered to Alex a fistful of keys wound around a simple iron ring. He allowed Alex to turn the lock, listening to the pins and drivers as his small hands opened the irritable latch. I was already inside, paring down our food inventory, economizing at every turn. We still needed to whittle down the mountain of debt, and I was determined to take the lead role in righting our ship. Someday this wretched war would end, and I for one, would be ready for business.

I heard the door squeak open and Alex's small footsteps shuffling across the tiled Greek key entryway. Behind him, my father threw the keys on the bar. He dumped an armful of buckets, broom and sponges on the floor, staring blankly at the cleaning equipment. He didn't know I watched him from behind the swinging doors to the kitchen.

Alex looked at the equipment and expectantly at the kitchen. "What are we gonna cook today, Papou?"

"We no cook today, Alexandros." My father's mind seemed miles beyond his bucket and brushes.

In the window, a sign screamed "Closed" To those waiting for a simple bacon-and-eggs breakfast, an unusually inhospitable message from The Classic Grill. My father motioned with a jerk of his index finger that Alex should sit at a back table to watch his cleaning show. I observed the little boy's dark gaze scrutinize the old man's scrubbing with admiration, and a little fear — exactly like me when I was young. After a few minutes, my father squirmed uncomfortably under the child's unblinking attention.

"I fix you something," he mumbled.

Daphne had asked my parents to watch Alex for the day. We had all observed that my mother was a ghost of her vibrant self, and certainly could use a day of rest. My father surprised her by taking Alex to the restaurant.

I watched him tenderly slice a loaf of fresh French bread and intensely examine the inside of the toaster until the bread glowed the perfect shade of golden-brown. His rough hands stacked up three oblong slices, slathering them with sweet, sticky strawberry jam. My father placed the towering dish of toast in front of Alex, who swung his legs from the seat of his bentwood chair, his joints like hinges.

"Thanks, Papou." Alex's voice reminded me of the tiny silver bells on the incense burner at church. I locked on my father's every move, tracking this odd streak of what seemed to be compassion. My eyes nearly fell out of my head as my father attended to his grandson's desire before his own need to start and finish his cleaning job. I was dizzy with this freshly minted father-and-grandson connection, jealous for the years that I had starved for a look, a nod, a pat on the back — anything to let me know my father saw me.

I loved this child and had given him my heart long before Daphne revealed her secret. I had played with Alex, nursed him to health, coaxed him, teased him and even helped him read from the primer books Demo and I had studied. While Demo was gone, Alex was my daily occupation. Every minute with him, I felt my bucket of love for Demo splash onto the boy, uniting us as brothers, although I was, in fact, his uncle. But now, resentment toward my father oozed out of my heart and slid hot and sticky down my chest.

I looked at my father, who always dreamed his grand plans. My father, whose life had been locked onto Demo's participation, never noticing that my nimble hands were always busy and helping. Always in the right place at the right time, never calling for glory. My father, who never gave me one lousy word of praise — in Greek or English. He was Zeus on his throne, thunderbolt in hand. And now Zeus was taking tender care of someone else. And it wasn't me! I had no guards on my tongue now. No filters. Nothing holding back the boiling truth erupting from my heart's core.

I slammed my way through the swinging doors to the dining room and stopped as they flapped shut behind me. I stood there with my arms folded across my heaving chest, across my cook's apron, across my heart like a shield.

"You here?" My father didn't bother to look up while tucking a napkin under Alex's chin.

You here? You here? He dished up those words carelessly, as if I was any dishwasher who had drifted in the back door, looking for an hour or two of work.

"You didn't tell me you were cleaning!" I roared. As if my life depended on it.

My father slowly turned to make sense of my thunderous voice, my weird intensity. He looked at my folded arms, his eyes narrowed.

He spoke to the floor, as if to guard Alex from his words.

"I need to do." He turned his back to me. "I clean out the old."

I uncorked my throat, slinging my next words into his back like a hatchet.

"Well, I want to do it with you!"

"Some dishes in the back." He stopped to find his bucket and broom. "You go do them."

Suddenly my hands reached beneath a large round dining table for six. Then and there, I flipped it and spun it across the room, several chairs crashing beneath it while others scattered across the room like bumper cars. My body was skinny but it was sinewy and strong. My hands were in motion, and my brain did not get in the way. I pulled back another chair and threw it across the room, crashing against a wall, far from Alex who watched wide-eyed and silent.

My father stood frozen, unsure if I would pull out a pistol or if I would tackle his old body to the ground.

"I am here, Pop! It's me, your son. *O défteros!* The second one!"

My father let out a low grunt, his eyes watching my hands. He'd faced many street fights with opponents stronger, faster and younger. Out of instinct, he watched my next move.

"I am here every day — but you don't see me. I make your Lamb Fricassee, and you don't taste it! I take your place at home when you are too busy for us — and you still don't see me."

With two long strides, I pushed my hot breath into his face.

"I am here!"

My father looked at the floor as if that would change me back to my obedient self.

"George!" He choked out the words. "You talk crazy!"

Talking? I was through with talking. I was yelling now.

"I love to cook. Just like you. I love The Classic Grill. Every inch of it. I'd have loved The Symposium too. *I am just like you!*"

"But you —"

"Not Demo. Me! I wanted to make Symposiums all across the country! I could taste it! I wanted what you wanted. Demo didn't care — but I am just like you!"

For once, he had no words. His throat let out a little rasp. But his silence was just weakness, I knew that now. And at that moment, I stepped to the front of the line, the head of the family.

"You think you miss Demo? I miss Demo more than you know. To you — I am nothing. But Demo loved me. Demo *was* my father."

I pulled my last arrow from the quiver I had lugged heavily on my back all my life, aimed it and let it fly.

"I will take over this restaurant. I will take over this family. I know how. I've been doing it for months!"

I slowly walked to my father and watched him shrink, like a beaten dog. Perhaps ready to obey, perhaps ready to bite. Then I walked to the center of the dining room, electric power zapping from my fingertips and from the ends of my hair. That day, my truth was my spiked club, and I swung it like a caveman.

"I would have worked with you today, cleaning." My voice was hoarse now. "We could have missed Demo — together."

Slowly I set one chair upright. Then I rocked the big round table back on its feet. Alex's eyes were wide, his lower lip trembling. I set a gentle hand on his shoulder. I felt a wind sweep through the restaurant and blow against my body. I was weary of my father and the enormous energy I had spent working around him, trying to please him.

"Tell me that you want to work with me. As your son. As your partner."

Still, my father was silent.

"Didn't you learn anything from Demo? Do you have to lose another son?"

My father hung his head, his shoulders like a rope bridge, slack from a lifetime of carrying the Pappayannis family's weight. Slowly he slouched to the bar and, placing both palms far apart on the counter, leaned heavily on them. Rivers of tears began to pour down my father's coarse cheeks. I was expecting a lash of words, but his eyes were weary, black circles beneath them, his usual fire extinguished. He turned his head and seemed to see Demo, Alex and me, all at once.

For a moment, I believed he would reach out and embrace me. But he did me one better.

He stared hard at me, his gaze locked on my hard, determined expression.

"George, I depend for you."

With a swipe of his shirtsleeve across his face, my father wiped his tears and refocused his gaze on the gleaming nickel bar. He shuffled to the back kitchen office and, with some rustling of paper, pulled out a checkbook and a folder jammed with receipts, leases, loans and bills. He planted himself on a stool and motioned for me to sit next to him.

"*Kathíste*. Sit."

My father's hands pulled back rubber bands that held together his mismatched paperwork and flattened out the accounting ledger on the counter. His fingers rummaged through his pockets for his reading glasses and carefully positioned them low on his nose. With a thumb, he wiped his eyes.

"The books," he said plainly, finally looking at me, man to man, partner to partner. "George, we look at the books together."

ONE HUNDRED

"So he came around to you!" Aman clasped her hands together, a slow smile spreading across her face. "I knew it!"

I figured Aman would love this turn of events, since she seemed to me the softest of the group. But it was Jesús who rushed to comfort me with one last fresh cup of coffee. Tears puddled in my eyes and one escaped, trickling down my ancient, craggy face. I realized I missed my father.

"Of course he was not that easy." I dragged a long white cotton sleeve across my face and slowly looked up. "He never said he loved me, but his wall was broken. And he didn't mind sharing the load—once he got used to it."

"So you took the restaurant over at seventeen-and-a-half?" Jason looked around at the fast-food restaurant, probably imagining what he would do if he owned it. "That's what I want to do. Have my own place."

"My father didn't move over immediately." I was not a bit ashamed I did not yank the reins and move him aside.

Zach slurped the last of his soda, then walked over in his dad-sandals with black socks to refill his cup with fresh ice and root beer. His eyes were cemented on me, waiting for a cheerful ending to my story.

"Whaddya mean?" Zach was instantly annoyed. "I thought you became the boss. What happened?"

If my group of new friends had lived through those years, they might have known. The relentless animal that was World War II waited in the shadows, plotting against me. When I wasn't looking, it leaped on my chest and bit me deep on the soft part of my neck, leaving me slack and bloody, gasping for breath. At least that's how it felt.

ONE HUNDRED ONE

My mother attempted to ignore my eighteenth birthday, with a desperate hope that the U.S. government would do the same. But a notice instructing me to appear for my physical examination sat menacingly on our kitchen table, everyone fearful to touch it. My mother's prayers and all the holy icons could not have protected me against the astonishing events that would soon consume my life.

I left at dawn for my physical on an unusually soggy and damp spring morning. My hand clutched the Greyhound bus ticket to San Francisco that accompanied my notice to appear. By this time, it was 1944 and I had resigned myself to some type of military service. I walked quickly to the bus station on York Street, hands hidden in my pockets to keep warm and contemplated that, if given the choice, the Navy was my cup of tea. I enjoyed chatting with the Navy brass we served nearly every day at the restaurant after their long day at The Yard. I figured if they could manufacture submarines and repair battleships, I could take orders from men like that.

The wheels of the bus shrieked to a stop in San Francisco and I walked downtown to the examination hall on Market Street. I stepped in the door and was overcome by a mammoth wall of orderly chaos. Long lines trailing everywhere. The military way.

I surveyed the boomy auditorium-sized ballroom with its drafty high ceiling, black wooden floors and dank, musty smell. I marched through each examination station following the lines of boys — I mean, young men — my age. I checked in and stripped down to my birthday suit and contributed my golden pee into a cup, crowded by other young men also making liquid donations. This was my first slice of privacy in the military. Next, a doctor peered into every dark cavity of my body, shoving a light up my nose, down my throat, into my slightly oversized ears and other uncomfortable places. My 99.8-degree temperature was recorded by another unemotional, unblinking doctor who checked the status of my feet — weeding out those lucky guys with feet as flat as the hotcakes we served at The Classic Grill.

Next, I was herded to a station where I spread my arms across a glass square surrounded with an icy, dark metal frame as X-rays zapped through my chest. Finally, I faced another poker-faced doctor who rested his reading glasses like a butterfly on the tip of his nose. He barked questions at me, asking how I would get along in the service. Could I stand to live in close quarters with other men? Did I have any previous mental problems? Did I like girls? My thoughts turned to Demo and how he had endured this process, changing his colors like a crab spider in enemy territory. As I had graduated from high school in January, I was not given the official, complete psychological exam. So I guess my diploma was good for something.

My bus trip home was another bumpy ride and my feet soon led me to The Classic Grill where I felt at home, at least for now. With my apron on, I made sure the day's special, or Mare Island Sub Sandwich — in truth, gluten meatballs in a hoagie roll with red sauce — was ready to serve. I walked slowly around the kitchen as the lunch orders stacked up and the onslaught began. Except for my family, I knew I would miss that kitchen more than anything, when I, hardly a man, was transformed into a soldier preparing to become a warrior.

The days after my exam I tried to shake off an overwhelming surge of black dread that pulled at my ankles, making each step weighty and slow. I realized I should beg to fight for my country like my friends did, and possibly die for it, as Demo had. But I simply didn't want to go. I was certain I was patriotic, but having just cleaned off the shovel I used to cover what was left of my brother's body, my heart was shut down. I was not ready to serve and my family was less prepared for me to leave than I was.

My mother had just begun to bake her cakes and pies again in the silence of our home, her sorrowful sanctuary. As the weeks slipped by, she began to work in her garden like a maniac, back to nurturing her children of the soil. She cooked our favorite foods at home and soon asked that Alex visit more often. And most impressive of all, my mother began to learn how to read English so that she could help Alex as he grew into his letters.

On a warm and golden September morning that miraculously brought no fog, I overslept again, a rare phenomenon that was becoming a habit.

Almost late for my duties at the restaurant, I flew down the red stairs of our house in a rush to get to work. Several weeks earlier, I caught a cold and never shook it, the cough rattling in my chest, with night sweats washing over my body. As a result, sleep rarely came to visit and only cast her silken net around me in the early morning hours.

A few blocks from our house, I collided with the plump, middle-aged woman who delivered our mail. She was a breakfast regular at The Classic Grill. Of course, women had taken over many jobs while the male postal workers served overseas. Recognizing me from the restaurant, she pressed a letter into my hand — another envelope from the medical examiner. I dashed back to our house, collapsed on the stairs and sat down to open it. Out of breath, wheezing a little from my cough, I read the words that slowly came into focus. The sentences made no sense and I scanned the letter looking for the date I would leave home and travel, like Demo, to miserable, soggy Fort Ord. Instead, my eyes read words that were not supposed to appear on the page addressed to me, a kid barely eighteen years old. The letter officially announced that the X-rays had detected symptoms consistent with tuberculosis and that I should immediately seek care. I would not be inducted into military service of any kind.

In one quick moment, the military system spat me out on the sidewalk. I felt both rejected and saved, like being slapped and kissed at the same time. I could hardly make sense of this coiled snake ready to strike, which I had passed off for weeks as a nagging, lingering cough. Breaking a nervous sweat, I felt airborne, in free-fall.

I called to my mother in her garden, her hands buried in the dark, loamy soil. We slowly walked inside and faced each other at our kitchen table, my mother shocked into silence with the news. She sat at the kitchen table for a moment with no words. Suddenly she leaped into action, with a powerful life force I had not seen since she made plans to revive our business. My mother ran to the phone and dialed Dr. Winston. As she spoke, I heard a power in her voice that had been absent for months. I realized that my mother now had a son to protect, a life to save — something she could not do for Demo. I was home, alive for now, and I knew my mother would employ every bit of maternal power, medicinal herbs and, of course, all the magic her saints could lend. Like the goddess Athena, she extended her long, golden spear towards the heavens to wage war on tuberculosis as she desperately attempted to save the life of her only remaining son.

At his office, Dr. Winston informed us that he would smear my phlegm on a glass slide, color it with a few special stains, and search under his microscope for the TB bacteria that skulked in the darkness like a street gang looking for trouble. After another round of X-rays, my family doctor pronounced his official diagnosis: I had contracted tuberculosis. The only decision that followed was in which sanatorium I would be housed. A conscription of another kind. In the Army I would have been constantly required to be on the move. Now, I looked at a future where I would be on ice — required to do nothing but rest and eat nutritious food — not cook it.

We were already in debt for thousands of dollars and now my disease had its mouth open, ready to consume the wads of cash my parents would soon have to toss down its gullet. I needed to rid the TB bacteria from my body but unfortunately the magic pill I could only dream about — the antibiotic streptomycin — had not yet been invented.

My mother insisted on paying for a sputum test for all our family, cooks and waitstaff, as she was terrified of spreading the ravenous disease to our customers. Understanding the gravity of the situation, Dr. Winston provided the lab services for free, hoping to avoid an epidemic in town. Every person on our The Classic Grill crew passed their health test and they returned to their daily dishing up of waffles, onion soup and meals that stretched our ration books and the provisions from my mother's garden.

I lay on my bed, practicing my rest position at home until we could locate a sanatorium we could afford. My father came to my room and gently sat down on my twin bed. Worry pinched the folds between his eyes. My father stumbled to find words, his voice raspy and dry from lack of use when it came to father-son chats.

"*Giorgi*." His face sagged from the strain. "You no deserve this. Not now. Not ever." He looked down at his shabby policeman's shoes, heels worn, a pair that should have been replaced months ago.

As if he were another person, the father I had dreamed of my entire life, he leaned over and hugged me just a little, risking contact with my deadly germs. "I wait for you at the restaurant. I need for you."

His tired eyes examined me, from my dark hair to my thinner-than-usual waistline. I gurgled a little with every breath.

"You a good boy." He mumbled more to himself than me. But it sounded like "I love you" to my ears, warm and ruddy with my low fever.

My father slowly rose from my bed, lightly patting me on my knee. His steps were plodding and slow, as if he anticipated tackling the mountain of work ahead of him, without my help.

ONE HUNDRED TWO

"I didn't think anyone caught that disease — even in your day." Mariam considered my situation. "So they had no pill to cure you? They did nothing?"

I told my group that I had missed a pharmaceutical cure by about a decade.

"The only thing I had in my corner was complete rest, eating good food and my young, strong body that I counted on to pull me through." My thoughts drifted away, remembering that wretched feeling in my stomach of becoming a financial burden to my parents.

"My dad got it bad in the sixties and they didn't diagnose it for a long time." Zach nervously bent his plastic straw into mangled shapes. "By that time, they had pills for TB. And, man, did he swallow a ton of them every day."

Aman turned to me. "How did you feel? I mean, how bad was it?"

"While I was home, I felt like a monster because I didn't want to expose my mother and father," I remembered. "Most of the time, I helped my mother call the sanatoriums from my bed. And I tried to pencil out how we could pay."

"I know that story." Zach looked down at his hands. "My father was stuck in Weimar, up there near Placerville."

I tried my best to smile, but maybe it came out like a grimace. "That's just the place I called home for the next year."

ONE HUNDRED THREE

The untouchable monthly price tag for a sanatorium might as well have been attached to a marble palace. My father, living at my uncle's place now, told my mother he felt the guilt of creating and then, singlehandedly, losing The Symposium and our family savings, leaving no pillow of safety for me.

On a relentlessly bright morning, I snuck out of bed to answer a telephone call as my mother was picking lemons in her garden. That was the call that changed everything. Dr. Winston, knowing about the painful crimp in our family budget, called to announce that he had completed an admissions card for me to become accepted at the Weimar Joint Sanatorium located up north in cool, piney Placer County, the place for those who could only afford to pay a small amount of the bill. The doctor's encouraging words slowly sank into my chest and a small rosebud began to slowly bloom, a flower I did not know could grow in the dark. I think it was called hope.

In five short days, I was rolling in Dr. Winston's shiny black Ford sedan on the state road. He had offered to drive me up there, since he knew my parents owned no vehicle. We cut through the coastal hills into the Central Valley, past the dusty outskirts of Fairfield, Vacaville, and the highway fruit stands outside of Dixon and Davis. The moist fog of my Bay Area home dried up and I breathed in the hot, crackly air that was supposed to help heal my infested lungs.

I read the pamphlets Dr. Winston delivered to our house that said I had a better chance of recovery if I kept up my spirits and stayed positive, not allowing my mind to wander aimlessly in the dark, cold rooms of despair. My mother believed that my sorrow for Demo had opened my body to this dangerous intrusion. I couldn't disagree.

Nothing happened at Weimar and nothing was expected to happen. As resting was the order of the day, my fellow inmates of all ages lay in their iron-framed beds, lined up like eggs in a carton. The Weimar literature mentioned that Placer County was "above the fog and below the snowline." This meant the location was specifically selected to avoid the cold, damp San Francisco Bay fog and was well below the level of icy snowfall from the Sierra Nevada mountains. Although I knew that rest was my only cure, the ball and chain of the slow remedy weighed me down and my teenage body began to feel like a sixty-year-old invalid.

Rest and nutritious food. Our headline entertainment was the highly anticipated meal service that was cooked up in the cafeteria three times a day. I am sure the cafeteria ladies did their best with the tight budget, but I dreamed of bold flavors — spicy sausage, tangy basil sauce for pasta and the perfect combination of salty feta cheese and dark, meaty Kalamata olives. I salivated over the thought of velvety, brown gravy splashed over the meatloaf served to us from the cafeteria. Wouldn't the fresh fruit offered on the lunch tray become delectable with a creamy sabayon sauce? I was just hallucinating after absorbing the recipes in James Beard's *Hors d'Oeuvre and Canapes*, *The Boston Cooking School Cookbook* by Fannie Farmer, *The Joy of Cooking* and of course, my favorite — *The Escoffier Cookbook*, which my mother mailed to me from home. Every minute I wasn't sleeping, I pored over the recipes in those books, my mind whipping up eggs for a soufflé or slowly stirring milk into a shortcake dough.

Besides mealtime, mail call was a beacon of pleasure in our monotonous, beige-colored lives. I purposely sunk my expectations, as no one in the family was adept at scrawling letters on a page. But on my one-month anniversary of moving to Weimar, the orderly called my name and gently tossed three letters in my direction.

I stared at the letters lying at the foot of my bed and did not recognize the handwriting. After reading a few lines of the first letter, I recognized the writer and instantly sprouted a new leaf of respect for Daphne. Upon first observing her, I had filed Daphne into the category of lost young women who would take whatever advantage they could. After she disclosed her secret of being my half-sister, neither Daphne nor I made an effort to connect as siblings. I suppose we assumed we had a lifetime to knit together memories that would make us a family — someday.

After Demo died, I was too busy wrapping bandages around my own wounds and offering triage to everyone around me. During that time, I vaguely remember hearing from my mother that Daphne was busy caring for Alex, holding down her job and she had even found herself a new boy-friend. But here in a hospital bed in Weimar, California, my eyes were grateful to see that Daphne was making a significant contribution to our family, and me in particular. She became the commander of the letter-writing campaign for my family and kitchen crew. In fact, the first letter I opened was one from Daphne herself — our first authentic communication.

She wrote that one afternoon, while she waited for Alex to devour a grilled cheese sandwich and a side of fried potatoes, Theo Vasili casually asked Daphne to write a card to me. He began to dictate his news: He had won a round in his alleyway craps game. A cousin died in Greece. Theo Vasili had taken up many of my duties at the restaurant but judged himself to be much slower than he'd ever been at the work. He sent his love to me. Soon after, Daphne timidly asked my mother if she would like to dictate a letter to me. My mother was overwhelmed with delight and Daphne soon developed writer's cramp during the hour she spent recording all of my mother's news and overflowing affection. She wrote that my father and Mr. Chris were in the queue for the next round of dictation. Daphne added that she was very pleased to give something back to my family — now her family — and said that she finally felt grown-up by offering this service. So there I lay, three letters — from Daphne, my mother and Theo Vasili — scattered across my rumpled blanket. I felt the warmth and love seeping out of each one.

Days melted into weeks. With nothing else to fill up my brain, I began to jot down a few ideas for recipes that I would prepare once I returned to my rightful spot at The Classic Grill. In my uneven handwriting, I fleshed out those sketchy ideas into complete recipes. Even after lights out, my brain continued to cook in the dark and I wanted to leap out of my bed every morning to open the restaurant in my mind. By the end of my twelve long months in Weimar, I had created a stack of tempting, and in my opinion, modern recipes.

I decided to utilize Daphne's communication pipeline to help this project that sustained my body and soul. So I sent detailed recipes to The Classic Grill instead of letters. Back at our restaurant in Vallejo, Daphne translated my ingredient list and cooking instructions from written to spoken English and my father and the crew followed my recipes. Amaz-ingly, my father clicked in with this project and established that testing my recipes was a kitchen priority. Of course, the cooks added a few of their own spices or herbs and Daphne noted the changes and sent them back to me. I was delighted that my father and the cooks were interested enough to become scientists in our mutual test kitchen. The kitchen crew revealed that my meatless recipes were much like their village cooking in Greece when slaughtering an animal was saved for feast days, not daily fare. True to my Hellenic heritage, the only ingredients I could never live without were olive oil and garlic, which slid their way into most of my creations.

My river of recipes kept me afloat that year. By the time I walked out of Weimar, my notebook was bursting. I had conquered boredom, kept my spirits from fragmenting and occupied my mind from missing Demo to the point of depression. Even more unexpectedly, I, George Pappayannis — a mere second son — had written a cookbook. My tubercular body and my operational brain had written *The Classic Grill Best Recipes Cookbook.* Now that tuberculosis was knocked out in the final round, my cookbook was the only remaining artifact of how I lived through twelve long months above the fog and below the snow.

ONE HUNDRED FOUR

"You published a — *cookbook*?" Jason was almost reverent.

"So where is it?" Mariam demanded.

Yes, I had written twenty recipes that were original, kitchen-tested, meatless and — in my own opinion — superb.

"I wrote it. But, no, I did not publish it. No self-publishing then." I sipped my coffee.

"I don't get it." Jesús seemed a little miffed. "You go to all the trouble to write a whole book, test the recipes and don't do anything with it?"

I sensed I had let my group down. I would have loved to go to my car and snatch a handful of my hardback cookbooks and autograph one for each person in my group.

"We did use my recipes in the restaurant, but not right away." My mind remembered the long days in Weimar. "But first, I had to get back to my family and The Classic Grill."

ONE HUNDRED FIVE

The cities of Hiroshima and Nagasaki became piles of radioactive ruins and dust, just about the time my doctor pronounced my final chest X-ray clear. I had patiently waited a year at my Placer County holding tank for a release date. That moment finally arrived in the form of Dr. Winston's dark sedan stationed at the sanitorium gates to take me home.

Daphne wrote that my mother asked Dr. Winston to bring me to the restaurant for a brief visit before going home. The kitchen crew wanted to say a quick hello. I wanted to be strong, resilient, like the young man I used to be. But I wasn't sure I *was* that person any longer. My legs were like soggy spaghetti and by four o'clock every day, my energy had drained through my feet.

I took a few halting steps from Dr. Winston's car after we parked beneath The Classic Grill neon sign that needed cleaning, a job I used to do every month. I pressed the latch on the front door and instantly remembered the feel of the heavy brass door handle of my second home. I inhaled the powerful smells of onions, garlic, coffee and toast.

My eyes first lit upon Theo Vasili's face. His beam of love nearly ripped open the seams of his cook's uniform. My mother snaked through the small crowd and silently looped her arms around me, resting her ear to my heart, soaking up the beats. In spite of my year of battling tuberculosis at Weimar, I had grown two inches taller and I easily gazed over her shoulder at my father. He slowly walked to me and patted my back, attempting to negotiate a space near me, but my mother's arms took up most of my real estate.

"Finally, you come." He spoke those quiet words for only me to hear.

That was the welcome party I needed. My gaze wandered to see the that restaurant was decorated with tables of food and candles everywhere. The atmosphere seemed to be a replica of the gathering we held after Demo's funeral, only inside out. This time, the celebration was for the living — for me. The back tables in the restaurant had been shoved together and my framed high school picture commanded the center.

But our usual Greek cuisine was not served on the platters that were jammed around my photo. From afar, I examined the food, the color, the texture and finally, the smell. Roasted okra, tomatoes and onions. Bulgur wheat salad with chopped mint and basil. Long green beans gently cooked with whole tomatoes and garlic. I recognized each dish as a recipe from my cookbook, all twenty of them. My eyes stung with the tears I tried to hold back. For a year, I had been isolated from my people, my family. Now they came together just for me, to bring me back to my work at the restaurant.

The cooks stood behind the food table, silently grinning, as my father, mother, uncle, Daphne and Alex joined them. Never one to keep his emotions sealed in his heart, Theo Vasili stretched out his long, skinny arms and pulled us together as if we were entwined in an ancient Greek folk dance, arms clasping arms, locked in a circle, moving to the same beat. I had not realized that my yearlong absence, in addition to Demo's death, had ripped two links from our family chain. It sat broken on the floor. While I suffered a lengthy, life-threatening disease in Weimar, so did my kin at The Classic Grill. Now, in our unbreakable circle of love, we held each other tightly with new strength and took our first steps in the dance to mend our psyches and our hearts.

ONE HUNDRED SIX

When the weight of the war finally slipped off my shoulders, I hadn't realized the load of worry I had carried on my young, unaccustomed back.
With the American victory in Japan, it seemed that the rest of the world
expected me to instantly click back into a joyous, normal existence. But
instead, the end of the war was another stinging reminder that Demo was
lost to the universe. I wondered how our Classic Grill family could ever
heal from his death. Our hearts were as empty as the glass milk jugs we set
on the back porch while we waited for the next delivery of happiness.

On an early winter evening, well after the restaurant closed, my mother,
father, Daphne, Alex and I gathered around our kitchen table at home
and dined on roasted lamb, rosemary potatoes and a Greek salad of tomatoes and cucumber. Having finished his plate, Alex rummaged around in
my bedroom and made a grand entrance into the kitchen, in all of my
brother's splendid finery — Demo's toga, his smiling mask of comedy and,
most importantly, Demo's hand-made wreath thrust on Alex's own crown
of curly dark hair. A Demo in miniature — with soft glowing eyes, gleeful
in his costume, ready to take the stage.

I was frozen, not knowing if I should scold my little nephew for digging
into Demo's cherished costumes or cheer him on. Should I snip the bud of
this new performer just because he rubbed Demo's memory on my wounds
like the sting of fresh lemons? Should I let the golden light of the dramatic
muses infuse another being in our house? But looking at Demo's robes
and flowered wreaths, I snapped back into my brother's intention for these
possessions he left behind and I quickly decided this surely was a sign from
Demo. He was telling us to get back to the land of the living, to celebrate
his spirit, to keep alive his love of theatre. To get on with life! *Amesos!* Now!

As I jumped up to arrange our kitchen chairs in a row, like a theatre, I
snuck a look at my parents' faces. It seemed that my mother immediately
made room for Alex's version of Demo, and probably had secretly waited

to adore a performing child since my brother's death. My father's expression was sweet and spongy, like angel food cake. The commanding Achilles Pappayannis appeared to be amused — and may I say — delighted by Alex's attempt at a dramatic performance. I could almost identify a sentimental, grandfatherly look of love in his eyes. My boyhood emotions flipped like a fish in my heart as I wished just a few grains of that delight had been sprinkled Demo's way. But Alex, standing in front of us, preparing to sing in the high soprano of a young child, reminded me that Demo was not here anymore. Perhaps because of that, my father miraculously softened the walls of his heart to include Alex.

So, just as I did for Demo, I pounded the table to create a drum roll for Alex's entrance. My miniature Greek god of a nephew sang and danced in Demo's costume with all the gusto my brother would have encouraged. For so many months, I had longed for Demo's dramatic performances. Now, one spontaneously sprang up and ignited a tiny spark of delight for our Pappayannis family. My father and mother applauded Alex, and of course, Daphne, like all Greek mothers, believed Alex's performance was brilliant and the work of genius.

That night I rested on my back in my twin bed, hands latched behind my head. Alex breathed quietly in the bed next to me while I faced the ceiling and studied the cracks and plaster. I would force my mind into a positive place and not look back at the emotional rubble our family had left behind. I would nimbly leap toward the future, like Demo did every day he was alive. I promised myself I would not forget my celestial brother who, I assumed, occupied his rightful stage somewhere in the universe. I was here — young and alive. I wanted to discover what the world had in store for me. I decided I would never be like my father and force my will on subjects around me. I would drive myself to happiness, whatever that meant. Like a durable good in the Sears Roebuck catalogue, I would weather all storms and bad news. Unshakable. People would look to me for my quiet strength, my dignity in seeing the best in people. I would envision that the next day would be a better one. At that moment, I knew I would die a fulfilled man.

ONE HUNDRED SEVEN

Jason's large frame squirmed in his plastic chair. Maybe he thought of himself as me, a young want-to-be restaurateur, not sure how to achieve it. Wondering if pushing a broom and sliding burgers into buns could somehow build his pathway to success.

"We don't even know what happened to the restaurant!" He demanded that I add the mortar to the bricks of my story.

I could see his point. To me, The Classic Grill always had extended welcoming arms and provided a comfortable lap for me. A warm kitchen, a place to cook and dream. Our restaurant was like a church and I could say with certainty we soothed the souls of our congregation with a delicious hot roast beef sandwich and, "You feeling better after the operation?" or "The weather — never been so hot!" We dispensed the communion of coffee and hot buttered toast to our parishioners who instantly were absolved of loneliness and hunger. We depended on our restaurant and our customers depended on us.

No, I had not forgotten the restaurant, or my story's ending. My favorite part.

ONE HUNDRED EIGHT

After my return from Weimar, I allowed myself a few months to regain my strength at The Classic Grill. I started with washing dishes and graduating to moving hefty crates packed with broccoli, potatoes and carrots. Next, I refreshed my mind with the accounting ledgers and tested my endurance with the cleaning ritual at closing time. Finally, I began to cook during the dinner shift, in the sweltering jungle of boiling pots set atop blazing burners and the ovens that opened to a red-hot furnace.

One April morning, the extraordinarily fogless sky flaunted a crystal clarity brought by the stiff westerly breeze. My father ambled into the restaurant, a little later than his customary start time at dawn. As usual, he fetched our bread in a cardboard box when the bread man did not deliver. I stood behind the counter where Theo Vasili was already seated. These days, my uncle spent most of his time on his stool, sipping coffee, helping less and less in the kitchen. My mother was again working as the host, dispensing menus and warm greetings to our customers.

My father breathed a sigh of exhaustion as he slumped onto his stool, an unlikely place for him, a bookend to my uncle. In recent weeks, I noticed that my father's pace had slackened, like the slow drip under the restaurant kitchen sink. This absence of spirit was a new phase for my father who always had been ready to fight the Trojan War. Now he seemed too tired to lift a spear.

I took this as a sign, the moment to toss out my lariat and snare him with my plan. I steadied myself for his reaction. Good or bad, I was ready to try.

"Pop, I've got an idea. A dream. *My* dream."

My short speech unrolled the map of the restaurant I had created in my mind. I described the latitude and longitude of my plan to make The Classic Grill into the chain he always preached about. But not a fancy Symposium, with oversized chandeliers and expensive marble floors. My Classic Grill would be the breakfast and lunch place of my imagination.

My midnight calculations told me we made more profit on eggs and toast than on roast beef dinners and the chicken fried steak special. We would welcome our customers from dawn to three o'clock in the afternoon. We would become everyone's favorite place for a quick breakfast or tasty lunch. Always the best coffee in town. Omelets, pancakes, sandwiches on fresh bread. Lots of food, all the best quality. A place to take the family. A place for lunch every day and for special occasions. A place to eat after church or to nurse a hangover on Sunday. We would invent daily lunch specials to keep our customers interested. And we would keep some of our old favorites like the Hot Turkey Sandwich or the Meatloaf Sandwich with Potato Salad and certainly would feature my mother's chocolate cake and pies. Of course, we would know each customer by name and — best of all — we would occupy more than one location. We would get it right in Vallejo and then build restaurants all over the Bay Area. And maybe a few locations in southern California.

With my father and uncle on the customer side of the counter, I kept my jaw moving and didn't hold back my enthusiasm for our future together. I sketched my idea in bright colors to kindle my father's imagination. Soon I could see the intense flame of a young, ambitious Greek restaurateur blaze in my father's eyes. For that one moment, it seemed Demo's death, World War II, loans gone bad and the devastating Symposium fire had evaporated into the mist for my father. To my eyes, my idea of a new Classic Grill massaged his throbbing wounds and began to magically erase his scars.

Breathing hard now, he stood up, and I knew he saw my vision. He was living my dream. His dream. My uncle cracked an oversized smile, showing a few missing teeth. I would always be grateful to my uncle, the beloved welcoming audience for my new recipes and ideas — he loved every one of them. My mother, already knowing and approving of my plan, bustled happily behind me in support.

"And we don't have to take out a loan. We will remake this restaurant as our model." I finished my speech, but I had to add one more ingredient. "Then — we expand!"

That was the clincher. My father slapped his hands on the counter.

"We do it! We start today!"

My father's fighting spirit was back, his heart beating wildly, his eyes looking years into the future. Now was his chance to move forward, the only acceptable direction for my father.

"This the best plan for us. For our family now." My mother purred in support of my idea.

My uncle reached over the counter and hugged me. "Best idea for a restaurant! *Tóso éxypnos!* So smart, my Georgie!"

So we remade The Classic Grill. But this time, I was the man in charge.

ONE HUNDRED NINE

"So The Classic Grill became *your* restaurant." Jesús smiled as he brought one last round of coffee and sodas to our table.

"Finally—you were the boss!" With a satisfied grin, Aman sat back in her chair and folded her arms.

I stood up to leave, but quickly sat down again. I wanted my loyal listeners to understand how I came to sit across from them, an old man in downtown Vallejo telling his patchwork story.

"After World War II spit us out onto the other side of the decade, it felt like the right time to make big changes." I began my explanation to fill in the final details.

"The Classic Grill—my version of it—was an instant success. The new early breakfast hours and invigorated lunch menu were popular with the Mare Island workers. Mare Island was buzzing with submarine repair for the underwater vessels that had been bruised in battle." I shifted in my seat, remembering. "Just because the war had been won on foreign soil didn't mean the U.S. War Department on the home front was dead and buried. Sometimes, while walking near the docks, overlooking The Yard, I wondered if they were simply preparing for the next war."

I told them I used many of the recipes I invented at Weimar to delight our customers. To supplement any income from the dinner service we might have lost, I invented a Take-Home Special of the Day that customers purchased for two dollars. The idea of dinners-to-go packed in the white cartons used by Chinese restaurants was new in our town. Our customers, especially single servicemen, loved them. So did our cash register.

I explained that after the war was over, Tetsuya and his wife were released from the Tule Lake camp and quietly returned to a small Vallejo apartment my father rented for them. Tetsuya took back his place in the restaurant kitchen and quickly perfected fluffy, golden omelets. He was grateful his sons returned whole from the war and quietly admired his oldest son Ted who was decorated for his service in the 442nd Division. But Tetsuya was no longer comfortable living in Vallejo, a Navy town. While Tetsuya and I walked down Georgia Street to catch some air between the breakfast and lunch rush, an angry woman shot her spit at Tetsuya and crossed the street, moving far away from The Enemy. He held his mouth in a tight line and I knew nothing could ever cool the sting of shame inflicted upon Tetsuya and his family. Tetsuya quietly told me one day that he, like my father, wanted to look forward. He could not do so in Vallejo where his Japanese face only brought him misery. He was forced to restart his life from nothing since his bank account was frozen and then confiscated.

With the help of a cousin in Butte County, north of Sacramento, Tetsuya and his family moved back to the land, where he felt more comfortable, more invisible, where the earth was his only judge. His cousin's sympathetic family friend rented Tetsuya a parcel of land and a tiny farmhouse. There the family would cultivate a variety of vegetables near Gridley, a small speck of a town in the Sacramento Valley. When the time came, I could only hug Tetsuya goodbye again and remember the hours of fatherly advice he poured into me before the war pulled our lives apart. I never told him that I had wanted to stand up for him — but didn't know how.

The Classic Grill held our family together through our transformation from the first half of the twentieth century to the last half, when the changes came like hotcakes off the griddle on a Sunday rush. A few years after the war, Daphne married a Navy officer who was stationed at Mare Island. I happily took the role of Alex's permanent older brother in the family and he was forever my shadow, just like I was to Demo. Alex swung by the restaurant on the way to school each day and I assembled a tall meat sandwich for him that put peanut butter and jelly to shame. Instead of going straight home to Daphne's house after school, Alex arrived to do the late-afternoon shutdown and cleaning with me, after a hearty roast beef sandwich or a bowl of clam chowder.

My mother established a small bakery case where we displayed her pastry and sold it by the box. As the years wore on, she and my father, like two trees in a gale force wind, grew closer together and helped each other edge into their older age. My dear Theo Vasili's lungs did not have the luck of a long life due to his days of breathing black, sooty air in the Nevada mines. We buried him near Demo's remains, the first old-timer to be laid down in America, not the rocky, mineral soil of Greece. We visited them both on Sundays and Demo received a crown of flowers I made with my own hands every week.

In the 1950s, we had finally realized our restaurant chain in other locations that were fertile ground for good food at good prices. In Santa Rosa, the locals nicknamed it "The Classic," a restaurant that ended up serving breakfast, lunch and dinner, like our original restaurant. In Napa, The Classic Grill, located downtown near the Napa River, was a central meeting place for the locals in the sleepy farm community we thought would never make much of itself. Taki passed away shortly after the war ended, but Nikko, who always wanted a more exotic life than Vallejo could offer, opened up two restaurants like ours in Redondo Beach, south and west of Los Angeles. Nikko never made his prosthetic leg his focus. His muscular build and Greek-godlike features were always accented with a pair of dark sunglasses that helped him slide into the southern California scene. Alex went off to college and returned with a diploma and a pretty young wife and we operated the restaurant shoulder-to-shoulder. Year after year. Decade after decade.

For better or for worse, the 1960s brought demolition to Lower Georgia. My uncle's gambling parlors, brothels, liquor stores and dives met with a wrecking ball and dynamite blasts. The wreckage was hauled away and concrete county buildings and apartments took over. The only images left of Lower Georgia were a handful of watercolor paintings from a talented and observant local artist and the memories in my mind.

While we revved up our restaurant for another decade of business, more changes came to Vallejo. African-Americans working at Mare Island, many of whom had immigrated from the South, secretly began to organize a protest for equal wages and promotions at The Yard. I learned much later that the "21-ers," actually twenty-five bold men, had petitioned the Navy brass for equal wages and promotions. After years — make that decades — of pressure, they finally gained equal pay while most of us in the town were barely aware of the changes at The Yard, as we went on with our daily postwar business.

The 1960s and 1970s brought new shopping plazas far from the town center and fewer people frequented our old downtown area. Hells Angels and hippie couples drifted to Vallejo from the East Bay and San Francisco in search of lower rents and sunnier skies. Business at The Classic Grill became slow, then non-existent. The old downtown was not renovated and second-hand stores took the place of Levy's, Crowley's, Karl Shoes and the lunch counter at Newberry & Co. By 1980, we shut the restaurant down for good. When Alex and I turned the key in the brass lock for the last time, I was content that The Classic Grill had its day. Closing our restaurant was like a woman placing her favorite party dress away in a hope chest, knowing that someday that vintage style would come back into fashion. It was just a matter of time when my town, downtown Vallejo, would regenerate and come back into style. Someone would appreciate the Alibi clock, the old hotels and turn of the century architecture. I was sure people would always be hungry for a good meal and a new crop of enterprising restaurateurs would feed them at good prices. I believed they would some-day recognize this jewel of a town set on the hillsides that could make San Francisco jealous. I knew the old downtown would be rebuilt and loved as we once loved our town and our restaurant. Maybe The Classic Grill would live again — under new management. I hoped I would live to see it.

ONE HUNDRED TEN

"So you never saw Tetsuya again?" I could tell Aman hoped to hear that we kept in close communication all our lives.

"You have to remember that my father and Tetsuya could not write English," I reminded her.

"And long distance calls were very expensive in those days," Zach added and then smiled. "No unlimited cell phone plans."

"From that small patch of land, Tetsuya, with his sons, built a business. Their company became the largest produce broker in northern California. I see the Togami & Sons produce trucks on the freeway now and again. I believe his grandchildren run the business now." I sat back in my chair, proud of their family.

Mariam chewed on that thought. A typical immigrant story of success against all adversity. She wasn't buying it and suspiciously scanned my face, looking for the catch.

"Why wouldn't they just go back to Japan?" she asked.

"He had no one there who cared about him and his sons were American. They were Nisei kids. This was their home — and they weren't leaving."

"I wouldn't want to go back to *Méjico* for anything," Jesús stated with certainty. "They couldn't drag me back. I'm American. But my parents…"

A gray cloud descended over our group. We could only guess that his parents may not be so lucky as to remain in this country. I was uneasy, first thinking about Tetsuya and now Jesús' parents. I shifted in my seat, my fingers fidgeting with my paper cup, as an overpowering sense of unfinished business draped over my shoulders and whispered in my ear. I tried to shake the feeling and concentrate on the treasured minutes I had left with my little group.

The truth was that I wanted this conversation to go on forever. I lived alone in our Pappayannis family home on Virginia Street where I collected my Social Security check. My only company came from watching television, cooking shows mostly. I didn't want to bore these young people with my current life of doctor appointments and the prostate cancer PSA numbers. I would love to return a few times a week and visit them again, but I didn't want to appear like a creepy old man who would hang around like gum on a shoe, with questionable intentions. I just wanted to be there to cheer for Aman, Mariam, Jesús and Jason as they stepped into the jaws of the real world.

It was well past six o'clock and that feeling of unfinished work remained heavy in my bones. But I was done. Out of story. Out of family. Out of coffee. Out of time. Time for an old man to leave these young, beautiful faces. I stood up, my worn out hat in my hand, unsure how to leave. I felt like I had shared a meaningful connection on a first date but didn't know how to ask for a second.

"Thank you," I said humbly, sincerely. I loved these young people.

I could never thank them enough for allowing me to bring Demo back to life. To talk about immigrants who made a little restaurant and, as my father said, "made it good." To tell someone how I treasured my bachelor Theo Vasili, my precious mother and my determined father who learned as he stumbled along. About how I loved Tetsuya and his humble strength, and even about Daphne who had transformed from girl to woman. I bowed just a little to my sweet group, my fellow children of immigrants, and turned my back to go. They remained seated but I heard a little clap. I turned to see the commotion, but I could only move slowly these days. When I turned my entire body around to see my young people, my friends were quietly applauding me as I left their restaurant. Aman flew to my side and shyly spoke.

"Will you come back to visit us?"

ONE HUNDRED ELEVEN

I walked on the bumpy gravel path to my car, almost dizzy from reliving my family story with my new friends. Parts of me were everywhere, my mind soaking up Demo's stories, my hands making phyllo-wrapped chicken and my heart waiting for Tetsuya to come home. My story left me wanting to go someplace other than home that June evening. I slid into the driver's seat and I knew what I had to do.

At seven o'clock, the sun took its time dipping below the Pacific where the fog had yet to appear. I drove my car back to the Golden Gate Bridge and felt lucky to find a parking space in the visitors' area. I buttoned my jacket as I walked slowly into the angry wind that slammed my face. Only a few protesters were left, but their signs told their story. A television news reporter wrapped up her coverage while the camera crew lingered to videotape the remaining signs, "Immigrants Are Americans," "Immigration — It's the American Way," and "Immigrants Make America Great." I took my place on the pedestrian sidewalk of the bridge, in the midst of the small remnants of the group, some with headscarves, most of them young women and men, and some children in strollers with their mothers.

I had no sign, but I planted my feet, dug my hands into my pockets and stood for my people. I stood for my new friends who would have a difficult road carving out their path to a contented life and their parents who might be living in the shadows of fear. I stood for my relatives, most of whom were buried, having given everything they could to this country. I stood for my brother Demo who would always be my hero because he lived unapologetically and unafraid. I stood for Tetsuya because he was my second father and I should have stood up for him so many years ago.

But now I did.

I stood like the Statue of Liberty but with my hands keeping warm in my pockets, my hat tight on my old man head. I stood until the last protesters packed up their signs and emptied the walkway. I stood in the dark as the lights sparked on across the bay in downtown San Francisco and Oakland, tiny fisheyes popping open in the ocean of navy-blue darkness. And because it was a clear night, I thought I saw a little light snap on, far away in the North Bay, in Vallejo. Perhaps in a small, friendly restaurant in the old downtown.

ACKNOWLEDGEMENTS

I thank my mother Georgia Econome and my sister Janet Econome for their inspiration and excellent editing contributions — and years of encouragement.

I thank my husband Dan Gutierrez and my children Jessica and Thomas for their love, support and for giving me the time to write.

A heartfelt thanks to my uncle (Theo) Bill Econome whose experiences during the early 1940s in Vallejo, CA added authenticity to the story — my technical advisor!

Many thanks to Lissa McLaughlin whose editing talent helped this story immensely. Thanks to Linda Jay who meticulously proofread the manuscript. And special thanks to Avery Econome who was my skillfull "on-call" editor.

Publishing Assistance

I wish to thank these people for their publishing expertise and professional guidance:

> Nancy Fish, Program Manager of the Path to Publishing Program, at Book Passage, Corte Madera, CA
>
> Maureen Forys at Happenstance Type-O-Rama

A special thank you to these colleagues for their support, friendship and creative assistance:

> William Sorensen & Stella Kwiecinski who created the videos on the website *nancyeconome.com*
>
> Allyson Pirenian who created graphic artwork
>
> Bill Walters who developed the website *nancyeconome.com*

My deepest thanks to these people for their critiques, historical insight and encouragement:

> Janet Andoe
>
> Andonia Cakouros
>
> Pauline Cazanis
>
> Dave Collins

George Econome

Nick Econome

Chef Timothy Garrow

Kim Malcolm

Gege Manolis

Ellen Martin

Angie Minkin

Rich Moreno, author of *Mysteries and Legends of Nevada; A Short History of Carson City, Nevada; The Roadside History of Nevada* and *A Short History of Reno, Nevada*

Joela Mueller

Doreen Pinelli

Georgia Plesha

Sacramento Annunciation Senior League of the Greek Orthodox Church

Bill Sevald

Claudia Stetler

Lori Tsukiji

Christine Walwyn

A Special Thank You

Thank you to Panera Bread restaurants in Santa Rosa and Rohnert Park, CA for offering me their hospitality and a friendly, safe place to write.

Historic Research

My sincere gratitude to the following institutions and people who generously contributed their time and knowledge about WWII, Vallejo and Bay Area life in 1942.

Ascension Episcopal Church, Vallejo, CA

Lisa & Ed Critchett

Kelsi Evans, Director of Archives and Special Collections at the Dr. John P. De Cecco Archives and Special Collections at the GLBT Historical Society

Steve Gilford, author of *Build 'Em by the Mile, Cut 'Em off by the Yard: How Henry J. Kaiser and the Rosies Helped Win World War II*

Elizabeth Gross

Sachiko Hori, Sachiko Hori Fine Art

Henry Kaku, lecturer on WWII internment camps, Origami Master and Judo Sensei

Masataka Katsumata

James Kern, Executive Director of the Vallejo Naval and Historical Museum

National Parks in the San Francisco Bay Area

The National WWII Museum, New Orleans assisted by Jason Dawsey & Walt Burgoyne

Father James Retelas, Annunciation Greek Orthodox Church, Sacramento

Brendan Riley, author of *Lower Georgia Street — California's Forgotten Barbary Coast*

Father Timothy Robinson, Annunciation Greek Orthodox Church, Sacramento

San Francisco Railway Museum

Alice & Ted Tsukiji

Andrea Waite

David Waite

ABOUT THE AUTHOR

Nancy Econome's debut novel is *The Classic Grill—A Tale of Greek Gods and Immigrant Heroes*, a work of historical fiction. As a Greek-American, Nancy Econome enjoyed creating a world that honors the past but reflects current events.

Nancy worked as Creative Services Director for a group of premium northern California wineries. She holds a Master's degree in Cinema from San Francisco State and a Bachelor of Arts degree in English from the University of California at Davis. Nancy worked as a reporter, has written several screenplays and has also found time to ride her bike across the continental United States. Living in northern California wine country, Nancy can be found at a local Panera Bread restaurant, writing her next novel.

The Classic Grill—A Tale of Greek Gods and Immigrant Heroes received Honorable Mention at the 15th Annual Maurice Prize for Fiction in 2020.